"*Lying on the Couch* is a witty, gripping and hugely entertaining novel from which the reader effortlessly learns a great deal about the theory and practice of psychotherapy."
—David Lodge, author of *Therapy* and *The Art of Fiction*.

ALSO BY IRVIN D. YALOM

Existential Psychotherapy

Every Day Gets a Little Closer: A Twice-Told Therapy
(with Ginny Elkin)

Encounter Groups: First Facts
(with Morton A. Lieberman and Matthew B. Miles)

Inpatient Group Psychotherapy

Concise Guide to Group Psychotherapy
(with Sophia Vinogradov)

The Theory and Practice of Group Psychotherapy
(Fourth Edition)

Love's Executioner

When Nietzsche Wept

Lying on the Couch

A Novel

IRVIN D. YALOM

HarperPerennial

A Division of HarperCollins*Publishers*

As a novel, this book is entirely a work of fiction. Though it contains incidental references to actual people, these references are used merely to lend the fiction an appropriate cultural and historical context. All other names, characters, and incidents portrayed in this book are fictitious. Any resemblance to actual events or persons, living or dead, is entirely coincidental.

A hardcover edition of this book was published in 1996 by BasicBooks, a division of HarperCollins Publishers.

First HarperPerennial edition published 1997.

Designed by Elliott Beard

The Library of Congress has catalogued the hardcover edition as follows:

Yalom, Irvin D., 1931–
    Lying on the couch / by Irvin D. Yalom. — 1st ed.
      p.   cm.
    ISBN 0-465-04295-3
    I. Title.
    PS3575.A39L95   1996
    813'.54—dc20   96-7377
                               CIP

ISBN 0-06-092851-4 (pbk.)

97 98 99 00 01 ❖/RRD 10 9 8 7 6

To the future—Lily, Alana, Lenore, Jason, Desmond.
May your lives be filled with wonder.

ACKNOWLEDGMENTS

*M*any have helped me in the precarious crossing from psychiatry to fiction: John Beletsis, Martel Bryant, Casey Feutsch, Peggy Gifford, Ruthellen Josselson, Julius Kaplan, Stina Katchadourian, Elizabeth Tallent, Josiah Thompson, Alan Rinzler, David Spiegel, Saul Spiro, Randy Weingarten, the guys of my poker game, Benjamin Yalom, and Marilyn Yalom (without whom this book could have been written with far greater comfort). To all, my deepest gratitude.

PROLOGUE

*E*rnest loved being a psychotherapist. Day after day his patients invited him into the most intimate chambers of their lives. Day after day he comforted them, cared for them, eased their despair. And in return, he was admired and cherished. And paid as well, though, Ernest often thought, if he didn't need the money, he would do psychotherapy for nothing.

Lucky is he who loves his work. Ernest felt lucky, all right. More than lucky. Blessed. He was a man who had found his calling—a man who could say, I am precisely where I belong, at the vortex of my talents, my interests, my passions.

Ernest was not a religious man. But when he opened his appointment book every morning and saw the names of the eight or nine dear people with whom he would spend his day, he was overcome with a feeling that he could only describe as religious. At these times he had the deepest desire to give thanks—to someone, to something—for having led him to his calling.

There were mornings when he looked up, through the skylight of his Sacramento Street Victorian, through the morning fog, and imagined his psychotherapy ancestors suspended in the dawn.

"Thank you, thank you," he would chant. He thanked them all— all the healers who had ministered to despair. First, the ur ancestors, their empyreal outlines barely visible: Jesus, Buddha, Socrates. Below them, somewhat more distinct—the great progenitors: Nietzsche, Kierkegaard, Freud, Jung. Nearer yet, the grandparent therapists: Adler, Horney, Sullivan, Fromm, and the sweet smiling face of Sandor Ferenczi.

A few years ago, they answered his cry of distress when, after his residency training, he fell into lockstep with every ambitious young neuropsychiatrist and applied himself to neurochemistry research—the face of the future, the golden arena of personal opportunity. The ancestors knew he had lost his way. He belonged in no science laboratory. Nor in a medication-dispensing psychopharmacological practice.

They sent a messenger—a droll messenger of power—to ferry him to his destiny. To this day Ernest did not know *how* he decided to become a therapist. But he remembered *when*. He remembered the day with astonishing clarity. And he remembered the messenger, too: Seymour Trotter, a man he saw only once, who changed his life forever.

Six years ago Ernest's department chairman had appointed him to serve a term on the Stanford Hospital Medical Ethics Committee, and Ernest's first disciplinary action was the case of Dr. Trotter. Seymour Trotter was a seventy-one-year-old patriarch of the psychiatric community and the former president of the American Psychiatric Association. He had been charged with sexual misconduct with a thirty-two-year-old female patient.

At that time Ernest was an assistant professor of psychiatry just four years out of residency. A full-time neurochemistry researcher, he was completely naive about the world of psychotherapy—far too naive to know he had been assigned this case because no one else would touch it: every older psychiatrist in Northern California greatly venerated and feared Seymour Trotter.

Ernest chose an austere hospital administrative office for the interview and tried to look official, watching the clock while waiting for Dr. Trotter, the complaint file on the desk in front of him, unopened. To remain unbiased, Ernest had decided to interview the accused with no previous knowledge and thus hear his story with no preconceptions. He would read the file later and schedule a second meeting, if necessary.

Presently he heard a tapping noise echoing down the hallway. Could Dr. Trotter be blind? No one had prepared him for that. The tapping, followed by shuffling, grew closer. Ernest rose and stepped into the hallway.

No, not blind. Lame. Dr. Trotter lurched down the hall, balanced uneasily between two canes. He was bent at the waist and held the canes widely apart, almost at arm's length. His good, strong cheekbones and chin still held their own, but all softer ground had been colonized by wrinkles and senile plaques. Deep folds of skin hung from his neck, and puffs of white hairy moss protruded from his ears. Yet age had not vanquished this man—something young, even boyish, survived. What was it? Perhaps his hair, gray and thick, worn in a crew cut, or his dress, a blue denim jacket covering a white turtleneck sweater.

They introduced themselves in the doorway. Dr. Trotter staggered a couple of steps into the room, suddenly raised his canes, twisted vigorously, and, as though by the sheerest chance, pirouetted into his seat.

"Bull's-eye! Surprised you, eh?"

Ernest was not to be distracted. "You understand the purpose of this interview, Dr. Trotter—and you understand why I'm taperecording it?"

"I've heard that the hospital administration is considering me for the Worker of the Month award."

Ernest, staring unblinking through his large goggle spectacles, said nothing.

"Sorry, I know you've got your job to do, but when you've passed seventy, you'll smile at good cracks like that. Yeah, seventy-one last week. And you're how old, Dr. . . . ? I've forgotten your name. Every minute," he said as he tapped his temple, "a dozen cortical neurons buzz out like dying flies. The irony is, I've published four papers on Alzheimer's—naturally I forget where, but good journals. Did you know that?"

Ernest shook his head.

"So you never knew and I've forgotten. That makes us about even. Do you know the two good things about Alzheimer's? Your old friends become your new friends, and you can hide your own Easter eggs."

Despite his irritation Ernest couldn't help smiling.

"Your name, age, and school of conviction?"

"I'm Dr. Ernest Lash, and perhaps the rest isn't germane just now, Dr. Trotter. We've got a lot of ground to cover today."

"My son's forty. You can't be more than that. I know you're a graduate of the Stanford residency. I heard you speak at grand rounds last year. You did well. Very clear presentation. It's all psychopharm now, isn't it? What kind of psychotherapy training you guys getting now? Any at all?"

Ernest took off his watch and put it on the desk. "Some other time I'll be glad to forward you a copy of the Stanford residency curriculum, but for now, please, let's get into the matter at hand, Dr. Trotter. Perhaps it would be best if you tell me about Mrs. Felini in your own way."

"Okay, okay, okay. You want me to be serious. You want me to tell you my story. Sit back, *boychik,* and I'll tell you a story. We'll start at the beginning. It was about four years ago—at least four years ago . . . I've misplaced all of my records on this patient . . . what was the date according to your charge sheet? What? You haven't read it. Lazy? Or trying to avoid unscientific bias?"

"Please, Dr. Trotter, continue."

"The first principle of interviewing is to forge a warm, trusting environment. Now that you've accomplished that so artfully, I feel a great deal freer to talk about painful and embarrassing material. Oh—*that* got to you. Gotta be careful of me, Dr. Lash, I've had forty years reading faces. I'm very good at it. But if you've finished the interruptions, I'll start. Ready?

"Years ago—let's say about four years—a woman, Belle, walks into, or I should say drags herself into, my office—or bedraggles herself in—bedraggles, that's better. Is *bedraggle* a verb? About midthirties, from a wealthy background—Swiss-Italian—depressed, wearing a long-sleeved blouse in the summertime. A cutter, obviously—wrists scarred up. If you see long sleeves in the summertime, perplexing patient, always think of wrist cutting and drug injections, Dr. Lash. Good-looking, great skin, seductive eyes, elegantly dressed. Real class, but on the verge of going to seed.

"Long self-destructive history. You name it: drugs, tried everything, didn't miss one. When I first saw her she was back to alcohol and doing a little heroin chipping. Yet not truly addicted. Somehow she didn't have the knack for it—some people are like that—but she was working on it. Eating disorder, too. Anorexia mainly, but occasional bulimic purging. I've already mentioned the cutting, lots of it up and down both arms and wrists—liked the pain and blood; that was the only time she felt alive. You hear patients say that all the time. A half-dozen hospitalizations—brief. She always signed out in a day or two. The staff would cheer when she left. She was good— a true prodigy—at the game of Uproar. You remember Eric Berne's *Games People Play?*

"No? Guess it's before your time. Christ, I feel old. Good stuff— Berne wasn't stupid. Read it—shouldn't be forgotten.

"Married, no kids. She refused to have them—said the world was too ghastly a place to inflict on children. Nice husband, rotten relationship. He wanted kids badly, and there was lots of fighting about that. He was an investment banker like her father, always traveling. A few years into the marriage, his libido shut off or maybe got channeled into making money—he made good money but never really hit the big time like her father. Busy busy busy, slept with the computer. Maybe he fucked it, who knows? He certainly didn't fuck Belle. According to her, he had avoided her for years, probably because of his anger about not having children. Hard to say what kept them married. He was raised in a Christian Science home and consistently refused couples therapy, or any other form of psychotherapy. But she admits she has never pushed very hard. Let's see. What else? Cue me, Dr. Lash.

"Her previous therapy? Good. Important question. I always ask that in the first thirty minutes. Nonstop therapy—or attempts at therapy—since her teens. Went through all the therapists in Geneva and for a while commuted to Zurich for analysis. Came to college in the U.S.—Pomona—and saw one therapist after another, often only for a single session. Stuck it out with three or four of them for as long as a few months, but never really took with anyone. Belle was—and is—very dismissive. No one good enough, or at least no one right for her. Something wrong with every therapist: too formal, too pompous, too judgmental, too condescending, too business-oriented, too cold, too busy with diagnosis, too formula-driven. Psych meds? Psychological testing? Behavioral protocols? Forget it—anyone suggest those and they were scratched immediately. What else?

"How'd she choose me? Excellent question, Dr. Lash—focuses us and quickens our pace. We'll make a psychotherapist of you yet. I had that feeling about you when I heard your grand rounds. Good, incisive mind. It showed as you presented your data. But what I liked was your case presentation, especially the way you let patients affect you. I saw you had all the right instincts. Carl Rogers used to say, 'Don't waste your time training therapists—time is better spent in *selecting* them.' I always thought there was a lot to that.

"Let's see, where was I? Oh, how she got to me: her gynecologist, whom she adored, was a former patient of mine. Told her I was a regular guy, no bullshit, and willing to get my hands dirty. She looked me up at the library and liked an article I wrote fifteen years ago discussing Jung's notion of inventing a new therapy language for each patient. You know that work? No? *Journal of Orthopsychiatry.* I'll send you a reprint. I took it even further than Jung. I suggested we invent a new therapy for each patient, that we take seriously the notion of the uniqueness of each patient and develop a unique psychotherapy for each one.

"Coffee? Yeah, I'll have some. Black. Thanks. So that's how she got to me. And the next question you should ask, Dr. Lash? *Why then?* Precisely. That's the one. Always a high-yield question to ask a new patient. The answer: dangerous sexual acting out. Even she could see it. She had always done some of this stuff, but it was getting very heavy. Imagine driving next to vans or trucks on the highway—high enough for the driver to see in—and then pulling up her skirt and masturbating—at eighty miles an hour. Crazy. Then she'd take the next exit and if the driver followed her off, she'd stop, climb into his cabin, and give him a blow job. Lethal stuff. And lots of it. She was so out of control that when she was bored, she'd go into some seedy San Jose bar, sometimes Chicano, sometimes black, and pick someone up. She got off on being in dangerous situations surrounded by unknown, potentially violent men. And there was danger not only from the men but from the prostitutes who resented her taking their business. They threatened her life and she had to keep moving from one place to another. And AIDS, herpes, safe sex, condoms? Like she never heard of them.

"So that, more or less, was Belle when we started. You get the picture? You got any questions or shall I just go on? Okay. So, somehow, in our first session I passed all her tests. She came back a second time and a third and we began treatment, twice, sometimes three times a week. I spent a whole hour taking a detailed history of her work with all her previous therapists. That's always a good strategy when you're seeing a difficult patient, Dr. Lash. Find out how they treated her and then try to avoid their errors. Forget that crap about the patient not being ready for therapy! *It's the therapy that's not ready for the patient.* But you have to be bold and creative enough to fashion a new therapy for each patient.

"Belle Felini was not a patient to be approached with traditional technique. If I stay in my normal professional role—taking a history, reflecting, empathizing, interpreting—poof, she's gone. Trust me. Sayonara. Auf Wiedersehen. That's what she did with every therapist she ever saw—and many of them with good reputations. You know the old story: the operation was a success, but the patient died.

"What techniques did I employ? Afraid you missed my point. *My technique is to abandon all technique!* And I'm not just being smart-assed, Dr. Lash—that's the first rule of good therapy. And that should be your rule, too, if you become a therapist. I tried to be more human and less mechanical. I don't make a systematic therapy plan—you won't either after forty years of practice. I just trust my intuition. But that's not fair to you as a beginner. I guess, looking back, the most striking aspect of Belle's pathology was her impulsivity. She gets a desire—bingo, she has to act on it. I remember wanting to increase her tolerance for frustration. That was my starting point, my first, maybe my major, goal in therapy. Let's see, how did we start? It's hard to remember the beginning, so many years ago, without my notes.

"I told you I lost them. I see the doubt in your face. The notes are gone. Disappeared when I moved offices about two years ago. You have no choice but to believe me.

"The main recollections I have are that in the beginning things went far better than I could have imagined. Not sure *why,* but Belle took to me immediately. Couldn't have been my good looks. I had just had cataract surgery and my eye looked like hell. And my ataxia did not improve my sex appeal . . . this is familial cerebellar ataxia, if you're curious. Definitely progressive . . . a walker in my future, another year or two, and a wheelchair in three or four. *C'est la vie.*

"I think Belle liked me because I treated her like a person. I did exactly what you're doing now—and I want to tell you, Dr. Lash, I appreciate your doing it. I didn't read any of her charts. I went into it blind, wanted to be entirely fresh. Belle was *never* a diagnosis to me, not a borderline, not an eating disorder, not a compulsive or antisocial disorder. That's the way I approach all my patients. And I hope I will never become a diagnosis to you.

"What, do I think there's a place for diagnosis? Well, I know you guys graduating now, and the whole psychopharm industry, live by diagnosis. The psychiatric journals are littered with meaningless discussions about nuances of diagnosis. Future flotsam. I know it's important in some psychoses, but it plays little role—in fact, a negative role—in everyday psychotherapy. Ever think about the fact that it's easier to make a diagnosis the first time you see a patient and that it gets harder the better you know a patient? Ask any experienced therapist in private—they'll tell you the same thing! In other words, certainty is inversely proportional to knowledge. Some kind of science, huh?

"What I'm saying to you, Dr. Lash, is not just that I didn't *make* a diagnosis on Belle; I didn't *think* diagnosis. I still don't. Despite what's happened, despite what she's done to me, I still don't. And I think she knew that. We were just two people making contact. And I liked Belle. Always did. Liked her a lot! And she knew that, too. Maybe *that's* the main thing.

"Now Belle was not a good talking-therapy patient—not by anyone's standard. Impulsive, action-oriented, no curiosity about herself, nonintrospective, unable to free-associate. She always failed at the traditional tasks of therapy—self-examination, insight—and then felt worse about herself. *That's* why therapy had always bombed. And that's why I knew I had to get her attention in other ways. That's why I had to invent a new therapy for Belle.

"For example? Well, let me give you one from early therapy, maybe third or fourth month. I'd been focusing on her self-destructive sexual behavior and asking her about what she really wanted from men, including the first man in her life, her father. But I was getting nowhere. She was real resistive to talking about the past—done too much of that with other shrinks, she said. Also she had a notion that poking in the ashes of the past was just an excuse to evade personal responsibility for our actions. She had read my book on psychotherapy and cited me saying that very thing. I hate that. When patients resist by citing your own books, they got you by the balls.

"One session I asked her for some early daydreams or sexual fantasies and finally, to humor me, she described a recurrent fantasy from the time she was eight or nine: a storm outside, she comes into a room cold and soaking wet, and an older man is waiting for her.

He embraces her, takes off her wet clothes, dries her with a large warm towel, gives her hot chocolate. So I suggested we role-play: I told her to go out of the office and enter again pretending to be wet and cold. I skipped the undressing part, of course, got a good-sized towel from the washroom, and dried her off vigorously—staying nonsexual, as I always did. I 'dried' her back and her hair, then bundled her up in the towel, sat her down, and made her a cup of instant hot chocolate.

"Don't ask me why or how I chose to do this at that time. When you've practiced as long as I have, you learn to trust your intuition. And the intervention changed everything. Belle was speechless for a while, tears welled up in her eyes, and then she bawled like a baby. Belle had never, never cried in therapy. The resistance just melted away.

"What do I mean by her resistance melting? I mean that she trusted me, that she believed we were on the same side. The technical term, Dr. Lash, is 'therapeutic alliance.' After that she became a real patient. Important material just erupted out of her. She began to live for the next session. Therapy became the center of her life. Over and over she told me how important I was to her. And this was after only three months.

"Was I *too* important? No, Dr. Lash, the therapist can't be too important early in therapy. Even Freud used the strategy of trying to replace a psychoneurosis with a transference neurosis—that's a powerful way of gaining control over destructive symptoms.

"You look puzzled by this. Well, what happens is that the patient becomes obsessed with the therapist—ruminates powerfully about each session, has long fantasy conversations with the therapist between sessions. Eventually the symptoms are taken over by therapy. In other words, the symptoms, rather than being driven by inner neurotic factors, begin to fluctuate according to the exigencies of the therapeutic relationship.

"No, thanks, no more coffee, Ernest. But you have some. You mind if I call you Ernest? Good. So to continue, I capitalized on this development. I did all I could to become even more important to Belle. I answered every question she asked me about my own life, I supported the positive parts of her. I told her what an intelligent, good-looking woman she was. I hated what she was doing to herself and told her so very directly. None of this was hard: all I had to do was tell the truth.

"Earlier you asked what my technique was. Maybe my best answer is simply: *I told the truth.* Gradually I began to play a larger role in her fantasy life. She'd slip into long reveries about the two of us—just being together, holding each other, my playing baby games with her, my feeding her. Once she brought a container of Jell-O and a spoon into the office and asked me to feed her—which I did, to her great delight.

"Sounds innocent, doesn't it? But I knew, even at the beginning, that there was a shadow looming. I knew it then, I knew it when she talked about how aroused she got when I fed her. I knew it when she talked about going canoeing for long periods, two or three days a week, just so she could be alone, float on the water, and enjoy her reveries about me. I knew my approach was risky, but it was a calculated risk. I was going to allow the positive transference to build so that I could use it to combat her self-destructiveness.

"And after a few months I had become so important to her that I could begin to lean on her pathology. First, I concentrated on the life-or-death stuff: HIV, the bar scene, the highway-angel-of-mercy blow jobs. She got an HIV test—negative, thank God. I remember waiting the two weeks for the results of the HIV test. Let me tell you, I sweated that one as much as she did.

"You ever work with patients when they're waiting for the results of the HIV test? No? Well, Ernest, that waiting period is a window of opportunity. You can use it to do some real work. For a few days patients come face to face with their own death, possibly for the first time. It's a time when you can help them to examine and reshuffle their priorities, to base their lives and their behavior on the things that really count. *Existential shock therapy,* I sometimes call it. But not Belle. Didn't faze her. Just had too much denial. Like so many other self-destructive patients, Belle felt invulnerable at anyone's hand other than her own.

"I taught her about HIV and about herpes, which, miraculously, she didn't have either, and about safe-sex procedures. I coached her on safer places to pick up men if she absolutely had to: tennis clubs, PTA meetings, bookstore readings. Belle was something—what an operator! She could arrange an assignation with some handsome total stranger in five or six minutes, sometimes with an unsuspecting wife only ten feet away. I have to admit I envied her. Most women don't appreciate their good fortune in this regard. Can you see men—especially a pillaged wreck like me—doing that at will?

"One surprising thing about Belle, given what I've told you so far, was her absolute honesty. In our first couple of sessions, when we were deciding to work together, I laid out my basic condition of therapy: *total honesty*. She had to commit herself to share every important event of her life: drug use, impulsive sexual acting out, cutting, purging, fantasies—everything. Otherwise, I told her, we were wasting her time. But if she leveled with me about everything, she could absolutely count on me to see this through with her. She promised and we solemnly shook hands on our contract.

"And, as far as I know, she kept her promise. In fact, this was part of my leverage because if there were important slips during the week—if, for example, she scratched her wrists or went to a bar—I'd analyze it to death. I'd insist on a deep and lengthy investigation of what happened just before the slip. 'Please, Belle,' I'd say, 'I must hear everything that preceded the event, everything that might help us understand it: the earlier events of the day, your thoughts, your feelings, your fantasies.' That drove Belle up the wall—she had other things she wanted to talk about and hated using up big chunks of her therapy time on this. That alone helped her control her impulsivity.

"Insight? Not a major player in Belle's therapy. Oh, she grew to recognize that more often than not her impulsive behavior was preceded by a feeling state of great deadness or emptiness and that the risk taking, the cutting, the sex, the bingeing, were all attempts to fill herself up or to bring herself back to life.

"But what Belle didn't grasp was that these attempts were futile. Every single one backfired, since they resulted in eventual deep shame and then more frantic—and more self-destructive—attempts to feel alive. Belle was always strangely obtuse at apprehending the idea that her behavior had consequences.

"So insight wasn't helpful. I had to do something else—and I tried every device in the book, and then some—to help her control her impulsivity. We compiled a list of her destructive impulsive behaviors, and she agreed not to embark on any of these before phoning me and allowing me a chance to talk her down. But she rarely phoned—she didn't want to intrude on my time. Deep down she was convinced that my commitment to her was tissue-thin and that I would soon tire of her and dump her. I couldn't dissuade her of this. She asked for some concrete memento of me to carry around with her. It would give her more self-control. Choose something in the office, I told her. She pulled my handkerchief out of my jacket. I gave it to her, but first wrote some of her important dynamics on it:

I feel dead and I hurt myself to know I'm alive.
I feel deadened and must take dangerous risks to feel alive.
I feel empty and try to fill myself with drugs, food, semen.
But these are brief fixes. I end up feeling shame—and even
more dead and empty.

"I instructed Belle to meditate on the handkerchief and the messages every time she felt impulsive.

"You look quizzical, Ernest. You disapprove? Why? Too gimmicky? Not so. It seems gimmicky, I agree, but desperate remedies for desperate conditions. For patients who seem never to have developed a definitive sense of object constancy, I've found some possession, some concrete reminder, very useful. One of my teachers, Lewis Hill, who was a genius at treating severely ill schizophrenic patients used to breathe into a tiny bottle and give it to his patients to wear around their necks when he left for vacation.

"You think that's gimmicky too, Ernest? Let me substitute another word, the proper word: *creative*. Remember what I said earlier about creating a new therapy for every patient? This is exactly what I meant. Besides, you haven't asked the most important question.

"Did it work? Exactly, exactly. That's the proper question. The *only* question. Forget the rules. Yes, it worked! It worked for Dr. Hill's patients and it worked for Belle, who carried around my handkerchief and gradually gained more control over her impulsivity. Her 'slips' became less frequent and soon we could begin to turn our attention elsewhere in our therapy hours.

"What? Merely a transference cure? Something about this is really getting to you, Ernest. That's good—it's good to question. You have a sense for the real issues. Let me tell you, you're in the wrong place in your life—you're not meant to be a neurochemist. Well, Freud's denigration of 'transference cure' is almost a century old. Some truth to it, but basically it's wrong.

"Trust me: if you can break into a self-destructive cycle of behavior—no matter *how* you do it—you've accomplished something important. The first step has *got to be* to interrupt the vicious circle of self-hate, self-destruction, and then more self-hate from the shame at one's behavior. Though she never expressed it, imagine the shame and self-contempt Belle must have felt about her degraded behavior. It's the therapist's task to help reverse that process. Karen Horney once said . . . do you know Horney's work, Ernest?

"Pity, but that seems to be the fate of the leading theoreticians of our field—their teachings survive for about one generation. Horney was one of my favorites. I read all of her work during my training. Her best book, *Neuroses and Human Growth,* is over fifty years old, but it's as good a book about therapy as you'll ever read—and not one word of jargon. I'm going to send you my copy. Somewhere, perhaps in that book, she made the simple but powerful point: 'If you want to be proud of yourself, then do things in which you can take pride.'

"I've lost my way in my story. Help me get started again, Ernest. My relationship with Belle? Of course, that's what we're really here for, isn't it? There were many interesting developments on that front. But I know that the development of most relevance for your committee is physical touching. Belle made an issue of this almost from the start. Now, I make a habit of physically touching all of my patients, male and female, every session—generally a handshake upon leaving, or perhaps a pat on the shoulder. Well, Belle didn't much care for that: she refused to shake my hand and began making some mocking statement like, 'Is that an APA-approved shake?' or 'Couldn't you try to be a little more formal?'

Sometimes she'd end the session by giving me a hug—always friendly, not sexual. The next session she'd chide me about my behavior, about my formality, about the way I'd stiffen up when she hugged me. And 'stiffen' refers to my body, not my cock, Ernest—I saw that look. You'd make a lousy poker player. We're not yet at the lascivious part. I'll cue you when we arrive.

"She'd complain about my age-typing. If she were old and wizened, she said, I'd have no hesitation about hugging her. She's probably right about that. Physical contact was extraordinarily important for Belle: she insisted that we touch and she never stopped insisting. Push, push, push. Nonstop. But I could understand it: Belle had grown up touch-deprived. Her mother died when she was an infant, and she was raised by a series of remote Swiss governesses. And her father! Imagine growing up with a father who had a germ phobia, never touched her, always wore gloves in and out of the home. Had the servants wash and iron all his paper currency.

"Gradually, after about a year, I had loosened up enough, or had been softened up enough by Belle's relentless pressure, to begin ending the sessions regularly with an avuncular hug. Avuncular? It means 'like an uncle.' But whatever I gave, she always asked for more, always tried to kiss me on the cheek when she hugged me. I always insisted on her honoring the boundaries, and she always insisted on pressing against them. I can't tell you how many little lectures I gave her about this, how many books and articles on the topic I gave her to read.

"But she was like a child in a woman's body—a knockout woman's body, incidentally—and her craving for contact was relentless. Couldn't she move her chair closer? Couldn't I hold her hand for a few minutes? Couldn't we sit next to each other on the sofa? Couldn't I just put my arm around her and sit in silence, or take a walk, instead of talking?

"And she was ingeniously persuasive. 'Seymour,' she'd say, 'you talk a good game about creating a new therapy for each patient, but what you left out of your articles was "as long as it's in the official manual" or "as long as it doesn't interfere with the therapist's middle-aged bourgeois comfort." She'd chide me about taking refuge in the APA's guidelines about boundaries in therapy. She knew I had been responsible for writing those guidelines when I was president of the APA, and she accused me of being imprisoned by my own rules. She'd criticize me for not reading my own articles. 'You stress the honoring of each patient's uniqueness, and then you pretend that a single set of rules can fit all patients in all situations. We all get lumped together,' she'd say, 'as if all patients were the same and should be treated the same.' And her chorus was always, 'What's more important: following the rules? Staying in your armchair comfort zone? Or doing what's best for your patient?'

"Other times she'd rail about my 'defensive therapy': 'You're so terrified about being sued. All you humanistic therapists cower before the lawyers, while at the same time you urge your mentally ill patients to grab hold of their freedom. Do you really think I would sue you? Don't you know me yet, Seymour? You're saving my life. And I love you!'

"And, you know, Ernest, she was right. She had me on the run. I *was* cowering. I was defending my guidelines even in a situation where I knew they were antitherapeutic. I was placing my timidity, my fears about my little career, before her best interests. Really, when you look at things from a disinterested position, there *was* nothing wrong with letting her sit next to me and hold my hand. In fact, every time I did this, without fail, it charged up our therapy: she became less defensive, trusted me more, had more access to her inner life.

"What? Is there any place at all for firm boundaries in therapies? Of course there is. Listen on, Ernest. My problem was that Belle railed at all boundaries, like a bull and a red flag. Wherever—*wherever*—I set the boundaries she pushed and pushed against them. She took to wearing skimpy clothes or see-through blouses with no brassiere. When I commented on this, she ridiculed me for my Victorian attitudes toward the body. I wanted to know every intimate contour of her mind, she'd say, yet her skin was a no-no. A couple of times she complained about a breast lump and asked me to examine her—of course, I didn't. She'd obsess about sex with me for hours on end, and beg me to have sex with her just once. One of her arguments was that one-time sex with me would break her obsession. She'd learn that it was nothing special or magical and then be freed to think about other things in life.

"How did her campaign for sexual contact make me feel? Good question, Ernest, but is it germane to this investigation?

"You're not sure? What seems to be germane is what I *did*—that's what I'm being judged for—not what I felt or thought. Nobody gives a shit about that in a lynching! But if you turn off the tape recorder for a couple of minutes, I'll tell you. Consider it instruction. You've read Rilke's *Letters to a Young Poet,* haven't you? Well, consider this my letter to a young therapist.

"Good. Your pen, too, Ernest. Put it down, and just listen for a while. You want to know how this affected me? A beautiful woman obsessed with me, masturbating daily while thinking of me, begging me to lay her, talking on and on about her fantasies about me, about rubbing my sperm over her face or putting it into chocolate chip cookies—how do you *think* it made me feel? Look at me! Two canes, getting worse, ugly—my face being swallowed up in my own wrinkles, my body flabby, falling apart.

"I admit it. I'm only human. It began to get to me. I thought of her when I got dressed on the days we had a session. What kind of shirt to wear? She hated broad stripes—made me look too self-satisfied, she said. And which aftershave lotion? She liked Royall Lyme better than Mennen, and I'd vacillate each time over which one to use. Generally I'd splash on the Royall Lyme. One day at her tennis club, she met one of my colleagues—a nerd, a real narcissist who's always been competitive with me—and as soon as she heard he had some connection to me, she got him to talk about me. His connection to me turned her on, and she immediately went home with him. Imagine, this schnook gets laid by this great-looking woman and doesn't know it's because of me. And I can't tell him. Pissed me off.

"But having strong feelings about a patient is one thing. Acting on them is another. And I fought against it—I analyzed myself continually, I consulted with a couple of friends on an ongoing basis, and I tried to deal with it in the sessions. Time after time I told her there was no way in hell I would ever have sex with her, that I wouldn't ever again be able to feel good about myself if I did. I told her that she needed a good, caring therapist much more than she needed an aging, crippled lover. But I did acknowledge my attraction to her. I told her I didn't want her sitting so close to me because the physical contact stimulated me and rendered me less effective as a therapist. I took an authoritarian posture: I insisted that my long-range vision was better than hers, that I knew things about her therapy that she couldn't yet know.

"Yes, yes, you can turn the recorder back on. I think I've answered your question about my feelings. So, we went along like this for over a year, struggling against outbreaks of symptoms. She'd have many slips, but on the whole we were doing well. I knew this was no cure. I was only 'containing' her, providing a holding environment, keeping her safe from session to session. But I could hear the clock ticking; she was growing restless and fatigued.

"And then one day she came in looking all worn-out. Some new, very clean stuff was on the streets, and she admitted she was very close to scoring some heroin. 'I can't keep living a life of total frustration,' she said. 'I'm trying like hell to make this work, but I'm running out of steam. I know me, I know me, I know how I operate. You're keeping me alive and I want to work with you. I think I can do it. But I *need some incentive!* Yes, yes, Seymour, I know what you're getting ready to say: I know your lines by heart. You're going to say that I already have an incentive, that my incentive is a better life, feeling better about myself, not trying to kill myself, self-respect. But that stuff is not enough. It's too far away. Too airy. I need to touch it. I need to touch it!'

"I started to say something placating, but she cut me off. Her desperation had escalated and out of it came a desperate proposition. 'Seymour, work with me. My way. I beg you. If I stay clean for a year—really clean, you know what I mean: no drugs, no purging, no bar scenes, no cutting, no *nothing*—then *reward me!* Give me some incentive! Promise to take me to Hawaii for a week. And take me there as man and woman—not shrink and sap. Don't smile, Seymour, I'm serious—dead serious. I need this. Seymour, for once, put *my* needs ahead of the rules. Work with me on this.'

"Take her to Hawaii for a week! You smile, Ernest; so did I. Preposterous! I did as you would have done: I laughed it off. I tried to dismiss it as I had dismissed all of her previous corrupting propositions. But this one wouldn't go away. There was something more compelling, more ominous in her manner. And more persistent. She wouldn't let go of it. I couldn't move her off it. When I told her it was out of the question, Belle started negotiating: she raised the good-behavior period to a year and a half, changed Hawaii to San Francisco, and cut the week first to five and then to four days.

"Between sessions, despite myself, I found myself thinking about Belle's proposition. I couldn't help it. I toyed with it in my mind. A year and a half—*eighteen months*—of good behavior? Impossible. Absurd. She could never do it. Why were we wasting our time even talking about it?

"But *suppose*—just a thought experiment, I told myself—suppose that she were really able to change her behavior for eighteen months? Try out the idea, Ernest. Think about it. Consider the possibility. Wouldn't you agree that if this impulsive, acting-out woman were to develop controls, behave more ego-syntonically for eighteen months, off drugs, off cutting, off all forms of self-destruction, *she'd no longer be the same person*?

"What? 'Borderline patients play games'? That what you said? Ernest, you'll never be a real therapist if you think like that. That's exactly what I meant earlier when I talked about the dangers of diagnosis. There are borderlines and there are borderlines. Labels do violence to people. You can't treat the label; you have to treat the person behind the label. So again, Ernest, I ask you: Wouldn't you agree that this person, not this label, but this Belle, this flesh and blood person, would be intrinsically, radically changed, if she behaved in a fundamentally different fashion for eighteen months?

"You won't commit yourself? I can't blame you—considering

your position today. And the tape recorder. Well, just answer silently, to yourself. No, let me answer for you: I don't believe there's a therapist alive who wouldn't agree that Belle would be a vastly different person if she were no longer governed by her impulse disorder. She'd develop different values, different priorities, a different vision. She'd wake up, open her eyes, see reality, maybe see her own beauty and worth. And she'd see me differently, see me as you see me: a tottering, moldering, old man. Once reality intrudes, then her erotic transference, her necrophilia, would simply fade away and with it, of course, all interest in the Hawaiian incentive.

"What's that, Ernest? Would I miss the erotic transference? Would that sadden me? Of course! Of course! I love being adored. Who doesn't? Don't you?

"Come on, Ernest. *Don't you?* Don't you love the applause when you finish giving grand rounds? Don't you love the people, especially the women, crowding around?

"Good! I appreciate your honesty. Nothing to be ashamed of. Who doesn't? Just the way we're built. So to go on, I'd miss her adoration, I'd feel bereft: but that goes with the territory. That's my job: to introduce her to reality, to help her grow away from me. Even, God save us, to forget me.

"Well, as the days and the weeks went on, I grew more and more intrigued with Belle's wager. *Eighteen months of being clean,* she offered. And remember that was still an early offer. I'm a good negotiator and was sure I could probably get more, increase the odds, provide even more room. Really cement the change. I thought about other conditions I could insist upon: some group therapy for her, perhaps, and a more strenuous attempt to get her husband into couples therapy.

"I thought about Belle's proposition day and night. Couldn't get it out of my mind. I'm a betting man, and the odds in my favor looked fantastic. If Belle lost the bet, if she slipped—by taking drugs, purging, cruising bars, or cutting her wrists—*nothing would be lost.* We'd merely be back to where we were before. Even if I got only a few weeks or months of abstinence, I could build on that. And if Belle won, she'd be so changed that she would never collect. This was a no-brainer. Zero risk downside and a good chance upside that I could save this woman.

"I've always liked action, love the races, bet on anything—baseball, basketball. After high school I joined the navy and put myself through college on my shipboard poker winnings; in my internship at Mount Sinai in New York I spent many of my free nights in a big game on the obstetrics unit with the on-call Park Avenue obstetricians. There was a continuous game going on in the doctors' lounge next to the labor room. Whenever there was an open hand, they called the operator to page 'Dr. Blackwood.' Whenever I heard the page, 'Dr. Blackwood wanted in the delivery room,' I'd charge over as fast as I could. Great docs, every one of them, but poker chumps. You know, Ernest, interns were paid almost nothing in those days, and at the end of the year all the other interns were in deep debt. Me? I drove to my residency at Ann Arbor in a new De Soto convertible, courtesy of the Park Avenue obstetricians.

"Back to Belle. I vacillated for weeks about her wager and then, one day, I took the plunge. I told Belle I could understand her needing incentive, and I opened serious negotiation. I insisted on two years. She was so grateful to be taken seriously that she agreed to all my terms, and we quickly fashioned a firm, clear contract. Her part of the deal was to stay entirely clean for two years: no drugs (including alcohol), no cutting, no purging, no sex pickups in bars or highways or any other dangerous sex behavior. Urbane sexual affairs were permitted. And no illegal behavior. I thought that covered everything. Oh, yes, she had to start group therapy and promise to participate with her husband in couples therapy. My part of the contract was a weekend in San Francisco: all details, hotels, activities were to be her choice—carte blanche. I was to be at her service.

"Belle treated this very seriously. At the finish of negotiation, she suggested a formal oath. She brought a Bible to the session and we each swore on it that we would uphold our part of the contract. After that we solemnly shook hands on our agreement.

"Treatment continued as before. Belle and I met approximately two times a week—three might have been better, but her husband began to grumble about the therapy bills. Since Belle stayed clean and we didn't have to spend time analyzing her 'slips,' therapy went faster and deeper. Dreams, fantasies—everything seemed more accessible. For the first time I began to see seeds of curiosity about herself; she signed up for some university extension courses on abnormal psychology, and she began writing an autobiography of her early life. Gradually she recalled more details of her childhood, her sad search for a new mother among the string of disinterested governesses, most of whom left within a few months because of her father's fanatical insistence on cleanliness and order. His germ phobia controlled all aspects of her life. Imagine: until she was fourteen she was kept out of school and educated at home because of his fear of her bringing home germs. Consequently she had few close friends. Even meals with friends were rare; she was forbidden to dine out and she dreaded the embarrassment of exposing her friends to her father's dining antics: gloves, hand washing between courses, inspections of the servants' hands for cleanliness. She was not permitted to borrow books—one beloved governess was fired on the spot because she permitted Belle and a friend to wear each other's dresses for a day. Childhood and daughterhood ended sharply at fourteen, when she was sent to boarding school at Grenoble. From then on, she had only perfunctory contact with her father, who soon remarried. His new wife was a beautiful woman but a former prostitute—according to a spinster aunt, who said the new wife was only one of many whores her father had known in the previous fourteen years. Maybe, Belle wondered—and this was her very first interpretation in therapy—*he* felt dirty, and that was why he was always washing and why he refused to let his skin touch hers.

"During these months Belle raised the topic of our wager only in the context of expressing her gratitude to me. She called it the 'most powerful affirmation' she'd ever gotten. She knew that the wager was a gift to her: unlike 'gifts' she had received from other shrinks— words, interpretations, promises, 'therapeutic caring'—this gift was real and palpable. Skin to skin. It was tangible proof that I was entirely committed to helping her. And proof to her of my love. Never before, she said, had she ever been loved like that. Never before had anyone put her ahead of his self-interests, ahead of the rules. Certainly not her father, who never gave her an ungloved hand and until his death ten years ago sent her the same birthday present every year: a bundle of hundred-dollar bills, one for every year of her age, each bill freshly washed and ironed.

"And the wager had another meaning. She was tickled by my willingness to bend the rules. What she loved best about me, she said, was my willingness to take chances, my open channel to my own shadow. 'There's something naughty and dark about you, too,' she'd say. 'That's why you understand me so well. In some ways I think we are twin brains.'

"You know, Ernest, that's probably why we hit it off so quickly, why she knew immediately that I was the therapist for her—just something mischievous in my face, some irreverent twinkle in my eyes. Belle was right. She had my number. She was a smart cookie.

"And you know, I knew exactly what she meant—exactly! I can spot it in others the same way. Ernest, just for a minute, turn off the recorder. Good. Thanks. What I wanted to say is that I think I see it in you. You and I, we sit on different sides of this dais, this judgment table, but we have something in common. I told you, I'm good at reading faces. I'm rarely wrong about such things.

"No? C'mon! You know what I mean! Isn't it precisely for this reason that you listen to my tale with such interest? More than interest! Do I go too far if I call it *fascination*? Your eyes are like saucers. Yes, Ernest, you and me. You could have been me in my situation. My Faustian wager could have been yours as well.

"You shake your head. Of course! But I don't speak to your head. I aim straight at your heart, and the time may come when you open yourself to what I say. And more—perhaps you will see yourself not only in me but in Belle as well. The three of us. We're not so different from one another! Okay, that's all—let's get back to business.

"Wait! Before you turn the recorder back on, Ernest, let me say one more thing. You think I give a shit about the ethics committee? What can they do? Take away hospital admitting privileges? I'm seventy, my career is over, I know that. So why do I tell you all this? In the hope that some good will come of it. In the hope that maybe you'll allow some speck of me into you, let me course in your veins, let me teach you. Remember, Ernest, when I talk about your having an open channel to your shadow, I mean that *positively*—I mean that you may have the courage and largeness of spirit to be a great therapist. Turn the recorder back on, Ernest. Please, no reply is necessary. When you're seventy, you don't need replies.

"Okay, where were we? Well, the first year passed with Belle definitely doing better. No slips whatsoever. She was absolutely clean. She placed fewer demands on me. Occasionally she asked to sit next to me, and I'd put my arm around her and we'd spend a few minutes sitting like that. It never failed to relax her and make her more productive in therapy. I continued to give her fatherly hugs at the end of sessions, and she usually planted a restrained, daughterly kiss on my cheek. Her husband refused couples therapy but agreed to meet with a Christian Science practitioner for several sessions. Belle told me that their communication had improved, and both of them seemed more content with their relationship.

"At the sixteen-month mark, all was still well. No heroin—no drugs at all—no cutting, bulimia, purging, or self-destructive behavior of any sort. She got involved with several fringe movements—a channeler, a past-lives therapy group, an algae nutritionist, typical California flake stuff, harmless. She and her husband had resumed their sexual life, and she did a little sexual acting out with my colleague—that jerk, that asshole, she met at the tennis club. But at least it was safe sex, a far cry from the bar and highway escapades.

"It was the most remarkable therapy turnabout I've ever seen. Belle said it was the happiest time of her life. I challenge you, Ernest: plug her into any of your outcome studies. She'd be the star patient! Compare her outcome with any drug therapy: Risperidone, Prozac, Paxil, Effexor, Wellbutrin—you name it—my therapy would win hands down. The best therapy I've ever done, and yet I couldn't publish it. Publish it? I couldn't even tell anyone about it. Until now! You're my first real audience.

"At about the eighteen-month mark, the sessions began to change. It was subtle at first. More and more references to our San Francisco weekend crept in, and soon Belle began to speak of it at every session. Every morning she'd stay in bed for an extra hour daydreaming about what our weekend would be like: about sleeping in my arms, phoning for breakfast in bed, then a drive and lunch in Sausalito, followed by an afternoon nap. She had fantasies of our being married, of waiting for me in the evenings. She insisted that she could live happily the rest of her life if she knew that I'd come back home to her. She didn't need much time with me; she'd be willing to be a second wife, to have me next to her for only an hour or two a week—she could live healthy and happy with that forever.

"Well, you can imagine that by this time I was growing a little uneasy. And then a lot uneasy. I began to scramble. I did my best to help her face reality. Practically every session I talked about my age. In three or four years I'd be in a wheelchair. In ten years I'd be eighty. I asked her how long she thought I would live. The males in my family die young. At my age my father had been in his coffin for fifteen years. She would outlive me at least twenty-five years. I even began exaggerating my neurological impairment when I was with her. Once I staged an intentional fall—that's how desperate I was growing. And old people don't have much energy, I repeated. Asleep at eight-thirty, I'd tell her. Been five years since I'd been awake for the ten o'clock news. And my failing vision, my shoulder bursitis, my dyspepsia, my prostate, my gassiness, my constipation. I even thought of getting a hearing aid, just for the effect.

"But all this was a terrible blunder. One hundred eighty degrees wrong! It just whet her appetite even more. She had some perverse infatuation with the idea of my being infirm or incapacitated. She had fantasies of my having a stroke, of my wife leaving me, of her moving in to care for me. One of her favorite daydreams involved nursing me: making my tea, washing me, changing my sheets and my pajamas, dusting me with talcum powder, and then taking off her clothes and climbing under the cool sheets next to me.

"At the twenty-month mark, Belle's improvement was even more pronounced. On her own she had gotten involved with Narcotics Anonymous and was attending three meetings a week. She was doing volunteer work at ghetto schools to teach teenage girls about birth control and AIDS, and had been accepted in an MBA program at a local university.

"What's that, Ernest? How did I know she was telling me the truth? You know, I never doubted her. I know she has her character flaws but truth telling, at least with me, seemed almost a compulsion. Early in our therapy—I think I mentioned this before—we established a contract of mutual and absolute truth telling. There were a couple of times in the first few weeks of therapy when she withheld some particularly unseemly episodes of acting out, but she couldn't stand it; she got into a frenzy about it, was convinced that I could see inside her mind and would expel her from therapy. In each instance she could not wait till the next session to confess but had to phone me—once after midnight—to set the record straight.

"But your question is a good one. Too much was riding on this to simply take her word for it, and I did what you would have done: I checked all possible sources. During this time I met with her husband a couple of times. He refused therapy but agreed to come in to help accelerate the pace of Belle's therapy, and he corroborated everything she said. Not only that but he gave me permission to contact the Christian Science counselor—who, ironically enough, was getting her Ph.D. in clinical psychology and was reading my work— and who also corroborated Belle's story: working hard on her marriage, no cutting, no drugs, community volunteer work. No, Belle was playing it straight.

"So what would you have done in this situation, Ernest? What? Wouldn't have been there in the first place? Yeah, yeah, I know.

Facile answer. You disappoint me. Tell me, Ernest, if you wouldn't have been there, where *would* you have been? Back in your lab? Or in the library? You'd be safe. Proper and comfortable. But where would the patient be? Long gone, that's where! Just like Belle's twenty therapists before me—they all took the safe route, too. But I'm a different kind of therapist. A saver of lost souls. I refuse to quit on a patient. I will break my neck, I'll put my ass on the line, I'll try anything to save the patient. That's been true my whole career. You know my reputation? Ask around. Ask your chairman. He knows. He's sent me dozens of patients. I'm the therapist of last resort. Therapists send me the patients they give up on. You're nodding? You've heard that about me? Good! It's good you know I'm not just some senile schnook.

"So consider my position! What the hell could I do? I was getting jumpy. I pulled out all the stops: I began to interpret like mad, in a frenzy, as if my life depended on it. I interpreted everything that moved. And I got impatient with her illusions.

"For example, take Belle's loony fantasy of our being married and her putting her life on hold waiting all week, in suspended animation, for an hour or two with me. 'What kind of life is that and what kind of relationship?' I asked her. It was not a relationship—it was shamanism. Think of it from my point of view, I'd say: What did she imagine I'd get out of such an arrangement? To have her healed by an hour of my presence—it was unreal. Was this a relationship? No! We weren't being real with each other; she was using me as an icon. And her obsession with sucking me and swallowing my sperm. Same thing. Unreal. She felt empty and wanted me to fill her up with my essence. Couldn't she see what she was doing, couldn't she see the error in treating the symbolic as if it were concrete reality? How long did she think my thimbleful of sperm would fill her up? In a few seconds her gastric hydrochloric acid would leave nothing but fragmented DNA chains.

"Belle gravely nodded at my frenetic interpretations—and then returned to her knitting. Her Narcotics Anonymous sponsor had taught her to knit, and during the last weeks she worked continuously on a cable-stitched sweater for me to wear during our weekend. I found no way to rattle her. Yes, she agreed that she might be basing her life on fantasy. Maybe she was searching for the wise old man archetype. But was that so bad? In addition to her MBA program, she was auditing a course in anthropology and reading *The*

Golden Bough. She reminded me that most of mankind lived according to such irrational concepts as totems, reincarnation, heaven, and hell, even transference cures of therapy, and the deification of Freud. 'Whatever works works,' she said, 'and the thought of our being together for the weekend works. This has been the best time in my life; it feels just like being married to you. It's like waiting and knowing you'll be coming home to me shortly; it keeps me going, it keeps me content.' And with that she turned back to her knitting. That goddamned sweater! I felt like ripping it out of her hands.

"By the twenty-two-month mark, I hit the panic button. I lost all composure and began wheedling, weaseling, begging. I lectured her on love. 'You say you love me, but love is a relationship, love is caring about the other, caring about the growth and the being of the other. Do you ever care about me? How *I* feel? Do you ever think about my guilt, my fear, the impact of this on my self-respect, knowing that I've done something unethical? And the impact on my reputation, the risk I'm running—my profession, my marriage?'

"'How many times,' Belle responded, 'have you reminded me that we are two people in a human encounter—nothing more, nothing less? You asked me to trust you, and I trusted you—I trusted for the first time in my life. Now I ask *you* to trust *me*. This will be our secret. I'll take it to my grave. No matter what happens. Forever! And as for your self-respect and your guilt and your professional concerns, well, what's more important than the fact that you, a healer, are healing me? Will you let rules and reputation and ethics take precedence over that?' You got a good answer for that, Ernest? I didn't.

"Subtly, but ominously, she alluded to the potential effects of my welching on the wager. She had lived for *two years* for this weekend with me. Would she ever trust again? Any therapist? Or *anyone*, for that matter? *That*, she let me know, would be something for me to feel guilty about. She didn't have to say very much. I knew what my betrayal would mean to her. She had not been self-destructive for over two years, but I had no doubt she had not lost the knack. To put it bluntly, I was convinced that if I welched, Belle would kill herself. I still tried to escape from my trap, but my wing beats grew more feeble.

"'I'm seventy years old—you're thirty-four,' I told her. 'There's something unnatural about us sleeping together.'

"'Chaplin, Kissinger, Picasso, Humbert Humbert and Lolita,' Belle responded, not even bothering to look up from her knitting.

"'You've built this up to grotesque levels,' I told her; 'it's all so inflated, so exaggerated, so removed from reality. This whole weekend cannot fail to be a downer for you.'

"'A downer is the best thing that could happen,' she replied. 'You know—to break down my obsession about you, my "erotic transference," as you like to call it. This is a no-loser for our therapy.'

"I kept weaseling. 'Besides, at my age, potency wanes.'

"'Seymour,' she chided me, 'I'm surprised at you. You still haven't gotten it, still haven't gotten that potency or intercourse is of no concern. What I want is you to be with me and hold me—as a person, a woman. Not as a patient. Besides, Seymour,' and here she held the half-knitted sweater in front of her face, coyly peeked over, and said, 'I'm going to give you the fuck of your life!'

"And then time was up. The twenty-fourth month arrived and I had no choice but to pay the devil his due. If I welched, I knew the consequences would be catastrophic. If, on the other hand, I kept my word? Then, who knows? Perhaps she was right, perhaps it *would* break the obsession. Perhaps, without the erotic transference, her energies would be freed to relate better to her husband. She'd maintain her faith in therapy. I'd retire in a couple of years, and she'd go on to other therapists. Maybe a weekend in San Francisco with Belle would be an act of supreme therapeutic agape.

"What, Ernest? My countertransference? Same as yours would have been: gyrating wildly. I tried to keep it out of my decision. I didn't act on my countertransference—I was convinced I had no other rational choice. And I'm convinced of that still, even in the light of what has happened. But I'll cop to being more than a little enthralled. There I was, an old man facing the end, with cerebellar cortical neurons croaking daily, eyes failing, sexual life all but over—my wife, who's good at giving things up, gave sex up long ago. And my attraction toward Belle? I won't deny it: I adored her. And when she told me she was going to give me the fuck of my life, I could hear my worn-out gonadal engines cranking up and turning over again. But let me say to you—and the tape recorder, let me say it as forcefully as I can—*that's not why I did it!* That may not be important to you or the ethics board, but it's of life-or-death importance to me. I never broke my covenant with Belle. I never broke my covenant with any patient. I never put my needs ahead of theirs.

"As for the rest of the story, I guess you know it. It's all in your chart there. Belle and I met in San Francisco for breakfast at Mama's in North Beach on Saturday morning and stayed together till Sunday dusk. We decided to tell our spouses that I had scheduled a weekend marathon group for my patients. I do such groups for ten to twelve of my patients about twice a year. In fact, Belle had attended such a weekend during her first year of therapy.

"You ever run groups like that, Ernest? No? Well, let me tell you that they are powerful . . . accelerate therapy like mad. You should know about them. When we meet again—and I'm sure we will, under different circumstances—I'll tell you about these groups; I've been doing them for thirty-five years.

"But back to the weekend. Not fair to bring you this far and not share the climax. Let's see, what can I tell you? What do I *want* to tell you? I tried to keep my dignity, to stay within my therapist persona, but that didn't last long—Belle saw to that. She called me on it as soon as we had checked into the Fairmont, and very soon we were man and woman and everything, everything, that Belle had predicted came to pass.

"I won't lie to you, Ernest. I loved every minute of our weekend, most of which we spent in bed. I was worried that all my pipes were rusted shut after so many years of disuse. But Belle was a master plumber, and after some rattling and clanging everything began to work again.

"For three years I had chided Belle for living in illusion and had imposed my reality on her. Now, for one weekend, I entered her world and found out that life in the magic kingdom wasn't so bad. She was my fountain of youth. Hour by hour I grew younger and stronger. I walked better, I sucked in my stomach, I looked taller. Ernest, I tell you, I felt like bellowing. And Belle noticed it. 'This is what you needed, Seymour. And this is all I ever wanted from you— to be held, to hold, to give my love. Do you understand that this is the first time in my life I have given love? Is it so terrible?'

"She cried a lot. Along with all other conduits, my lachrymal ducts, too, had unplugged, and I cried too. She gave me so much that weekend. I spent my whole career giving, and this was the first time it came back, really came back, to me. It's like she gave for all the other patients I've ever seen.

"But then real life resumed. The weekend ended. Belle and I went back to our twice-weekly sessions. I never anticipated losing that wager, so I had no contingency plans for the postweekend therapy. I tried to go back to business as usual, but after one or two sessions I saw I had a problem. A big problem. It is almost impossible for intimates to return to a formal relationship. Despite my efforts, a new tone of loving playfulness replaced the serious work of therapy. Sometimes Belle insisted on sitting in my lap. She did a lot of hugging and stroking and groping. I tried to fend her off, I tried to maintain a serious work ethic, but, let's face it, it was no longer therapy.

"I called a halt and solemnly suggested we had two options: either we try to go back to serious work, which meant returning to a non-physical and more traditional relationship, or we drop the pretense that we're doing therapy and try to establish a purely social relationship. And 'social' didn't mean sexual: I didn't want to compound the problem. I told you before, I helped write the guidelines condemning therapists and patients having post-therapy sexual relationships. I also made it clear to her that, since we were no longer doing therapy, I would accept no more money from her.

"Neither of those options were acceptable to Belle. A return to formality in therapy seemed a farce. Isn't the therapy relationship the one place where you don't play games? As for not paying, that was impossible. Her husband had set up an office at home and spent most of his time around the house. How could she explain to him where she was going for two regular hours a week if she were not regularly writing checks for therapy?

"Belle chided me for my narrow definition of therapy. 'Our meetings together—intimate, playful, touching, sometimes making good love, real love, on your couch—that *is* therapy. And good therapy, too. Why can't you see that, Seymour?' she asked. 'Isn't effective therapy good therapy? Have you forgotten your pronouncements about the 'one important question in therapy'? *Does it work?* And isn't my therapy working? Aren't I continuing to do well? I've stayed clean. No symptoms. Finishing grad school. I'm starting a new life. You've changed me, Seymour, and all you have to do to maintain the change is continue to spend two hours a week being close to me.'

"Belle was a smart cookie, all right. And growing smarter. I could marshal no counterargument that such an arrangement was not good therapy.

"Yet I knew it couldn't be. I enjoyed it too much. Gradually, much too gradually, it dawned on me that I was in big trouble. Anyone looking at the two of us together would conclude that I was exploiting the transference and using this patient for my own pleasure. Or that I was a high-priced geriatric gigolo!

"I didn't know what to do. Obviously I couldn't consult with anyone—I knew what they would advise and I wasn't ready to bite the bullet. Nor could I refer her to another therapist—she wouldn't go. But to be honest, I didn't push that option hard. I worry about that. Did I do right by her? I lost a few nights' sleep thinking about her telling another therapist all about me. You know how therapists gossip among themselves about the antics of previous therapists—and they'd just love some juicy Seymour Trotter gossip. Yet I couldn't ask her to protect me—keeping that kind of secret would sabotage her next therapy.

"So my small-craft warnings were up but, even so, I was absolutely unprepared for the fury of the storm when it finally broke. One evening I returned home to find the house dark, my wife gone, and four pictures of me and Belle tacked to the front door: one showed us checking in at the registration desk of the Fairmont Hotel, another of us, suitcases in hand, entering our room together, the third was a close-up of the hotel registration form—Belle had paid cash and registered us as Dr. and Mrs. Seymour. The fourth showed us locked in an embrace at the Golden Gate Bridge scenic overlook.

"Inside, on the kitchen table, I found two letters: one from Belle's husband to my wife, stating that she might be interested in the four enclosed pictures portraying the type of treatment her husband was offering his wife. He said he had sent a similar letter to the state board of medical ethics and ended with a nasty threat suggesting that if I ever saw Belle again, a lawsuit would be the least important thing the Trotter family would have to worry about. The second letter was from my wife—short and to the point, asking me not to bother to explain. I could do my talking to her lawyer. She gave me twenty-four hours to pack up and move out of the house.

"So, Ernest, that brings us up to now. What else can I tell you?"

"How'd he get the pictures? Must've hired a private eye to tail us. What irony—that her husband chose to leave only when Belle had improved! But, who knows? Maybe he'd been looking for an escape for a long time. Maybe Belle had burned him out.

"I never saw Belle again. All I know is hearsay from an old buddy of mine at Pacific Redwood Hospital—and it ain't good hearsay. Her husband divorced her and ultimately skipped the country with the family assets. He had been suspicious of Belle for months, ever since he had spotted some condoms in her purse. That, of course, is further irony: it was only because therapy had curbed her lethal self-destructiveness that she was willing to use condoms in her affairs.

"The last I heard, Belle's condition was terrible—back to ground zero. All the old pathology was back: two admissions for suicidal attempts—one cutting, one a serious overdose. She's going to kill herself. I know it. Apparently she tried three new therapists, fired each in turn, refuses further therapy, and is now doing hard drugs again.

"And you know what the worst thing is? I know I could help her, even now. I'm sure of it, but I'm forbidden to see her or speak to her by court order and under the threat of severe penalty. I got several phone messages from her, but my attorney warned me that I was in great jeopardy and ordered me, if I wanted to stay out of jail, not to respond. He contacted Belle and informed her that by court injunction I was not permitted to communicate with her. Finally she stopped calling.

"What am I going to do? About Belle, you mean? It's a tough call. It kills me not to be able to answer her calls, but I don't like jails. I know I could do so much for her in a ten-minute conversation. Even now. Off the record—shut off the recorder, Ernest. I'm not sure if I'm going to be able to just let her sink. Not sure if I could live with myself.

"So, Ernest, that's it. The end of my tale. *Finis.* Let me tell you, it's not the way I wanted to end my career. Belle is the major character in this tragedy, but the situation is also catastrophic for me. Her lawyers are urging her to ask for damages—to get all she can. They will have a feeding frenzy—the malpractice suit is coming up in a couple of months.

"Depressed! Of course I'm depressed. Who wouldn't be? I call it an appropriate depression: I'm a miserable, sad old man. Discouraged, lonely, full of self-doubts, ending my life in disgrace.

"No, Ernest, not a drug-treatable depression. Not that kind of depression. No biological markers: psychomotor symptoms, insomnia, weight loss—none of that. Thanks for offering.

"No, not suicidal, though I admit I'm drawn to darkness. But I'm a survivor. I crawl into the cellar and lick my wounds.

"Yes, very much alone. My wife and I had been living together by habit for many years. I've always lived for my work; my marriage has always been on the periphery of my life. My wife always said I fulfill all my desires for closeness with my patients. And she was right. But that's not why she left. My ataxia's progressing fast, and I don't think she relished the idea of becoming my full-time nurse. My hunch is that she welcomed the excuse to cut herself loose from that job. Can't blame her.

"No, I don't need to see anyone for therapy. I told you I'm not clinically depressed. I appreciate your asking, Ernest, but I'd be a cantankerous patient. So far, as I said, I'm licking my own wounds and I'm a pretty good licker.

"It's fine with me if you phone to check in. I'm touched by your offer. But put your mind at ease, Ernest. I'm a tough son of a bitch. I'll be all right."

And with that, Seymour Trotter collected his canes and lurched out of the room. Ernest, still sitting, listened to the tapping grow fainter.

~

When Ernest phoned a couple of weeks later, Dr. Trotter once again refused all offers of help. Within minutes he switched the conversation to Ernest's future and again expressed his strong conviction that, whatever Ernest's strengths as a psychopharmacologist, he was still missing his calling: he was a born therapist and owed it to himself to fulfill his destiny. He invited Ernest to discuss the matter further over lunch, but Ernest refused.

"Thoughtless of me," Dr. Trotter had responded without a trace of irony. "Forgive me. Here I am advising you about a career shift and at the same time asking you to jeopardize it by being seen in public with me."

"No, Seymour," for the first time Ernest called him by first name, "that is absolutely not the reason. The truth is, and I am embarrassed to say this to you, I'm committed already to serve as an expert witness at your civil suit trial for malpractice."

"Embarrassment is not warranted, Ernest. It's your duty to testify. I would do the same, precisely the same, in your position. Our profession is vulnerable, threatened on all sides. It is our to duty to protect it and to preserve standards. Even if you believe nothing else about me, believe that I treasure this work. I've devoted my entire life to it. That's why I told you my story in such detail—I wanted you to know it is not a story of betrayal. I acted in good faith. I know it sounds absurd, yet even to this moment I think I did the right thing. Sometimes destiny pitches us into positions where the right thing is the wrong thing. I never betrayed my field, nor a patient. Whatever the future brings, Ernest, believe me. I believe in what I did: I would never betray a patient."

Ernest did testify at the civil trial. Seymour's attorney, citing his advanced age, diminished judgment, and infirmity, tried a novel, desperate defense: he claimed that Seymour, not Belle, had been the victim. But their case was hopeless, and Belle was awarded two million dollars—the maximum of Seymour's malpractice coverage. Her lawyers would have gone for more but there seemed little point to it since, after his divorce and legal fees, Seymour's pockets were empty.

That was the end of the public story of Seymour Trotter. Shortly after the trial he silently left town and was never heard from again, aside from a letter (with no return address) that Ernest received a year later.

⌇

Ernest had only a few minutes before his first patient. But he couldn't resist inspecting, once again, the last trace of Seymour Trotter.

> Dear Ernest,
>   You, alone, in those demonizing witch hunt days, expressed concern for my welfare. Thank you—it was powerfully sustaining. Am well. Lost, but don't want to be found. I owe you much—certainly this letter and this picture of Belle and me. That's her house in the background, incidentally: Belle's come into a good bit of money.
>
> Seymour

Ernest, as he had so many times before, stared at the faded picture. On a palm-studded lawn, Seymour sat in a wheelchair. Belle stood behind him, forlorn and gaunt, fists clutching the handles of the wheelchair. Her eyes were downcast. Behind her a graceful colonial home, and beyond that the gleaming milky-green water of a tropical sea. Seymour was smiling—a big, goofy, crooked smile. He held on to the wheelchair with one hand; with the other, he pointed his cane jubilantly toward the sky.

As always, when he studied the photograph, Ernest felt queasy.

He peered closer, trying to crawl into the picture, trying to discover some clue, some definitive answer to the real fate of Seymour and Belle. The key, he thought, was to be found in Belle's eyes. They seemed melancholy, even despondent. Why? She had gotten what she wanted, hadn't she? He moved closer to Belle and tried to catch her gaze. But she always looked away.

ONE

$\mathcal{T}$hree times a week for the past five years, Justin Astrid had started his day with a visit to Dr. Ernest Lash. His visit today had begun like any of the previous seven hundred therapy sessions: at 7:50 A.M. up the outdoor stairs of the Sacramento Street Victorian, handsomely painted in mauve and mahogany, through the vestibule, up to the second floor, into Ernest's dimly lit waiting room, permeated with the rich, moist aroma of Italian dark roast. Justin inhaled deeply, then poured coffee into a Japanese mug adorned with a hand-painted persimmon, and sat on the stiff green leather sofa and opened the *San Francisco Chronicle* sports section.

But Justin could not read about yesterday's baseball game. Not on this day. Something momentous had happened—something that demanded commemoration. He folded his newspaper and stared at Ernest's door.

At eight A.M. Ernest put Seymour Trotter's folder into his file cabinet, glanced quickly at Justin's chart, straightened his desk, placed his newspaper in a drawer, put his coffee cup out of sight, rose, and, just before opening his office door, looked back to scan his office. No visible signs of habitation. Good.

He opened his door and for a moment the two men looked at each other. Healer and patient. Justin with his *Chronicle* in hand, Ernest's newspaper hidden deeply in his desk. Justin in his dark blue suit and Italian striped silk tie. Ernest in a navy blue blazer and Liberty flowered tie. Both were fifteen pounds overweight, Justin's flesh spilling into chins and jowls, Ernest's belly bulging over his belt. Justin's mustache curled upward, stretching for his nostrils. Ernest's manicured beard was his tidiest feature. Justin's face was mobile, fidgety, his eyes jittery. Ernest wore large goggle spectacles and could go for long periods without blinking.

"I've left my wife," Justin began, after taking a seat in the office. "Yesterday evening. Just moved out. Spent the night with Laura." He offered these first words calmly and dispassionately, then stopped and peered at Ernest.

"Just like that?" Ernest asked quietly. No blinking.

"Just like that." Justin smiled. "When I see what has to be done, I don't waste time."

A little humor had entered their interaction over the past few months. Ordinarily, Ernest welcomed it. His supervisor, Marshal Streider, had said that the appearance of humorous byplay in therapy was often a propitious sign.

But Ernest's "just like that" comment had not been good-natured byplay. He was unsettled by Justin's announcement. And irritated! He had been treating Justin for five years—five years of busting his ass trying to help him leave his wife! And today Justin casually informs him that he left his wife.

Ernest thought back to their very first session, to Justin's opening words: "I need help getting out of my marriage!" For months Ernest had painstakingly investigated the situation. Finally he concurred: Justin *should* get out—it was one of the worst marriages Ernest had ever seen. And for the next five years Ernest had used every known psychotherapy device to enable Justin to leave. Every one had failed.

Ernest was an obstinate therapist. No one had ever accused him of not trying hard enough. Most of his colleagues considered him too active, too ambitious in his therapy. His supervisor was forever remonstrating him with, "Whoa, cowboy, slow down! Prepare the soil. You can't *force* people to change." But, finally, even Ernest was forced to give up hope. Though he never stopped liking Justin and never stopped hoping for better things for him, he gradually grew convinced that Justin would never leave his wife, that he was immovable, rooted, that he would be stuck for life in a tormented marriage.

Ernest then set more limited goals for Justin: to make the best of a bad marriage, to become more autonomous at work, to develop better social skills. Ernest could do this as well as the next therapist. But it was boring. Therapy grew more and more predictable; nothing unexpected ever happened. Ernest stifled yawns and pushed his glasses up the bridge of his nose to keep himself awake. He no longer discussed Justin with his supervisor. He imagined conversations with Justin in which he raised the question of referring him to another therapist.

And here, today, Justin saunters in and nonchalantly announces he has left his wife!

Ernest tried to conceal his feelings by cleaning his goggle spectacles with a Kleenex yanked from the box.

"Tell me about it, Justin." Bad technique! He knew it instantly. He put his glasses back on and jotted on his notepad: "mistake—asked for information—countertransference?"

Later, in supervision, he would go over these notes with Marshal. But he knew himself that it was nuts for him to be pulling for information. Why should *he* have to coax Justin to continue? He should not have given in to his curiosity. *Incontinent*—that's what Marshal had called him a couple of weeks earlier. "Learn to wait," Marshal would say. "It should be more important for Justin to tell you this than for you to hear it. And if he chooses *not* to tell you, then you should focus on why he comes to see you, pays you, and yet withholds information from you."

Ernest knew Marshal was right. Yet he did not care about technical correctness—this was no ordinary session. The sleeping Justin had awakened and left his wife! Ernest looked at his patient; was it his imagination or did Justin appear more powerful today? No obsequious head bowing, no slouching, no fidgeting in his chair to adjust his underwear, no hesitancy, no apologies about dropping his newspaper on the floor next to his chair.

"Well, I wish there were more to tell—it all went so easily. Like I was on automatic pilot. I just did it. I just walked out!" Justin fell silent.

Again, Ernest couldn't wait. "Tell me more, Justin."

"It's got to do with Laura, my young friend."

Justin rarely spoke of Laura, but when he did she was always, simply, "my young friend." Ernest found that irritating. But he gave away nothing and remained silent.

"You know I've been seeing her a lot—maybe I've minimized that a bit to you. I don't know why I've kept it from you. But I've been seeing her almost daily, for lunch, or a walk, or going up to her apartment for a romp in the hay. I've just been feeling more and more together, at home, with her. And then, yesterday, Laura said, very matter-of-factly, 'It's time, Justin, for you to move in with me.'

"And you know," Justin continued, brushing away the mustache hairs tickling his nostrils, "I thought, she's right, it *is* time."

Laura tells him to leave his wife and he leaves his wife. For a moment Ernest thought about an essay he had once read on the mating behavior of coral reef fish. Apparently marine biologists can easily identify the dominant female and male fish: they simply watch the female swim and observe how she visibly disrupts the swim patterns of most male fish—all but the dominant males. The power of the beautiful female, fish or human! Awesome! Laura, barely out of high school, had simply told Justin it was time to leave his wife, and he had obeyed. Whereas he, Ernest Lash, a gifted, a highly gifted therapist, had wasted five years trying to pry Justin out of his marriage.

"And then," Justin went on, "at home last night Carol made it easy for me by being her usual obnoxious self, hammering at me for not being *present*. 'Even when you're present, you're absent,' she said. 'Pull your chair up to the table! Why are you always so far away? Talk! Look at us! When was the last time you made a single unsolicited comment to me or the children? Where are you? Your body's here—you're not!' At the end of the meal, when she was clearing the table and banging and clattering the dishes, she added, 'I don't even know why you bother to bring your body home.'

"And then suddenly, Ernest, it came to me: Carol's right. She's right. *Why do I bother?* I said it again to myself, *Why do I bother?* And then, just like that, I said it out loud. 'Carol, you're right. In this, as in all other things, you are right! I don't know *why* I bother coming home. You're absolutely right.'

"And so, without another word, I went upstairs and packed up everything I could in the first suitcase I found and walked out of the house. I wanted to take more, to come back in for another suitcase. You know Carol—she'll slash and burn everything I leave behind. I wanted to come back for my computer; she'll take a hammer to it. But I knew it was then or never. Walk back into the house, I told myself, and you're lost. I know me. I know Carol. I didn't look to the right or the left. I kept on walking, and just before I closed the front door I leaned my head in and yelled, not knowing where Carol or the kids were, 'I'll call you.' And then I got the hell away!"

Justin had been leaning forward in his chair. He took a deep breath, leaned back exhausted, and said, "And that's all there is to tell."

"And that was last night?"

Justin nodded. "I went directly to Laura's and we held each other all night. God, it was hard to leave her arms this morning. I can hardly describe it, it was so hard."

"Try," Ernest urged.

"Well, as I started to unfold myself from Laura, I suddenly had an image of an amoeba dividing in two—something I hadn't thought about since high school biology class. We were like the two halves of the amoeba separating bit by bit until there was just one thin strand connecting us. And then, *pop*—a painful pop—and we were separate. I got up, got dressed, looked at the clock, and thought, 'Only fourteen more hours until I'll be back in bed folded together again with Laura.' And then I came here."

"That scene with Carol last evening—you've dreaded it for years. Yet, you seem high-spirited."

"Like I said, Laura and I fit together, belong together. She's an angel—made in heaven for me. This afternoon we go apartment hunting. She has a small studio on Russian Hill. Great view of the Bay Bridge. But too small for us."

Made in heaven! Ernest felt like gagging.

"If only," Justin continued, "Laura had come along years ago! We've been talking about what rent we could afford. On my way here today I started to calculate what I've spent on therapy. Three times a week for five years—how much is that? Seventy, eighty thousand dollars? Don't take this personally, Ernest, but I can't help wondering what would have happened if Laura had come along five years ago. Maybe I would've left Carol then. And finished therapy, too. Maybe I'd be looking for an apartment now with eighty thousand dollars in my pocket!"

Ernest felt his face flush. Justin's words clanged in his mind. *Eighty thousand dollars! Don't take this personally, don't take this personally!*

But Ernest gave nothing away. Nor did he blink or defend himself. Nor point out that, five years ago, Laura would have been about fourteen and Justin couldn't have wiped his ass without asking Carol's permission, couldn't get to noon without calling his therapist, couldn't order from a menu without his wife's guidance, couldn't dress in the morning if she didn't lay out his clothes. And it was his wife's money, anyway, that paid the bills, not his—Carol earned three times as much as he did. If not for five years of therapy, he'd have eighty thousand dollars in his pocket! Shit, five years ago Justin couldn't have figured out which pocket to put it in!

But Ernest said none of these things. He took pride in his restraint, a clear sign of his maturation as a therapist. Instead he innocently asked, "Are you high-spirited all the way down?"

"What do you mean?"

"I mean, this is a momentous occasion. Surely you must have many layers of feelings about it?"

But Justin did not give Ernest what he wished. He volunteered little, seemed distant, distrustful. Finally Ernest realized that he must focus not on *content* but on *process*—that is, on the *relationship* between patient and therapist.

Process is the therapist's magic amulet, always effective in times of impasse. It is the therapist's most potent trade secret, the one procedure that makes talking to a therapist materially different and more effective than talking to a close friend. Learning to focus on process—on what was happening between patient and therapist— was the most valuable thing he had gotten from his supervision with Marshal and, in turn, was the most valuable teaching he himself offered when he supervised residents. Gradually, over the years, he had come to understand that *process* was not only an amulet to be used in times of trouble; it was the very heart of therapy. One of the most useful training exercises Marshal had given him was to focus on process at least three different times during each session.

"Justin," Ernest ventured, "can we take a look at what's happening today between the two of us?"

"What? What do you mean 'what's happening'?"

More resistance. Justin playing dumb. But, Ernest thought, maybe rebellion, even passive rebellion, wasn't a bad thing. He remembered

those scores of hours they had worked on Justin's maddening obse-
quiousness—the sessions spent on Justin's tendency to apologize for
everything and to ask for nothing, not even to complain about the
morning sun in his eyes or to ask if the blinds could be lowered.
Given *that* background, Ernest knew he should applaud Justin, support him for taking a stand. The task today was to help him convert
this back-assed resistance into overt expression.

"I mean, how do you feel about talking to me today? Something's
different. Don't you think?"

"What do *you* feel?" Justin asked.

Whoops, another very un-Justin response. A declaration of independence. *Be happy,* Ernest thought. *Remember Geppetto's glee
when Pinocchio first danced without strings?*

"Fair enough, Justin. Well, I feel distant, left out, as though something important has happened to you—no, that's not right. Let me
put it this way: as though *you have made something important happen* and you want to keep it separate from me, as though you don't
want to be here, as though you want to exclude me."

Justin nodded appreciatively. "That's accurate, Ernest. *Real* accurate. Yeah, I *do* feel that. I *am* staying away from you. I want to
hang on to feeling good. I don't want to be brought down."

"And I'll bring you down? I'll try to take it away from you?"

"You've already tried," said Justin, uncharacteristically looking
directly into Ernest's eyes.

Ernest raised his eyebrows quizzically.

"Well, isn't that what you were doing when you asked if I were
high-spirited all the way down?"

Ernest caught his breath. Whoa! A real challenge from Justin.
Maybe he had learned something from therapy after all! Now
Ernest played dumb. "What do you mean?"

"*Of course* I don't feel good all the way down—I've got lots of
feelings about leaving Carol and my family forever. Don't you know
that? How could you not know? I've just walked away from everything: my home, my Toshiba laptop, my kids, my clothes, my bicycle, my racquetball racquets, my neckties, my Mitsubishi TV, my
videotapes, my CDs. You know Carol—she'll give me nothing, she'll
destroy everything I own. Owww . . ." Justin grimaced, crossed his
arms and crouched over as if he had just been slammed in the belly.
"That pain's there—I can reach it—you see how close it is. But
today, for one day, I wanted to forget, even for a few hours. And you

didn't want me to. You don't seem even pleased that I finally left Carol."

Ernest was staggered. Had he given away so much? What would Marshal do in this spot? Hell, Marshal wouldn't *be* in this spot!

"Are you?" Justin repeated.

"Am I what?" Like a stunned boxer, Ernest clenched his opponent while his head cleared.

"Pleased at what I've done?"

"You think," Ernest weaseled, trying hard to regulate his voice, "I'm not pleased with your progress?"

"Pleased? You don't act like it," Justin responded.

"And what about *you*?" Ernest weaseled again. "Are *you* pleased?"

Justin let up and ignored the weaseling this time. Enough was enough. He needed Ernest and he backed off: "Pleased? Yes. And scared. And resolved. And wavering. Everything all mixed up. The main thing now is for me never to go back. I've broken away and the important thing now is to stay away, to stay away forever."

For the rest of the hour, Ernest tried to make amends by supporting and exhorting his patient: "Hold your ground . . . remember how long you yearned to make such a move . . . you've acted in your best interests . . . this may be the most important thing you've ever done."

"Should I go back to discuss this with Carol? After nine years, don't I owe it to her?"

"Let's play it out," Ernest suggested. "What would happen if you went back now to talk?"

"Mayhem. You know what she's capable of doing. To me. To herself."

Ernest didn't have to be reminded. He vividly remembered an incident Justin had described a year ago. Several of Carol's law partners were coming over for a Sunday brunch and, early in the morning, Justin, Carol, and the two children had gone out shopping. Justin, who did all the cooking, wanted to serve smoked fish, bagels, and leo (lox, scrambled eggs, and onions). Too vulgar, Carol said. She wouldn't hear of it, even though, as Justin reminded her, half the partners were Jewish. Justin decided to take a stand and began to turn the car toward the delicatessen. "No, you don't, you son of a bitch," Carol shouted, and jerked at the steering wheel to turn it back. The struggle in moving traffic ended when she crashed the car into a parked motorcycle.

Carol was a wildcat, a wolverine, a madwoman who tyrannized through her irrationality. Ernest remembered another car adventure that Justin had described a couple of years ago. While driving on a warm summer night, she and Justin had argued about the choice of a movie—she for *The Witches of Eastwick*, he for *Terminator II*. Her voice rose, but Justin, who had been encouraged by Ernest that week to assert himself, refused to give in. Finally she opened the car door, again in moving traffic, and said, "You miserable fucker, I'm not going to spend another minute with you." Justin grabbed at her, but she sank her nails into his forearm and, as she jumped out into the traffic, plowed four violent red furrows into his flesh.

Once out of the car, which had been moving about fifteen miles per hour, Carol lurched forward for three or four jolting steps and then slammed into and over the hood of a parked car. Justin stopped the car and rushed to her, parting the crowd that had already gathered. She lay on the street, dazed but serene—stockings ripped and bloodied at the knees, abrasions on her hands, elbows and cheeks, and an obviously fractured wrist. The rest of the evening was a nightmare: the ambulance, the emergency room, the humiliating interrogation by the police and the medical staff.

Justin was badly shaken. He realized that even with Ernest's help he could not outbid Carol. No stakes were too high for her. That dive out of the moving car was the event that had broken Justin for good. He could not oppose her, nor could he leave her. She was a tyrant, but he had a need for tyranny. Even a single night away from her filled him with anxiety. Whenever Ernest had asked him, as a thought experiment, to imagine walking away from the marriage, Justin became filled with dread. Breaking his bond to Carol seemed inconceivable. Until Laura—nineteen, beautiful, ingenuous, brash, unafraid of tyrants—had come along.

"What do you think?" Justin repeated. "Should I act like a man and try to talk this over with Carol?"

Ernest reflected on his options. Justin needed a dominant woman: Was he merely exchanging one for another? Would his new relationship resemble, in a few years, his old one? Still, things had been so frozen with Carol. Perhaps, once pried away from her, Justin might be open, even briefly, for therapeutic work.

"I really need some advice now."

Ernest, like all therapists, hated to give direct advice—it was a no-win situation: if it worked, you infantilized the patient; if it failed, you looked like a jerk. But in this instance he had no choice.

"Justin, I don't think it's wise just yet to meet with her. Let some time pass. Let her collect herself. Or perhaps try seeing her with a therapist in the room. I'll make myself available or, better yet, give you the name of a marital therapist. I don't mean the ones you've seen already—I know they didn't work out. Someone new."

Ernest knew that his advice would not be taken: Carol had always sabotaged marital couples therapy. But *content*—the precise advice he gave—was not the issue. What was important at this point was *process*: the relationship behind the words, his offering Justin support, his atoning for weaseling, his making the hour wholesome again.

"And if you feel pressed and need to talk before our next session, call me," Ernest added.

Good technique. Justin appeared soothed. Ernest regained his poise. He had salvaged the hour. He knew his supervisor would approve of his technique. But he himself did not approve. He felt soiled. Contaminated. He had not been truthful with Justin. They had not been *real* with each other. And that was what he valued about Seymour Trotter. Say what you will about him—and Lord knows a lot had been said—but Seymour knew how to be *real*. He still remembered Seymour's response to his question about technique: *"My technique is to abandon technique. My technique is to tell the truth."*

As the hour ended, something unusual transpired. Ernest had always made a point of physically touching each of his patients at every session. He and Justin customarily parted with a handshake. But not this day: Ernest opened the door and somberly bowed his head to Justin as he left.

TWO

*I*t was midnight, and Justin Astrid was less than four hours out of her house, when Carol Astrid began cutting him out of the rest of her life. She began on the closet floor with Justin's shoelaces and a pair of pinking shears and ended four hours later in the attic cutting the big red *R* out of Justin's tennis sweater from Roosevelt High School. In between she went from room to room methodically destroying his clothes, his flannel sheets, his fur-lined slippers, his glass-covered beetle collection, his high school and college diplomas, his porno video library. Photos of his summer camp where he and his co-counselor posed with their group of eight-year-old campers, his high school tennis team, the senior prom with his horse-faced date—all were slashed to pieces. Then she turned to their wedding album. With the help of a razor-blade knife that her son used for model plane construction, she soon left no trace of Justin's presence at St. Marks, the favorite site of fashionable Episcopal weddings in Chicago.

While she was at it, she carved out the faces of her in-laws from the wedding photos. If it hadn't been for them and their promises, empty promises, of big, big money, she'd probably never have married Justin. A snowy day in hell before they would see their grandchildren again. And her brother Jeb, too. What was his picture still doing there? She slashed it. She had no use for him. And all the pictures of Justin's relatives, table after table of the cretins: fat, grinning, raising glasses to make idiotic toasts, pointing their lumpish children toward the camera, shambling over to the dance floor. To hell with them all! Soon every trace of Justin and his family smoldered in the fireplace. Now her wedding, as well as her marriage, had turned to ashes.

All that remained in the album were a few pictures of herself, her mother, and a handful of friends, including her law partners, Norma and Heather, whom she would phone in the morning for help. She stared hard at her mother's picture, desperately craving her help. But her mother was gone, fifteen years in her grave. Gone even long before that. As her breast cancer slowly invaded all the crawl spaces of her body, her mother had become frozen with terror, and for years Carol had become her mother's mother. Carol tore out the pages with the pictures she wanted, ripped apart the album, and threw it into the fire as well. A minute later she thought better of it—the white plastic album covers might give off fumes toxic to her eight-year-old twins. She snatched it out of the fire and carried it to the garage. Later, with other debris, she'd make a package of it to return to Justin.

Next, Justin's desk. She was in luck: it was the end of the month and Justin, who worked as the CPA for his father's chain of shoe stores, had brought work home. All his paper records—ledgers and payroll receipts—fell quickly to the scissors. The important stuff, Carol knew, was locked in his laptop. Her impulse was to take a hammer to it, but she thought better of it—she could make use of a five-thousand-dollar computer. File erasure was the proper technique. She tried to get into his documents, but Justin had encrypted them. Paranoid bastard! Later she would get some help on that. Meanwhile she locked the computer into her cedar chest and made a mental note to get all the house locks changed.

Before dawn she fell into bed after checking on her twins for the third time. Their beds were crowded with dolls and stuffed animals. Deep, peaceful breathing. Such innocent, gentle sleep. God, she envied them. She slept fitfully for three hours until awakened by an aching jaw. She had ground her teeth in her sleep. Cupping her face in her hands while slowly opening and closing her jaws, she could hear the crepitations.

She looked across to Justin's vacant side of the bed and muttered, "You son of a bitch. You aren't worth my teeth!" Then, shivering and holding her knees, she sat up in bed and wondered where he was. The tears running down her cheeks and onto her nightgown startled her. She dabbed at the tears and stared at her glistening fingertips. Carol was a woman of extraordinary energy and quick and decisive action. She had never found relief from looking within, and considered those who did, like Justin, pusillanimous.

But no further action was possible: she had broken all that remained of Justin, and now she felt so heavy she could barely move. But she could still breathe and, remembering some breathing exercises from yoga class, she inhaled deeply and let out half the breath slowly. Then she exhaled half the remaining breath and half of that, and half again of that. It helped. She tried another exercise that her yoga teacher had suggested. She thought of her mind as a stage and sat back in the audience, dispassionately viewing the parade of her thoughts. Nothing came—only a progression of painful and inchoate feelings. But how to differentiate and grasp them? Everything seemed matted together.

An image wafted into her mind—the face of a man she hated, a man whose betrayal had scarred her for life: Dr. Ralph Cooke, the psychiatrist she had seen at her college mental health service. A well-scrubbed pink face, round as a moon, topped with wispy blond hair. She had gone to him in her sophomore year because of Rusty, a boy she had dated since she was fourteen. Rusty had been her first boyfriend and, for the next four years, had served her well, permitting her to skip all the awkwardness of looking for dates and prom escorts and, later, sexual partners. She followed Rusty to Brown University, enrolled in every course he took, bartered her way into a dorm room close to his. But perhaps her grip was too tight: ultimately Rusty began dating a beautiful French-Vietnamese student.

Never had Carol known such pain. At first she turned everything inward: wept every night, refused to eat, skipped classes, got hooked on speed. Later, rage erupted: she trashed Rusty's room, slashed his bicycle tires, stalked and harassed his new girlfriend. Once, she followed the two of them into a bar and overturned a pitcher of beer onto them.

At first, Dr. Cooke helped. After winning her confidence, he helped her to mourn her loss. The reason her pain was so intense, he explained, was that the loss of Rusty tore open the big wound of her life: being abandoned by her father. Her father was a "Woodstockian MIA"; when she was eight, he went to the Woodstock concert and never returned. There were a few holiday cards at first from Vancouver, Sri Lanka, and San Francisco, but then he stopped even that contact. She remembered watching her mother tear and burn his pictures and clothes. After that, her mother never again spoke of him.

Dr. Cooke insisted that Carol's loss of Rusty drew its power from her father's desertion. Carol resisted, claiming she had no positive memories of her father. Perhaps no *conscious* memories, Dr. Cooke responded, but may there not have been a host of forgotten nurturing episodes? And what about the father of her wishes and dreams— the loving, supporting, protecting father she never had? She mourned that father, too, and Rusty's abandonment opened the crypt of that pain as well.

Dr. Cooke also comforted her by helping her to assume a different perspective—to consider the loss of Rusty in her entire life trajectory: she was only nineteen, memories of Rusty would fade away. A few months hence she would rarely think of him; in a few years she would have only a vague recollection of a nice young lad named Rusty. Other men would come along.

In fact, another man *was* coming along, for, as he spoke, Dr. Cooke insidiously edged his chair closer. He assured Carol that she was an attractive, a *very* attractive woman, held her hand when she wept, hugged her tightly at the end of the sessions, and assured her that a woman with her grace would have no difficulty attracting other men. He spoke for himself, he said, and told her that he was drawn toward her.

Dr. Cooke rationalized his actions with theory. "Touch is necessary for your healing, Carol. Rusty's loss has fanned the embers of early, preverbal losses, and the treatment approach, too, has to be nonverbal. You can't talk to these kind of body memories—they have to be assuaged by physical comforting and cradling."

Physical comforting soon progressed to sexual comforting, offered on the sad, worn Kashan rug that separated their two chairs.

Thereafter, sessions took on a prescribed ritual: a few minutes of checking in on her week's events, empathic "tch-tchs" from Dr. Cooke (she never called him by his first name), then an exploration of her symptoms—obsessive thinking about Rusty, insomnia, anorexia, problems concentrating—and then finally a reiteration of his interpretation that her catastrophic reaction to Rusty drew its strength from her father's desertion of the family.

He was skillful. Carol felt calmer, cared for, and grateful. And then, about halfway through each hour, Dr. Cooke would move from words to action. It might be in the context of Carol's sexual fantasies: he'd say that it was important to make some of those fantasies come true; or, responding to Carol's anger at men, he'd say that his job was to prove that not all men were bastards; or when Carol talked about feeling ugly and unattractive to men, he'd say that he could personally prove that hypothesis wrong, that indeed Carol was stunningly attractive to him. Perhaps it might follow Carol's crying when he'd say, "There, there, it's good to let it out, but you need some holding."

Whatever the transition, the remainder of the session was the same. He'd slip off his chair, down to the frayed Persian rug, crook his finger at her to follow him. After holding and caressing her for a few minutes, he'd hold out his hands, a different-colored condom in each, and ask her to choose. Perhaps her choosing allowed him to rationalize that she was in control of the act. Carol would then open the condom, slip it on his primed cock, the same color as his scrubbed pink cheeks. Dr. Cooke always took a passive position, lying on his back and allowing Carol to impale herself on him and to control the pace and depth of their sexual dance. Perhaps that, too, was to foster the illusion that she was in charge.

Were these sessions helpful? Carol thought so. Each week for five months she left Dr. Cooke's office feeling cared for. And, precisely as Dr. Cooke had predicted, thoughts of Rusty did indeed fade from her mind, a sense of calm returned, and she resumed attending classes. All seemed well until, one day, after about twenty such sessions, Dr. Cooke declared her healed. His job was done, he told her, and it was time to terminate treatment.

Terminate therapy! His desertion dumped her back to where she had begun. Though she had not regarded their relationship as permanent, she had never, not for a moment, anticipated being cast off in this fashion. She phoned Dr. Cooke daily. At first cordial and gentle, he grew sharper and more impatient as the calls continued. He reminded her that the student health service only provided brief therapy, and discouraged her from calling him again. Carol was convinced that he had found another patient to treat with sexual affirmation. So everything had been a lie: his concern, his caring for her, his calling her attractive. Everything had been manipulation, everything had been for his gratification, not for her benefit. She no longer knew what or whom to trust.

The next few weeks were nightmarish. She desperately wanted Dr. Cooke and waited outside his office hoping for some glimpse, some scrap of his attention. Evening after evening was spent dialing his number or straining to see him through the wrought-iron fence of his enormous home on Prospect Street. Even now, almost twenty years later, she could still feel the impress of the twisted cold iron bars upon her cheeks as she watched his silhouette, and those of his family, moving from room to room. Soon her hurt turned to anger and to thoughts of retribution. She had been raped by Dr. Cooke— a nonviolent rape, but a rape just the same. She turned for help to a female teaching assistant, who advised her to drop it. "You have no case," she told her; "no one will take you seriously. And even if they do, think of the humiliation—having to describe the rape, especially your participation in it and why you freely returned for more rape, week after week."

That was fifteen years ago. That was the moment Carol decided to become an attorney.

In her senior year Carol excelled in political science, and her professor agreed to write her a sterling letter of recommendation to law school—but insinuated strongly that he would expect sexual favors in return. Carol could hardly control her rage. Finding herself slipping once again into a state of helplessness and depression, she sought the help of Dr. Zweizung, a psychologist in private practice. For the first two sessions Dr. Zweizung was helpful, but then he took on an ominous resemblance to Dr. Cooke, as he edged his chair closer and insisted on talking about how very, very attractive she was. This time Carol knew what to do and immediately stalked out of the office, yelling at the top of her lungs, "You scumbag!" That was the last time Carol had ever asked for help.

She shook her head vigorously, as though to dislodge the images. Why think of those bastards now? Especially that little shit, Ralph Cooke? It was because she was trying to sort out matted feelings.

Ralph Cooke had given her one good thing—a mnemonic to help identify feelings by starting with the four primary feelings: bad, mad, glad, and sad. It had been helpful more than once.

She propped a pillow behind her and concentrated. "Glad" she could eliminate immediately. It had been a long time since she had known glad. She turned to the other three. "Mad"—that was easy; she knew mad: mad was where she lived. She curled her hands into a fist and clearly and cleanly felt the anger surging through her. Simple. Natural. She reached over, pounded Justin's pillow, and hissed, "Fucker, fucker, fucker! Where in the fuck did you spend the night?"

And Carol knew "sad" too. Not well, not vividly, but as a vague, shadowy companion. Today she realized clearly its former presence by its present absence. For months she had hated the mornings: her waking groan as she thought about the day's schedule, her enervation, her queasy stomach, her stiff joints. If that was "sad," it had vanished today; she felt different this morning—energized, bristling. And mad!

"Bad"? Carol didn't know much about "bad." Justin often spoke of "bad" and pointed to his chest, where he felt the oppressive pressure of guilt and anxiety. But she had little experience with "bad"— and little tolerance for those, like Justin, who whined about it.

The room was still dark. Starting toward the bathroom, Carol stumbled against a soft mound. A flip of the light switch reminded her of last evening's clothing massacre. Slices of Justin's neckties and trouser cylinders were strewn across the bedroom floor. She stuck her toe into a section of sliced trouser and kicked it into the air. It felt right to her. But the ties—stupid to have slashed them. Justin had five treasured ties—his art collection, he called them—hanging separately in a suede zippered case she had once given him for his birthday. He wore a tie from his art collection rarely, only for very special occasions, so they had lasted for years. Two of the ties he had bought even before they married, nine years ago. Last night Carol had destroyed all of his everyday ties and then started on the art collection ties. But after slicing up two of them, she stopped and gazed at Justin's favorite: an exquisite Japanese design arranged around a bold and glorious forest-green layered blossom. This is stupid, she thought. There must be something more hurtful, more potent, that she could do with these ties. She locked it and the two remaining ones on top of the computer in her cedar chest.

~

She phoned Norma and Heather and asked them to come over that night for an urgent meeting. Though the three did not regularly socialize—Carol had no intimate friends—they considered themselves a standing war council and often convened in time of great need, generally some crisis of gender discrimination at the law firm of Kaplan, Jarndyce, and Tuttle where they had all worked for the past eight years.

Norma and Heather arrived after dinner, and the three women met in the family room with its exposed beams and Neanderthal chairs made from massive slabs of redwood burl and covered with thick animal skins. Carol started a fire of eucalyptus and pine logs and asked Norma and Heather to help themselves to wine or beer in the fridge. Carol was so agitated that she sprayed beer over her sleeve when opening her can. Heather, seven months pregnant, jumped up, ran into the kitchen, returned with a wet cloth, and wiped Carol's arm. Carol sat next to the fire attempting to dry her sweater and described the details of Justin's exodus.

"Carol, it's a blessing. Think of it as a *mitzvah,*" Norma said, as she poured herself some white wine. Norma was tiny, intense, with black bangs framing a small, perfectly proportioned face. Though her ancestry was straight Irish Catholic—her father had been an Irish cop in South Boston—her ex-husband had taught her Yiddish expressions for every occasion. "He's been a millstone around your neck ever since we've known you."

Heather, a long-faced, enormous-bosomed Swede, who had gained over forty pounds with her pregnancy, agreed: "That's right, Carol. He's gone. You're free. The house is yours. This is no time for despair; this is a time for changing the locks. Mind your sleeve, Carol! I smell singeing."

Carol moved away from the fire and plunked down into one of the fur-covered chairs.

Norma took a deep gulp of wine, "*L'chaim,* Carol. To liberation. I know you're shook up now, but remember *this is what you've wanted.* In all the years I've known you, I can't remember a positive word from you—not a single one—about Justin or your marriage."

Silence from Carol, who had taken off her shoes and sat hugging her knees. She was a thin woman with a long graceful neck and thick short black curly hair, pronounced jaw- and cheekbones, and eyes that blazed like hot embers. She wore tight black Levi's and an oversized cable-stitched sweater with an enormous cowl.

Norma and Heather searched for the right tone. They proceeded haltingly and glanced frequently at each other for guidance.

"Carol," said Norma, leaning over and rubbing Carol's back, "think of it this way: you've been cured of the plague. Hallelujah!"

But Carol shrank from Norma's touch and held her knees more tightly. "Yes, yes. I know this. I know all this. This is not helping. I know what Justin is. I know he wasted nine years of my life. But he's not going to get away with this."

"Get away with *what*?" said Heather. "Don't forget, you want him gone. You don't *want* him back. This is a *good* thing that's happened to you."

"That's not the point," said Carol.

"You've just burst a boil. You want the pus back? Let it go," said Norma.

"That's not the point, either," said Carol.

"What *is* the point?" asked Norma.

"Revenge is the point!"

Heather and Norma overspoke each other. "What?! He's not worth the time! He's gone, let him stay gone. Don't let him continue to run your life."

Just then Jimmy, one of Carol's twins, called. She rose to go to him, muttering, "I love my kids, but when I think of being on twenty-four-hour call for the next ten years . . . Christ!"

Norma and Heather felt awkward in Carol's absence. Best, each thought, to avoid conspiratorial chatter. Norma added a small eucalyptus log to the fire and they watched it sizzle until Carol returned. She resumed immediately: "Of course, I'll let him stay gone. You're still missing the point. I'm glad he's gone—I wouldn't take him back. But I want him to pay for leaving me like this."

Heather had known Carol since law school and was accustomed to her antagonistic ways. "Let's try to understand," she said. "I want to get the point. Are you angry that Justin walked out? Or are you just angry at the *idea* of his walking out?"

Before Carol could respond, Norma added, "More likely, you're angry at yourself for not throwing him out!"

Carol shook her head. "Norma, you know the answer to that. For years he's tried to provoke me into throwing him out because he was too weak to leave, too weak to bear the guilt of breaking up the family. I wouldn't give him the satisfaction of throwing him out."

"So," Norma asked, "are you saying you stayed in the marriage simply to punish him?"

Carol shook her head irritably. "I swore a long, long time ago that no man would ever walk out on me again. *I'll* let him know when he can leave. I decide that! Justin didn't walk out—he doesn't have the guts: he was carried out or wheeled out by someone. And I want to find out who she was. A month ago my secretary told me she saw him at the Yank Sing happily eating dim sum with a very young woman, about eighteen. You know what pissed me off most about that? The dim sum! I love dim sum, but not once has he ever taken me out for dim sum. With me, the bastard gets MSG tremors and headaches whenever he sees a map of China."

"Did you ask him about the woman?" asked Heather.

"Of course I asked him! What do you think? I'm going to ignore it? He lied. He claimed it was a client. The next evening I settled the score by picking up some guy at the Sheraton bar. I had forgotten all about the dim sum woman. But I'll find out who she is. I can guess. Probably someone who works for him. Someone poor. Someone stupid or myopic enough to adore that tiny dick of his! He wouldn't have the nerve to approach a real woman. I'll find her."

"You know, Carol," Heather said, "Justin ruined your legal career—how many times have I heard you say that? That his fear of being home alone sabotaged your whole career. Remember the offer from Chipman, Bremer, and Robey you had to turn down?"

"Do I remember? Of course I remember! He *did* ruin my career! You guys know about the offers I had when I graduated. I could've done anything. That position was a dream offer, but I *had* to turn it down. Whoever heard of anyone in international law who couldn't travel? I should have hired a fucking baby-sitter for him. And then the twins came, and they were the nails in the coffin of my career. If I had gone over to C, B, and R ten years ago, I'd be a partner there now. Look at that nerd, Marsha—she did it. You think I couldn't have made partner? Hell, yes, I could've done it by now."

"But," Heather said, "that's my point! His weakness controlled your life. Spend your time and energy on revenge and he'll continue to control you."

"Right," Norma chipped in. "Now you've got a second chance. Just get on with it!"

"Just get on with it," Carol snapped. "Easy to say. But not so simple to do. He sucked up nine years! I was stupid enough to get sucked in by promises of things to come. When we married, his father was ill and was about to turn over their shoe-store chain to him—worth millions. Here it is nine years later and his goddamn father is healthier than ever! Hasn't even retired. And Justin's still working for peanuts as Daddy's bookkeeper. Guess what I'm going to get now when Daddy croaks? After all these years of waiting? As an ex-daughter-in-law? Nothing! Absolutely nothing.

"'Just get on with it,' you say. You don't 'just get on with it' after blowing off nine years." Carol angrily threw a cushion to the floor and got up and began pacing behind Norma and Heather. "I've given him everything, clothed him—the helpless bastard—he could never buy his underwear alone, or socks! Black socks he wears, and I had to buy them for him because the ones he bought were not soft enough and always slipped down. I've mothered him, wifed him, sacrificed for him. And given up other men for him. It makes me sick when I think of the men I could've had. And now a tug on the leash by some airhead and he just saunters away."

"Do you know that for sure?" asked Heather, turning her chair to face Carol. "I mean the woman. Has he said anything to that effect?"

"I'd bet on it. I know that jerk. Could he possibly have moved out on his own? Bet me: a thousand to five hundred that he's moved in with someone already—last night."

No takers. Carol usually won her bets. And if she lost, it wasn't worth it—she was a nasty loser.

"You know," said Norma, also turning her chair, "when my first husband left me I went into a six-month funk. I'd be there yet if not for therapy. I saw a psychiatrist, Dr. Seth Pande, in San Francisco, an analyst. He was terrific for me, and then I met Shelly. We were great together, especially in bed, but Shelly had a gambling problem and I asked him to work on his habit with Dr. Pande before we married. Pande was marvelous. Changed Shelly around. Used to bet his whole salary on anything that moved: horses, greyhounds, football. Now he's satisfied with a small social poker game. Shelly swears by Pande. Let me give you his number."

"No! Christ, no! A shrink's the last thing I need," Carol said, as she rose and paced behind them. "I know you're trying to help, Norma—both of you—but trust me, this is not help! And therapy is not help. And how much did he help you and Shelly, anyway? Get your story straight—how many times have you told us that Shelly's a lead weight around your neck? That he's gambling as much as ever? That you have to keep a separate bank account to stop him from raiding it?" Carol grew impatient anytime Norma praised Shelly. She knew a great deal about Shelly's character—and about his sexual prowess: it had been with *him* that she had settled the dim sum score. But she was good at keeping secrets.

"I admit it was no permanent cure," said Norma, "but Pande helped. Shelly settled down for years. It wasn't till he got laid off from his job that some of the old stuff's come back. Things'll be okay when he gets work. But, Carol, why are you so tough on therapists?"

"Someday, I'll tell you about my shit list of therapists. One thing I learned from my experience with them: don't swallow your anger. Believe me, that is one mistake I won't make again."

Carol sat down and looked at Norma. "When Melvin left, maybe you still loved him—maybe you were confused, or wanted him back, or maybe your self-esteem was shot. Maybe your shrink helped with that. But that's *you*. And that's not where I am. I'm not confused. Justin stole almost ten years from me, my best decade—my make-or-break professional decade. He deposited the twins in me, let me support him, whined day and night about his two-bit bookkeeping job for his daddy, spent a ton of our money—my money—on his fucking shrink. Can you believe three, sometimes four times a week? And now, when the fancy strikes him, he just walks away. Tell me, do I exaggerate?"

"Well," said Heather, "maybe there's another way to look at—"

"Believe me," Carol interrupted, "I'm not confused. I sure as hell don't love him. And I don't want him back. No, that's not right. I *do* want him back—so I can throw him the fuck out! I know exactly where I am and what I really want. I want to *hurt* him—and the airhead, too, when I find her. You want to help me? Tell me how to hurt him. Really hurt him."

Norma picked up an old Raggedy Andy lying next to the wood chest (Alice and Jimmy, Carol's twins, now eight, had outgrown most of their dolls) and set it on the fireplace mantel, saying, "Pins, anyone?"

"Now you're talking," said Carol.

They brainstormed for hours. First it was money—the old-fashioned remedy—make him pay. Put him in debt for the rest of his life, yank his ass out of that BMW and those Italian suits and ties. Ruin him—tamper with his business accounts and have his father nailed for tax evasion, cancel his auto and medical insurance.

"Cancel his medical insurance. Hmm, that's interesting. Insurance pays only thirty percent of his shrink's fee, but that's something. What I wouldn't give to cut off his visits to his shrink. That would make him desperate. That would bust his balls! He always says Lash is his best friend—I'd like him to see how good a friend Lash would be if Justin can't pay his fees!"

But all this was playacting: these were professional, knowledgeable women; they all knew that money was going to be part of the problem, not part of the revenge. Finally it fell to Heather, a divorce attorney, to remind Carol gently that she earned far more than Justin and that any divorce settlement in California would, without doubt, require her to pay *him* alimony. And, of course, she personally would have no claim to the millions he would ultimately inherit. The sad truth was that any scheme they concocted to ruin Justin financially would only result in Carol having to fork over more money to him.

"You know, Carol," said Norma, "you're not alone in this; I may be facing the same problem soon. Let me be up front with you about Shelly. It's been six months since he lost his job: I *do* feel he's a millstone around my neck. Bad enough he's not killing himself to find a new job, but you're right: he *is* gambling again—money is disappearing. He's nickel-and-diming me to death. And every time I confront him he's got some slick rationalization. God knows what's missing; I'm afraid to take an inventory of our goods. I wish I could lay down an ultimatum: look for a job and no more gambling, or this marriage is over. I should. But I just can't. Christ, I wish he could get his act together."

"Maybe," said Heather, "it's because you like the guy. That's no secret—he's fun, he's beautiful. You say he's a great lover. Everyone says he looks like a young Sean Connery."

"I won't deny it. He's great in bed. The greatest! But expensive. Yet a divorce is even more expensive. It'll cost big bucks: I figure I'll have to pay more alimony to him than he's throwing away in poker. And there's a strong chance—there was precedent in Sonoma County Court last month—that my partnership in the firm—yours, too, Carol—may be considered a tangible, and very valuable, joint asset."

"You're in a different situation, Norma. You're getting *something* out of the marriage. At least you like your husband. Me, I'll resign my job, move to another state, before I pay alimony to that prick."

"Give up your home, give up San Francisco, give us up—me and Heather—and then start a practice in Boise, Idaho, on top of a dry cleaner?" Norma said. "Good thinking! That'll show him!"

Carol angrily flung a handful of kindling into the fire and watched the flames flare.

"I'm feeling worse," she said. "This whole evening is making me worse. You guys don't understand—you don't have a clue how serious I am. Especially you, Heather, you're calmly explaining the technicalities of divorce law and I've spent all day thinking about hit men. There are plenty of them out there. And how much money are we talking about? Twenty, twenty-five thousand? I've got it. I've got that much offshore and untraceable! I can't imagine money better spent. Would I like him dead? You bet!"

Heather and Norma were silent. They avoided eye contact with each other and with Carol, who studied their faces intently. "I shock you?"

Her friends shook their heads. They denied shock, but inwardly they grew concerned. It was too much for Heather, who stood, stretched, went into the kitchen for a few minutes, and returned with a pint of burgundy cherry ice cream and three forks. The others declined her offer, and she started on the ice cream, methodically picking out the cherries.

Carol suddenly grabbed a fork and pushed her way in. "Here, let me have some before it's too late. I hate when you do that, Heather. The cherries are the only good thing."

Norma went into the kitchen for more wine, pretending gaiety and lifting her glass. "To your hit man—I'll drink to that! I should've thought of that when Williams voted against my partnership."

"Or, if not murder," continued Norma, "how about a major beating? I have a Sicilian client who offers a special: tire-chain maulings for five thousand."

"Tire chains for five thou? Sounds attractive. You trust this guy?" Carol asked.

Norma caught Heather's stern glance.

"I saw that look," said Carol. "What's going on?"

"We need to keep our balance," said Heather. "Norma, I don't think you're helping by feeding Carol's anger, even by joking. If it is a joke. Carol, think about timing. Anything illegal—*anything*—that might happen to Justin over the next few months has *got* to implicate you. Automatically. Your motives, your temper . . ."

"My what?"

"Well, put it this way," Heather continued, "your proclivity for impulsive behavior leaves you—"

Carol jerked her head and looked away.

"Carol, let's be objective. You have a short fuse: you know it, we know it, it's a matter of public record. Justin's attorney would have no difficulty demonstrating that in court."

Carol did not respond. Heather went on: "What I meant to say is that you'd be in an exposed position, and, if it came to any vigilante activity, you're highly vulnerable to disbarment."

A silence again. The base of the fire gave way and the logs tumbled noisily into new, sloppy positions. No one rose to stoke or add wood.

Norma gamely held up the Raggedy Andy. "Pins, anyone? Safe, legal pins?"

"Anyone know any good books on revenge?" asked Carol. "A hands-on how-to book?"

Head shaking by Heather and Norma. "Well," Carol said, "there's a market out there. Maybe I ought to write one—with personally tested recipes."

"That way the hit man's fee could be written off as a business expense," said Norma.

"I once read a biography of D. H. Lawrence," said Heather, "and I vaguely remember some macabre story about his widow, Frieda, who defied his last wishes and had him cremated, then stirred his ashes into a block of cement."

Carol nodded appreciatively. "The free spirit of Lawrence imprisoned forever in cement. *Chapeau*, Frieda! *That's* what I call revenge! Creative revenge!"

Heather looked at her watch. "Let's get practical, Carol, there are safe and legal ways to punish Justin. What does he love? What does he care about? *That's* got to be our starting place."

"Not very much," said Carol. "That's the problem with him. Oh, his comforts, his clothes—he loves his clothes. But I don't need your help in carving up his wardrobe. I've taken care of that, but I don't think it will affect him. He'll just go shopping with my money and a new lady who'll pick out a new wardrobe to her taste. I should've done something else with his clothes, like send them to his worst enemy. Problem is, he's too much of a nerd to have enemies. Or give them to the next man in my life. If there is a next man. I've saved his favorite ties. And, if he had a boss, I'd sleep with the boss and give him the ties.

"What else does he love? Maybe his BMW. Not the kids—he's unbelievably indifferent to them. Denying him visiting privileges would be a favor, not a punishment. Naturally, I'll poison their minds against him—that goes without saying. But I don't think he'll notice. I could trump up some sex-abuse charges against him, but the children are too old to brainwash. Besides, that would make it impossible for him to take care of them and give me time off."

"What else?" asked Norma. "There's got to be something."

"Not much! This is a big-time self-centered man. Oh, there's his racquetball—two, three times a week. I thought of sawing his racquets halfway through, but he keeps them in the gym. He could have met the woman in the gym, maybe one of the aerobics class leaders. And with all that exercise, he's still a pig. I think it's the beer—oh, yes, he loves his beer."

"People?" asked Norma. "There's got to be people!"

"About fifty percent of his conversation is to sit around and complain—what's that Yiddish term you use, Norma?"

"*Kvetch!*"

"Yeah, sit around and kvetch about his lack of friends. He has no intimates, except of course the dim sum girl. She's the best bet for getting to him."

"If she's as bad as you imagine," said Heather, "it might be best to do nothing, to let them get completely enmeshed. It'll be *No Exit*—they'll make their own personal hell."

"You still don't understand, Heather. I don't just want him to be miserable: that's not revenge. *I want him to know it's my doing.*"

"So," said Norma, "we've established the first step: find out who she is."

Carol nodded. "Right! And next I'll find a way to get him through her. Bite the head off and the tail will die. Heather, you got a good private eye you've used in divorce cases?"

"Easy: Bat Thomas. He's great—he'll tail Justin and identify her in twenty-four hours."

"And Bat's cute, too," Norma added. "Maybe offer you some sexual affirmation—no extra charge."

"Twenty-four hours?" responded Carol. "He could get the name in one hour if he were good enough to bug the couch of Justin's shrink. Justin probably talks about her all the time."

"Justin's shrink. Justin's shrink," said Norma. "You know, it's curious how we've neglected Justin's shrink. How long did you say Justin's seen him?"

"Five years!"

"Five years at three times a week," Norma continued. "Let's see . . . with vacations, that's about a hundred forty hours a year—multiply by five, that's about seven hundred hours total."

"Seven hundred hours!" exclaimed Heather. "What on earth have 6they been talking about for seven hundred hours?"

"I can guess," said Norma, "what they've been discussing lately."

In the last few minutes, in an effort to conceal her irritation with Heather and Norma, Carol had slumped so deeply into the cowl of her sweater that only her eyes were visible. As so often before, she felt more alone than ever. This came as no surprise—many times friends traveled part of the way with her, many times they had promised loyalty; yet, in the end, they always misunderstood.

It was the mention of Justin's shrink that caught her attention. Now, like a tortoise emerging from its shell, she slowly extended her head. "What do you mean? What *have* they been discussing?"

"The great exodus, of course. What else?" said Norma. "You seem surprised, Carol."

"No! I mean yes. I know Justin *had* to have been discussing me with his shrink. Funny how I manage to forget that. Maybe I have to forget. Creepy to think of being continually bugged, of Justin reporting to his shrink on every conversation with me. But of course! Of course! Those two planned every step of this together. I told you! I told you before that Justin could never have walked out on his own."

"He ever tell you what he talks about?" asked Norma.

"Never! Lash advised him not to tell me, said I was too controlling and he needed his private sanctum where I wasn't permitted to enter. I stopped asking long ago. But you know there was a time two or three years ago when he was down on his shrink and bad-mouthed him for a couple of weeks. He said that Lash was so off base that he was urging a marital separation. At the time, I don't know why—maybe 'cause Justin's so obviously pathetic—I thought Lash was on my side, maybe trying to show Justin that, if he were away from me, he'd realize how much he really gets from me. But now I see everything differently. Shit, I've had a mole in my home for years!"

"Five years," said Heather. "That's a long time. I don't know a soul who's stayed in therapy for so long. Why five years?"

"You don't know much about the therapy industry," replied Carol. "Some of the shrinks will keep you coming in perpetuity. And, oh yeah, I didn't tell you that's five years with *this* therapist. There were others before him. Justin's always had problems: indecisive, obsessive, has to check everything twenty times. We leave the house and he goes back and forth to the door to see if he locked it. By the time he gets back to the car, he forgets if he checked and out he goes again. Dumb shit! Can you imagine an accountant like that? It's a joke. He was dependent on pills—couldn't sleep without them, fly without them, meet an auditor without them."

"Still?" asked Heather.

"He's gone from pill addict to shrink addict. Lash is his nipple. Can't get enough of him. Even at three times a week, he can't get through the week without phoning Lash. Someone criticizes him at work, five minutes later he's whining about it on the phone to his shrink. Sickening."

"It's sickening also," said Heather, "to think of medical exploitation of that kind of dependency. Great for the shrink's bank account. What motivation does he have for helping a patient function on his own? Is there a malpractice angle?"

"Heather, you're not listening. I told you that the industry considers five years as normal. Some analyses go on for eight, nine years, four or five times a week. And have you ever tried to get one of these guys to testify against another? It's a closed shop."

"You know," said Norma, "I think we're making headway." She picked up a second doll, placed it next to the other on the mantel, and wrapped some twine around both. "They're Siamese twins. Get one, we get the other. Hurt the doc, we hurt Justin."

"Not quite," said Carol, her long neck now fully emerged from her cowl, her voice steely and impatient. "Hurting Lash alone wouldn't do anything. It might even bring them closer together. No, the real target is the relationship: I destroy *that,* and I'll get to Justin."

"You ever met Lash, Carol?" asked Heather.

"No. Several times Justin told me he wanted me to come in for a couples session, but I've had it with shrinks. Once, about a year ago, curiosity got the better of me, though, and I went to one of his lectures. Arrogant blimp. I remember thinking how I'd like to set off a bomb under his couch or put my fist right into that sanctimonious face. It would settle some scores. Old ones and new ones."

As Heather and Norma brainstormed about how to nail a shrink, Carol grew still. She stared at the fire, thinking of Dr. Ernest Lash, her cheeks glistening and reflecting the glow of the eucalyptus embers. And then it came to her. A door opened in her mind; an idea, a stupendous idea, swiveled into view. Carol knew exactly what she had to do! She rose, took the dolls from the mantel, and tossed them onto the fire. The delicate twine binding them together flared briefly, then became an incandescent thread before falling into ash. The dolls seeped smoke, turned dark with heat, and soon burst into flame. Carol stoked the ashes and then announced, "Thank you, my friends. I know my way now. Let's see how Justin does with his shrink out of business. Conference adjourned, ladies."

Heather and Norma didn't budge.

"Trust me," said Carol, closing the fire screen. "Better not to know more. If you don't know, you'll never have to perjure yourselves."

THREE

*E*rnest entered Printers Inc. bookstore in Palo Alto and glanced at the poster on the door.

DR. ERNEST LASH
Assoc. Clin. Prof. of Psychiatry, U. of Cal. San Francisco
Speaking on his new book:

BEREAVEMENT: FACTS, FADS, AND FALLACIES
Feb. 19.   8 – 9 PM – followed by book signing

Ernest glanced at the list of speakers from the previous week. Impressive! He was traveling in good company: Alice Walker, Amy Tan, James Hillman, David Lodge. *David Lodge*—from England? How had they snared *him*?

As he strolled in, Ernest wondered whether the customers milling about in the store recognized him as the evening's speaker. He introduced himself to Susan, the owner, and accepted her offer of a cup of coffee from the bookstore café. Heading toward the reading room, Ernest scanned the new titles for his favorite writers. Most stores allowed speakers to choose a free book for their efforts. Ah, a new book by Paul Auster!

Within minutes, his bookstore blues descended. Books everywhere, shrieking for attention on large display tables, shamelessly exhibiting their iridescent green and magenta jackets, heaped on the floor patiently awaiting shelving, spilling off tables, splashing onto the floor. Against the far wall of the store, great mounds of failed books glumly awaited return to their maker. Next to them stood unopened cartons of bright young volumes eager for their moment in the sun.

Ernest's heart went out to his little baby. What chance did it have in this ocean of books, one frail little spirit, swimming for its life?

He turned into the reading room, where fifteen rows of metal chairs had been unfolded. Here his *Bereavement: Facts, Fads, and Fallacies* was prominently displayed; several stacks, perhaps a total of sixty books, awaited signing and purchase next to the podium. Fine. Fine. But what about his book's future? What about two or three months hence? Perhaps one or two copies filed inconspicuously under *L* in the psychology or the self-help section. Six months hence? Vanished! "Available only on special order; should arrive in three to four weeks."

Ernest understood that no store had room enough to display all books, even those of great merit. At least, he could understand it for other writer's books. But surely it was not reasonable that *his* book should have to die—not the book he had worked on for three years, not his exquisitely honed sentences and the graceful manner by which he took readers by the hand and led them gently through some of the darkest realms of life. Next year, ten years hence, there would be widows and widowers, plenty of them, who would need his book. The truths he wrote would be as profound and as fresh then as now.

"Do not confuse value and permanence—that way lies nihilism," Ernest murmured as he tried to shake off his blues. He invoked his familiar catechisms: "Everything fades," he reminded himself. "That's the nature of experience. Nothing persists. Permanence is an illusion, and one day the solar system will lie in ruins." Ah yes, that felt better! And better yet when Ernest invoked Sisyphus: a book fades? Well then, write a fresh book! And then yet another and another.

Though there were still fifteen minutes left, the seats were beginning to fill. Ernest settled down in the last row to scan his notes and to check whether he had placed them back in the proper order after his reading in Berkeley the previous week. A woman carrying a cup of coffee sat down a couple of seats away. Some force caused Ernest to look up, and when he did he saw that she was gazing at him.

He checked her out and liked what he saw: a large-eyed handsome woman, about forty, with long blond hair, heavy dangling silver earrings, a silver serpent necklace, black net stockings, and a burnt orange angora sweater valiantly trying to contain commanding breasts. Those breasts! Ernest's pulse quickened; he had to rip his eyes away from them.

Her gaze was intense. Ernest rarely thought of Ruth, his wife who had died six years before in an auto accident, but he remembered with gratitude one gift she had given him. Once, in their early days, before they had stopped touching and loving each other, Ruth had revealed to him the woman's ultimate secret: how to capture a man. "Such a simple matter," she had said. "One has only to look into a man's eyes and hold his gaze for a few extra seconds. That's all!" Ruth's secret had proven accurate: time and again he had identified women trying to pick him up. This woman passed that test. He looked up again. She was still staring. Absolutely no doubt about it—this woman was coming on to him! And at a most opportune time: his relationship with the current woman in his life was quickly unraveling, and Ernest was ravenously horny. All atwitter, he sucked in his belly and boldly gazed back.

"Dr. Lash?" She leaned toward him and extended her hand. He clasped it.

"My name is Nan Swensen." She held his hand two or three seconds longer than expected.

"Ernest Lash." Ernest tried to modulate his voice. His heart pounded. He loved the sexual chase but hated the first stage—the ritual, the risk. How he envied Nan Swensen's bearing: her absolute command, absolute self-confidence. How lucky such women are, he thought. No necessity to speak, no fumbling for cute opening lines, no awkward invitations for drinks, dance, or conversation. All they have to do is let their beauty do the talking.

"I know who *you* are," she said. "The question is, do you know who *I* am?"

"Should I?"

"I'll be shattered if you don't."

Ernest was puzzled. He looked her up and down, trying not to let his eyes linger on her bosom.

"I think I need a harder and longer look—later." He smiled and glanced significantly at the growing audience, which would soon call him away.

"Perhaps the name Nan *Carlin* might help."

"Nan Carlin! Nan Carlin! Of course!" Ernest excitedly squeezed her shoulder, which jiggled her hand and splashed her coffee over her purse and skirt. He sprang up, circled the room awkwardly in search of a napkin, and finally returned with a wad of paper towels.

While she blotted the coffee out of her skirt, Ernest riffled through his recollections of Nan Carlin. She had been one of his very first patients ten years ago, in the very beginning of his residency. The chief of training, Dr. Molay, a group therapy fanatic, had insisted that all residents start a therapy group during their first year. Nan Carlin had been one of the members of that group. Though it was years ago, it all came back clearly. Nan had been quite obese then—that was why he hadn't recognized her now. He remembered her also as shy and self-denigrating, again no resemblance to this self-possessed woman gazing at him. If he recalled, Nan was in the midst of a disintegrating marriage—yes, that was it. Her husband actually told her he was leaving her because she had gotten too fat. He charged her with breaking her marriage vows, claiming that she was deliberately dishonoring and disobeying him by making herself repulsive.

"Do I remember?" Ernest responded. "I remember how shy you were in the group, how long it took you to utter a word. And then I remember how you changed, how angry you got at one of the men—Saul, I believe. You accused him, with good justification, of hiding behind his beard and lobbing grenades into the group."

Ernest was showing off. He had a prodigious memory with near total retention, even years later, of individual and group psychotherapy sessions.

Nan smiled and nodded vigorously. "I remember that group too: Jay, Mort, Bea, Germana, Irinia, Claudia. I was only in it for two or three months before I was transferred to the East Coast, but I think it saved my life. That marriage was destroying me."

"What a pleasure to learn you're in a better place. And that the group played a role in that. Nan, you look wonderful. Can it really be ten years? Honestly, honestly, and this is no therapist malarkey—wasn't *malarkey* one of your favorite words?"—showing off again. "You look more confident, younger, more attractive. You feel that way, too?"

She nodded and touched his hand as she spoke. "I'm in a very good place. Single, healthy, lean."

"I remember you were always fighting the weight!"

"That battle's been won. I'm really a new woman."

"How have you done it? Maybe I should use your method." Ernest pinched a fold of belly between his fingers.

"You don't need it. Men are lucky. They wear weight well—they even get rewarded with terms like *powerful* and *husky*. But my method? If you must know, I've had the help of a good doctor!"

That was discouraging news to Ernest. "You've been in therapy all this time?"

"No, I've stayed true to you, my one and only shrink!" She gave his hand a playful pat. "I'm talking about a doctor doctor, a plastic surgeon who carved me a new nose and waved his magic liposuction wand over my tummy."

The room had filled, and Ernest listened to the introduction, which ended with the familiar "so please join me in welcoming Dr. Ernest Lash."

Before rising, Ernest leaned over, clasped Nan's shoulder, and whispered, "Really good to see you. Let's talk some more later."

He walked to the podium with his head in a swirl. Nan was beautiful. Absolutely stunning. And his for the taking. No woman had ever made herself more available to him. It was only a matter of finding the nearest bed—or couch.

Couch. Yes, precisely! And therein lies the problem, Ernest reminded himself: ten years ago or not, she is still a patient and is off-limits. In the forbidden zone! No, not *is*—she *was* a patient, he thought, one of eight members of a therapy group for a few weeks. *Aside from a pregroup screening session, I don't think I ever saw her in a one-to-one session.*

What difference does that make? A patient's a patient.

Forever? After ten years? Sooner or later, patients graduate to full adulthood with all the concomitant privileges.

Ernest yanked himself from his internal monologue and turned his attention to the audience.

"Why? Ladies and gentlemen, why write a book about bereavement? Look at the bereavement and loss section of this bookstore. The shelves groan with volumes. Why yet another book?"

Even as he spoke, he continued the internal debate. *She says she's never been better. She is not a psychiatric patient. She hasn't been in therapy for nine years! It's perfect. Why not, for chrissakes? Two consenting adults!*

"As a psychological ailment, bereavement occupies a unique place. First of all, it is universal. No one our age . . . "

Ernest smiled and made eye contact with many people in the audience; he was good at that. He noted Nan in the last row, nodding and smiling. Sitting right next to Nan was a severe, attractive woman with short curly black hair, who seemed to be studying him intently. Was this another woman coming on? He caught her eye for just an instant. She turned away quickly.

"No one our age," Ernest continued, "escapes bereavement. It is the one universal psychiatric ailment."

No, that's the problem, Ernest reminded himself: *Nan and I are not two consenting adults. I know too much about her. Because she's confided so much to me, she feels unusually tied to me. I remember her father died when she was a teenager—I filled her father's role. I'd betray her if I got involved sexually with her.*

"Many have noted that it is easier to lecture to medical students about bereavement than about other psychiatric syndromes. Medical students understand it. Of all the psychiatric conditions, it most closely resembles other medical ailments, for example, infectious diseases or physical trauma. No other psychiatric ailment has such a precise onset, a specific identifiable cause, a reasonably predictable course, an efficient, time-limited treatment, and a well-defined specific end point."

No, Ernest argued with himself, *after ten years all bets are off. She may once have considered me fatherly. So? That's then, this is now. She's experiencing me as an intelligent, sensitive male. Look at her: she's inhaling my words. She's incredibly attracted to me. Face it. I am sensitive. I am deep. How often does a single woman her age, any age, meet a man like me?*

"But, ladies and gentlemen, the fact that medical students or physicians or psychotherapists yearn for simple, straightforward diagnosis and treatment of bereavement does not make it so. To attempt to understand bereavement using a medical disease model is to omit precisely that which is most human about us. Loss is not like a bacterial invasion, not like physical trauma; psychic pain is not analogous to somatic dysfunction; mind is not body. The amount, the nature, of the anguish we experience is determined not by the (or not *only* by the) nature of the trauma but by the *meaning* of the trauma. And *meaning* is precisely the difference between soma and psyche."

Ernest was hitting his stride. He checked the faces in his audience to assure himself of their attention.

Remember, Ernest chattered to himself, *how she feared divorce because of her earlier experience with men, who used her sexually and then simply went on their way? Remember how empty she felt? If I went home with her tonight, I'd simply be doing the same thing to her—I'd be another in a long string of exploiting men!*

"Let me give you an example of the importance of 'meaning' from my research. Consider this puzzle: two widows, recently bereaved, each having been married for forty years. One of the widows had gone through much suffering but had gradually reclaimed her life and enjoyed some periods of equanimity and, on occasion, even great pleasure. The other fared much worse: a year later, she was mired in deep depression, at times suicidal, and required ongoing psychiatric attention. How can we account for the difference in outcome? It *is* a puzzle. Now let me offer a clue.

"Though these two women resembled each other in many ways, they differed greatly in one significant respect: the nature of their marriages. One woman had had a tumultuous, conflicted marital relationship, the other a loving, mutually respectful, growing relationship. Now my question for you is: Which was which?"

As Ernest waited for an answer from the audience, he caught Nan's eye again and thought, *How do I know she'd feel empty? Or exploited? How about grateful? Maybe our relationship would lead somewhere. Maybe she's as sexually itchy as I am! Don't I ever get to be off duty? Do I have to be a shrink twenty-four hours a day? If I have to worry about the nuances of every single act, every relationship, I'll never get laid!*

Women, big boobs, getting laid . . . you're disgusting—he said to himself. *Don't you have anything more important to do? Anything more elevated to think about?*

"Yes, exactly!" said Ernest to a woman in the third row who had ventured a reply. "You're right: the woman with the conflicted relationship had the worse outcome. Very good. I bet you've already read my book—or maybe you don't need to." Adoring smiles from the audience. Ernest guzzled them and continued. "But doesn't that seem counterintuitive? One might think that the widow who had had a deeply gratifying, loving, forty-year relationship might fare less well. After all, hasn't she had the greater loss?

"Yet, as you suggest, the reverse is often the case. There are several explanations. I think 'regret' is the key concept. Think of the anguish of the widow who feels, deep down, that she has spent forty years married to the wrong man. So her grief is not, or not *only,* for her husband. She is in mourning for her own life."

Ernest, he admonished himself, *there are millions, billions, of women in the world. There are probably a dozen in the audience tonight who'd love to make it with you, if you had enough guts to approach them. Just stay away from patients! Stay away from patients!*

But she's not a patient. She's a free woman.

She saw you, and still sees you, unrealistically. You helped her; she trusted you. The transference was powerful. And you're trying to exploit it!

Ten years! Transference is immortal? Where is that writ?

Look at her! She's gorgeous. She adores you. When has a woman like that ever picked you out of a crowd and come on to you like that? Look at yourself. Look at your paunch. A few more pounds and you won't be able to see your fly. You want proof? There's your proof!

Ernest's attention was so split that he began to feel dizzy. The split was a familiar one for him. On the one hand, genuine concern for patients, students, his public. And genuine concern, as well, for the real issues of existence: growth, regret, life, death, meaningfulness. On the other hand, his shadow: selfishness and carnality. Oh, he was adept at helping his patients reclaim their shadows, draw strength from them: power, vital energy, creative drive. He knew all the words; he loved Nietzsche's proclamation that the mightiest trees must sink deep roots, deep into darkness, deep into evil.

Yet those fine words held little meaning for him. Ernest hated his dark side, hated its dominion over him. He hated thralldom, hated being driven by animal instinct, hated being enslaved by early programming. And today was the perfect example: his barnyard sniffing and crowing, his primitive lust for seduction and conquest—what *were* they if not fossils direct from the dawn of history? And his passion for the breast, for the kneading and the sucking. Pathetic! A relic from the nursery!

Ernest clenched his fist and dug his nails into his palm, hard! *Pay attention! You've got a hundred people out there! Give them as much as you can.*

"And another thing about the conflicted marital relationship: death freezes it in time. It is forever conflicted, forever unfinished, unsatisfactory. Think of the guilt! Think of the times the bereaved widow or widower says, *'If only I had. . . . '* I think that's one reason that bereavement as a result of sudden death, for example an automobile accident, is so very difficult. In these instances husband and wife had no time to say good-bye, no time for preparation—too much unfinished business, too much unresolved conflict."

Ernest was rolling now, and his audience was attentive and quiet. He no longer looked at Nan.

"Let me leave you with one last point before stopping for questions. Think for a moment of how mental health professionals evaluate the process of spousal bereavement. What is successful mourning? When is it over? One year? Two years? Common sense has it that the work of mourning is over when the bereaved person has sufficiently detached from the dead spouse to resume a functional life again. But it's more complex than that! Far more complex!

"One of the most interesting findings of my research is that a substantial proportion of bereaved spouses—perhaps twenty-five percent—don't just resume life or return to their previous level of functioning but instead undergo a substantial amount of personal growth."

Ernest loved this part; audiences always found it meaningful.

"*Personal growth* is not the perfect term. I don't know what to call it—maybe *heightened existential awareness* would be better. I only know that a certain proportion of widows, and occasionally widowers, learn to approach life in a very different fashion. They develop a new appreciation for the preciousness of life. And a new set of priorities. How to characterize it? One might say that they learn to trivialize the trivialities. They learn to say no to the things they do not want to do, to devote themselves to those aspects of life that provide meaning: love of close friends and family. They also learn to sip from their own creative springs, to experience the changing of the seasons and the natural beauty around them. Perhaps most important of all, they gain a keen sense of their own finiteness and, as a consequence, learn to live in the immediate present, instead of postponing life for some future moment: the weekend, summer vacation, retirement. I describe all this at greater length in my book and also speculate about the causes and antecedents of this existential awareness.

"Now, for some questions." Ernest enjoyed fielding questions: "How long have you worked on the book?" "Were the case histories real and, if so, what about confidentiality?" "Your next book?" "The usefulness of therapy in bereavement?" Questions about therapy were always asked by someone in the midst of personal bereavement, and Ernest took great care to treat such questions delicately. Thus he pointed out that bereavement is self-limited—bereaved individuals, for the most part, are going to improve with or without therapy—and that no proof exists that, for the average bereaved person, those in therapy are better off at the end of a year than those not in therapy. But, lest he appear to be trivializing therapy, Ernest hastened to add that there is evidence that therapy may make the first year less painful and indisputable evidence for efficacy of therapy with bereaved people who suffer from intense guilt or anger.

The questions were all routine and genteel—he had expected no less from a Palo Alto audience—not like the quarrelsome, irritating questions from a Berkeley crowd. Ernest glanced at his watch and signaled to his hostess that he was finished, closed his folder of notes, and sat down. After a formal statement of gratitude from the bookstore proprietor, a robust burst of applause broke out. A swarm of book purchasers surrounded Ernest. He smiled graciously as he signed each book. Perhaps it was sheer fancy, but it seemed to him that several attractive women looked at him with interest and held his gaze an extra second or two. He did not respond: Nan Carlin was waiting for him.

Slowly the crowd dispersed. Finally he was free to rejoin her. How should he handle this? A cappuccino in the bookstore café? A less public spot? Or perhaps simply a few minutes of conversation in the bookstore and let the whole confounded matter drop? What to do? Ernest's heart started pounding again. He looked around the room. Where was she?

Ernest closed his briefcase and rushed, searching, through the bookstore. No sign of Nan. He poked his head back into the reading room to take one last look. It was entirely empty aside from a woman sitting quietly in the seat that Nan had occupied—the severe, slender woman with short curly black hair. She had angry, penetrating eyes. Even so, Ernest tried again to catch her gaze. Again, she looked away.

FOUR

A last-minute patient cancellation gave Dr. Marshal Streider a free hour before his weekly supervisory appointment with Ernest Lash. He had mixed feelings about the cancellation. He felt troubled about the depth of the patient's resistance: not for a minute did he buy the feeble excuse of a business trip, yet he welcomed the free time. The money was the same in either case: he would, of course, bill the patient for the hour regardless of the excuse.

After returning phone calls and answering correspondence, Marshal stepped outside onto his small deck to water the four bonsai that sat on a wooden shelf outside his window: a snow rose with miraculously delicate exposed roots (some meticulous gardener had planted it so that it grew over a rock, and then four years later meticulously chipped away the rock); a gnarled five-needle pine, at least sixty years old; a nine-tree maple grove; and a juniper. Shirley, his wife, had spent the previous Sunday helping him shape the juniper, and it looked transformed, much like a four-year-old after his first real haircut; they had clipped off all the shoots on the underside of the two opposing main branches, amputated a maverick forward-growing branch, and trimmed the tree into a jaunty scalene-triangle shape.

Then Marshal indulged himself with one of his great pleasures: he turned to the stock tables of the *Wall Street Journal* and extracted from his wallet the two credit-card-sized accoutrements that permitted him to calculate his profits: a magnifying sheet to read the small print of the market prices and a solar-powered calculator. A low-volume market yesterday. Nothing had moved except his largest holding, Silicon Valley Bank—bought on a good tip from an ex-patient—which was up one and an eighth; with fifteen hundred shares, that came to almost seventeen hundred dollars. He looked up from the stock tables and smiled. Life was good.

Picking up the most recent issue of *The American Journal of Psychoanalysis,* Marshal skimmed the table of contents but closed it quickly. Seventeen hundred dollars! Christ, why hadn't he bought more? Leaning back in his leather swivel chair, he surveyed the view in his office: the Hundertwasser and the Chagall prints, the collection of eighteenth-century wineglasses with delicately twisted, ribboned stems brilliantly displayed in a highly polished rosewood cabinet. Most of all he enjoyed his three glorious pieces of glass sculpture by Musler. He rose to dust them with an old feather duster his father had once used to dust the shelves in his tiny grocery store on Fifth and R streets in Washington.

Though he rotated the paintings and prints of his large collection at home, the delicate sherry glasses and the fragile Musler pieces were permanent office fixtures. After checking the earthquake-proof mountings of the glass sculptures, he lovingly caressed his favorite one: The Golden Rim of Time, a huge, glowing, wafer-thin orange bowl with edges resembling some futuristic metropolitan skyline. Since acquiring it twelve years ago, he had hardly passed a day without caressing it; its perfect contours and its extraordinary coolness were wonderfully soothing. More than once he had been tempted, only tempted of course, to encourage a distraught patient to stroke it and soak up its cool, calming mystery.

Thank God he had overridden his wife's wishes and bought the three pieces: they had been his best purchases. And possibly his last. Musler's prices had escalated so much that another piece would cost him six months' salary. But if he could catch another market surge with Standard and Poor futures, as he had last year, perhaps then—but of course his best tipster had been inconsiderate enough to finish therapy. Or perhaps when his two children finished college and graduate school, but that was at least five years away.

Three minutes after eleven. Ernest Lash was late, as usual. Marshal had supervised Ernest for the past two years, and even though Ernest paid ten percent less than a patient, Marshal almost always looked forward to his weekly hour. Ernest was a refreshing break in the day from his clinical caseload—a perfect student: a seeker, bright, receptive to new ideas. A student possessing a vast curiosity—and an even vaster ignorance about psychotherapy.

Though Ernest was old, at thirty-eight, to be still in supervision, Marshal considered that a strength, not a weakness. During Ernest's psychiatric residency, completed over ten years ago, he had staunchly resisted learning anything about psychotherapy. Instead, heeding the siren call of biological psychiatry, he had focused on pharmacological treatment of mental illness, and after residency had elected to spend several years in molecular biological laboratory research.

Ernest was not alone in this. Most of his peers had taken the same stance. Ten years ago psychiatry appeared to be poised on the brink of major biological breakthroughs in biochemical causes of mental disease, in psychopharmacology, in new imaging methods of studying brain anatomy and function, in psychogenetics and the imminent discovery of the chromosomal location of the specific gene for each of the major mental disorders.

But Marshal had not been swayed by these new developments. At sixty-three, he had been a psychiatrist long enough to have lived through several such positivistic swings. He remembered wave after wave of ecstatic optimism (and subsequent disappointment) surrounding the introduction of Thorazine, psychosurgery, Miltown, Reserpine, Pacatal, LSD, Tofranil, lithium, Ecstasy, beta-blockers, Xanax, and Prozac—and was not surprised when some of the molecular biological fervor began to wane, when many extravagant research claims were not substantiated and when scientists began to acknowledge that perhaps, after all, they had not yet located the corrupt chromosome behind every corrupt thought. Last week Marshal had attended a university-sponsored seminar in which leading scientists presented the cutting edge of their work to the Dalai Lama.

Though no advocate of nonmaterialistic worldviews, he was tickled by the Dalai Lama's response to the scientists' new photos of individual atoms and their certainty that nothing existed outside of matter. "And what about time?" the Dalai Lama had sweetly asked. "Have those molecules been seen yet? And, please, show me the photos of the self, the enduring sense of self?"

After working for years as a researcher in psychogenetics, Ernest grew disenchanted both with research and with academic politics and had entered private practice. For two years, he practiced as a pure psychopharmacologist, seeing patients for twenty-minute appointments and dispensing medications to all. Gradually, and here Seymour Trotter played a role, Ernest realized the limitations, even the vulgarity, of treating all patients with drugs and, at the sacrifice of forty percent of his income, gradually shifted into a psychotherapy practice.

So it was to Ernest's credit, Marshal felt, that he now sought out expert psychotherapy supervision and planned to apply for candidacy to the psychoanalytic institute. Marshal shuddered when he thought of all the psychiatrists out there—and all the psychologists, social workers, and counselors as well—who practiced therapy without proper analytic training.

Ernest, as always, rushed into the office, precisely five minutes late, poured himself a cup of coffee, fell into Marshal's white Italian leather chair, and riffled through his briefcase for his clinical notes.

Marshal had stopped inquiring into Ernest's lateness. For months, without satisfaction, he had questioned it. Once Marshal had even gone outside and timed the one-block walk between his office and Ernest's. Four minutes! Since Ernest's 11:00 appointment ended at 11:50, there was easily time enough, even with a toilet stop, for Ernest to arrive at noon. Yet some obstacle invariably arose, Ernest claimed: a patient ran overtime, or a phone call demanded attention, or Ernest forgot his notes and had to run back to his office. There was always something.

And that something was obviously resistance. To pay a great deal of money for fifty minutes and then systematically squander ten percent of that money and time, thought Marshal, obviously is patent evidence of ambivalence.

Ordinarily Marshal would have been rocklike in his insistence that the lateness be fully explored. But Ernest wasn't a patient. Not exactly. Supervision lay in the no-man's-land between therapy and education. There were times the good supervisor had to probe beyond the case material and go deeply into the student's unconscious motivations and conflicts. But, without a specific therapy contract, there were limits beyond which the supervisor could not go.

So Marshal let the matter drop, though he made a statement by invariably ending their fifty-minute supervision hour precisely on time—almost to the second.

"A lot to talk about," Ernest began. "I'm not sure where to begin. I want to discuss something different today. No new developments with the two regulars we're following—just had workaday sessions with Jonathan and Wendy; they're doing okay.

"I want to describe a session with Justin in which a lot of countertransference material came up. And also about a social encounter with a former patient I had last night at a bookstore reading."

"Book still selling well?"

"The bookstores are still displaying it. All my friends are reading it. And I've had a few good reviews—one came out this week in the AMA newsletter."

"Great! It's an important book. I'm going to send a copy to my older sister, who lost her husband last summer."

Ernest thought of saying that he'd be glad to autograph that book with a little personal note. But the words froze in his throat. It seemed presumptuous to say that to Marshal.

"Okay, let's get to work . . . Justin . . . Justin. . . . " Marshal flipped through his notes. "Justin? Refresh my memory. Wasn't he your long-term obsessive-compulsive? The one with so many marital problems?"

"Yeah. Haven't talked about him for a long time. But you remember we followed his treatment closely for several months."

"I didn't know you were still seeing him. I've forgotten—what was the reason we stopped following him in supervision?"

"Well, to be honest, the real reason is that I lost interest in him. It became clear he couldn't go much farther. We haven't really been doing therapy . . . more of a holding action. Yet he's still coming in three times a week."

"A holding action—three visits a week? That's a lot of holding." Marshal sat back in his chair and stared at the ceiling, as he usually did when listening hard.

"Well, I worry about that. That's not why I chose to talk about him today, but maybe it's just as well that we address that, too. I can't seem to cut him down—and that's three times a week plus a phone call or two!"

"Ernest, do you have a waiting list?"

"A short one. Actually, just one patient. Why?" But Ernest knew exactly where Marshal was heading, and admired his way of asking hard questions with perfect aplomb. Damn, he was tough!

"Well, my point is that many therapists get so threatened by open hours that they unconsciously keep their patients dependent."

"I'm on top of that—and I repeatedly talk to Justin about cutting down our hours. If I were keeping a patient in therapy for the sake of my pocketbook, I wouldn't be sleeping very well at night."

Marshal nodded his head slightly, signaling he was satisfied, for the time being, with Ernest's response. "A couple of minutes ago you said you *didn't* think he could go farther. Past tense. And now something has happened to change your mind about that?"

Marshal was listening all right—total retention. Ernest looked admiringly at him: rusty-blond hair, alert dark eyes, unblemished skin, the body of a man twenty years younger. Marshal's physique was like his persona: no fat, no waste, solid muscle. He had once played defensive linebacker for the University of Rochester. His thick muscular biceps and freckled forearms completely filled his jacket sleeves—a rock! And a rock, too, in his professional role: no waste, no doubt, always confident, always certain of the right way. Some of the other training analysts also had an air of certainty—a certainty begat by orthodoxy and belief—but none was like Marshal, none spoke with such an informed, flexible authority. Marshal's certainty sprang from some other source, some instinctive sureness of body and mind that dispelled all doubt, that invariably provided him with an immediate and penetrating awareness of the larger issues. Ever since their first meeting ten years ago when Ernest heard Marshal's lecture on analytic psychotherapy, he had used Marshal as a model.

"You're right. To fill you in, I'll need to backtrack a bit," Ernest said. "You may remember that from the beginning Justin explicitly asked my help in leaving his wife. You felt I got overinvolved, that Justin's divorce became my mission, that I became a vigilante. That was when you referred to me as 'therapeutically incontinent,' remember?"

Marshal remembered, of course. He nodded with a smile.

"Well, you were right. My efforts were misdirected. Everything I did to help Justin leave his wife came to naught. Whenever he came close to leaving, whenever his wife suggested that perhaps they should consider separation, he went into a panic. I came close to hospitalizing him more than once."

"And his wife?" Marshal took out a blank sheet of paper and started taking notes. "Sorry, Ernest, I don't have my old notes."

"What about his wife?" Ernest asked.

"You ever meet with them as a couple? What was she like? She also in therapy?"

"Never met her! Don't even know what she looks like, but I think of her as a demon. She wouldn't come in to see me, said that it was Justin's pathology, not hers. Nor would she get into individual therapy—same reason, I guess. No, there was something else . . . I remember Justin telling me she hated shrinks—had seen two or maybe even three of them when she was younger, and each one ended up screwing her or trying to screw her. As you know, I've seen several abused patients, and no one feels more outrage than I at this unconscionable betrayal. Still, if it happened to the same woman twice or three times . . . I don't know—maybe we ought to wonder about *her* unconscious motivations."

"Ernest," Marshal said, shaking his head forcefully, "this is the only time you'll ever hear me say this, but in this one instance, unconscious motivations are irrelevant! When patient-therapist sex occurs, we should forget about dynamics and only look at behavior. Therapists who sexually act out with their patients are invariably irresponsible and destructive. There's no defending them—they should be out of the field! Maybe some patients have sexual conflicts, maybe they want to seduce men—or women—in authority positions, maybe they are sexually compulsive, but that's why they're in therapy. And if the therapist can't understand that and deal with it, then he ought to change professions.

"I've told you," Marshal continued, "I'm on the state medical ethics board. Well, I spent last night reading the cases for next week's monthly meeting in Sacramento. Incidentally, I was going to talk to you about that. I want to nominate you to serve a term on the board. My three-year term is up next month, and I think you'd do an outstanding job. I remember the stand you took in that Seymour Trotter case several years ago. That showed courage and integrity; everyone else was so cowed by the old disgusting bastard that they wouldn't testify against him. You did the profession a great service. But what I was going to say," Marshal continued, "was that therapist-patient sexual abuse is getting epidemic. There's a new scandal reported almost every day in the papers. A friend mailed me a story in the *Boston Globe* that reports on sixteen psychiatrists who have been charged with sexual abuse in the last few years, including some well-known figures: the former chairman at Tufts and one of the senior training analysts of the Boston Institute. And then, of course, there is the case of Jules Masserman—who, like Trotter, was a past president of the American Psychiatric Association. Can you believe what he did—giving patients sodium pentothal and then having sex with them while they were unconscious? It's unthinkable!"

"Yes, that was the one that shook me up the most," said Ernest. My internship roommates often kid me about spending that year soaking my feet—I had terrible ingrown toenails—and reading Masserman: his *Principles of Dynamic Psychiatry* was the best textbook I ever read!"

"I know, I know," said Marshal, "all the fallen idols. And it's getting worse! I don't understand what's happening. Last night I read the charges against eight therapists—shocking, disgusting stuff. Can you believe a therapist who slept with—and charged!—his patient for every session, twice a week, for *eight* years! Or a child psychiatrist, caught in a motel with a fifteen-year-old patient? He was covered with chocolate syrup, and his patient was licking it off! Disgusting! And there was a voyeuristic offense—a therapist treating multiple personality states who hypnotized his patients and encouraged more primitive personalities to emerge and to masturbate in front of him. The therapist's defense was that he never touched his patients—and also that it was proper treatment, first to give these personalities free expression in a safe environment and then gradually to encourage reality testing and integration."

"And all the while getting off sexually while watching them masturbate," Ernest added, sneaking a look at his watch.

"You looked at your watch, Ernest. Can you put that into words?"

"Well, time is going by. I had wanted to get into some material about Justin."

"In other words, though this discussion may be interesting, it's not what you came for. In fact, you'd rather not squander your supervision time and money on it?"

Ernest shrugged his shoulders.

"Am I close?"

Ernest nodded.

"Then why not say so? It's your time; you're paying for it!"

"Right, Marshal, it's that old business of wanting to please. Of still holding you too much in awe."

"A little less awe and a little more directness will serve this supervision better."

Like a rock, Ernest thought. A mountain. These little exchanges, generally quite separate from the formal task of discussing patients, were often the most valuable teaching that Marshal did. Ernest hoped that sooner or later he would internalize Marshal's mental toughness. He also took note of Marshal's draconian attitudes about patient-therapist sexual relations; he had intended to talk about his dilemma involving Nan Carlin at his bookstore reading. Now he wasn't so sure.

Ernest returned to Justin. "Well, the more I worked with Justin, the more I was convinced that any progress made in our hours was immediately undone at home in his relationship with his wife, Carol—an absolute gorgon."

"It's coming back to me. Wasn't she the borderline who threw herself out of the car to stop him from buying bagels and lox?"

Ernest nodded. "That's Carol, all right! The meanest, toughest lady I ever encountered, even indirectly, and I hope never to meet her face to face. As for Justin, for about two to three years I did good traditional work with him: good therapeutic alliance, clear interpretations of his dynamics, the right professional detachment. Yet I could not budge this guy. I tried everything, raised all the right questions: Why had he chosen to marry Carol? What payoff did he get for staying in the relationship? Why had he chosen to have kids? But nothing we talked about ever got translated into behavior.

"It became apparent to me that our usual assumptions—that enough interpretation and insight will ultimately lead to external change—weren't the answer. I interpreted for years but Justin had, it seemed to me, a total paralysis of the will. You may remember that, as a result of my work with Justin, I became fascinated with the concept of will and began reading everything I could about it: William James, Rollo May, Hannah Arendt, Allen Wheelis, Leslie Farber, Silvano Arieti. I guess it was about two years ago that I gave a grand rounds presentation on paralysis of the will."

"Yes, I remember that lecture—you did well, Ernest. I still think you should write that up for publication."

"Thanks. I've got a little will paralysis myself on finishing that paper. Right now it's stacked up behind two other writing projects. You may remember that in grand rounds I concluded that, if insight doesn't kick-start the will, then therapists have to find some other way to mobilize it. I tried exhortation: in one way or another, I began to whisper in his ear, 'You have to try, you know.' I understood, oh, did I understand, Allen Wheelis's comment that some patients have to get their backs off the couch and their shoulders to the wheel.

"I tried visual imagery," Ernest continued, "and urged Justin to project himself into the future—ten, twenty years from now—and to imagine himself still stuck in this lethal marriage, to imagine his remorse and regret for what he had done with his own life. It didn't help.

"I became like a second in a boxer's corner, offering advice, coaching him, helping him rehearse declarations of marital liberation. But I was training a featherweight, and his wife was a cruiser-class heavyweight. Nothing worked. I guess the last straw was the great backpacking caper. Did I tell you about that?"

"Go on; I'll stop you if I've heard it."

"Well, about four years ago Justin decided it would be a great thing for the family to go backpacking—he's got twins, a boy and girl aged eight or nine now. I encouraged him. I was delighted with anything that had the aroma of initiative. He always felt guilty about not spending enough time with his children. I suggested he think of a way to change that, and he decided that a backpacking trip might be an exercise in good fathering. I was delighted and told him so. But Carol wasn't delighted! She refused to go—no particular reason, just sheer perversity—and she forbade the kids to go with Justin. She didn't want them sleeping in the woods—she's phobic about everything, you name it: insects, poison oak, snakes, scorpions. Besides, she has problems staying home alone, which is strange, since she has no problem traveling alone for business—she's an attorney, a tough trial lawyer. And Justin can't stay home alone, either. A folie à deux.

"Justin, with my vehement urging, of course, insisted that he would go camping and he would go with or without her permission. He was putting his foot down this time! '*Atta boy, 'atta boy,* I whispered. *Now we're moving.* She raised hell, she wheedled, she bargained, she promised that if they all went to Yosemite and stayed in the Ahwahnee Hotel this year, then next year she'd go camping with them. '*No deal,*' I coached him, '*hold firm.*'

"So, what happened?"

"Justin stared her down. She caved in and invited her sister to come stay with her while Justin and the kids went camping. But then . . . twilight zone set in . . . odd things began to happen. Justin, dazzled by his triumph, became concerned that he was not in good enough physical shape for such a venture. It would be necessary, first, to lose weight—he set twenty pounds for his goal—and then to strengthen his back. So he began working out, mainly by climbing forty stories to get to and from his office. During one workout he developed acute shortness of breath and got an extensive medical workup."

"Which was negative, of course," said Marshal. "I don't remember your telling me this story, but I think I can fill in the rest. Your patient became morbidly concerned about the camping trip, couldn't lose weight, grew convinced his back wouldn't hold up and that he wouldn't be able to take care of his children. Finally he developed full-blown panic attacks and forgot about backpacking. The family went off to the Ahwahnee Hotel, and everyone wondered how his idiot shrink ever came up with such a harebrained scheme."

"The Disneyland Hotel."

"Ernest, this is an old, old story. And an old, old error! You can count on this scenario whenever the therapist mistakes the symptoms of the family system for the symptoms of the individual. So that was when you gave up?"

Ernest nodded. "That's when I switched to a holding action. I assumed he was stuck forever in his therapy, his marriage, his life. That's when I stopped talking about him in our supervision."

"But now comes a major new development?"

"Yes. Yesterday he came in and, almost nonchalantly, told me he had left Carol and moved in with a much younger woman—someone he had hardly mentioned to me. Three times a week he sees me and he *forgets* to talk about her."

"Oh-ho, that's interesting! And?"

"Well, it was a bad hour. We were out of sync. I felt diffusely annoyed most of the session."

"Run through the hour quickly with me, Ernest."

Ernest recounted the events of the session, and Marshal went straight for the countertransference—the therapist's emotional response to the patient.

"Ernest, let's focus first on your annoyance with Justin. Try to relive the hour. When your patient tells you he has left his wife, what do you begin to experience? Just free-associate for a minute. Don't try to be rational—stay loose!"

Ernest took the plunge. "Well, it was as if he were making light of, even mocking, our years of good work together. I worked like hell for years with this guy—I broke my ass. For years he was a deadweight around my neck . . . this is raw stuff, Marshal."

"Go on. It's *supposed* to be raw stuff."

Ernest searched his feelings. Plenty there, but which ones dare he share with Marshal? He wasn't in therapy with Marshal. And he wanted Marshal's collegial respect—and his referrals, and his sponsorship for the analytic institute. But he also wanted the supervision to be supervision.

"Well, I was pissed—pissed about his throwing the eighty thousand dollars in my face, pissed that he would just mosey out of that marriage without discussing it with me. He knew how much I had invested in his leaving her. Not even a phone call to me! And, let me tell you, this guy has phoned me about incredibly trivial stuff. Also, he had hidden the other woman from me, and that pissed me off, too. And also I was pissed about her ability, the ability of any woman, to simply crook her finger or twitch her little cunt and enable him to do what I had failed to do for four years."

"And what about your feelings about the fact that he actually left his wife?"

"Well, he did it! And that's good. No matter *how* he did it, it's good. But he didn't do it the right way. Why in hell couldn't he have done it the right way? Marshal, this is nuts—primitive stuff, practically primary process. I'm really uncomfortable verbalizing this."

Marshal leaned over and put his hand on Ernest's arm, a very uncharacteristic act for him. "Trust me, Ernest. This is not easy. You're doing great. Try to keep going."

Ernest felt encouraged. It was interesting for him to experience that strange paradox of therapy and supervision: the more unlawful, shameful, dark, ugly stuff you revealed, the more you were rewarded! But his associations had slowed: "Let's see, I'll have to dig. I hated it that Justin allowed himself to be led around by his pecker. I had hoped for better things from him, hoped he could leave that dragon the right way. That wife of his, Carol . . . she gets to me."

"Free-associate to her, just for one or two minutes," Marshal requested. His reassuring "just for one or two minutes" was one of Marshal's few concessions to a supervisory rather than a therapy contract. A clear and short time limit put boundaries around the self-disclosure and made the process feel safer to Ernest.

"Carol? . . . bad stuff . . . gorgon's head . . . selfish, borderline, vicious woman . . . sharp teeth . . . eye slits . . . evil incarnate . . . the nastiest woman I ever met. . . . "

"So you *did* meet her?"

"I mean the nastiest woman I *never* met. I only know her through Justin. But after several hundred hours, I know her pretty well."

"What did you mean when you said he didn't do it the *right* way. What's the right way?"

Ernest squirmed. He looked out the window, avoiding Marshal's eyes.

"Well, I can tell you the *wrong* way: the wrong way is to go from one woman's bed to another woman's bed. Let's see . . . if I had my wish for Justin, what would it be? That, for once, just once, he'd be a *mensch*! And that he'd leave Carol like a *mensch*! That he would decide that this was the wrong choice, the wrong way to spend his one and only life, that he would simply move out—face his own isolation, come to terms with who he is, as a person, as an adult, as a separate human being. What he's done is pathetic: shucking his responsibility, falling into a trance, swooning in love with some young pretty face—'an angel made in heaven,' he put it. Even if it does work for a while, he's not going to grow, not going to learn a goddamned thing from it!

"Well, there it is, Marshal! Not pretty! And I'm not proud of it! But if you want primitive stuff, there it is. Plenty of it—and it's patent. I can see through most of it myself!" Ernest sighed and leaned back, exhausted, awaiting Marshal's response.

"You know, it's been said that the goal of therapy is to become one's own mother and father. I think we could say something analogous about supervision. The goal is to become your own supervisor. Sooo . . . let's take a look at what you see about yourself."

Before looking inside, Ernest took a look at Marshal and thought, "*Be my own mother and father, be my own supervisor*—goddamn, he's good."

"Well, the most obvious thing is the depth of my feelings. I'm overinvested, for sure. And this crazy sense of outrage, of proprietorship—of *how dare he* make this decision without consulting me first."

"Right!" Marshal nodded vigorously. "Now juxtapose outrage with your goal of diminishing his dependency on you and cutting down his hours."

"I know, I know. The contradiction is glaring. I want him to break his attachment to me, yet I get angry when he acts independently. It's a healthy sign when he insists on his private world, even concealing this woman from me."

"Not only a healthy sign," Marshal said, "but a sign that you've been doing good therapy. Damn good therapy! When you work with a dependent patient, your reward is rebellion, not ingratiation. Take pleasure in it."

Ernest was moved. He sat in silence, holding back tears, gratefully digesting what Marshal had given him. A caregiver for so many years, he was not used to being nourished by others.

"What do you see," Marshal continued, "in your comments about the right way for Justin to leave his wife?"

"My arrogance! Only one way: *my* way! But it's very strong—I feel it even now. I'm disappointed in Justin. I wanted better things for him. I sound like a demanding parent, I know!"

"You're taking a strong position, so extreme you yourself don't believe it. Why so strong, Ernest? Where's the push coming from? What about your demands on yourself?"

"But I *do* believe it! He's gone from one dependent position to another, from wife-devil-mother to angel-mother. And the swooning, falling in love, 'angel from heaven' business—he's in bliss-merger, like an incompletely divided amoeba, he said . . . anything to avoid facing his own isolation. And it's the fear of isolation that's kept him in this lethal marriage all these years. I've got to help him see that."

"But so strong, Ernest? So demanding? Theoretically, I think you're right, but what divorcing patient can ever match up to that standard? You demand the existential hero. Great for novels but, as I think back over my years of practice, I cannot recall a single patient who left a spouse in that noble fashion. So let me ask you again, where's all that push coming from? What about similar issues in your own life? I know that your wife was killed in a car accident several years ago. But I don't know much else about your life with women. Did you remarry? Have you been through a divorce?"

Ernest shook his head and Marshal continued: "Let me know if I'm intruding too far, if we're crossing the line between therapy and supervision."

"No, you're on the right track. Never remarried. My wife, Ruth, has been dead six years. But the truth is that our marriage was over long before that. We were living separately but in the same house, just staying together for convenience. I had a lot of trouble leaving Ruth, even though I knew very early—we both knew—that we were wrong for each other."

"Sooo," Marshal persisted, "going back to Justin and your countertransference . . . "

"Obviously I've got some work to do and I've got to stop asking Justin to do my work for me." Ernest looked up at the ornate gold-plated Louis XIV clock on Marshal's mantel only to be reminded, once again, that it was purely decorative. He looked at his watch: "Five minutes left—let me discuss one other point."

"You mentioned something about a bookstore reading and a social encounter with a former patient."

"Well, first something else. The whole question of whether I should have owned up to my irritation to Justin when he called me on it. When he accused me of trying to bring him down from his love bliss, he was absolutely right—he was reading reality correctly. I think that, by *not confirming his accurate perceptions,* I was doing antitherapy."

Marshal shook his head sternly. "Think about it, Ernest: What would you have said?"

"Well, one possibility was to have simply told Justin the truth— more or less what I told you today." That was what Seymour Trotter would have done. But of course Ernest did not mention that.

"Like what? What do you mean?"

"That I had become unwittingly possessive; that I may have been confusing him by discouraging his independence from therapy; and also that I may have permitted some of my own personal issues to have clouded my view."

Marshal had been staring at the ceiling and suddenly looked at Ernest, expecting to see a smile on his face. But there was no smile.

"Are you serious, Ernest?"

"Why not?"

"Don't you see that you're too much involved as it is? Whoever said that the point of therapy is to be truthful about everything? *The point, the one and only point, is to act always in the patient's behalf.* If therapists discard structural guidelines and decide instead to do their own thing, to improvise willy-nilly, to be truthful all the time, why, imagine it—therapy would become chaos. Imagine a long-faced general walking among his troops wringing his hands on the eve of battle. Imagine telling a severe borderline that, no matter how hard she tries, she's in for another twenty years of therapy, another fifteen admissions, another dozen wrist slashings or overdoses. Imagine telling your patient you're tired, bored, flatulent, hungry, fed up with listening, or just itching to get onto the basketball court. Three times a week I play basketball at noon, and for an hour or two before I am flooded with fantasies of jump shots and spinning drives to the basket. Shall I tell the patient those things?

"Of course not!" Marshal answered his own question. "I keep these fantasies to myself. And if they get in the way, then I analyze my own countertransference or I do exactly what you're doing right now—and doing well, I want to add: working on it with a supervisor."

Marshal looked at his watch. "Sorry to go on so long. We're running out of time—and some of that is my fault for talking about the ethics committee. Next week let me give you the details about your beginning a term on the committee. But now, please, Ernest, take two minutes about the bookstore meeting with your former patient. I know that was part of your agenda."

Ernest started to pack his notes into his briefcase. "Oh, it was nothing dramatic, but the situation was interesting—the kind of thing that might generate a good discussion at an institute study group. In the beginning of the evening a very attractive woman came on to me very strongly and I, for a moment or two, reciprocated and flirted back. Then she told me that she had been my patient briefly, very briefly, in a group about ten years ago, in my first year of residency, that the therapy had been successful, and that she was doing extremely well in her life."

"And?" asked Marshal.

"Then she invited me to meet her after my reading, just for coffee in the bookstore café."

"And what did you do?"

"I begged off, of course. Told her I had a commitment for the evening."

"Hmm . . . yes, I see what you mean. It *is* an interesting situation. Some therapists, even some analysts, might have met with her briefly for coffee. Some might say, given that you saw her only in brief therapy and in a group, that you were being too rigid. But—" Marshal rose to signify the end of their hour—"I agree with you, Ernest. You did the right thing. I would have done exactly the same."

FIVE

ith forty-five minutes to spare before his next patient, Ernest set off for a long walk down Fillmore toward Japantown. He was unsettled in many ways by the supervisory session, especially by Marshal's invitation, or rather edict, to join the State Medical Ethics Committee.

Marshal had, in effect, ordered him to join the profession's police force. And if he wanted to become an analyst, he could not alienate Marshal. But why was Marshal pushing it so hard? He must have known the role wasn't right for Ernest. The more he thought about it, the more anxious he grew. This was no innocent suggestion. Surely Marshal was sending him some kind of wry, coded message. Perhaps, "See for yourself the fate of incontinent shrinks."

Calm down, don't make too much of it, Ernest said to himself. Maybe Marshal's motives were entirely benign—probably serving on this committee would facilitate acceptance as a candidate for the analytic institute. Even so, Ernest didn't like the idea. His nature was to understand someone in human terms, not to condemn. He had acted as policeman only once before, with Seymour Trotter, and, though his behavior had been publicly impeccable on that occasion, he had resolved never again to sit in judgment of another.

Ernest checked his watch: only eighteen minutes before the first of his four afternoon patients. He bought two crisp fuji apples from a grocery store on Divisadero and devoured them as he rushed back to his office. Brief lunch breaks of apples or carrots were the latest in a long series of weight-losing strategies, each hugely unsuccessful. Ernest was so ravenous by the evening that he wolfed down the equivalent of several lunches during dinner.

The simple truth: Ernest was a glutton. He consumed far too much food and would never lose weight merely by shifting the proportions around during the day. Marshal's theory (which Ernest secretly considered analytic bullshit) was that he did too much mothering in therapy, permitted himself to be sucked so dry by his patients, that he gorged himself to fill his emptiness. In supervision, Marshal had repeatedly urged him to give less, and to say less, limiting himself to only three or four interpretations each hour.

Glancing about—Ernest would hate for a patient to see him eating—he continued to reflect on the supervisory hour. "The General wringing his hands before the troops on the eve of battle!" Sounded good. Everything Marshal said in that confident Bostonian accent sounded good. Almost as good as the Oxonian speech of the two British analysts in the Psychiatry Department. Ernest marveled at the way he and everyone else hung on their every word, even though he had yet to hear either of them express an original thought.

And so, too, Marshal sounded good. But what had he really said? That Ernest should conceal himself, that he should hide any doubts or uncertainties. And as for the general wringing his hands—what kind of analogy was that? What the hell did the battlefield have to do with him and Justin? Was there a war going on? Was he a general? Justin a soldier? Sheer sophistry!

These were dangerous thoughts. Never before had Ernest permitted himself to be so critical of Marshal. He reached his office and began scanning his notes in preparation for his next patient. Ernest permitted no slack time for personal reverie when he was about to see a patient. Heretical thoughts about Marshal would have to wait. One of Ernest's cardinal rules of therapy was to give each patient one hundred percent of his attention.

Often he cited this rule when patients complained that they thought of him far more than he thought of them, that he was but a friend rented by the hour. He generally responded that when he was with them in the here-and-now of the therapy hour, he was entirely and fully with them. Yes, of course they thought more about him than he about them. How could it be otherwise? He had many patients, they only one therapist. Was it any different for the teacher with many students, or the parent with many children? Ernest often was tempted to tell patients that when he had been in therapy he had experienced the same feelings for *his* therapist, but that was precisely the type of disclosure that brought the severest criticism from Marshal.

"For chrissakes, Ernest," he would say. "Keep something for your friends. Your patients are professional clients, *not* your friends." But lately Ernest was beginning to question more seriously the discrepancy between one's personal and professional personae.

Is it so impossible for therapists to be genuine, to be authentic in all encounters? Ernest thought of a tape he had heard recently of the Dalai Lama speaking to an audience of Buddhist teachers. One member of the audience had asked him about teacher burnout and the advisability of structured off-duty time. The Dalai Lama giggled and said, "The Buddha *off duty*? Jesus Christ *off duty*?"

Later that evening during dinner with his old friend, Paul, he returned to these thoughts. Paul and Ernest had known each other since the sixth grade, and their friendship had solidified during medical school and residency at Johns Hopkins when they had roomed in a small, white-stepped house on Mount Vernon Place in Baltimore.

For the past few years their friendship had been conducted largely by telephone, since Paul, reclusive by nature, lived on a twenty-acre wooded lot in the Sierra foothills, a three-hour drive from San Francisco. They had made a commitment to spend one evening a month together. Sometimes they met halfway, sometimes they alternated the drive. This had been Paul's month to travel and they met for an early dinner. Paul never spent the night anymore; always misanthropic, he had grown more so as he aged and recently had developed a strong aversion to sleeping anywhere but in his own bed. He was unperturbed by Ernest's interpretations about homosexual panic or his gibes about packing his beloved blanket and mattress in his car.

Paul's growing contentment with inner journeys was a source of annoyance to Ernest, who missed his travel companion of earlier years. Though Paul was extremely savvy about psychotherapy—he had once spent a year as a candidate at the Jungian institute in Zurich—his preference for rural life limited his supply of long-term psychotherapy patients. He earned his living primarily as a psychopharmacologist at a county psychiatric clinic. But sculpting was his real passion. Working in metal and glass, he gave graphic form to his deepest psychological and existential concerns. Ernest's favorite piece was one that had been dedicated to him: a massive earthenware bowl containing a small brass figure who grasped a large boulder as he peered inquisitively over the lip. Paul had titled it Sisyphus Enjoying the View.

They dined at Grazie, a small restaurant in North Beach. Ernest came directly from his office, dressed nattily in a light gray suit with a black and green plaid vest. Paul's clothing—cowboy boots, checked western shirt, and string tie clasped by a large turquoise stone—clashed with his pointed professorial beard and thick wire-rimmed spectacles. He seemed like a cross between Spinoza and Roy Rogers.

Ernest ordered an enormous meal while Paul, a vegetarian, displeased the Italian waiter by refusing all his entreaties and ordering only a salad and grilled marinated zucchini. Ernest wasted no time filling Paul in on the events of his week. Dipping his focaccia in olive oil, he described his bookstore encounter with Nan Carlin and proceeded to complain about striking out with three women he had approached that week.

"Here you are, horny as hell," said Paul, peering through his thick glasses and picking lightly at his radicchio salad, "and listen to yourself: a beautiful woman comes after you, and because of some cockamamie excuse of having seen her twenty years ago. . . . "

"Not 'seen' her, Paul; I was her therapist. And it was ten years ago."

"Ten years, then. Because she was a member of your group for a few sessions ten years ago—a goddamned half-generation ago—you can't have a different relationship with her now. She's probably sex-starved, and the best thing you could have offered her was your cock."

"C'mon, Paul, be serious. . . . Waiter! More focaccia, olive oil, and Chianti, please."

"I *am* serious," Paul continued. "You know the reason you never get laid? Ambivalence. An ocean, large ocean, of ambivalence. It's a different reason every time. With Myrna you were afraid she'd fall in love with you and get permanently hurt. With what's-her-name last month you were afraid she'd catch on that you were only interested in her big boobs and she'd feel used. With Marcie you were afraid one romp in bed with you would destroy her marriage. The lyrics are different but the music is always the same: the lady admires you, you act nobly, you don't get laid, the lady respects you even more, and then she goes home to bed with her vibrator."

"I can't turn it on and off. I can't be a paragon of responsibility during the day and join a gang-bang line at night."

"Gang-bang line? Listen to yourself! You can't believe that there are plenty of women as interested in casual sexual release as we are. All I'm saying is that you've worked yourself into a corner of pious horniness. You take so much 'therapeutic' responsibility for every woman, you won't give them what they might really want."

Paul's point struck home. In a curious way it was a close cousin to what Marshal had been saying for years: don't usurp everyone else's personal responsibility. Don't aspire to be the universal breast. If you want people to grow, help them learn to become their own mother and father. Despite Paul's misanthropic crotchetiness, his insights were invariably incisive and creative.

"Paul, I don't exactly see you ministering to the needs of sexually deprived female pilgrims."

"But you don't see me complaining. I'm not the one who's being led around by his pecker. Not anymore—and I don't miss it. Aging isn't all bad. I've just finished an ode to 'gonadal tranquillity.'"

"Yuck! 'Gonadal tranquillity'! I can just see it inscribed on the tympanum of your mausoleum."

"*Tympanum?* Good word, Ernest." Paul jotted it down on his napkin and stuffed it in the pocket of his checkered flannel shirt. He had begun writing poetry to accompany each of his pieces of sculpture and collected arresting words. "But I'm not dead, just tranquil. Pacific. I'm also not the one who's running away from stuff tossed in my lap. That one in the bookstore who wants some shrink sex? Send her up to me. I guarantee I won't excavate some excuse not to lay her. Tell her she can count on a man both enlightened and engorged."

"I was serious about introducing you to Irene, that neat woman I met through the personal ads. Are you really interested?"

"Just so long as she's grateful for what she gets, doesn't nosy around my house, and drives back home the same night. She can squeeze anything she wants as long as it's not orange juice in the morning."

Ernest looked up from his minestrone to engage Paul's smile. But there was no smile. Just Paul's magnified eyes peering through his thick spectacles. "Paul, we're going to have to deal with this—you're drifting into terminal misanthropy. Another year and you'll have moved into a mountain cave with a picture of Saint Jerome on the wall."

"Saint Anthony, you mean. Saint Jerome lived in the desert and consorted with beggars. I detest beggars. And what do you have against caves?"

"Not much, just insects, cold, dampness, darkness, cavernous-ness—oh, hell, this is too big a project for tonight, especially with no cooperation from the afflicted one."

The waiter approached, weighted down with Ernest's entree. "Let me guess who gets what. The osso buco, fagiolini, and side order of gnocchi al pesto must go to you?" he asked, playfully putting it in front of Paul. "And you"—turning to Ernest—"you're gonna love these cold dry vegetables."

Ernest laughed. "Too much zucchini—I can't eat all that!" He switched plates and dug in. "Talk to me seriously about my patient Justin," he said between mouthfuls, "and the direction I'm getting from Marshal. This is really agitating me, Paul. On the one hand, Marshal seems to know what he's doing—I mean, after all, there's a corpus of real knowledge in this business. The science of psy-chotherapy is almost a hundred years old. . . . "

"Science? Are you kidding? Shit, about as scientific as alchemy. Maybe less!"

"Okay. The art of therapy . . . " Ernest noted Paul's frown and tried to correct himself. "Oh, you know what I mean—the field, the endeavor—what I mean is that for a hundred years there have been a lot of bright people in this field. Freud was no slouch intellectually, you know—not many to match him. And all these analysts spend-ing decades, thousands, tens of thousands, of hours listening to patients. That's Marshal's point: that it would be the height of arro-gance to ignore all they have learned, to simply make it all up anew, to make it up as I go along."

Paul shook his head. "Don't accept this crap that listening invariably begets knowledge. There are such things as undisciplined listening, as the concretization of error, as selective inattention, as self-fulfilling prophecies, as unconsciously prompting the patient to give you the material you want to hear. You want to do something interesting? Go to the library stacks, pick up a nineteenth-century text on hydrotherapy—not a historical overview but the original text. I've seen texts of a thousand pages with the most precise instructions—you know, water temperature, length of immersion, force of spray, proper sequence of heat and cold—and all calibrated for each specific kind of diagnosis. Very impressive, very quantitative, very scientific—but it doesn't have a goddamn thing to do with reality. So I'm not impressed with 'tradition,' and you shouldn't be either. The other day some enneagram expert responded to a challenge by claiming that the enneagram had its roots in ancient sacred Sufi texts. As though that meant it should be taken seriously. All it probably meant, and he didn't appreciate my telling him so, was that at a bull session a long, long time ago some camel drivers, sitting on heaps of dried camel dung, poked their camel prods in the sand and drew diagrams of the personality."

"Strange—I wonder why he didn't appreciate that," said Ernest, as he wiped up the last of the pesto sauce with a hunk of focaccia.

Paul went on. "I know what you're thinking—terminal misanthropy, especially about experts. Did I tell you my New Year's resolution? To piss off an expert every day! This posturing of experts, it's all a charade. The truth is, we often don't know what the fuck we're doing. Why not be real, why not admit it, why not be a human being with your patient?

"Have I ever told you," Paul continued, "about my analysis in Zurich? I saw a Dr. Feifer, an old-timer, who had been a close associate of Jung. Talk about therapist self-disclosure! This guy would tell me *his* dreams, especially if a dream involved me or even remotely involved some theme even remotely relevant to my therapy. You read Jung's *Memories, Dreams, Reflections*?"

Ernest nodded. "Yeah, bizarre book. Dishonest, too."

"Dishonest? Dishonest how? Put that on the agenda for next month. But, for now, do you remember his comments about the wounded healer?"

"That only the wounded healer can truly heal?"

"The old bird went further than that. He said the ideal therapeutic situation occurred when the patient brought the perfect plaster for the therapist's wound."

"The *patient* ministers to the therapist's wound?" asked Ernest.

"Exactly! Just imagine the implications of that! It blows your fucking mind! And whatever else you think of Jung, Christ knows he was no dummy. Not in Freud's class, but close. Well, many of Jung's early circle took that idea quite literally and worked on their own issues as they arose in therapy. So not only did my analyst tell me his dreams; he went into some very personal material in his inter- pretations of them, including at one time his homosexual yearnings for me. I almost bolted from his office right then. I found out later he wasn't really interested in my hairy ass—he was too busy screw- ing two of his female patients."

"Learned that from the doyen, I'm sure," said Ernest.

"No doubt. Old Jung had no compunctions about hitting on his female patients. Those early analysts were absolutely predatory, almost every single one of them. Otto Rank was screwing Anaïs Nin, Jung was screwing Sabina Spielrein and Toni Wolff, and Ernest Jones screwed everybody, had to leave at least two cities because of sexual scandal. And of course, Ferenczi had trouble keeping his hands off his patients. About the only one who didn't was Freud himself."

"Probably because he was too busy sticking it to Minna, his sister-in-law."

"No, I don't think so," Paul replied. "No real evidence for that. I think Freud had a premature arrival into gonadal tranquillity."

"Obviously you've got as strong feelings as I do about preying on female patients. So how come you were on my case, a few minutes ago, when I told you about the ex-patient I met in the bookstore?"

"You know what that scene reminded me of? My orthodox uncle Morris, who kept so kosher he wouldn't eat a cheese sandwich in a nonkosher sandwich shop: he feared it might have been cut with a knife that had previously cut a ham sandwich. There's responsibility and then there's fanaticism masquerading as responsibility. Hell, I remember our social hours at Hopkins with the student nurses: without fail you'd get out of there quickly and run back to your novel, or else go after the homeliest one there. Remember Mathilda Shore—we called her 'Mathilda Shorething'? That's who you'd pick! And that gorgeous one who used to follow you around, you avoided her like the plague. What was her name?"

"Betsy. She looked fragile as hell and, what's more, her boyfriend was a police detective."

"See, that's what I mean! Fragility, boyfriend—Ernest, those are *her* problems, not yours. Who appointed you world therapist laureate? But let me finish telling you about this Dr. Feifer. On several occasions he used to change chairs with me."

"Change chairs?"

"Literally. Sometimes right in the middle of the hour he'd get up and suggest that I sit in his chair and he in mine. He might start talking about his personal difficulties with the problem I was discussing. Or he might disclose some strong countertransference and work on it on the spot."

"This part of the Jungian canon?"

"In a way, yes. I've heard that Jung did some experimentation with this in collaboration with a strange bird named Otto Gross."

"Anything written on this?"

"Not sure. I know Ferenczi and Jung talked about changing chairs and experimented with it. I'm not even sure who got it from whom."

"So what did your analyst disclose to you? Give me an example."

"The one I remember best had to do with my being Jewish. Though he personally was not anti-Semitic, his father was a Swiss Nazi sympathizer and he carried a lot of shame about that. He told me that was his main reason for marrying a Jewish woman."

"And how'd it affect your analysis?"

"Well, look at me! Have you ever seen anyone more integrated?"

"Right. A couple more years with him and you'd have bricked up the entrance to your cave by now! Seriously, Paul, what did it do?"

"You know how difficult attribution is, but my best reading is that his disclosure never hurt the process. Generally it helped. It freed me up, allowed me to trust him. Remember that in Baltimore I saw three or four cold fish analysts and never went back for a second session."

"I was a lot more compliant than you. Olivia Smithers was the first analyst I saw, and I stuck with her for about six hundred hours. She was a training analyst, so I figured she's got to know what she's doing and if I didn't get it, then it was my problem. Big mistake. I wish I had those six hundred hours back. She shared nothing about herself. We never had an honest moment between us."

"Well, I don't want to give you the wrong idea about my relationship with Feifer. Revealing à la suisse doesn't necessarily mean real. For the most part, he didn't relate to *me*. His self-revelation was punctated. He didn't look at me, sat about ten feet away, and then suddenly he'd snap open like a Jack-in-the-box and tell me how much he wanted to decapitate his father or fuck his sister. Then the next minute he'd snap back to his stiff, arrogant persona."

"I'm more interested in the ongoing realness of the relationship," said Ernest. "Think about that session I told you about with Justin. He's *got* to have realized that I was piqued at him, that I was being petty. Look at the paradox I put him in: first, I tell him the purpose of my therapy is to improve his mode of relating to others. Second, I try to form an authentic relationship with him. Third, along comes a situation in which he perceives, quite accurately, some problematic aspect of our relationship. Now I ask you, if I deny his accurate view, what else can you call it but antitherapy?"

"Jesus, Ernest, don't you think you might be perseverating on one minuscule event in the history of humankind? Do you know how many patients I saw today? Twenty-two! And that's with stopping early to drive down here. Give this guy a little Prozac and see him fifteen minutes every other week. You really think he'd be worse off?"

"Dammit, forget that, Paul, we've been through that discussion. Stay with me this one time."

"Well, just do it, then. Run the experiment; change chairs during the session and be a total truth teller. Start tomorrow. You say you see him three times a week. You want to wean him from you, to de-idealize you, so show him some of your limitations. What would the risks be?"

"Probably few risks with Justin, except that after so many years, he'd be bewildered by a radical change in technique. Idealization is tenacious. It might even backfire—knowing Justin, he'd probably idealize me even more for being so honest."

"So? Then you'd bring *that* to his attention."

"You're right, Paul. The truth is that the real risk is not to the patient, but to *me*. How can I be supervised by Marshal and do something he's so opposed to? And I certainly can't lie to a supervisor. Imagine paying a hundred sixty dollars an hour to lie."

"Maybe you're grown up professionally. Maybe the time has come to stop seeing Marshal. Maybe he'd even agree. You've served your apprenticeship."

"Hah! In the world of analysis I haven't even started. I need a full training analysis, maybe four or five years, years of classes, years of intensive supervision on my training cases."

"Well, that neatly takes care of the rest of your life," Paul responded. "That's the modus operandi of orthodoxy. They smother a blooming, dangerous young brain in the manure of doctrine for a few years until it goes to seed. Then when the last dandelion fluff of creativity has blown away, they graduate the initiate and rely on him in his dotage to perpetuate the holy book. That's the way it works, isn't it? Any challenge by a trainee would be interpreted as resistance, wouldn't it?"

"Something like that. For sure, Marshal would interpret any experimentation as acting out or, as he puts it, as my therapeutic incontinence."

Paul signaled the waiter and ordered an espresso. "There's a long history to therapists experimenting with self-disclosure. I just started to read the new Ferenczi clinical diaries. Fascinating. Only Ferenczi of Freud's inner circle had the courage to develop more effective treatment. The old man himself was too concerned with theory and the care and preservation of his movement to pay much attention to outcome. Besides, I think he was too cynical, too convinced of the inexorability of human despair, to expect that any real change could occur from any form of psychological treatment. So Freud tolerated Ferenczi, loved him in a way, as much as he could love anyone—used to take Ferenczi on vacations with him and analyze him as they walked together. But any time Ferenczi went too far in his experimentation, any time his procedures threatened to give psychoanalysis a bad name, then Freud came down hard, very hard. There's a letter of Freud's chastising Ferenczi for entering his third puberty."

"But didn't Ferenczi deserve that? Wasn't he sleeping with his patients?"

"I'm not so sure. It's possible, but I think he was after the same goal as you: some way of humanizing the therapeutic procedure. Read the book. I think it's got some interesting stuff on what he calls 'double' or 'mutual' analysis: he analyzes the patient one hour, and the next hour the patient analyzes him. I'll lend you the book—once you return the other fourteen. And all overdue fines."

"Thanks, Paul. But I already have it. It's on my nightstand waiting its turn. But your offer of a loan . . . I am touched, not to mention staggered, by it."

For twenty years Paul and Ernest had recommended books to each other, mainly novels but also nonfiction. Paul's specialty was contemporary novels, especially those overlooked or dismissed by the New York establishment, while Ernest was delighted to be able to surprise Paul with dead, largely forgotten writers like Joseph Roth, Stefan Zweig, or Bruno Shulz. Lending books was out of the question. Paul didn't like to share—even food, always frustrating Ernest's wish to share entrees. The walls of Paul's house were lined with books and he frequently browsed through them, pleasantly reexperiencing old friendships with each. Ernest did not like to lend books either. He read even evanescent page-turners with pencil in hand, underlining sections that moved him or made him think, possibly to use in his own writing. Paul scavenged for interesting poetic words and images, Ernest for ideas.

When he got home that night, Ernest spent an hour skimming Ferenczi's journal. He also began thinking about Seymour Trotter's comments about truth telling in therapy. Seymour said we must show patients that we eat our own cooking, that the more open, the more genuine *we* become, the more they will follow suit. Despite Trotter's terminal disgrace, Ernest sensed that there was something of the wizard in him.

What if he followed Trotter's suggestion? Revealed himself totally to a patient? Before the night was out, Ernest made a bold decision: he would conduct an experiment using a radically egalitarian therapy. He would reveal himself entirely, having one objective only: to establish an authentic relationship with that patient and assume that the relationship, *in and by itself,* would be healing. No historical reconstruction, no interpretations of the past, no explorations of psychosexual development. He would focus on nothing but what was in between him and the patient. And he would begin the experiment immediately.

But who would be the experimental patient? Not one of his ongoing patients; the transition from his old to his new method would be awkward. Better, much better, to make a fresh start with a new patient.

He picked up his appointment book and looked at the next day's schedule. There was a new patient coming in at ten A.M.—a Carolyn Leftman. He knew nothing about her other than that she was self-referred, having heard him lecture at the Printer's Inc. bookstore in Palo Alto. "Well, whoever you are, Carolyn Leftman, you're in for a unique therapeutic experience," he said, then turned out the light.

SIX

t 9:45 Carol arrived at Ernest's office and, following the instructions given her when she phoned for an appointment, let herself into the waiting room. Like most psychiatrists, Ernest used no receptionist. Carol had deliberately come early to allow a few minutes to calm herself, to rehearse the clinical history she had invented, and to sink into her role. She sat down on the same green leather sofa that Justin habitually used. Only two hours previously Justin had jauntily bounced up the stairs and creased the very cushion upon which Carol now sat.

She poured some coffee, sipped it slowly, and then took several deep breaths to savor Ernest's antechamber. *So this is it,* she thought, as her eyes circled the room; *this is the war room where this odious man and my husband have plotted against me for so long.*

She scanned the furnishings. Hideous! The tacky woven wall hanging—a refugee from a sixties Haight Street fair—the musty armchairs, the amateur photos of San Francisco, including the mandatory scene of the Victorian homes at Alamo Square. God spare me from any more psychiatrist home photos, Carol thought. She shivered at the memory of Dr. Cooke's Providence office, of lying on that worn Persian rug and staring at wall photos of bleary Truro sunrises while her doctor cupped her buttocks with his frosty hands and, with joyless, muted grunts, thrust into her the sexual affirmation he insisted she needed.

She had spent over an hour dressing. Wanting to appear sensuous, yet needy and vulnerable, she had gone from silk slacks to long, patterned skirt, from sheer satin blouse to magenta cashmere sweater. Finally, she decided on a short black skirt, a tight ribbed sweater, also black, and a simple twisted gold chain. Under that a brand-new lace bra, heavily padded and smartly uplifting, purchased specially for the occasion. Not for nothing had she studied Ernest's interaction with Nan in the bookstore. Only a blind fool would have missed his puerile interest in breasts. That unctuous creep—and those quivering, spittle-dripping lips. He had practically leaned over and started suckling. Worse yet, he was so pompous, so full of himself, that it probably had never even occurred to him that women notice his leering. Since Ernest was not tall, about Justin's height, she wore flats. She considered black patterned stockings but rejected them. Not yet.

Ernest entered the waiting room and offered his hand. "Carolyn Leftman? I'm Ernest Lash."

"How do you do, Doctor?" said Carol, shaking his hand.

"Please come in, Carolyn," said Ernest, gesturing for her to sit in the armchair facing his. "This being California, I'm on a first-name basis with my patients. 'Ernest' and 'Carolyn' okay with you?"

"I'll try to get used to it, Doctor. It may take me a while." She followed him into the office and quickly took in her surroundings. Two cheap leather armchairs set at ninety-degree angles so that both doctor and patient had to turn slightly to face each other. On the floor a worn, fake Kashan rug. And against one wall the mandatory couch—good!—over which hung a couple of framed degrees. The wastepaper basket was full, with some crumpled, grease-stained tissues visible—probably straight from Burger King. A ratty, piss-colored Mexican floor screen made of plywood and frayed rope stood in front of Ernest's disheveled desk, which was piled high with books and papers and crowned with a huge computer monitor. No evidence of any aesthetic sensibility. Nor the slightest trace of a woman's touch. Good!

Her chair felt stiff and uninviting. At first she resisted putting her full weight on it by bracing herself with her arms. Justin's chair. For how many hours—hours she had paid for—had Justin sat in this chair and violated her? She shivered when she imagined him and this ass, sitting in this office, fat heads together, scheming against her.

In a most grateful voice she said, "Thank you for seeing me so quickly. I felt I was at the end of my rope."

"You sounded pressed on the phone. Let's start from the beginning," said Ernest, taking out his notepad. "Tell me everything I need to know. From our brief conversation I know only that your husband has cancer and that you called me after hearing me read at a bookstore."

"Yes. And then I read your book. I was very impressed. By many things: your compassion, your sensitivity, your intelligence. I've never had much respect for therapy or for the therapists I've met. With one exception. But when I heard you speak, I had a strong feeling that you and only you might be able to help me."

Oh, God, Ernest thought, here's the patient I designated for truth-telling therapy, for an uncompromisingly honest relationship, and here we are, in the very first minute, off to the falsest of beginnings. Only too well he remembered his struggle with his shadow that evening in the bookstore. But what could he say to Carolyn? Certainly not the truth! That he shuttled back and forth between his cock and his brain, between lust for Nan and concern for his topic and his audience. No! Discipline! Discipline! Then and there Ernest began developing a set of guiding principles for his truth-telling therapy. First principle: *Reveal yourself only to the extent it will be helpful to the patient.*

Accordingly, Ernest gave an honest but measured response: "I have a couple of different responses to your comment, Carolyn. Naturally I feel pleased by your compliments. But I also feel uncomfortable with your feeling that *only* I can help you. Because I am also an author and in the public eye, people tend to imbue me with more wisdom and therapeutic expertise than I possess.

"Carolyn," he continued, "I say this to you because, if we find that we don't work well together for whatever reason, I want you to know that there are plenty of therapists in this community as competent as I. Let me add, though, I'll do my best to live up to your expectations."

Ernest felt a warm glow. Pleased with himself. Not bad. Not bad at all.

Carol flashed an appreciative smile. Nothing worse, she thought, than ingratiating false humility. Pompous bastard! And if he keeps saying "Carolyn" every other sentence, I'm going to throw up.

"So, Carolyn, let's begin at the beginning. First a few basic facts about yourself: age, family, living, work situation."

Carol had decided to steer a mid-course between deception and truth. To avoid trapping herself in lies, she would stay as close as possible to the truth about her life and would alter the facts only as much as necessary to prevent Ernest from realizing she was Justin's wife. At first she planned to use the name Caroline, but it felt too alien and she settled upon Carolyn, hoping it was sufficiently removed from Carol. The deception came easy to her. She glanced again at the couch. This wouldn't take long, she thought—maybe only two to three hours.

She delivered her well-rehearsed story to the unsuspecting Ernest. She had prepared carefully. She had taken a new phone line at home, lest Ernest notice that she had the same number as Justin. She paid in cash to avoid the trouble of opening an account under her maiden name of Leftman. And she had prepared a story line about her life that was as close to the truth as possible without arousing Ernest's suspicions. She was thirty-five, she told Ernest, an attorney, mother of an eight-year-old daughter, married unhappily for nine years to a man who several months ago underwent radical surgery for prostate cancer. The cancer recurred and he had been treated by orchiectomy, hormones, and chemotherapy. She also had planned to say that the hormones and the surgical removal of his testicles had rendered him impotent and her sexually frustrated. But now that seemed too much all at once. No rush. All in due time.

Instead, she had decided to focus in this first visit on her desperate sense of entrapment. Her marriage, she told Ernest, had never been a satisfying one, and she had been seriously contemplating separation when his cancer was diagnosed. Once the diagnosis was made, her husband fell into deep despair. He was terrified by the thought of dying alone, and she could not bring herself to raise the question of ending the marriage. And then, only a few months later, the cancer recurred. The prognosis was grim. Her husband begged her not to let him die alone. She agreed, and now, for the rest of his life, she was trapped. He had insisted they move from the Midwest to San Francisco to be near the University of California cancer treatment center. So, a couple of months ago, she left all her friends in Chicago, abandoned her law career, and moved to San Francisco.

Ernest listened carefully. He was struck by the similarity of her story with that of a widow he had treated a few years before, a schoolteacher who had been on the verge of asking for a divorce when her husband also developed prostate cancer. She promised him that she would not let him die alone. But the horror of it was that he took nine years to die! Nine years of nursing him as the cancer slowly spread through his body. Horrible! And after his death, she was devastated by rage and regret. She had tossed away the best years of her life for a man she did not like. Did that lie in store for Carolyn? Ernest's heart went out to her.

He tried to empathize, to imagine himself into her situation. He noticed his reluctance. Like diving into a cold pool. What a dreadful trap!

"Now tell me all the ways this has affected you."

Carol reeled off her symptoms: insomnia, anxiety, loneliness, crying spells, a sense of futility about her life. She had no one to talk to. Certainly not her husband—they had never talked in the past and now, more than ever, a great gulf loomed between them. Only one thing helped—marijuana—and since moving to San Francisco, she smoked two or three joints a day. She sighed deeply and fell silent.

Ernest looked closely at Carolyn. An attractive, sad woman, with thin lips twisted at the corners into a bitter grimace; large, tearful, cow-brown eyes; short, curly black hair; long, graceful neck rising from a tight ribbed sweater that cradled sturdy, tidy breasts and was stretched thin at the tips by plucky nipples; a tight skirt; a flash of jet-black underpants visible when she slowly crossed her slender legs. Under social circumstances Ernest would have checked out this woman diligently, but today he was impervious to her sexual allure. While in medical school he had acquired the knack of flicking a switch and turning off all sexual arousal, even sexual interest, when working with patients. He did pelvic exams all afternoon in the gynecology clinic with hardly a sexual thought, and then later that evening made a complete idiot of himself trying to plead his way into some nurse's underpants.

What could he do for Carolyn? he wondered. Was this even a psychiatric problem? Perhaps she was simply an innocent victim who happened to be in the wrong place at the wrong time. No doubt in an earlier age, she would have consulted her priest for consolation.

And perhaps priestly consolation was exactly what he should be offering. Surely there was something to be learned from the church's two thousand years in the therapy business. Ernest had always wondered about priests' training. How good were they really at providing consolation? Where did they learn their technique? Courses in consolation? Courses in confession-booth counseling? Ernest's curiosity had once led him to do a literature search at the library on Catholic confession counseling. He had come up with nothing. Another time he had inquired at a local seminary and learned that the curricula offered no explicit psychological training. Once, while visiting a deserted cathedral in Shanghai, Ernest sneaked into the confessional booth and, for thirty minutes, sat in the priest's seat, inhaling the Catholic air and murmuring, again and again, "You are forgiven. My child, you are forgiven!" He emerged from the booth full of envy. What powerful Jovian weapons against despair the priests wielded; in contrast, his own secular armamentarium of interpretations and creature comforts seemed puny, indeed.

A widow whom he had guided through bereavement and who still returned now and then for a tune-up session once referred to his role as that of a compassionate witness. Maybe, Ernest thought, compassionate witnessing is all I'll be able to offer Carolyn Leftman.

But maybe not! Maybe there are some openings for real work here.

Ernest silently formulated a checklist of areas to explore. First of all, why such a poor relationship with her husband before he got cancer? Why stay for ten years with someone you don't love? Ernest mused about his own loveless marriage. If Ruth had not been crushed to death in her automobile, would he have been able to make the break? Perhaps not. Still, if Carolyn's marriage were so bad, why no attempts at marital therapy? And should her assessment of the marriage be accepted at face value? Perhaps there was still a chance to salvage the relationship. Why move to San Francisco for cancer treatment? Plenty of patients come to the cancer center for treatment for brief periods and then return home. Why so meekly give up her career and her friends?

"You've been feeling trapped for a long time, Carolyn, first maritally, now maritally *and* morally," ventured Ernest. "Or maritally *versus* morally."

Carol tried to nod in rapt agreement. *Oh, how brilliant,* she thought. *Shall I genuflect?*

"You know, I'd like you to fill me in, to tell me everything about yourself, everything you think I should know to help us make sense of your life predicament."

Us, Carol thought, *hmm, interesting. They are so slick. They get the hook in so deftly. Fifteen minutes into the session and already it's "us," it's "tell me everything"; already "we" seem to have agreed that making sense of my "predicament" will offer salvation. And he needs to know everything, everything. There's no rush. Why should there be, at a hundred and fifty dollars an hour? And that's a hundred and fifty clear—no fifty percent overhead, no law clerks, no conference room, no office library, no paralegals, not even a secretary.*

Swiveling her attention back to Ernest, Carol began to recount her personal history. Safety lay in truth. Within limits. Surely, she reasoned, Justin was too self-centered to have talked much about the details of his wife's life. The fewer lies she told, the more convincing she would be. Hence, aside from shifting her education from Brown and Stanford Law School to Radcliffe and Chicago Law, she merely told Ernest the truth about her early life, about a frustrated and bitter mother who taught elementary school and never recovered from her husband's abandoning her.

Memories of her father? Left when she was eight. According to her mother, he went crazy at age thirty-five, fell in with a grubby flower child, left everything, followed the Grateful Dead for a few years, and stayed stoned in a San Francisco commune for the next fifteen years. He sent her birthday cards (with no return address) for a few years and then . . . nothing. Until her mother's funeral. Then he suddenly reappeared, dressed, as though in a time warp, in a threadbare Haight-Ashbury uniform with rotting sandals, faded, shredded jeans, and a tie-dyed shirt, and claimed that only his wife's presence had stood in the way, all these years, of his assuming his natural paternal role. Carol desperately wanted and needed a father but began to suspect his judgment when he whispered to her at the cemetery service that she shouldn't delay in getting out all her anger toward her mother.

Any remaining illusion of a father's return evaporated the following day when, stuttering, scratching his lice-filled hair, and filling the room with the stench of his hand-rolled cigarettes, he presented a business proposition that consisted of her turning over to him her small inheritance to invest in a Haight Street head shop. When she refused, he countered by insisting that her mother's house "properly" belonged to him—by "human law" if not "legal law"—since he had paid the down payment twenty-five years before. Naturally she had suggested he leave (her words, which she didn't tell Ernest, had been, "Hit the road, creep"). She'd been lucky enough never to have heard from him again.

"So you lost your father and mother at the same time?"

Carol nodded, bravely.

"Siblings?"

"One brother, three years older."

"His name?"

"Jeb."

"Where is he?"

"New York or New Jersey, I'm not sure. Somewhere on the East Coast."

"He doesn't call you?"

"He better not!"

Carol's answer was so sharp and bitter that Ernest involuntarily winced.

"Why had he 'better not'?" he asked.

"Jeb got married at nineteen and joined the navy at twenty-one. At thirty-one he sexually molested his two young daughters. I went to the trial: he only got a three-year prison sentence and a dishonorable discharge. He's under court injunction not to live within a thousand miles of Chicago, where his daughters live."

"Let's see." Ernest consulted his notes and calculated: "He's three years older . . . you must have been twenty-eight . . . so all this happened ten years ago. You haven't seen him since he was sentenced to prison?"

"A three-year term is short. He got a longer sentence from me."

"How long?"

"Life!"

A chill ran through Ernest. "Life is a long sentence."

"For a capital offense?"

"How about *before* the offense? Did you have much anger toward your brother then?"

"His daughters were eight and ten when he abused them."

"No, no, I mean anger toward him that existed *before* the offense."

"His daughters were *eight* and *ten* when he abused them," Carol repeated through clenched teeth.

Whoa! Ernest had stumbled into a land mine. He knew he was doing a "wildcat" session—one he could never describe to Marshal. He could anticipate the criticism: "What in hell are you doing by pressing her about her brother before even taking a decent systematic past history? You haven't even explored her marriage, the manifest reason for her coming." Yes, he could hear Marshal's words: "Sure, there's something there. But, for chrissakes, can't you wait? Store it; come back to it at the appropriate time. You're incontinent again."

But Ernest knew he had to put Marshal out of mind. His resolution to be entirely open and honest with Carolyn demanded that he be spontaneous, that he share *what* he felt *when* he felt it. No tactics, no storing ideas with this patient! The object today was "Be yourself. Give yourself."

Besides, Ernest was fascinated by the suddenness of Carolyn's rage—so immediate, so real. Earlier he had had trouble reaching her: she seemed so bland, matter-of-fact. Now there was juice: she had come alive; her face and her words were in sync. To reach this woman he had to keep her real. He decided to trust his intuition and go where the emotion was.

"You're angry, Carolyn, and not only at Jeb, but at me, too."

Finally, jerk—you got something right, Carol thought. *Christ, you're worse than I imagined. No wonder you never thought twice about what you and Justin were doing to me. You don't even flinch at the thought of an eight-year-old girl being violated by her father!*

"I'm sorry, Carolyn, to have poked so hard into such a tender area. Perhaps I was premature. But let me be up front with you. What I was getting at was this: if Jeb could be so barbarous as to do that to his own young daughters, what might he have done to his younger sister?"

"What do you mean . . . ?" Carol put her head down; she suddenly felt faint.

"Are you all right . . . some water?"

Carol shook her head and quickly regained her composure. "Sorry, I suddenly felt faint. Don't know what it was."

"What do you think?"

"Don't know."

"Don't lose the feeling, Carolyn. Stay with it just for another couple of minutes. It happened when I asked about Jeb and you. I was thinking of you as a ten-year-old and what your life was like with an older brother like that."

"I've been the counsel in a couple of lawsuits involving childhood sexual abuse. It's the most brutal process I've ever witnessed. Not only the awful recovered memories but the violent upheaval in the families and all the controversy about implanted memories—it's brutal for everyone. I guess I blanched at the thought of going through all this stuff myself. I'm not sure if you were steering me in that direction. If you were, I've got to tell you that right now I remember no particular trauma involving Jeb: my recollection is only of the typical amount of brother-sister torment. But it is also true that I remember very little of my early childhood."

"No, no—I'm sorry, Carolyn, I wasn't clear. I wasn't thinking about some major childhood trauma and subsequent post-traumatic stress. Not at all, although I agree with you about that type of thinking being very much in fashion today. What I had in mind was less dramatic, more insidious, more ongoing. Something like this: What might it have been like for you to have grown up, to have spent considerable part of every day with an uncaring or even abusive brother?"

"Yes, yes, I see the difference."

Ernest glanced at the clock. Dammit, he thought, only seven minutes left. So much to do! I've *got* to start examining her marriage.

Though Ernest's glance at the clock was sly, Carol caught it. Her first reaction was inexplicable. She felt hurt. But that passed quickly and she thought, *Look at him—the sneaky, greedy bastard—figuring out how many minutes are left before he can chuck me out and start the meter clicking for the next hundred and fifty dollars.*

Ernest's clock was deep in a bookshelf out of the patient's view. In contrast, Marshal placed his clock in plain view on the small table between himself and the patient. "Only being honest," Marshal said. "It's open knowledge that the patient pays for fifty minutes of my time, so why keep the clock secret? To hide the clock is to collude in a pretense that you and the patient have a personal, not a professional, relationship." Typical Marshal: solid, irrefutable. Just the same, Ernest kept his clock obscured.

Ernest tried to devote the remaining few minutes to Carolyn's husband: "I'm impressed that all the men you've mentioned, the pivotal men in your life, have badly disappointed you, and I know 'disappointment' is too tepid a word: your father, your brother, and, of course, your husband. But I really don't know much about your husband yet."

Carol ignored Ernest's invitation. She had her own agenda.

"While we're talking about men in my life who have disappointed me, I should mention one important exception. When I was an undergraduate student at Radcliffe, I was in a dangerous psychological place. I've never been worse: down on myself, depressed, feeling inadequate, ugly. And then, the last straw: I was dumped by Rusty, my boyfriend since junior high. I really hit bottom, drinking, using drugs, considering dropping out of college, even suicide. Then I saw a therapist, a Dr. Ralph Cooke, who saved my life. He was extraordinarily kind and gentle and affirming."

"How long did you see him?"

"About a year and a half, as a therapist."

"There's more, Carolyn?"

"I'm a little hesitant to go into it. I really value this man and don't want you misunderstanding." Carol reached for a Kleenex and squeezed out a tear.

"Can you go on?"

"Well . . . I'm very uncomfortable talking about this. . . . I'm afraid you'll judge him. I should never have mentioned his name. I know therapy is confidential. But . . . but . . . "

"Is there a question in there for me, Carolyn?" Ernest wanted to waste no time letting her know that he was a therapist whom she could question and who would answer all questions.

Dammit, Carol thought, squirming with irritation in her chair. *"Carolyn, Carolyn, Carolyn." Every goddamned sentence he has to say "Carolyn"!*

She continued, "A question . . . well, yes. More than one. First, is this entirely confidential? Not to be shared with anyone? And, second, will you judge or stereotype him?"

"Confidential? Absolutely. Count on me."

Count on you? Carol thought. *Yeah, like I could count on Ralph Cooke.*

"And as for judging, my task here is to understand, not to judge. I'll do my best and I'll promise to be open with you about it. I'll answer any of your questions," said Ernest, weaving his truth-telling resolve tightly into the fabric of this first session.

"Well, I'll just spit it out. Dr. Cooke and I became lovers. After I had seen him for a few sessions, he began to hug me from time to time to comfort me, and then it just happened—there on that glorious Persian rug in his office. It was the best thing that ever came my way. I don't know how to talk about it except to say it saved my life. Every week I saw him and every week we made love, and all the pain and all the misery just vanished. Finally he didn't think I needed any more therapy, but we kept on being lovers for another year. With his help I graduated college and got into law school. The best: University of Chicago Law."

"Your relationship ended when you went to law school?"

"For the most part. But a few times when I needed him I flew into Cambridge, and every time he was there and he gave me the comforting I needed."

"He still in your life?"

"Dead. He died young, about three years after I graduated from law school. I think I've never stopped looking for him. I met my husband, Wayne, shortly afterward and decided to marry him. A hasty decision. And a bad one. Maybe I wanted Ralph so much I imagined I saw him in my husband."

Carol grabbed more Kleenex, emptying Ernest's box. She didn't have to squeeze tears out now; they flowed of their own accord. Ernest reached into a desk drawer for another box of tissues, tore off the plastic cover, and started the paper flow by pulling out the first tissue, which he handed to Carol. She was astounded at her tears: a tragic and romantic view of her own life swept over her as her fiction became her truth. How sublime to have been loved so much by this all-giving, magnificent man; and how awful, how unbearable—here Carol wept harder—never to have seen him again, to have lost him forever! When Carol's sobbing subsided, she put away the Kleenex and looked up expectantly at Ernest.

"Now I've said it. Aren't you judging? You said you'd tell me the truth."

Ernest was in a jam. The truth was that he felt little charity toward this dead Dr. Cooke. He quickly considered his options. Remember, he reminded himself: total disclosure. But he balked. Total disclosure in this instance would not have been in his patient's best interests.

His interview with Seymour Trotter had been his first exposure to therapist sexual abuse. In the ensuing eight years he had worked with several patients who had been sexually involved with previous therapists, and in every case the result had been calamitous for the patient. And, despite Seymour's photograph, despite his arm raised jubilantly toward the sky, who can say what the outcome was for Belle? Of course there was the money she was awarded at the trial, but what else? Seymour's cerebellar deterioration was progressive. Probably after a year or two she had been trapped into full-time caretaking for the rest of his life. No, no way one could say the outcome was good, in the long run, for Belle. Nor for any patient he had ever heard of. And yet, here today, Carolyn says that she and her therapist had an ongoing sexual relationship and it saved her life. Ernest was stunned.

His first impulse was to discredit Carolyn's claim: maybe the transference to this Dr. Cooke was so strong that she hid the truth from herself. After all, it was clear that Carolyn wasn't home free. Here it is, fifteen years later, and she is still sobbing about him. Furthermore, as a result of her Dr. Cooke encounter, she made a bad marriage, which has plagued her since.

Careful, Ernest warned himself, don't prejudge this. Take a moralistic, righteous stand and you'll lose your patient. Be open; try to enter Carolyn's experiential world. And above all, don't bad-mouth Dr. Cooke now. Marshal had taught him that. Most patients feel a deep bond toward the offending therapists and need time to work through the remnants of their love. It is not unusual for sexually abused patients to go through several new therapists before they find one with whom they can work.

"So your father and brother and husband ended up abandoning or betraying or trapping you. And the one man you really cared for died. Sometimes death feels like abandonment, too." Ernest was disgusted with himself, with this therapy cliché, but under the circumstances it was the best he could do.

"I don't think Dr. Cooke was too happy about dying."

Carol immediately regretted her words. *Don't be stupid!* she chastised herself. *You want to seduce this guy, to suck him in, what in hell are you doing getting testy and defending this wonderful Dr. Cooke, who is a sheer figment of your imagination?*

"Sorry, Dr. Lash . . . I mean, Ernest. I know that wasn't what you meant. I guess I'm missing Ralph a lot now. I'm feeling pretty much alone."

"I know that, Carolyn. That's just why it's important for us to be close."

Ernest noted Carolyn's eyes widen. *Careful,* he warned himself, *she could see that statement as seductive.* In a more formal voice, he continued: "And that's precisely why the therapist and patient must examine all the things that get in the way of their relationship—like, for example, your irritation at me a couple of minutes ago." *Good, good, much better,* he thought.

"You said you'd share your thoughts with me. I guess I was wondering if you *were* being judgmental of him or me."

"Is there a question in there for me, Carolyn?" Ernest was stalling for time.

Good God! I have to spell it out in big letters? thought Carol. "*Were* you being judgmental? How *do* you feel?"

"About Ralph?" More stalling.

Carol nodded, silently groaning.

Ernest threw caution to the winds and told the truth. Mostly. "I admit that I *am* thrown off balance by what you tell me. And I guess I *do* feel judgmental of him. But I'm working on it—I don't want to close down; I want to stay entirely open to your experience.

"Let me tell you why I'm thrown off balance," Ernest continued. "You tell me he was enormously helpful to you, and I believe you. Why would you come here, pay me a great deal of money, and not tell the truth? So I don't doubt your words. Yet what am I supposed to do with my own experience—not to mention a large professional literature and powerful clinical consensus—which leads to different conclusions: namely, that sexual contact between patient and therapist is invariably destructive to the patient—and ultimately to the therapist as well."

Carol had prepared well for this argument. "You know, Dr. Lash . . . sorry, Ernest—I'll get it soon; I'm not used to shrinks being real people with first names. They usually hide behind their titles. They're usually not up front with their humanity like you. What was I saying . . . oh, yes, I took the liberty, while in the process of deciding to see you, of checking out your bibliography in the library—old work habit: checking out the credentials of doctors who are testifying in court as expert witnesses."

"And?"

"And I found out you were well trained in the natural sciences and published a number of reports of your psychopharmacological research."

"And?"

"Well, is it possible you're neglecting your scientific standards here? Consider the data which you're using to form conclusions about Ralph. Look at your evidence—a totally uncontrolled sample. Be honest: Would it pass any kind of scientific muster? *Of course* your sample of patients who have been involved sexually with therapists consists of injured or dissatisfied patients—but that's because *they're the ones that come for help.* But the others—satisfied customers like me—they don't come in to see you, and you have no idea how large a population that might be. In other words, all you know is the numerator, just those who come for therapy. You know nothing about the denominator—the number of patients and therapists who have sexual contact or the number who were helped or the number for whom the experience was irrelevant."

Impressive, Ernest thought. *Interesting to see her professional persona; I would not like to be on the wrong side of this woman in a courtroom.*

"Do you see my point, Ernest? Is it possible I'm right? Be honest with me. Have you ever run into someone before me who wasn't harmed by such a relationship?"

His mind again drifted to Belle, Seymour Trotter's patient. *Would Belle fit into the category of those who were helped?* Again, the faded picture of Seymour and Belle flitted across his mind. *Those sad eyes. But maybe she was better off. Who knows, maybe they both ended up better off? Or temporarily better off. No, who can be sure of anything in that case, least of all how they ended up together?* For years Ernest had wondered when they first decided to retreat to an island together. Had Seymour decided at the very end to rescue her? Or had they schemed together much earlier? Perhaps from the very beginning?

No, these were not thoughts to be shared. Ernest swept Seymour and Belle out of his mind and gently shook his head in response to Carolyn's question. "No, I haven't, Carolyn. I've never seen a patient who wasn't harmed by it. But nonetheless your point about objectivity is well taken. It will help me not to prejudge." Ernest took a long look at his watch. "We're already over our time, but I still need to check in with a couple of questions."

"Sure." Carol brightened. Another hopeful sign. *First he asked me to ask him questions. No reputable shrink does that. There's even an implication he will respond to personal questions about his life—I'm going to test that next time. And now he's bending the rules by running well over the fifty minutes.*

She had read the APA guidelines to psychiatrists about how to avoid charges of sexual abuse: hold firm to all boundaries, avoid the slippery slope, don't call your patients by first names, start and end sessions promptly. Every single therapist abuse case she had been counsel for had started with the therapist extending the fifty minutes. *Aha,* she thought, *a little slip here, a slope there, who knows where we'll be after a couple of sessions?*

"First, I want to know about any discomfort you're going to be taking home from today's session. What about the powerful feelings earlier when we talked about Jed?"

"Not Jed—*Jeb.*"

"Sorry. Jeb. You felt faint briefly when we spoke of him."

"I'm still a little shaky, but not upset. I think you were onto something important."

"Okay. Second, I want to find out something about the space between us. You worked hard today, you took some big risks, revealed really important parts of yourself. You trusted me a great deal and I appreciate your trust. Do you think we can work together? How are you feeling about me? What's it like to have revealed so much to me?"

"I feel good about working with you. Real good, Ernest. You're personable and flexible; you make it easy to talk, and you have an impressive ability to focus on the wounded spots, spots I don't know about myself. I feel I'm in very good arms. And here is your fee." She handed him three fifty-dollar bills. "I'm in the midst of switching banks from Chicago to San Francisco, and it's more convenient to pay everything in cash."

In good arms, mused Ernest as he escorted her to the door. *Isn't the expression "in good hands"?*

At the door Carol turned. With moist eyes she said, "Thank you. You're a godsend!"

Then she leaned over, gave the surprised Ernest a light hug for two or three seconds, and walked out.

As Carol descended the stairs, a wave of sadness crashed over her. Unwanted images from long ago passed through her: she and Jeb having a pillow fight; jumping and yelling in her parents' bed; her father carrying her books as he walked her to school; her mother's casket sinking into the ground; Rusty's boyish face grinning at her as he fetched her books from her high school locker; her father's calamitous reentry into her life; the sad, worn Persian rug in Dr.

Cooke's office. She squeezed her eyes to brush them all away. Then she thought about Justin, perhaps at this very moment walking hand in hand with his new woman somewhere else in the city. Perhaps near here. She reached the front entrance of the Victorian and looked up and down Sacramento Street. No sign of Justin. But a young, attractive man with long blond hair, dressed in sweat pants, a pink shirt, and an ivory sweater jogged by and charged up the stairs two at a time. *Probably Lash's next sucker,* she thought. She began to walk away, then turned to glance up at Ernest's office window. *Goddamnit,* she thought, *that son of a bitch is trying to help me!*

Upstairs, Ernest sat at his desk recording his notes from their session. The pungent citrus aroma of Carolyn's perfume lingered for the longest time.

SEVEN

*A*fter Ernest's supervisory hour, Marshal Streider sat back in his chair and thought about victory cigars. Twenty years ago he had heard Dr. Roy Grinker, an eminent Chicago analyst, describe his year on Freud's couch. That was in the twenties, in the days when analytic respectability required a pilgrimage to the master's couch—sometimes for a couple of weeks, sometimes, if one dreamed of becoming an analytic mover and shaker, as long as a year. According to Grinker, Freud never concealed his glee when he made an incisive interpretation. And if Freud thought he had made a monumental interpretation, he opened up his box of cheap cigars, offered one to his patient, and suggested they have a "victory" smoke. Marshal smiled at Freud's lovable, naive handling of the transference. If he still smoked, he would have lit a celebratory cigar after Ernest's departure.

His young supervisee had been coming along nicely the past few months, but today had been a landmark session. Putting Ernest on the medical ethics board was nothing short of inspired. Marshal often thought that Ernest's ego was riddled with lacunae: he was grandiose and impulsive. Unruly bits of his sexual id jutted out at odd angles. But worst of all was his juvenile iconoclastic stubble: Ernest had far too little respect for discipline, for legitimate authority, for knowledge worked out over decades by diligent analysts with minds more penetrating than his.

And what better method, Marshal thought, *of helping to resolve iconoclasm than appointing Ernest to judgeship? Brilliant!* It was on occasions like this that Marshal yearned for observers, an audience to appreciate the work of art he had fashioned. Everyone recognized the traditional reasons for the analyst to be fully analyzed. But Marshal intended, sooner or later (his to-do list of papers had grown and grown), to write a paper about an unappreciated aspect of maturity: the ability to be creative year after year, decade after decade, in the absence of any external audience. After all, what other artists—who can still take seriously Freud's claim that psychoanalysis is a science?—can devote a lifetime to an art that is never viewed by others? Imagine Cellini casting a silver chalice of luminous beauty and sealing it into a vault. Or Musler spinning glass into a masterpiece of grace and then, in the privacy of his studio, shattering it. Horrible! *Isn't "audience,"* Marshal thought, *one of the unheralded but important nutrients that supervision provides for the not-yet-mature therapist? One needs decades of seasoning to be able to create sans spectators.*

And true for life as well, Marshal reflected. *Nothing worse than living the unobserved life.* Again and again, in his analytic work, he had noted his patients' extraordinary thirst for his attention—indeed, the need for an audience is a major unsung factor in prolonged interminal therapy. In work with his bereaved patients (and in this he agreed with Ernest's observations in his book), he had often seen them fall into despair because they had lost their audience: their lives were no longer observed (unless they were lucky believers in a deity who had the leisure time to scrutinize their every action).

Wait! Marshal thought. *Is it really true that analytic artists work in solitude? Aren't patients an audience? No, in this matter they do not count. Patients are never sufficiently disinterested. Even the most elegantly creative analytic utterances are lost on them! And they are greedy! Watch how they suck out the marrow of an interpretation without an admiring glance at the magnificence of its container. What about students or supervisees? Are they not audience? Only rarely is a student perspicacious enough to grasp the artistry of an analyst. Usually the interpretation is beyond them; later in their clinical practice, maybe months, even years afterward, something will jar their memory and suddenly, in a flash, they will apprehend and gasp at the subtlety and greatness of their teacher's art.*

Certainly that would be true for Ernest. The time would come when he would arrive at understanding and gratitude. By forcing him now to identify with the aggressor, I've saved him at least a year on his training analysis.

Not that he was in a rush for Ernest to finish. Marshal wanted him around for a long time.

Later that evening, after he had seen his five afternoon analytic patients, Marshal rushed home only to find the house empty and a note from his wife, Shirley, saying dinner was in the fridge and she would be back from the flower-arranging exposition around seven. As always, she had left an ikebana arrangement for him: a long, tubular ceramic bowl containing a nest of gray, angular, bare, downward-facing euonymus branches. At one end of the nest emerged two long-stemmed Easter lilies facing away from each other.

Goddamnit, he thought, as he shoved the arrangement down to, and almost over the end of, the table. *I had eight patient hours and one supervisory hour today—fourteen hundred dollars—and she can't put dinner out for me because she's too busy with these fucking flower arrangements!* Marshal's anger dissipated as soon as he opened the plastic containers in the fridge: gazpacho with a knockout aroma, a gaily colored salad niçoise made with fresh pepper-seared tuna, and a mango, green grapes, and papaya fruit salad in a passion fruit sauce. Shirley had taped a note to the gazpacho bowl: "Eureka! At last—a negative calorie recipe: the more you eat, the skinnier you get. Only two bowlfuls—don't disappear on me." Marshal smiled. But only for a moment. He vaguely recalled some other "disappearing" joke Shirley had made only a few days ago.

As he ate, Marshal opened the afternoon *Examiner* to the financial section. The Dow had risen twenty. Of course the *Examiner* only had the one P.M. quotes, and lately the market had gyrated wildly at the end of the day. But no matter: he enjoyed checking the quotes twice daily and would see the closing quotes in the *Chronicle* tomorrow morning. He held his breath as he hastily punched in the rise of each of his stocks on his calculator and computed the day's profits. Eleven hundred dollars—and it could be more by the time the market closed. A warm flush of satisfaction swept over him, and he took his first spoon of thick, crimson gazpacho studded with small gleaming green-white cubes of onion, cucumber, and zucchini. Fourteen hundred dollars from clinical billings and eleven hundred from stock profits. It had been a good day.

After the sports page and a quick glance at the world news, Marshal hastily changed his shirt and charged out into the night. His passion for exercise almost equaled his love of profits. He played basketball at the YMCA on Mondays, Wednesdays, and Fridays during his lunch break. On weekends he bicycled and played tennis or racquetball. On Tuesdays and Thursdays he had to fit in aerobic time any way he could—there was a meeting of the Golden Gate Psychoanalytic Institute at eight, and Marshal left early enough for the brisk thirty-minute walk to the institute.

With each powerful stride, Marshal's anticipation grew as he thought about the meeting that evening. It was going to be an extraordinary session. No doubt about it: there was going to be high drama. There was going to be blood spilled. Oh, the blood—yes, that was the exciting part. Never before had he so clearly apprehended the lure of horror. The carnival atmosphere at public executions in olden days, the peddlers hawking toy gallows, the buzz of excitement as the drums rolled and the doomed shuffled up the stairs of the scaffold. The hanging, the beheadings, the burnings, the drawing and quarterings—imagine a man's four limbs being tied to a team of horses who were whipped and spurred and cheered by onlookers until he was ripped into quarters, all major arteries gushing at once. Horror, yes. But someone else's horror—someone who provided a view of the precise juncture of being and nonbeing at the moment, the very instant, that spirit and flesh are wrenched asunder.

The grander the life to be annihilated, the greater the lure. The excitement during the Reign of Terror must have been extraordinary, as noble heads rolled and blood gushed crimson from royal torsos. And the excitement, too, about those sacred last words. As that juncture between being and nonbeing approaches, even freethinkers speak in hushed voices, listening, straining to hear the dying person's final syllables—as if in that very moment, when life is wrested away and flesh begins its transformation into meat, there will be a revelation, a clue to the great mysteries. It reminded Marshal of the avalanche of interest in near-death experiences. Everyone knew it was sheer charlatanism, but the craze lasted twenty years and sold millions of books. God! Marshal thought, the money made on that rot!

Not that there was regicide on that night's institute agenda. But the next best thing: excommunication and banishment. Seth Pande, one of the institute's founding members and a senior training analyst, was on trial and certain to be expelled because of diverse anti-analytic activities. Not since Seymour Trotter's excommunication many years ago for screwing a patient had there been an occasion like this.

Marshal knew his personal political position was delicate and that he had to proceed this evening with great caution. It was public knowledge that Seth Pande had been his training analyst fifteen years before and had been enormously helpful to Marshal both personally and professionally.

Yet Seth's star was waning; he was over seventy and, three years before, had had extensive lung cancer surgery. Always grandiose, Seth had considered it his privilege to disregard all rules of technique and morality. And now his illness and confrontation with death had freed him from any remaining strains of conformity. His analytic colleagues had grown increasingly embarrassed and irritated by his extreme anti-analytic positions on psychotherapy and his outrageous personal behavior. But he was still a presence: his charisma was so great that he was immediately sought out by the press and TV for statements on almost any breaking news story—the impact of TV violence on children, municipal indifference to the homeless, attitudes toward public panhandling, gun control, politicians' sexual imbroglios. About each of these Seth had some newsworthy, often scandalously irreverent comment. Over the last months it had gone too far and the institute's current president, John Weldon, and the old anti-Pande analytic contingent had finally worked up the guts to challenge him.

Marshal pondered his strategy: of late, Seth had so overstepped himself, been so flagrant in his sexual and financial exploitation of patients, that it would be political suicide to support him now. Marshal knew that his voice had to be heard. John Weldon was counting on his support. It would not be easy. Though Seth was a dying man, he still had his allies. Many of his present and past analysands would be present. For forty years he had played a leading intellectual role in institute affairs. Along with Seymour Trotter, Seth was one of the two living founding members of the institute—that is, assuming Seymour was still alive. No Seymour sightings had been reported in years—thank God! The damage that man had done to the reputation of the field! Seth, on the other hand, was a living menace and had served so many three-year terms as president he would have to be crowbarred from power.

Marshal wondered if Seth could exist without the institute: it was so enmeshed with his identity. Banishing Seth would be like delivering a death sentence. Too bad! Seth should have thought about that before casting the good name of psychoanalysis into disrepute. There was no other way: Marshal had to cast his vote against Seth. Yet Seth was his former analyst. How to avoid appearing ruthless or parricidal? Tricky. Very tricky.

Marshal's future prospects in the institute were excellent. So certain was he of ultimate leadership that his only concern was how to make that happen as quickly as possible. He was one of the few key members who had entered the institute during the seventies, when the star of analysis appeared to be waning and the number of applicants had dropped off significantly. In the eighties and nineties the pendulum had swung back, and many had applied for candidacy in the seven- to eight-year program. Thus the institute essentially had a bimodal age distribution: there were the old-timers, the aging pundits headed by John Weldon, who had joined together to challenge Seth, and a number of novitiates, some of them Marshal's analysands, admitted to full membership only within the past two to three years.

In his own age bracket Marshal had little challenge: two of the most promising of the group had died untimely deaths of coronary artery disease. Indeed, it was their deaths that spurred Marshal's frantic aerobic attempts to flush out the arterial debris that was a consequence of the sedentary profession of psychoanalysis. Marshal's only real competition came from Bert Kantrell, Ted Rollins, and Dalton Salz.

Bert, a sweet guy but lacking any political sense, had compromised himself by his deep involvement with nonanalytic projects, especially his supportive therapy work with AIDS patients. Ted was entirely ineffectual: his training analysis had taken eleven years, and everyone knew he was finally graduated sheerly because of analytic fatigue and pity. Dalton had recently gotten so involved with environmental issues that no analyst took him seriously anymore. When Dalton read his idiotic paper on analyzing archaic environmental destructive fantasies—raping Mother Earth and pissing on the walls of our planetary home—John Weldon's first comment was, "Are you serious or are you putting us on?" Dalton held his ground and ultimately—after rejection by every analytic journal—published the paper in a Jungian journal. Marshal knew all he had to do was wait and make no mistakes. All three of these clowns were fucking up their chances with no help from him.

But Marshal's ambition went much further than the presidency of Golden Gate Analytic Institute. That office would serve as a springboard for national office, possibly even head of the International Psychoanalytic Association. The time was ripe: there had never been a president of IPA who had graduated from an institute in the western United States.

But there was one hitch: Marshal needed publications. He had no shortage of ideas. One of his current cases, a borderline patient who had an identical twin who was schizoid with no borderline features, had enormous implications for mirroring theory and was crying to be written up. His ideas on the nature of the primal scene and execution audiences would result in a major revision of basic theory. Yes, Marshal knew his ideas flowed in abundance. The problem was his writing: his ungainly words and sentences hobbled far behind his ideas.

That's where Ernest came in. Ernest lately had become irritating—his immaturity, his impulsivity, his sophomoric insistence that the therapist be authentic and self-revealing would try any supervisor's patience. But Marshal had good reason to be patient: Ernest had an extraordinary literary talent. Graceful sentences flew off his keyboard. Marshal's ideas and Ernest's sentences would be an unbeatable combination. All he needed was to restrain Ernest enough to get him accepted into the institute. Persuading Ernest to collaborate on journal articles, even book projects, would be no problem. Marshal had already planted the seeds by systematically exaggerating the difficulty Ernest would face in attaining admission to the institute and the importance of Marshal's sponsorship. Ernest would be grateful for years. Besides, Ernest was so ambitious, Marshal believed, he would snatch at the opportunity for coauthorship with Marshal.

As Marshal neared the building, he took several deep breaths of cold air to clear his mind. He would need his wits about him; a battle for control was sure to erupt this evening.

John Weldon, a tall, stately man in his mid-sixties with a ruddy complexion, thinning white hair, and a long, wrinkled neck fronted by a formidable Adam's apple, was already standing at the podium of the book-lined room that served double duty as the library and conference room. Marshal glanced around at the large turnout and was unable to think of any institute member who was absent. Except Seth Pande, of course, who had been interviewed at length by a subcommittee and who had been specifically asked not to attend this meeting.

In addition to the members, there were three student candidates present, analysands of Seth's who had petitioned to be present. This was unprecedented. And their stakes were high: if Seth were expelled or banished or, indeed, if he simply lost his training analyst status, they would lose credit for their years of analytic work with him and be forced to begin anew with another training analyst. All three had made it clear that they might refuse to change analysts, even if that meant resigning their candidacy. There was even talk about forming a splinter institute. Given these considerations the governing committee, in the hope that the three would discover their loyalty to Seth was misplaced, took the extraordinary and highly controversial step of permitting them to attend as non-voting participants.

The instant Marshal took a seat in the second row, John Weldon, as though he had been waiting for Marshal's entrance, pounded his small lacquered gavel and called the meeting to order.

"Each of you," he began, "has been informed about the purpose of this extraordinary meeting. The painful task confronting us tonight is to consider serious, very serious, charges against one of our most venerable members, Seth Pande, and to see what action, if any, the institute should take. As you were all informed by letter, the ad hoc subcommittee investigated each of these charges with great care, and I think it would be expedient to proceed directly to their findings."

"Dr. Weldon, a point of procedure!" It was Terry Fuller, a brash young analyst admitted only a year ago. He had been analyzed by Seth.

"The chair recognizes Dr. Fuller." Weldon addressed his comments to Perry Wheeler, a seventy-year-old, partially deaf analyst who served as institute secretary and was furiously scribbling minutes.

"Is it proper for us to consider these 'charges' in the absence of Seth Pande? Not only is a trial in absentia morally repugnant but it violates the institute's by-laws."

"I spoke to Dr. Pande and we both agreed it would be best for all concerned if he did not attend tonight."

"Correction! *You*, not we, thought it would be best, John." Seth Pande's powerful voice boomed out. He stood in the doorway surveying the audience and then picked up a chair in the rear and carried it to the front row. On his way he gave Terry Fuller an affectionate pat on the shoulder and continued, "I said I would consider the matter and let you know my decision. And my decision, as you see, is to be here in the bosom of my loving brethren and distinguished colleagues."

Seth's six-foot, three-inch frame had been bowed by his cancer, but he was still an imposing man with gleaming white hair, bronzed complexion, fine hooked nose, and regal chin. He had come from royal lineage and in his early years had been reared in the royal court of Kipoche, a Northeast Indian province. When his father was appointed as India's representative to the UN, Seth moved to the United States and continued his education at Exeter and Harvard.

Holy shit, thought Marshal. *Get out of the way and let the big dogs eat*. He ducked into his collar as far as possible.

John Weldon's face flushed purple, but his voice remained calm. "I regret your decision, Seth, and I sincerely believe you'll have reason to regret it as well. I was merely protecting you against yourself. It may be humiliating for you to listen to a detailed public discussion of your professional—and nonprofessional—behavior."

"I have nothing to hide. I have always been proud of my professional work." Seth looked over the audience and continued: "If you need proof, John, I suggest you look about you. The presence in this room of at least a half-dozen of my former analysands, and three current ones—each creative, integrated, a credit to his, or her"—and here he bowed deeply and gracefully toward Karen Jaye, one of the female analysts—"profession—attests to the solidity of my work."

Marshal winced. *Seth was going to make this as difficult as possible. Oh, my God!* In his sweep of the room, Seth had momentarily caught his gaze. Marshal looked in another direction only to find

Weldon's gaze awaiting him. He closed his eyes, squeezed his buttocks together, and shrank even more.

Seth continued. "What would really humiliate me, John, and here I may be different from you, is to be falsely charged, possibly slandered, and make no effort to defend myself. Let's get down to business. What are the charges? Who are my accusers? Let's hear them one by one."

"The letter each of you, and that includes you, Seth, received from the education committee," John Weldon responded, "catalogues the grievances. I'll read them off. Let's start with bartering: trading analytic hours for personal service."

"I'm entitled," Seth demanded, "to know who has brought which charge."

Marshal winced. *My time has come,* he thought. It was he who had brought Seth's practice of bartering to Weldon's attention. He had no choice but to rise and speak with all the directness and confidence he could muster.

"I take responsibility for the grievance about bartering. A few months ago I saw a new patient, a professional financial adviser, and in our discussion about fees he suggested an exchange of services. Since our hourly fees were similar, he said, "Why not simply exchange services without the necessity of taxable money changing hands?" Naturally, I declined and explained why such an arrangement would, on a number of levels, sabotage therapy. He accused me of small-mindedness and rigidity and named two people, one of his associates and a client, a young architect, who had a bartering arrangement with Seth Pande, the former president of the psychoanalytic institute."

"I'll respond substantively to that grievance in due course, Marshal, but naturally one cannot first but wonder why a colleague, friend, and, even more, former analysand chose not to speak to me, not to raise the question with me directly!"

"Where is it written," Marshal responded, "that the properly analyzed analysand must forever treat his former analyst with filial partiality? I learned from you that the goal of treatment and of the working through of transference is to help the analysand leave his parents, to develop autonomy and integrity."

Seth flashed a broad smile, like a parent beaming when his child checkmates him for the first time. "Bravo, Marshal. And touché. You've learned your lessons well, and I take pride in your performance. But still, I wonder whether, despite our scrubbing, our five years of psychoanalytic rubbing and polishing, there still remain stains of sophistry?"

"Sophistry?" Marshal dug in stubbornly. As a college football linebacker, his powerful, churning legs drove men twice his size relentlessly backward. Once he engaged an opponent, he never gave way.

"I see no sophistry. Am I expected, for the sake of the analytic father, to put parentheses around my conviction—a conviction I am certain everyone in this room shares—that bartering analytic hours for personal services is wrong? Wrong in every sense. It is wrong legally and morally: it is expressly forbidden by the tax laws of this country. It's wrong technically: it plays havoc with transference and countertransference. And its wrongness is compounded when the services enjoyed by the analyst are of a personal kind: for example, financial advising, where the patient must know the most intimate details of your financial life. Or, as I understand it in the case of the architect patient, designing a new home where the patient must be privy to the innermost details of your domestic habits and preferences. You cover your own mistakes with smokescreen accusations of my character."

And with that Marshal sat down, pleased with himself. He refrained from looking around. It wasn't necessary. He could almost hear the gasps of admiration. He knew he had established himself as a man to be reckoned with. He also knew Seth well enough to predict what would happen. Whenever Seth was attacked, he invariably attacked back in a manner that implicated him even deeper. There was no need to explicate further the destructive nature of Seth's behavior; he would do the damage to himself.

"Enough," said John Weldon, pounding his gavel. "This issue is too important for us to become embroiled in an ad hominem squall. Let us stick to substance: a systematic review of the charges and a substantive discussion of each."

"Bartering," said Seth, entirely ignoring Weldon's comment, "is but an ugly term insinuating that an act of analytic agape is something else, something invidious."

"How can you defend bartering, Seth?" asked Olive Smith, an elderly analyst whose major claim to fame was her psychoanalytic regal lineage: forty-five years before, she had been analyzed by Frieda Fromm-Reichman, who, in turn, had been analyzed by Freud

himself. Moreover she had once had a brief friendship and correspondence with Anna Freud and knew some of the Freud grandchildren. "Obviously, an uncontaminated frame, especially concern-
ing fees, is integral to the analytic process."

"You talk about analytic agape as a way to justify bartering. Surely,
you're not serious," said Harvey Green, a rotund, smug analyst who
rarely failed to make an irritating comment. "Suppose your client
worked as a prostitute? How then does your bartering system work?"

"A venal and original comment, Harvey," shot back Seth. "The
venality, well, that is, of course, not surprising from you. But the
originality, the cleverness, of your question, that is indeed unexpected. But a question of no merit whatsoever. Sophistry has made
a home in the Golden Gate Institute, I see." Seth turned his head
toward Marshal and then glared back at Harvey. "Tell us, Harvey,
how many prostitutes have you analyzed recently? Any of you?"
Seth's dark eyes swept the room. "How many prostitutes can take a
deep analytic look at themselves and still be prostitutes?

"Grow up, Harvey!" Seth continued, obviously relishing the confrontation. "You confirm something I've written about in the *International Journal,* namely, that we old analytic denizens—what's the
official term you Yids use? *Alte cockers!*—should be required to
have regular maintenance analyses, say, about every ten years or so.
In fact, we could serve as control cases for the candidates. That
would be a way of preventing ossification. Surely this organization
needs that."

"Order," Weldon said, pounding his gavel. "Let us return to the
business at hand. As president I insist . . . "

"Barter!" continued Seth, who had turned his back to the podium
and now faced the members. "Barter! What a crime! A capital
offense! A highly troubled young architect, a male anorexic, whom
I have treated for three years and brought to the brink of major
characterologic change, suddenly lost his position when his firm was
ingested by another company. It will take him a year or two to establish himself independently. Meanwhile he has practically no income.
What is the proper analytic move? To abandon him? To allow him
to incur a debt of several thousand dollars, an alternative fundamentally unacceptable to him? Meanwhile, for reasons relating to
my personal health, I had planned to build a wing to my home
including an office and a waiting room. I was searching for an architect. He was searching for a client.

"The solution—the proper, the moral solution, according to my judgment, which I do not have to justify to this or any other audience—was obvious. The patient designed my new structure. The fee problem was alleviated, and he was positively therapeutically affected by my trust in him. I plan to write up this case: the act of designing my home—the father's inner lair—delivered him into the deepest layers of archaic memories and fantasies of his father, layers inaccessible by conservative techniques. Do I, have I ever, needed your permission to practice creatively?"

Here Seth dramatically scanned the audience again, allowing his glare to rest for a few moments on Marshal.

Only John Weldon dared answer: "Boundaries! Boundaries! Seth, are you beyond all established technique? Having the patient inspect and design your home? You may call this creative. But I tell you, and I know I am joined in this by all, *it is not analysis.*"

"'Established technique.' 'Not analysis.'" Seth parodied John Weldon, repeating his words in a high-pitched singsong manner. "The mewling of small minds. Do you think technique comes from Moses' tablets? Technique is fashioned by visionary analysts: Ferenczi, Rank, Reich, Sullivan, Searles. Yes, and Seth Pande!"

"A self-proclaimed visionary status," Morris Fender, a bald, pop-eyed, gnomelike man with enormous spectacles and no neck, pitched in, "is a clever, a diabolical, vehicle to conceal and rationalize a multitude of sins. I have some deep concerns, Seth, about your behavior. It undermines the good name of analysis to the general public, and frankly I shudder to think of you training young analysts. Consider your own writing—like your statements in the *London Literary Review.*"

Morris drew some newspaper pages from his pocket and tremulously unfolded them. "This," he said, wagging the pages in front of him, "is from your own review of the Freud-Ferenczi correspondence. Here you publicly proclaim that you tell patients you love them, that you hold them and discuss intimate details of your life with them: your impending divorce, your cancer. You tell them they are your best friends. You invite them to your home for tea, you talk to them about your sexual preferences. Now, your sexual preference is your own business—and its nature is not at issue here—but why does the entire reading public as well as your analysands have to know of your bisexuality? You can't deny this." Again Morris rattled the papers in front of him. "These are your own words."

"Of course, they are my own words. Is plagiarism also a charge on the docket?" Seth picked up the letter from the ad hoc committee and mockingly pretended to pore over it: "Plagiarism, plagiarism—oh, so many other capital offenses, so many other varieties of capital wickedness, but no plagiarism. Of that at least I have been spared. Yes, of course, my own words. And I stand by them. Does there exist a more intimate bond than that between analyst and analysand?"

Marshal listened expectantly. *Good for you, Morris,* he thought. *Perfect goading. First intelligent thing I've ever seen you do!* Seth's rockets were smoking; he was about to blast off into self-destruct orbit.

"Yes," Seth continued, his one lung laboring, his voice growing hoarse. "I stand by my words that my patients are my closest friends. And that is true for all of you. You too, Morris. My patients and I spend four hours a week in the most intimate possible discussion. Tell me, which of you spends that much intimate time with a friend? I'll answer for you: *not one of you*—certainly not you, Morris. We all know about American male friendship patterns. Perhaps some, a few, of you have a weekly lunch with a friend and, between ordering and chewing, spend thirty minutes in intimate congress.

"Will you deny"—Seth's voice filled the room—"that the therapy hour is designed to be a temple of honesty? If your patients are your most intimate connections, *then have the courage to drop the hypocrisy and tell them!* And what difference does it make if they know the details of your personal life? Not once has my self-disclosure interfered with the analytic procedure. On the contrary, it speeds up the process. Perhaps, due to my cancer, speed has become important to me. My only regret is that I waited so long to discover this. My new analysands sitting in this room can attest to the speed with which we work. Ask them! I am now convinced that no training analysis need exceed three years. Go ahead, let them speak!"

Marshal stood up. "I object! It is improper and incontinent"—that word again, his favorite word!—"to involve your analysands in any way whatsoever in this deplorable discussion. It is a sign of poor judgment even to consider it. Their viewpoint is doubly encumbered: by transference and by self-interest. You ask them about speed, about a quick and dirty analysis—*of course* they will agree. Of course they will be enticed by the idea of a brief, three-year training analysis. What candidate wouldn't be? But aren't we avoiding the real issue: your illness and the impact it has upon your views and your work. As you yourself suggest, Seth, your illness has imbued you with an urgency to finish patients quickly. None among us fails to understand and to be sympathetic with that. Your illness changes your perspective in many ways, perfectly understandable ways, given the situation.

"But that does not mean," Marshal continued with a growing confidence, "that your new perspective, born out of personal urgency, should be presented to students as psychoanalytic doctrine. I'm sorry, Seth, but I must agree with the Education Committee that it is right and timely to raise the question of your training status and your ability to serve further in that status. A psychoanalytic organization can ill afford to neglect the issue of succession. If analysts cannot do it, how can we expect other organizations who seek our help—corporations, governments—to attend to the process of the transfer of responsibility and power from the old and powerful to the next generation?"

"Nor," Seth roared, "can we afford to ignore a raw grasping for power by those too mediocre to merit it!"

"Order!" John Weldon pounded his gavel. "Let us return to substance. The ad hoc committee has brought our attention to your public and published comments attacking and derisively dismissing some of the central pillars of psychoanalytic theory. For example, in your recent interview in *Vanity Fair* you ridicule the oedipal complex and dismiss it as a 'Jewish error'—and then you go on to say it is one of many in the fundamental canons of psychoanalysis. . . . "

"Of course," Seth shot back, all attempts at banter or humor gone, "*of course it's a Jewish error*. The error of elevating the little Viennese Jewish family triangle to universal familyhood and then attempting to solve for the world what guilt-ridden Jews cannot solve for themselves!"

By now the hall was buzzing, and several analysts tried to speak at once. "Anti-Semitic," said one. Many other comments could be heard: "massaging patients," "sex with patients," "self-aggrandizement," "not analysis—let him do any damn thing he wants, but don't call it analysis."

Seth spoke right over them. "Of course, John, I said and wrote these things. And I stand by those comments, too. Everyone, deep down, knows I am right. Freud's little Jewish ghetto family represents a tiny minority of mankind. Take my own culture, for exam-

ple. For every Jewish family left on earth, there are thousands of
Muslim families. Analysis knows nothing about these families and
these patients. Knows nothing about the different and overweening
role of the father, about the deep unconscious desire for the father,
for a return to the comfort and safety of the father, for merger with
the father."

"Yes," Morris said, and opened up a journal, "here it is in a letter to the editor in *Contemporary Psychoanalysis*. You discuss your
interpretation to a young bisexual of his craving, and I quote, 'which
was a universal craving to return to the ultimate world sinecure—
the womb-rectum of the father.' You refer to that with your usual
modesty as"—here Morris read further—"'a transforming seminal
interpretation which has been entirely obscured by the racial bias of
psychoanalysis.'"

"Exactly! But that article, published only a couple of years ago,
was written six years ago. It doesn't go far enough. It's a universal
interpretation; I make it central now in my work with *all* my
patients. Psychoanalysis is no Jewish provincial endeavor. It must
recognize and embrace the truths of East as well as West. Each of
you has a great deal to learn, and I have grave doubts about both
your desire and your ability to absorb new ideas."

It was Louise Saint Clare, a silver-haired, gentle analyst of great
integrity, who made the first decisive challenge. She spoke directly to
the chair. "I think I've heard enough, Mr. President, to convince me
that Dr. Pande has moved too far away from the corpus of psychoanalytic teachings to be responsible for the training of young analysts. I move that he be removed from his status as training analyst!"

Marshal raised his hand: "I second that motion."

Seth stood menacingly and glowered at the members. "*You*
remove *me*? I expected no less from the Jewish analytic Mafia."

"Jewish Mafia?" questioned Louise Saint Clare. "My parish
priest will be astonished to hear this."

"Jew, Christian, no difference—a Jew-Christian Mafia. And you
think you can remove *me*. Well, I shall remove *you*. I made this institute. I *am* this institute. And where I go—and believe me, I am leaving—*there* shall be the institute." With that Seth shoved his chair
aside, seized his hat and coat, and noisily strode out.

Rick Chapton broke the silence after Seth Pande left. Naturally
Rick, as one of Seth's ex-analysands, would feel the effects of Seth's
removal particularly keenly. Even though his training was entirely

finished and he was a full institute member, Rick, like most, continued to take pride in the status of his training analyst.

"I wish to speak in defense of Seth," said Rick. "I have some grave misgivings about the spirit and the propriety of this evening's proceedings. Nor do I think that Seth's last several statements are germane. They prove nothing. He is a sick and a proud man and we all know that when he is pressed, and one might suspect he was pressed intentionally tonight, he has been known to respond in a defensive and arrogant manner."

Rick stopped for a moment to consult a three-by-five-inch card and then continued: "I'd like to offer an interpretation about the process of this evening's proceedings. I see a lot of you whipping yourselves up into a frenzy of self-righteousness about Seth's theoretical stand. But I wonder if it is truly the *content* of Dr. Pande's interpretations that is the issue, and not his style and his visibility! Is it possible that many of you are threatened by his brilliance, by his contributions to our field, by his literary ability, and above all by his ambition? Is the membership not envious of Seth's frequent appearance in magazines and newspapers and on TV? Can we tolerate a maverick? Can we tolerate someone who challenges orthodoxy in much the same way that Sandor Ferenczi challenged analytic doctrine seventy-five years ago? I suggest that the controversy tonight is not directed toward the *content* of Seth Pande's analytic interpretations. The discussion of his father-focused theory is a red herring, a classic example of displacement. No, this is a vendetta, a personal attack—and an unworthy one at that. I submit that the real motives at play here are envy, defense of orthodoxy, fear of the father, and fear of change."

Marshal responded. He knew Rick well, having supervised one of his analytic cases for three years. "Rick, I respect your courage, your loyalty, and your willingness to speak your mind, but I must disagree with you. Seth Pande's interpretive content is very much *my* issue here. He has moved so far from analytic theory that it is our responsibility to differentiate ourselves from him. Examine the content of his interpretations: the drive to merge with the father, to return to the father's womb-rectum. Indeed!"

"Marshal," Rick countered, "you're taking one interpretation entirely out of context. How many of you have made some idiosyncratic interpretation that, out of context, would seem foolish or indefensible?"

"That may be. But that's not the situation with Seth. He's often lectured and written for the profession and for the general public that he considers this motif a key dynamic in the analysis of every male. He's made it clear tonight that this was not some single interpretive occasion. A 'universal interpretation,' he called it. He boasted that he has made this same dangerous interpretation to all his male patients!"

"Hear, hear." Marshal was supported by a chorus of voices.

"'Dangerous,' Marshal?" Rick chided. "Aren't we overreacting?"

"Underreacting, if anything." Marshal's voice grew stronger. He had now clearly emerged as a powerful spokesman of the institute. "Do you question the paramount role or the power of interpretation? Do you have any idea how much damage this interpretation may have caused? Every adult male who has some craving for a regressive sojourn, some temporary return to a tender, caring resting place, receives the interpretation that he desires to crawl through the father's anus back into the womb-rectum. Think of the iatrogenic guilt and anxiety of homosexual regression."

"I agree completely," added John Weldon. "The Education Committee was unanimous in their recommendation that Seth Pande be relieved of his status as training analyst. It was only Seth Pande's severe illness and his previous contributions to this institute that prompted them not to expel him from membership entirely. The general membership must vote on their acceptance of the Education Committee's recommendation."

"I call for the question," said Olive Smith.

Marshal seconded, and the vote would have been unanimous but for Rick Chapton's nay vote. Mian Khan, a Pakistani analyst who often collaborated with Seth, and four of Seth's previous analysands, abstained.

The cluster of the three nonvoting, current analysands of Seth whispered together and one said that they needed time to decide their future course, but that they as a group felt great dismay at the tenor of the meeting. Then they left the room.

"I feel more than dismay," said Rick, who noisily gathered his things and proceeded to walk out. "This is scandalous—sheer hypocrisy." As he got to the door, he added, "I believe with Nietzsche that the only real truth is the lived truth!"

"What does that mean in this context?" asked John Weldon, pounding his gavel for silence.

"Does this organization truly believe with Marshal Streider that Seth Pande has inflicted serious damage to his male patients with his form of father-fusion interpretations?"

"I believe I can speak for the institute," John Weldon replied, "in saying that no responsible analyst would disagree with the view that Seth has inflicted grievous harm to a number of patients."

Rick, standing in the doorway, said, "Then Nietzsche's meaning for you is very simple. If this organization truly and sincerely believes that terrible damage has been done to Seth's patients, and if this organization has any integrity left, then there is only one course open to you—that is, if you desire to act in a morally and legally responsible fashion."

"And that is?" asked Weldon.

"Recall!"

"Recall? What's that?"

"If," responded Rick, "General Motors and Toyota have the integrity, and the balls—excuse me, ladies, there's no politically correct equivalent term—to recall poorly constructed vehicles, vehicles with some glitch that will ultimately cause harm to its owners, then certainly *your* path is clear."

"You mean . . . ?"

"You know exactly what I mean." Rick stomped out and did not hesitate to slam the door behind him.

Three former analysands of Seth's and Mian Khan departed immediately after Rick. At the door Terry Fuller left this warning: "Take this very seriously, gentlemen. There's a real threat of irreversible schism."

John Weldon needed no reminder to take the exodus seriously. The last thing he wanted on *his* watch was a schism and the formation of a splinter psychoanalytic institute. It had happened many times in other cities: New York had three institutes after splitting by the followers of Karen Horney and later by Sullivanian interpersonalists. It had happened in Chicago, in Los Angeles, in the Washington-Baltimore school. It probably should have happened in London, where, for decades, three gangs, the followers of Melanie Klein, Anna Freud, and the "middle school"—the object relations disciples of Fairbairn and Winnicott—had engaged in relentless warfare.

The Golden Gate Analytic Institute had lived in peace for fifty years, perhaps because its aggressive energies were effectively released toward more visible enemies: a robust Jungian Institute and a succession of alternative therapy schools—transpersonal, Reichian, past lives, holotrophic breathing, homeopathic, Rolfing—that rose relentlessly and miraculously from the steaming springs and hot tubs of Marin County. Moreover, John knew that there would be some literate journalist who would not resist a story on a psychoanalytic institute split. The spectacle of well-analyzed analysts unable to live together, posturing, straining for power, bickering over trivialities, and finally divorcing in a huff, made for wonderful literary buffoonery. John did not want to be remembered as presiding over the institute's fragmentation.

"Recall?" exclaimed Morris. "Such a thing has never been done."

"Desperate remedies for desperate times," murmured Olive Smith.

Marshal watched John Weldon's face vigilantly. Upon seeing a slight nod in response to Olive, he took the cue.

"If we don't accept Rick's challenge—which I'm sure will become part of the public domain shortly—then our chance of healing this breech is very slim."

"But *recall*," said Morris Fender, "because of a wrong interpretation?"

"Don't minimize a serious issue, Morris," said Marshal. "Is there any analytic tool more powerful than interpretation? And are we not in agreement that Seth's formulation is both wrong and dangerous?"

"It is dangerous *because* it is wrong," ventured Morris.

"No," said Marshal; "it could be wrong but passive—wrong because it doesn't move the patient along. But this is wrong *and* actively dangerous. Imagine! Every one of his male patients who craves some slight comfort, some slight human contact, is led to believe that he is experiencing a primitive desire to crawl back through his father's anus into the comfort of his bowel-womb. It's unprecedented, but I believe it's right that we take steps to protect his patients." A quick glance assured Marshal that John not only supported but appreciated his stand.

"Womb-rectum! Where did this shit, this heresy, this . . . this . . . this *mishugas* come from?" said Jacob, a fierce-looking analyst with hanging jowls and enormous gray sideburns and eyebrows.

"From his own analysis, he told me, with Allen Janeway," said Morris.

"And Allen's been dead for three years now. You know I never trusted Allen. I had no evidence, but his misogyny, his foppery, those bow ties, his gay friends, his taking a condominium in the Castro, his building his whole life around the opera . . . "

"Let's stay focused, Jacob," John Weldon interrupted. "The issue at this moment is not Allen Janeway's sexual preference. Nor Seth's. We must be very circumspect about this. In today's climate it would be a political catastrophe if we were perceived as censuring or bouncing a member because he was gay."

"He or *she* were gay," said Olive.

John impatiently nodded assent and continued. "Nor, for that matter, is the issue Seth's alleged sexual misconduct with patients—which we have not yet discussed tonight. We've had reports of sexual misconduct from therapists who've treated two of Seth's ex-patients, but neither patient, as yet, has agreed to file charges. One is unconvinced that it caused lasting harm to her; the other states that it introduced an insidious and destructive duplicity into her marriage but, either because of some perverse transferential loyalty to Seth or because she is loath to face the publicity, has refused to press charges. I agree with Marshal: our proper course is to stay with one issue, namely, that under the aegis of psychoanalysis, he has made incorrect, nonanalytic, and dangerous interpretations."

"But look at the problems," said Bert Kantrell, one of Marshal's cohorts in his analytic class, "think of the confidentiality issues. Seth could sue us for slander. And what about malpractice? If Seth were sued for malpractice by one of his former patients, what would prevent other patients from coming after the deep pockets of our institute or even the national institute? After all, they could easily enough say that we sponsored Seth, that we appointed him to a major training position. This is a hornet's nest; we'd best keep our hands out of it."

Marshal loved seeing his competition appear weak and indecisive. To highlight the contrast, he spoke with all his confidence. "*Au contraire,* Bert. We are far *more* vulnerable if we do *not* act. The very point you make *not* to act is the reason we *must* act and act with dispatch to dissociate ourselves from Seth, and to do all we can to correct damage. I can just see Rick Chapton, damn him, bringing a suit against us—or at the very least siccing a *Times* reporter on us—if we censure Seth and then do nothing to protect his patients."

"Marshal's right," said Olive, who often served as the moral conscience of the institute. "Believing, as we do, that our treatment is potent and that the misapplication of psychoanalysis—wild analysis—is powerfully injurious, then we have no choice but to live by our words. We must get Seth's ex-patients back into a course of remedial psychotherapy."

"Easier said than done," warned Jacob. "No power on earth could persuade Seth to give out the names of his ex-patients."

"That won't be necessary," said Marshal. "Our preferred procedure, it seems to me, is to make a public appeal in the popular press to all his patients of the last several years, or at least all males." With a smile, Marshal added, "Let us assume that he handled females differently."

Smiles went through the audience at Marshal's double entendre. Though the rumors of Seth's sexual acting out with female patients had been known to the membership for years, it was a great relief finally to have it out in the open.

"Are we agreed, then," said John Weldon, pounding his gavel, "that we should attempt to offer remedial therapy to Seth's patients?"

"I so move," said Harvey.

After a unanimous vote, Weldon addressed Marshal: "Would you be willing to take responsibility for this move? Simply check in with the steering committee with your precise plans."

"Yes, of course, John," said Marshal, barely able to contain his joy and his wonder at how far his star had risen that night. "I'll also clear any of our actions with the International Psychoanalytic Association—I've got to talk to the secretary, Ray Wellington, about another matter this week."

EIGHT

*F*our-thirty in the morning. Tiburon was dark except for one brightly lit house perched high on a promontory overlooking San Francisco Bay. The lights of the mighty Golden Gate were obscured by milky fog, but the delicate skyline lights of the city shimmered in the distance. Eight weary men hunched over a table and paid no attention to bridge, fog, or skyline; they had eyes only for the cards dealt them.

Len, hefty, red-faced, wearing broad yellow suspenders decorated with dice and playing cards, announced, "Last hand." It was dealer's choice and Len called for seven-card high-low: the first two cards down, four up, and the final one down. The pot was shared by two winners, the highest and the lowest hands.

Shelly, whose wife, Norma, was one of Carol's law partners, was the big loser that evening (and every evening, at least for the past five months), but he picked up his cards eagerly. He was a handsome, powerful man, with doleful eyes, irrepressible optimism, and a bad back. Before looking at his first two cards, Shelly stood and adjusted the ice pack strapped around his waist. As a young man, he had toured as a tennis pro and even now, despite the pointed objections of some bulging intervertebral discs, still played almost every day.

He picked up the two cards, one atop the other. The ace of diamonds! Not bad. Slowly he slid the second card into view. The two of diamonds. An ace and deuce of diamonds! Perfect hole cards! Was it possible, after a run of such miserable cards? He put them down and a few seconds later couldn't resist looking at them again. Shelly didn't notice the other players watching him—that second, loving look was one of Shelly's many "tells"—tiny sloppy mannerisms that gave away his hand.

The next two up cards were just as good: a five and then a four of diamonds. Holy Christ! A million-dollar hand. Shelly almost burst into a chorus of "Zip-a-dee-doo-dah, zip-a-dee-ay, my oh my— what a wonderful day." One, two, four, and five of diamonds—a hand to die for! Finally his luck had turned. He knew it had to happen, if he just hung in there. And God knows he had hung in.

Three more cards coming, and all he needed for an ace-high flush was another diamond, or a three of diamonds for a straight flush— that would take the high half of the pot. Any low card—a three, six, even a seven—would take the low half of the pot. If he got both a diamond *and* a low card, he could win *both* high and low—the entire pot. This hand would make him healthier but not entirely whole; he was down twelve thou.

Usually, on the rare occasions he had a decent hand, most of the guys folded early. Bad luck! Or was it? That was where his "tells" did him in—the players dropped in droves when they picked up his excitement, his silently counting the pot, his guarding his cards more tightly, his betting more promptly than usual, his looking away from the bettor to encourage more betting, his pathetic attempts at camouflage by pretending to be studying the high hands when, in fact, he was going low.

But no one was folding this time! Everyone seemed fascinated with their hands (that was not unusual for the last hand—the guys loved to play so much that they characteristically drained the dregs of the last game). There should be a humungous pot.

To build himself as big a pot as possible, Shelly started betting on the third card. On the fourth card he bet a hundred (betting was a twenty-five-dollar limit on the first round, a hundred on the next rounds, and two hundred on the last two) and was startled when Len raised. Len didn't show much on the table: two spades, a two and a king. The best Len could do was a king-high spade flush (the ace of spades was sitting in front of Harry).

Keep raising, Len, Shelly prayed. *Please keep raising. God grant you your king-high flush! It'll suck hind titty to my ace-high diamond flush.* He raised back and all seven players called. All seven—amazing! Shelly's heart beat faster. He was going to win a goddamn fortune. God, it was good being alive! God, he loved to play poker!

Shelly's fifth card was disappointing, a useless jack of hearts. Still, he had two more cards coming. Time to dope out this hand. Hastily he looked around the table and tried to figure the odds. Four diamonds in his hand and three more showing around the table. That meant seven of the thirteen diamonds were out. Six diamonds left. Great odds to get the flush. And then there was the low. Very few low cards on the table—plenty, plenty left in the deck, and he had two cards coming.

Shelly's head whirled—too complicated to figure out precisely, but the odds were fabulous. Way in his favor. To hell with figuring the odds—he was going all in on this hand no matter what. With seven players in the pot, he would get three and a half dollars back for every one invested. And a good chance of winning the whole pot— a seven to one return.

The next card was an ace of hearts. Shelly winced. A pair of aces was not much use. He started to worry. Everything rode on the last card. Still, only one diamond and only two low cards had turned up on the last round; his chances were still fabulous. He bet the max: two hundred. Len and Bill both raised. There was a three-raise limit, and Shelly raised back for the third raise. Six players called. Shelly studied the hands. Nobody showed much. Only two small pairs on the whole table. What the hell were they all betting on? Were there going to be some nasty little surprises? Shelly kept trying to sneak-count the pot. Gigantic! Probably over seven thou, and another big round of betting left.

The seventh and last card was dealt down. Shelly picked up his three down cards, shuffled them thoroughly, and then slowly squeezed them open. He had seen his father do it that way a thousand times. An ace of clubs! Shit! The worst card he could get. Starting off with four small diamonds and ending up with trip aces. They were nothing—worse than nothing because he probably couldn't win and yet they were too good to fold. This hand was a fucking curse! He was trapped; he had to stay in! He checked. Len, Arnie, and Willy bet, raised, reraised, and reraised again. Ted and Harry dropped. Eight hundred to him. Should he cough it up? Five players in. No chance to win. Inconceivable that one of them wouldn't have three aces beat.

And yet . . . and yet . . . there were no high hands showing. Maybe, just maybe, Shelly thought, all the other four players were going for low! Len had a pair of threes showing; maybe he was trying to push through two pair or trip threes. He was known for that. No! Wake up, dreamer! Save the eight hundred. No chance to win with trip aces—there had to be hidden flushes or straights. *Had* to be. What the hell could they be betting on? How much was the pot? At least twelve thou, maybe more. He could go home to Norma a winner.

And to fold his hand now—and to learn that his trip aces would have won—Christ, he'd never forgive himself that failure of nerve. He'd never recover. Goddamnit! Goddamnit! He had no fucking choice. He was too deep into this pot to go back. Shelly coughed up the eight hundred.

The denouement was quick and merciful. Len turned over a king-high flush, and Shelly's trip aces were dead in the water. And even Len's flush didn't win: Arnie had a full house, completely hidden— that meant he drew it on the last card. Shit! Shelly saw that even if he had drawn his diamond flush, he would have lost. And even if he had gotten his three or four, he still would have lost for low—Bill turned a perfect "nuts" low: five, four, three, two, ace. For an instant Shelly felt like crying, but instead he flashed his great smile and said, "Tell me that wasn't two thousand dollars' worth of fun!"

Everyone counted his chips and cashed in with Len. The game rotated from home to home, every two weeks. The host acted as banker and settled all accounts at the end of the evening. Shelly was down fourteen thou, three hundred. He wrote a check and apologetically explained that he was postdating it a few days. Taking out an enormous wad of hundred-dollar bills, Len said, "Forget it, Shelly, I'll cover it. Bring the check to the next game." That was the way this game was. The trust ran so deep that the guys often said that in case of a flood or an earthquake, they could play poker by telephone.

"Naw, no problem," Shelly replied nonchalantly. "I brought the wrong checks and just have to transfer funds into this account."

But Shelly did have a problem. A very big problem. Four thousand dollars in his bank account and he owed fourteen thousand dollars. And if Norma found out about his losses, his marriage would be over. This just might be his last poker game. On his way out he took a nostalgic stroll around Len's home. Maybe his last walk around Len's home, or any of the guys' homes. Tears came to his eyes as he looked at the antique carousel horses on the stairwell landings, and the gloss of the enormous polished koa wood dining room table, the six-foot-square slab of sandstone teeming with impressions of prehistoric fish frozen for all time.

Seven hours ago, the evening had started at that table with a feast of hot corned beef, tongue, and pastrami sandwiches, which Len sliced and piled high and surrounded with half green pickles and slaw and sour cream potato salad—all specially flown in earlier that day from the Carnegie Deli in New York. Len ate hugely and entertained hugely. And then he exercised it off, most of it, on the Stair-Master and treadmill in his well-equipped gym.

Shelly walked into the salon and joined the rest of the guys as they stood admiring an old painting Len had just bought at auction in London. Not recognizing the artist, and afraid of showing his ignorance, Shelly remained silent. Art was only one of the topics from which Shelly felt excluded; there were others: wine (several of his poker mates had restaurant-sized cellars and often traveled together to wine auctions), opera, ballet, cruise ships, three-star Parisian restaurants, casino betting limits. All too rich for Shelly's blood.

He took a good look at each of the players, as though to impress each indelibly into his memory. He knew these were the good old days, and sometime in the future—maybe after a stroke, while sitting on the lawn of a nursing home some autumn day, dried leaves tumbling in the wind, faded plaid blanket in his lap—he wanted to be able to conjure up each smiling face.

There was Jim, the Iron Duke or Rock of Gibraltar, as he was often called. Jim had gigantic hands and a mighty jaw. God, he was tough. No one had bluffed Jim out of a hand, ever.

And Vince: enormous. Or *sometimes* enormous. Sometimes he was not. Vince had a yo-yo relationship with the Pritikin health and weight-loss centers: always either going to one (a couple of times his wake-up call had been settling into a chair at one of the games only to break it) or coming from one, slim and sleek—and bringing diet peach sodas, fresh apples, and fat-free fudge cookies. Most of the time he put out lavish buffets when the game was at his house—his wife made great Italian food—but for the first couple of months after leaving a Pritikin center, the guys dreaded the food he served: *baked* tortilla chips, raw carrots and mushrooms, Chinese chicken salad without the sesame oil. Most of the guys ate before they came. They liked heavy food—the richer the better.

Next Shelly thought about Dave, a balding, bearded shrink, who had bad vision and would go ballistic when the host didn't provide jumbo index poker cards. He'd run out of the house and roar away in his bright red, dented Honda Civic to the nearest variety store—not an easy feat, since some of the homes were in deep, deep suburbia. Dave's insistence on the proper cards was a source of great merriment. He was such a bad player, spewing "tells" all over the table, that most of the guys thought he was better off when he didn't see his cards. And the most comical thing was that Dave actually thought he was a good poker player! Funny thing was, Dave usually ended up ahead. That was the great mystery of the Tuesday game: *Why in hell didn't Dave lose his ass in this game?*

It was an endless source of amusement that a shrink should be much more out of touch with himself than anyone else at the table was. Or at least *had been* more out of touch. Dave was coming around. No more haughty intellectual holier-than-thou shit. No more ten-syllable words. What were they? "Penultimate hand" or "duplicitous strategy." Or instead of a "stroke" he'd say "cerebrovascular accident." And the food he used to serve—sushi, melon kabobs, cold fruit soup, pickled zucchini. Worse than Vince's. Nobody touched a bite, but still it took Dave a year to get the point—and then only after he started getting anonymous faxes of brisket, brownie, and cheesecake recipes.

He's so much better now, Shelly thought, acts like a real person. We should have billed him for our services. Several guys took him in hand. Arnie sold him a five percent interest in one of his racehorses, took him to workouts and races, taught him how to read the racing form and how to dope out horses from watching their workouts. Harry introduced Dave to pro basketball. When they first met, Dave didn't know a point guard from a free safety or a shortstop. Where had he spent his first forty years? Now Dave drives a burgundy Alfa, shares season basketball tickets with Ted and hockey tickets with Len, lays down his bets with the rest of the guys with Arnie's Vegas bookie, and almost forked out a thousand bucks to go to Streisand's Vegas concert with Vince and Harry.

Shelly watched Arnie walk out the door wearing his idiotic Sherlock Holmes hat. He always wore a hat during the game and, if he won, continued wearing the same hat until its luck wore out. Then he went out and bought a new one. That goddamn Sherlock Holmes hat had made him about forty thou. Arnie drove his custom-made Porsche two and a half hours to the game. A couple of years ago he moved to L.A. for a year to manage his cellular phone company and flew up regularly to see his dentist and play in the game. Just as a gesture, the guys took out his airfare from the first couple of pots. Sometimes his dentist, Jack, played, too—until he lost too much. Jack was a terrible player but a terrific dresser. One time Len took a great fancy to Jack's western metallic-stitched shirt and made a side bet on a hand: two hundred dollars against the shirt. Jack lost: a "queens over" boat to Len's straight flush. Len let him wear the shirt home but came to collect it the next morning. That was Jack's last game. And every game for about the next year Len came dressed in Jack's shirt.

Even during his best times, Shelly had by far the least money of the group. By a factor of ten. Or more. And now, with the Silicon Valley slump, was not one of the best times; he had been out of work since Digilog Microsystems had gone belly-up five months ago. At first he hounded the headhunters and scoured the classified ads every day. Norma billed two hundred fifty an hour for her legal services. That was great for family finances but made Shelly ashamed to accept a job paying twenty or twenty-five an hour. He set his demands so high that the headhunters ultimately dropped him, and he gradually became acclimated to the idea of being supported by his wife.

No, Shelly was not gifted at making money. And it ran in the family. His father had worked and scratched for years to save two stakes when Shelly was young. And blew them both. He sank the first in a Japanese restaurant in Washington, D.C., which opened two weeks before Pearl Harbor. The second, ten years later, he used to buy an Edsel dealership.

Shelly kept up the family tradition. He was an all-American college tennis player but won only three matches in three years on the pro satellite tour. He was handsome, he'd play brilliantly, the crowds loved him, he'd always get the first service break—but he just couldn't put his opponent away. Maybe he was just too nice a guy. Maybe he needed a "closer." When he retired from the pro circuit, he invested his modest inheritance in a tennis club near Santa Cruz a month before the '89 earthquake swallowed up his whole valley. He received a small insurance settlement, most of which he invested in Pan Am Airlines stock just before it went belly-up; some went into junk bonds with Michael Milken's brokerage firm, the rest he invested in the San Jose Nets of the American Volleyball League.

Perhaps that was one of the game's attractions for Shelly. These guys knew what the hell they were doing. They knew how to make money. Maybe some of it would rub off on him.

Of all the guys, Willy was by far the richest. When he sold his start-up personal finance software company to Microsoft, he walked off with about forty million. Shelly knew that from reading the newspapers; none of the guys ever talked openly about it. What he loved about Willy was the way he enjoyed his money. He made no bones about it: his mission on earth was to have a good time. No guilt. No shame. Willy spoke and read Greek—his folks were Greek immigrants. He especially loved the Greek writer Kazantzakis and tried to pattern himself after Zorba, one of his characters, whose purpose in life was to leave death "nothing but a burned-out castle."

Willy loved action. Whenever he folded a hand, he'd rush into the other room to snatch a peek on the TV at some game—basketball, football, baseball—on which he had bet a bundle. Once he rented a Santa Cruz war games ranch for the whole day, the kind of place where groups play Capture the Flag using guns that shoot paint bullets. Shelly smiled as he remembered driving out to the place and seeing the guys standing around watching a duel. Willy, wearing goggles and a World War I fighter pilot's hat, and Vince, both with guns in hand, were pacing off ten steps. Len, the referee, wore Jack's shirt and held a fistful of hundred-dollar bills from the betting. Those guys were nuts—they'd bet on anything.

Shelly followed Willy outside where Porsches, Bentleys, and Jags were revving up and waiting for Len to open up the massive iron gates. Willy turned and put his arm around Shelly's shoulders; the guys did a lot of touching. "How's it going, Shelly? Job search moving?"

"Comme çi, comme ça."

"Hang in there," said Willy. "Business is turning. I've got a feeling the Valley's going to open up again soon. Let's have lunch." The two had become close friends over the years. Willy loved to play tennis and Shelly often gave him a few pointers and had, for years, informally coached Willie's kids, one of whom now played on Stanford's team.

"Great! Next week?"

"No, after that. Away a lot the next two weeks but real free the end of the month. My schedule's in the office. I'll call you tomorrow. I want to talk about something with you. I'll see you at the next game."

No comment from Shelly.

"Right?"

Shelly nodded. "Right, Willy."

"So long, Shelly, so long, Shelly." "So long, Shelly." "So long, Shelly." The calls rang out as the big sedans pulled away. Shelly ached as he watched them drive off into the night. Oh, how he would miss them. God, he loved those guys!

Shelly drove home in deep grief. *Losing fourteen thou. Dammit— takes talent to lose fourteen grand.* But it wasn't the money. Shelly didn't care about the fourteen thou. What he cared about was the guys and the game. But there was no way he could continue playing. Absolutely no way! The arithmetic was simple: there was no more money. *I have to get a job. If not in software sales, then I'm going to have to go into another field—maybe back to selling yachts in Monterey. Yuck. Can I do that? Sitting around for weeks waiting for my one sale every month or two would be enough to send me back to the horses.* Shelly needed action.

In the past six months he had lost a lot of money in the game. Maybe forty, fifty thousand dollars—he had been afraid to keep an exact count. And there was no way to get more money. Norma deposited her paycheck in a separate bank account. He had borrowed on everything. And from everyone. Except, of course, from one of the guys. That would be bad form. Only one last possession he could get his hands on—a thousand shares of Imperial Valley Bank stock, worth about fifteen thousand bucks. His problem was how to cash them in without Norma finding out. Somehow or other she'd get wise. He had run out of excuses. And she was running out of patience. It was only a matter of time.

Fourteen thou? That fucking last hand. He kept reliving it. He was sure he had played it right: when you got the odds, you have to push . . . lose your nerve and it's over. It was the cards. He knew they would turn soon. That's the way it went. He had the long view. He knew what he was doing. He had gambled heavily since he was a teenager and ran a baseball bookie operation throughout high school. And a damn profitable operation, too.

When he was fourteen he read, he forgot where, that the odds on picking any three ballplayers to get a combined total of six hits on any given day was about twenty to one. So he offered nine or ten to one and had plenty of takers. Day after day the suckers kept believing that three players selected from the likes of Mantle, Musial, Berra, Pesky, Bench, Carew, Banks, McQuinn, Rose, and Kaline *had* to get six hits between them. Suckers! They never learned.

Maybe now it was *he* who wasn't learning. Maybe *he* was the sucker and shouldn't be in this game. Not enough money, not enough nerve, not a good enough player. But Shelly had a hard time believing he could be that bad. Suddenly, after holding his own over fifteen years in this game, he'd turned into a bad player? It didn't compute. But maybe there were some small things he was doing differently. Maybe the bad run of cards was affecting his play.

His worst sin, he knew, during the whole bad streak was to get too impatient and try to force through mediocre hands. Yes, no doubt. It was the cards. And without question they would turn. Just a matter of time. It could happen any game—probably the next game—and then he could take off on a fantastic winning tear. He had played in the game for fifteen years and sooner or later things balanced out. Just a matter of time. But now Shelly could buy no more time.

A light rain started. His window fogged. Shelly flipped on the wipers and defroster, stopped to pay his three dollars at the toll booth on the Golden Gate, and headed down Lombard Street. He was not good at planning ahead, but now, the more he thought about it, the more he realized how much was at stake: his membership in the game, his pride, his self-esteem as a player. Not to mention his marriage—that was at stake, too!

Norma knew about his gambling. Before they married eight years before, she had had a long talk with his first wife—who had left him six years earlier when, in a marathon game on a Bahamas cruise, four jacks wiped out their entire savings.

Shelly really loved Norma and sincerely meant the vows he made to her: to give up all gambling, to attend Gamblers Anonymous, to turn over his paychecks, and to allow her to manage all finances.

And then, in a show of good faith, Shelly even proposed to work on his problem with any therapist she chose. Norma selected a psychiatrist she had seen a couple of years before. He saw the shrink—kind of a jerk—for a few months. A total waste of time; he remembered nothing of what they discussed. But a good investment—it clinched the deal, proving to Norma that he took his vows seriously.

And, for the most part, Shelly had kept his vows. He gave up gambling except for the poker game. No betting on football or basketball, he said good-bye to Sonny and Lenny, his long-time bookies; no more Vegas or Reno. He discontinued his subscriptions to *The Sporting Life* and *Card Player*. The only sporting event he bet on was the U.S. Open; he knew how to read tennis form. (But dropped a bundle betting McEnroe over Sampras.)

And, until Digilog went under six months ago, he faithfully turned over his paychecks to Norma. She knew about the poker game, of course, and gave him a special dispensation for it. She thought it was a five- and ten-dollar game and willingly advanced him a couple of hundred at times—Norma rather liked the idea of her husband socializing with some of the richest and most influential businessmen in Northern California. Furthermore, a couple of the guys retained her for legal counsel.

But there were two things Norma didn't know. First, the stakes. The guys were very discreet about that—no cash on the table, only the chips they always called "quarters" (twenty-five dollars), "half-bucks" (fifty dollars), and "bucks" (hundred dollars). Occasionally one of the guys' kids would watch the game for a few hands and would have no idea of the real stakes. Sometimes when Norma met one of the players or their wives socially—at weddings, confirmations, bar mitzvahs—Shelly braced himself for her learning about his losses or the magnitude of risk. But the guys, bless their hearts, knew their lines: no one ever slipped. It was one of those rules that no one ever mentioned but everyone knew.

The other thing Norma didn't know about was his poker account. Between marriages Shelly built up sixty thousand dollars in capital. He had been a super software salesman . . . whenever he decided to work. Twenty thousand dollars he brought into the marriage, but forty thousand was his poker fund and he kept it hidden from Norma in a secret Wells Fargo bank account. He thought that forty thousand could last forever, that it could ride out any losing streak. And so it had. For fifteen years. Until this one—this losing streak from hell!

The stakes had gradually risen. He subtly opposed the increases but was ashamed to make a big deal about it. To have a thrill in the game, everyone needs high stakes. Losses have to smart a bit. The problem was that the other guys had too much money: high stakes for him were like penny ante for them. What could he do? Endure the humiliation of saying, "Sorry, guys, I don't have enough money to play cards with you. I'm too poor, too gutless, too much of a fucking failure to keep up with you"? No way he would ever say that.

But now his poker fund was gone, all but four thousand of it. Thank God that Norma had never learned about the forty thou. Otherwise she'd be long gone. Norma hated gambling because her father had lost the family home in the stock market: he didn't play poker (he was a church deacon, a straight arrow, broomstick up his ass) but stock market, poker—same thing! The markets, Shelly had always thought, were for pussies without the guts for poker!

Shelly tried to focus; he needed ten thou in a hurry: he had post-dated the check just four days ahead. What he had to do was get the money from somewhere Norma wouldn't think of looking for two weeks. Shelly *knew,* he absolutely *knew,* as he had known few things in his life before, that if he could only raise a stake and play in the next game, the cards would turn, he'd win a mint, and everything would fall into place again.

By the time Shelly reached home at five-thirty he had decided what to do. The best solution, the *only* solution, was to sell some of his Imperial Bank stock. About three years ago Willy had bought the Imperial Bank and dropped an insider tip to Shelly that it was sure-fire. Willy was thinking he'd at least double his investment in a couple of years, when it went public. So Shelly bought a thousand shares with the twenty-thousand-dollar nest egg he had brought into the marriage, crowing to Norma about the insider tip and the money he and Willy were going to make.

Shelly's record for being in the wrong place at the wrong time remained intact: this time it was the savings and loan scandal. Willy's bank was hurt bad: the stock skidded from twenty a share to eleven. Now it was back to fifteen. Shelly took the loss in stride and knew that Willy had lost a bundle, too. Still he wondered why, immersed in the old boys' network, he couldn't once, just once, cash in. Everything he touched turned to shit.

He stayed awake till six so that he could call Earl, his broker, to place an order to sell at market price. At first he planned to sell just six hundred and fifty shares—that would've netted him the ten thousand dollars he needed. But while on the phone he decided to sell the whole thousand shares, to give him the ten thousand payback and an extra five thousand to stake him into one last game.

"Want a callback for confirmation of the sale, Shelly?" Earl asked in that squeaky voice of his.

"Yeah, buddy, I'll be in all day. Let me know the exact amount. And, oh yeah, rush it for me, and don't mail the check into our account. That's important—don't mail it. Hold it for me and I'll stop by and pick it up."

This was going to be okay, Shelly thought. In two weeks, after the next game, he'd buy the shares back with his winnings and Norma would never be the wiser. His good spirits returned. He softly whistled a couple of bars of "Zip-a-dee-doo-dah" and got into bed. Norma, a light sleeper, was sleeping in the guest room as was usual on poker nights. He read a little from *Tennis Pro* magazine to calm down, switched off the ringer on the phone, put earplugs in so as not to hear Norma getting ready for work, and turned off the light. With a little luck he would sleep till noon.

⌒

It was almost one P.M. when he stumbled into the kitchen and put on some coffee. As soon as he turned the phone ringer back on, it rang. It was Carol, Norma's friend, who was an attorney at the same firm.

"Hi, Carol, you looking for Norma? She's long gone. She's not at the office? Listen, Carol, I'm glad to get you on the phone. I heard about Justin leaving. Norma said you were shook up. What an idiot to walk out on a class act like you. He was never in your league. Sorry I never called to talk. But the offer is now open. Lunch? A drink? A cuddle?" Ever since the afternoon Carol had picked him up for a quick revenge lay, Shelly had had hot fantasies of a repeat performance.

"Thanks, Shelly," said Carol in her steeliest voice, "but I've got to table the social talk. This is a professional call."

"What do you mean? I told you, Norma's not here."

"Shelly, it's you I'm calling, not Norma. Norma has engaged me as counsel to represent her. It's an awkward situation, of course, given our little encounter, but Norma asked and there was no way I could refuse.

"To the point, now," Carol continued in her clipped professional voice. "My client has asked me to file separation papers and I hereby instruct you to be out of the house, completely out, by seven this evening. She wishes no further direct contact with you. You are not to attempt to speak to her, Mr. Merriman. I have advised her that all necessary transactions between you are to be executed through me, your wife's counsel."

"Cut this legalese shit, Carol. Once I make it with a broad, I'm not going to be intimidated by her highfalutin language! Plain English. What the fuck is going on?"

"Mr. Merriman, I am instructed by my client to direct your attention to your fax machine. The answer to all your questions will become apparent. Even to you. Remember, we have a court injunction, seven P.M. this evening.

"Oh, yes, one other thing, Mr. Merriman. If this counsel may be permitted one short personal comment: you're a shit. Grow up!" And with that Carol slammed down the phone.

Shelly's ears rang for a moment. He ran to the fax machine. There, to his horror, was a copy of his morning's stock transaction with a note that Shelly could pick up the check the following day. And beneath that something even worse: a Xerox of the balance statement of Shelly's secret Wells Fargo poker fund. And attached to that a yellow Post-it with a terse note from Norma: "You don't want me to see it? Figure out how to cover your tracks! We're history."

Shelly called his broker. "Hey, Earl, what the fuck's going on? I asked you to call *me* with the confirmation. Some pal!"

"Back off, jerk," said Earl. "You asked for a confirmation call at home. We sold at seven-fifteen. My secretary called at seven-thirty. Your wife answered and my secretary gave her the message. She asked us to fax it to her office. My secretary should know not to tell your wife? Remember, the bonds were held in a joint account. We should conceal it from her? I should lose my license for your lousy fifteen thousand account?"

Shelly hung up. His head reeled. He tried to make sense of what had happened. He should never have asked for a confirmation call. And those goddamned earplugs. When Norma learned about the stock sale, she must have started looking through all his papers and found his Wells Fargo account. And now she knew everything. It was all over.

Shelly reread Norma's fax and then yelled, "Fuck it all, fuck it all!" and tore it to shreds. He returned to the kitchen, warmed up his coffee, and opened the morning *Chronicle*. Classified ad time. Only now it was not only a job that he needed, but a furnished apartment as well. However, a strange headline on the first page of the Metropolitan section caught his eye.

MOVE OVER, FORD, TOYOTA, CHEVROLET!
NOW PSYCHIATRISTS RECALL PRODUCT!

Shelly read on.

> Taking a page from the notebooks of the giant auto makers, the Golden Gate Psychoanalytic Institute has posted a recall bulletin (see page D2). In an unruly meeting on October 24 the institute censored and suspended one of its luminaries, Dr. Seth Pande, "for conduct detrimental to psychoanalysis."

Seth Pande! Seth Pande! Hey, Shelly thought, wasn't that the shrink Norma asked me to see before we got married? Seth Pande— yes, I'm sure of it: How many *Pandes* can there be? Shelly read on:

> Dr. Marshal Streider, the institute's spokesman, would not elaborate further except to say that members believed that Dr. Pande's patients may not have received the best treatment psychoanalysis had to offer and possibly may have suffered some harm as a result of their analytic work with Dr. Pande. Dr. Pande's patients are being offered a free "Psychoanalytic tune-up!" Was it the fuel pump? this reporter asked. Power train? Spark plugs? Exhaust system? Dr. Streider would not comment.
>
> Dr. Streider says the action is evidence of the Psychoanalytic Institute's commitment to the highest possible standards of patient care, professional responsibility, and integrity.
>
> Maybe so. But doesn't this development raise further questions about the presumptuousness of the entire psychiatric enterprise? How much longer can psychiatrists pretend to provide guidance for individuals, groups, and organizations when there is once again—remember the scandalous Seymour

Trotter case a few years ago?—graphic evidence of
its inability to govern itself?

Dr. Pande was contacted. His comment (surprise!):
"Talk to my lawyer."

Shelly flipped to page D2 for the formal notice.

PSYCHIATRIC PATIENT RECALL

The Golden Gate Psychoanalytic Institute urges all
male patients who saw Dr. Seth Pande in treatment
after 1984 to call 415–555–2441 for a psychological
evaluation and, if necessary, a course of remedial
psychiatric treatment. It is possible that Dr. Pande's
treatment may have significantly deviated from psychoanalytic guidelines and may have had deleterious
effects. All services will be offered free of charge.

Within seconds Shelly was on the phone with the Psychoanalytic
Institute secretary.

"Yes, Mr. Merriman, you're entitled, in fact encouraged, to
undergo a free course of therapy with one of our members. Our
therapists are offering their services on a rotating basis. You're the
first person to call. May I offer you an appointment with Dr. Marshal Streider, one of our senior analysts? Friday nine A.M. at 2313
California Street."

"Could you tell me what this is about, exactly? This is making me
nervous. I don't want to have a panic attack waiting."

"I can't tell you too much. Dr. Streider will fill you in, but the
institute feels that some of Dr. Pande's interpretations might not
have been helpful to some patients."

"So, if I had a symptom—let's say, an addiction—you're saying he
might have screwed me over."

"Well . . . something like that. We are not saying that Dr. Pande
intentionally harmed you. The institute has simply gone on record
as strongly disagreeing with his methods."

"Okay, nine A.M. Friday would be fine. But you know, I'm very
subject to panic attacks. This all is upsetting to me and I don't want
to end up at the emergency room; it would be a relief—a lifesaving
relief—to have in writing what you just told me, including the time
and place of my appointment. What's his name? See what I mean?

I'm losing it already. I think I need it now. Could you fax it to me right away?"

"Gladly, Mr. Merriman."

Shelly went to the fax machine and waited. Finally *something* had gone right. He quickly scribbled a note:

> Norma,
>   Read these! A mystery solved! Remember your therapist, Dr. Pande? And how I got to him? And how opposed I was to therapy? And how I put myself in his hands at your request? This has caused me, and you, and us, a lot of grief. I tried to do the right thing. No wonder therapy didn't help! Now we know why. I'm trying again to do the right thing—going in for full repairs. And I'm going to do it! Whatever it takes. However long it takes. Hang in there with me. Please!
>   Your one and only husband

Shelly then faxed his note to Norma, along with the newspaper article and the letter from the Analytic Institute secretary. A half-hour later the fax machine clattered again and a message from Norma glided out.

> Shelly,
>   Willing to talk. See you at six.
>   Norma

Shelly returned to his coffee, closed the classified section, and turned to the sports page.

"Zip-a-dee-doo-dah, zip-a-dee-ay."

NINE

*M*arshal checked his appointment book. His next patient, Peter Macondo, a Mexican businessman residing in Switzerland, was coming in for his eighth and final session. Mr. Macondo, visiting San Francisco for a month, had called requesting brief therapy for a family crisis. Until two or three years ago, Marshal accepted only long-term analytic cases, but times had changed. Now, like every other therapist in town, he had open hours and was happy to see Mr. Macondo twice weekly for a month.

Mr. Macondo had been a pleasure to work with and had made good use of therapy. Exceptionally good use. Moreover, he paid cash on the barrelhead. At the end of the first session he handed Marshal two hundred-dollar bills and said, "I prefer to simplify life with cash. Incidentally, you may wish to know that I don't file U.S. income taxes and don't claim medical expenses on my Swiss taxes."

With that he started out the door.

Marshal knew exactly what to do. It would be an egregious error to begin therapy under the shadow of some collusion in a dishonest project, even such a widespread one as concealing cash income. Though Marshal wished to be firm, he spoke in a gentle tone: Peter Macondo was a gentle man who had an air of innocent nobility about him.

"Mr. Macondo, I must say two things to you. First, let me say that I always report all income. It's the right thing to do. I'll give you a receipt at the end of each month. Second, you've paid me too much. My fee is one hundred seventy-five. Here, let me see if I have change." He reached into his desk.

Mr. Macondo, one hand on the doorknob, turned and held up his other hand, his palm facing Marshal. "Please, Dr. Streider, in Zurich the fee is two hundred dollars. And Swiss therapists are less quali-fied than you. Far less qualified. I beg you, please extend me the courtesy of setting the same fee. It will set me at ease and thus facil-itate my work with you. Until Thursday."

Marshal, his hand still in his pocket, gaped after the departing fig-ure. Many patients had considered his fee too high, but never before had Marshal encountered one who insisted it was too low. *Oh, well,* he thought, *he's European. And there are no long-term transference implications; it's just brief therapy.*

It wasn't just that Marshal had little respect for brief therapy. He held it in contempt. Focused, symptom-relieving therapy . . . the satisfied-customer model . . . the hell with that! What counted for Marshal, and for most analysts, was the *depth* of change. Depth was everything. Psychoanalysts everywhere knew that the deeper the exploration, the more effective the therapy. "Go deep"—Marshal could hear the voice of Bob McCallum, his own psychoanalytic supervisor—"go deep into the most ancient realms of consciousness, into primitive feelings, archaic fantasies; go back to the earliest lay-ers of memory, then and only then will you be able to uproot the neurosis entirely and to effect an analytic cure."

But deep therapy was losing the battle: the barbarian hordes of expediency were everywhere. Marching to the starched new banners of managed care, the battalions of brief therapy darkened the land-scape and hammered at the gates of the analytic institutes, the last armed enclaves of wisdom, truth, and reason in psychotherapy. The enemy was close enough for Marshal to see its many faces: biofeed-back and muscular relaxation for anxiety disorders; implosion or desensitization for phobias; drugs for dysthymia and obsessive/compulsive disorders; cognitive group therapy for eating disorders; assertiveness training for the timid; diaphragmatic breathing groups for panicked patients; social skills training for the socially avoidant; one-session hypnotic interventions for smoking; and those goddamned twelve-step groups for everything else!

The economic juggernaut of managed care had overwhelmed medical defenses in many parts of the country. Therapists in subjugated states were forced, if they wished to stay in practice, to genuflect to the conqueror, who paid them a fraction of their customary fee and assigned them patients to treat for five or maybe six sessions when, in actuality, fifty or sixty sessions were needed.

When therapists used up their meager allotted rations, the charade began in earnest and they were forced to beg their case manager for additional sessions to continue treatment. And, of course, they had to document their request with mountains of phony, time-consuming paperwork in which they were forced to lie by exaggerating the patient's suicidal risk, substance abuse, or propensity for violence; those were the only magic words that caught the attention of the health plans—not because administrators felt any concern for the patient but because they were cowed by the threat of some future litigation.

Thus, therapists were not only ordered to treat patients in impossibly brief periods, but also had the added, humiliating chore of placating and accommodating the case managers—often brash young administrators with only the most rudimentary knowledge of the field. The other day Victor Young, a respected colleague, received a note from his twenty-seven-year-old case manager granting him four more sessions in his treatment of a severely schizoid patient. In the margin was scribbled the case manager's cryptic, idiotic instruction: "Break through denial!"

Not only was the dignity of psychiatrists being assaulted, but their pocketbooks were, as well. One of Marshal's office mates had left psychiatry and, at forty-three, entered a radiology residency. Others, who had invested well, were considering early retirement. Marshal no longer had a waiting list and gratefully accepted patients he would have referred away in the past. He often worried about the future—his future and the future of the field.

Ordinarily Marshal felt the most he might accomplish in brief therapy was some slight amelioration of symptoms that, with luck, might hold the patient until the next fiscal year, when case managers might permit another few sessions. But Peter Macondo had been a striking exception. Only four weeks ago he had been highly symptomatic: guilt-ridden, with severe anxiety, insomnia, and gastric distress. And now he was virtually symptom-free. Rarely had Marshal had a patient whom he had helped so much in such a brief period.

Did that change Marshal's opinion about the efficacy of brief therapy? In no way! The explanation for Peter Macondo's remarkable success was simple and clear: Mr. Macondo had no significant neurotic or characterological problems. He was an unusually resourceful, well-integrated individual whose symptoms emanated from stress that was, for the most part, situation-bound.

Mr. Macondo was a highly successful businessman who, Marshal believed, was confronted with the typical problems of the mega-wealthy. Divorced a few years ago, he was now contemplating marriage with Adriana, a beautiful younger woman. Though he loved Adriana very much, he was crippled by hesitation—he had known of too many nightmarish divorces involving wealthy businessmen and trophy wives. He felt his only alternative—a nasty, awkward one—was to insist on a prenuptial agreement. But how to present it without commercializing and contaminating their love? He circled, he obsessed, he procrastinated. That was the major problem that had brought him into therapy.

Peter's two children represented another problem. Heavily influenced by Evelyn, his angry ex-wife, the children steadfastly opposed the marriage and refused even to meet Adriana. Peter and Evelyn had been inseparable in college and had married the day following graduation. But the marriage had tarnished quickly, and within a few years Evelyn had sunk into severe alcoholism. Peter had heroically kept the family intact, made sure his children had a good Catholic education, and then, when they graduated from high school, filed for divorce. But the years of living amid bitter conflict had taken their toll on the children. In retrospect Peter knew that he would have done better to divorce earlier and to have fought for custody of the children.

The children, in their early twenties, openly accused Adriana of scheming to take over the family fortune. Nor were they timid in expressing their resentment toward their father. Even though Peter had put almost three million dollars into trust for each, they insisted he had not done right by them. To bolster their claim, they pointed to a recent story in the London *Financial Times* describing a highly profitable two-hundred-million-pound venture of his.

He was paralyzed by conflicting sentiments. By nature a generous man, he wanted nothing more than to share his assets with his children—they were his whole reason for amassing property. Yet the money had turned into a curse. Both children had dropped out of college, had deserted the church, and were floundering with no career interests, no ambition, no vision of the future, and no guiding set of moral values. To top it off, his son was seriously abusing drugs.

Peter Macondo was slumping into nihilism. What had he been working for these past twenty years? His own religious faith had waned, his children no longer represented a meaningful project for the future, and even his philanthropic ventures had begun to feel meaningless. He had given money to several universities in his native Mexico but felt overwhelmed by the poverty, the political corruption, the runaway population explosion in Mexico City, the environmental catastrophe. The last time he had visited Mexico City he had to wear a cloth mask because he could not breathe the air. What could his few millions do?

Marshal had no doubt he was the perfect therapist for Peter Macondo. He was accustomed to working with ultra-wealthy patients and their children and understood their problems. He had given public addresses to several venture capital and philanthropic groups on the subject and dreamed someday of writing a book. But this book—which he already had a title for, *Affluenza: The Curse of the Ruling Class*—like Marshal's other good ideas for books, remained a dream. Carving time out of a busy practice to write a book seemed impossible. How had the great theoreticians—Freud, Jung, Rank, Fromm, May, Horney—done it?

Marshal used a number of brief, focused therapy techniques with Peter Macondo and, to his great pleasure, every one he tried worked to perfection. He normalized his patient's dilemma and eased his guilt by informing him about the universality of these problems among the very wealthy. He depressurized Peter's relationship to his children by helping him grow more aware of the children's experiential world, in particular, their entrapment in the ongoing struggle between their mother and father. He suggested that the best way to improve his relationship with the children was to improve his relationship with his ex-wife. Gradually he reestablished a more respectful relationship with her and, after the fourth hour of therapy, Mr. Macondo invited his ex-wife to a lunch during which the two of them had their first nonconfrontative talk in years.

Again at Marshal's suggestion, Peter urged his ex-wife to join with him in acknowledging that, though they no longer could live together, they had loved each other for many years and the reality of that past love still existed: it was important to treasure it, not to trash it. Peter offered, at Marshal's suggestion, to pay the twenty thousand dollars for her to stay a month in the Betty Ford Alcohol Rehabilitation Center. Though she had received an extremely generous divorce settlement and could easily have afforded to sponsor herself, she had always resisted treatment. But Peter's caring gesture moved her a great deal and, to his surprise, she accepted his offer.

Once Peter and his ex-wife began to communicate better, his relationship with the children improved. With Marshal's help, he drew up a plan for an additional five-million-dollar trust for each child, to be distributed over the next ten years when certain specific targets were achieved: graduation from college, marriage, two years in some established, intrinsically worthy professional endeavor, and service on boards of community-oriented projects. This generous but strictly structured trust worked wonders for the children, and in a remarkably short time their attitude toward their father changed drastically.

Marshal devoted a couple of the sessions to Mr. Macondo's propensity for guilt assumption. He hated to disappoint anyone and, though he tended to minimize the scores of brilliant investment decisions he had made for his investors—a faithful group of Swiss and Scottish bankers—he vividly remembered every single poor decision and grew sad in Marshal's office as he recalled the faces of his few disappointed investors.

Marshal and Mr. Macondo spent most of the fifth session on a single investment incident. About a year earlier his father, a distinguished professor of economics at the University of Mexico, had flown to Boston from Mexico to have triple coronary bypass surgery.

After the operation, the surgeon, Dr. Black, to whom Mr. Macondo was exceedingly grateful, asked for a donation to the cardiovascular research program at Harvard. Not only did Mr. Macondo readily agree but he expressed a wish, as well, to make a gift to Dr. Black personally. Dr. Black declined, stating that the surgical fee of ten thousand dollars adequately compensated him. However, in a conversation Mr. Macondo casually mentioned that he expected to make a considerable profit in a large position he had taken the day before in Mexican peso futures. Dr. Black immediately made the same investment, only to lose seventy percent of it the following week when Luis Colosio, the presidential candidate, was assassinated.

Mr. Macondo was awash in guilt about Dr. Black. Marshal made strenuous efforts to confront him with reality, reminding his patient that he had acted in good faith, that he had also lost heavily, that Dr. Black had made an independent decision to invest. But Mr. Macondo continued to ruminate about how he could make things right again. Following the session, and despite Marshal's protests, he impulsively sent Dr. Black a personal check for thirty thousand dollars, the amount he had lost in the investment.

But Dr. Black, to his credit, sent the check right back with thanks but a curt reminder that he was a grown-up and knew how to deal with reversals. Besides, Dr. Black added, he could use the losses to offset some capital gains from investments in sugar futures. Eventually Mr. Macondo settled his conscience with an additional thirty-thousand-dollar donation to Harvard's cardiovascular research program.

Marshal got a charge from his work with Mr. Macondo. None of his patients had been in quite this stratospheric a financial league. It was thrilling to have an intimate, insider glimpse of great wealth and to share in decisions about dispensing a million here, a million there. He couldn't help salivating at Peter's account of his generosity to his father's doctor. More and more he daydreamed about his grateful patient directing money his way. But each time Marshal hastily brushed away the fantasy; the memory of Seth Pande's excommunication for professional misconduct was all too vivid. It was malpractice to accept sizable gifts from *any* therapy patient, but especially from a patient who was pathologically generous and scrupulous. Any ethics board, certainly any ethics board on which *he* was a member, would strongly condemn a therapist for exploiting such a patient.

The most difficult challenge in Mr. Macondo's therapy was his irrational fear of discussing the prenuptial agreement with his fiancée. Marshal took a systematic and disciplined approach. First, he helped work out the terms of the prenuptial contract: a flat million-dollar sum that would increase sharply according to the longevity of the marriage and would change after ten years to a one-third share of his entire estate. Then he and his patient role-played the discussion several times. But, even so, Mr. Macondo expressed doubt about confronting Adriana. Finally Marshal offered to facilitate the discussion and asked him to bring in Adriana for a three-way session.

When the two arrived a few days later, Marshal feared he had made a mistake: never had he seen Mr. Macondo so agitated—he could barely stay in his chair. Adriana, however, was the epitome of grace and calm. When Mr. Macondo opened the session with a painfully fumbling statement about conflicts between his matrimonial wishes and family claims to his estate, she immediately interrupted and commented that she had been thinking that a prenuptial marital agreement would be not only appropriate but desirable.

She said that she could well understand Peter's concerns. In fact, she shared many of them. Just the other day her father, who was quite ill, had spoken to her of the wisdom of keeping her own estate outside of marital community property. Even though her holdings were small compared to Peter's, she would eventually come into a much larger estate—her father was a major shareholder in a large chain of California movie houses.

The matter was resolved on the spot. Peter nervously presented his terms and Adriana enthusiastically accepted, with the additional proviso that her personal resources remain in her own name. Marshal noted, with displeasure, that his patient had doubled the amounts that they had previously discussed, probably out of gratitude to Adriana for making things so easy. *Incurable generosity,* Marshal thought. *But there are worse diseases, I guess.* As the couple left, Peter turned back, clasped Marshal's hand, and said, "I shall never forget what you did for me today."

⌇

Marshal opened his door and invited Mr. Macondo to enter. Peter wore a luxuriously soft auburn cashmere jacket to match the silky brown hair that slipped gracefully over his eyes and had to be guided back into place again and again.

Marshal devoted their final session to reviewing and solidifying their gains. Mr. Macondo regretted the end of their work and stressed how incalculably indebted he felt to Marshal.

"Dr. Streider, all my life I've paid consultants considerable sums for what usually amounted to be of little or no value. With you I've had the opposite experience: you've given me something of inestimable value and in return I've given you practically nothing. In these few sessions you've changed my life. And how have I reciprocated? Sixteen hundred dollars? If I am willing to endure the tedium, I can make that kind of money in fifteen minutes investing in financial futures."

He rushed on, speaking faster and faster: "You know me well, Dr. Streider, well enough to realize that this inequality doesn't sit well with me. It's an irritant: it'll stick in my throat. We can't ignore it because—who knows?—it may even cancel out some of the gains I've made as a result of our work. I want, I *insist,* that we even the score.

"Now you know," he continued, "I'm not good at direct interpersonal communication. And I'm not too good at fathering. Or at confronting females. But there's one thing I'm very good at, and that's making money. You would be doing me a great honor by allowing me to make you a gift of a portion of one of my new investments."

Marshal flushed. He felt faint, overcome by a clash of greed and propriety. But he gritted his teeth, did the right thing, and declined the opportunity of a lifetime: "Mr. Macondo, I'm touched but it's entirely out of the question. I'm afraid that in my field it is considered unethical to accept a monetary gift, or any other gift, from patients. One issue we never discussed in therapy is your discomfort in accepting help. Perhaps if we ever work together in the future that should be on the agenda. For now there is only time for me to simply remind you that I have set, and you have paid, a fair fee for my services. I embrace the same position as your father's surgeon, and assure you there is no debt."

"Dr. Black? What a comparison. Dr. Black charged ten thousand dollars for a few hours' work. And thirty minutes after surgery, he put a bite on me for a million for a Harvard chair in cardiovascular surgery."

Marshal shook his head emphatically. "Mr. Macondo, I admire your generosity; it's wonderful. And I'd love to accept. I enjoy the idea of financial security as much as anyone—more than most, since I yearn for the free time to write; I have several projects on analytic theory struggling to be born. But I cannot accept. It would violate the ethical code of my profession."

"Another suggestion," Mr. Macondo countered quickly, "not a monetary gift. Please permit me to open a futures account for you and trade for you for a month. We'll converse daily and I will teach you the art of making money by daily trading in currency futures. Then I take back my original investment and turn over the profits to you."

Now this suggestion, this possibility of learning insider trading technique, was extraordinarily appealing to Marshal. It was so painful to refuse that his eyes filled with tears. But he bolstered his resolve and shook his head even more vigorously. "Mr. Macondo, if we were in some other . . . uh . . . situation . . . I'd gladly accept. I'm touched by your offer, and would like to learn trading techniques from you. But no. No. It's not possible. Also, something I forgot to say before. I've gotten more than my fee from you. There's something else, and that's the pleasure of seeing your improvement. It's very gratifying to me."

Mr. Macondo slumped back helplessly in his chair, his eyes filled with admiration for Marshal's professionalism and integrity. He held out his hands palms up, as though to say, "I surrender; I've tried everything." The hour was over. The two men shook hands for the last time. On the way out the door, Mr. Macondo seemed lost in thought. Suddenly he stopped and turned.

"One last request. This you cannot refuse. Please be my guest for lunch tomorrow. Or Friday. I leave for Zurich on Sunday."

Marshal hesitated.

Mr. Macondo quickly added: "I know there are rules against socializing with patients, but with that final handshake a minute ago we are no longer doctor and patient. Thanks to your good services, I'm over my illness and we are both again fellow citizens."

Marshal considered the invitation. He liked Mr. Macondo and his insider stories of the making of wealth. What was the harm? There was no ethics violation here.

Seeing Marshal's hesitation, Mr. Macondo added, "Though I will briefly return to San Francisco from time to time for business—certainly twice a year for board meetings, to see my children, and to see Adriana's father and sisters—we will be inhabiting different continents. Surely there is no rule against a post-therapy luncheon."

Marshal reached for his diary. "One o'clock Friday?"

"Excellent. The Pacific Union Club. You know it?"

"Know *of* it. But I've never been there."

"On California, top of Nob Hill. Next to the Fairmont. There's parking in the back. Just mention my name. See you then."

∼

On Friday morning Marshal received a fax: a copy of a fax Mr. Macondo had received from the University of Mexico.

> Dear Mr. Macondo,
>   We are delighted with your generous gift to endow the annual Marshal Streider Endowed Lecture Series: Mental Health in the Third Millennium. We will, of course, per your suggestion, invite Dr. Streider to serve on the three-member committee to select the annual speakers. The president of the university, Raoul Menendez, will be contacting him shortly. President Menendez asked me to send you his personal greetings; incidentally, he lunched with your father earlier this week.
>   We are indebted to you for this and your many other gifts in support of Mexican research and education. It is painful to imagine the plight of this university without the sustaining force of you and a small group of like-minded, visionary benefactors.
>
> Sincerely,
Raoul Gomez
Provost, University of Mexico

Peter Macondo's accompanying note:

> I never say no. Here is a gift even you cannot refuse! See you tomorrow.

Marshal read the fax twice, slowly, sorting out his feelings. The Marshal Streider endowed lecture series—a memorial that would extend into perpetuity. Who wouldn't be pleased? The perfect self-esteem insurance policy. Years from now, whenever he felt diminished, he could think of his endowed lecture series. Or fly to Mexico City for the lecture and rise, reluctantly, hand held aloft, turning slowly and modestly to acknowledge the applause of a grateful audience.

But it was a bittersweet gift, poor solace for letting the financial opportunity of a lifetime slip through his fingers. When would he ever again have a mega-wealthy patient who wanted nothing more

than to make him a wealthy man? Mr. Macondo's offer of a gift—
"a portion of one of his investments"—Marshal wondered what it
might have been. Fifty thousand? A hundred thousand? God, what
a difference that would make in his life! And he could parlay that
quickly. Even his own investment strategy—using a computer program to time the market and moving in and out of the Fidelity select
funds—had netted him sixteen percent each of the last two years.
With Mr. Macondo's offer to trade in the foreign exchange currency
markets, he could probably double or triple that. Marshal knew he
was the puny trading outsider—any scraps of information that came
his way were invariably too late. Here, for the first time in his life,
he had been given the chance to be an insider.

Yes, as an insider he could set himself up for life. He didn't need
much. All he really wanted was to free up time and devote three or
four afternoons a week to research and writing. And the money!

And yet he had had to turn all this down. Damn! Damn! Damn!
But what choice did he have? Did he want to go the way of Seth
Pande? Or Seymour Trotter? He knew he had done the right thing.

~

On Friday, as he approached the massive marble doorway of the
Pacific Union Club, Marshal was thrilled, almost awed. For years he
had felt closed out of such fabled places as the P.U. Club, the
Burlingame Club, and the Bohemian Grove. Now doors were opening for him. He paused at the doorstep, took a breath, and strode
into the deepest lair of the insiders.

It was the end of a journey, Marshal thought, a journey that had
begun in 1924 in the crowded, foul-smelling steerage class of a
transatlantic barge that brought his parents, still children, from
Southampton to Ellis Island. No, no, it started before that, in
Prussina, a shtetl near the Polish-Russian border built of rickety
wooden homes with earthen floors. In one of those homes his father
had slept, as a child, in a small warm nook atop the large, clay-
bricked oven that filled much of the common room.

How had they gotten from Prussina to Southampton? Marshal
wondered. Overland? Boat? He had never asked them that. And it
was too late now. His mother and father had turned to dust, side
by side, long ago, in the tall grass of an Anacostia cemetery just
outside Washington, D.C. There was only one survivor of that long
journey who might still know—his mother's brother, Label, rocking

out his final years on the long, wooden porch of a urine-reeking Miami Beach nursing home with pink stucco walls. Time to phone Label.

The central rotúnda, a graceful octagon, was rimmed by stately mahogany leather sofas and capped, ninety feet up, by a magnificent ceiling of translucent glass etched with a delicate floral pattern. The majordomo, clad in tuxedo and patent leathers, greeted Marshal with great deference and, upon hearing his name, nodded and directed him into the sitting room. There, at the far end, before an enormous fireplace, sat Peter Macondo.

The sitting room was huge—half of Prussina would probably have fit under the soaring ceiling supported by walls of gleaming oak alternating with scarlet satin panels of *fleur-de-lis*. And leather everywhere—Marshal quickly counted twelve long sofas and thirty massive chairs. On some of the chairs sat wizened, gray-haired, pin-striped men holding newspapers. Marshal had to peer closely to determine if they were still breathing. Twelve candelabra on one wall—that meant forty-eight in the room, each with three rows of bulbs, the innermost with five, the next with seven, the outermost with nine, a total of twenty-one bulbs, a grand total of . . . Marshal stopped multiplying as he noticed a pair of three-foot-tall metal bookends on one of the fireplaces, replicas of Michelangelo's bound slaves; in the center of the room stood a massive table piled high with newspapers, mostly financial, from around the world; along one wall a glass case containing an enormous porcelain bowl of the late eighteenth century with a plaque stating that it had been donated by a member and was Ching-te Cheng pottery. Its painted scenes depicted episodes from the novel *Dream of the Red Chamber*.

The real thing. Yes, this was the real thing, Marshal thought, as he approached Peter, who was on a sofa chatting amiably with another member—a tall, stately man wearing a red checkered jacket, a pink shirt, and a brightly flowered ascot. Marshal had never seen anyone dress like that—never seen anyone who *could* dress in clothes that clashed so shockingly and yet have the grace and dignity to pull it off.

"Ah, Marshal," said Peter, "good to see you. Let me introduce Roscoe Richardson. Roscoe's father was the best mayor San Francisco ever had. Roscoe, Dr. Marshal Streider, San Francisco's leading psychoanalyst. There's a rumor, Roscoe, that Dr. Streider has just been honored by having a university lecture series named after him."

After a brief exchange of pleasantries, Peter led Marshal toward the dining room, then turned back for one last comment.

"Roscoe, I *don't* believe there's market room for another main-frame system, but I'm not entirely closed to it; if Cisco really decides to invest, I could be interested, too. Convince me and I'll convince my own investors. Please send the business plan to Zurich and I'll turn to it on Monday when I return to the office."

"Fine man," Peter said as they walked away. "Our fathers knew each other. And a great golfer. His home is right on the Cypress Point course. Interesting investment possibility but I wouldn't recommend it to you: these start-ups are such long shots. Very expensive to play the game—you hit only one start-up in twenty. Of course, when you *do* hit, they pay better, far better, than twenty to one. Incidentally, I hope I'm not presumptuous in calling you Marshal."

"No, of course not. First names. We're no longer in a professional relationship."

"You say you've never been to the Club before?"

"No," said Marshal. "Walked by it. Admired it. Not a part of the grazing grounds of the medical community. I know almost nothing about the Club. What's the profile of its members? Mostly business-men?"

"Mostly old San Francisco money. Conservative. Most are coupon clippers, hanging on to inherited wealth. Roscoe's an excep-tion—that's why I like him. At seventy-one he's still a high flyer. Let's see . . . what else? All male, mostly WASPs, politically incorrect—I first raised objections ten years ago, but things move slowly around here, especially after lunch. See what I mean?" Peter subtly gestured toward chairs on which two tweeded octogenarians snoozed, still clutching for dear life their copies of the London *Financial Times*.

As they arrived at the dining room, Peter addressed the major-domo, "Emil, we're ready. Any chance for some of that salmon en croute today? *Il est toujours délicieux.*"

"I believe I can persuade the chef to prepare some especially for you, Mr. Macondo."

"Emil, I remember how wonderful it was at the Cercle Union Interalliée in Paris." Peter then whispered to Emil, "Tell my secret to no one French, but I prefer the preparation here."

Peter continued to chat animatedly with Emil. Marshal did not hear the conversation because he was staggered by the magnificence of the dining room, including a mammoth porcelain bowl holding the mother of all Japanese flower arrangements—glorious cymbid-ium orchids cascading down a scarlet-leafed maple branch. If only my wife could see that, Marshal thought. They paid someone plenty for that arrangement—that might be a way for her to turn her little hobby into something useful.

"Peter," Marshal said after Emil had seated them, "you're in San Francisco so rarely. You keep a continuously active membership in this club and in Zurich and Paris also?"

"No, no, no," said Peter, smiling at Marshal's naïveté. "At that rate lunch here would cost around five thousand a sandwich. All these clubs—the Circolo dell'Unione in Milan, the Atheneum in London, the Cosmos Club in Washington, the Cercle Union Interal-liée in Paris, the Pacific Union in San Francisco, the Baur au Lac in Zurich—they're all in a network: membership in one club grants privileges in all. Actually, that's how I know Emil: he used to work at the Cercle Union Interalliée in Paris." Peter lifted his menu. "So, Marshal, start with a drink?"

"Just some Calistoga water. I've still got four patients to see."

Peter ordered a Dubonnet and soda and, when the drinks arrived, held up his glass. "To you, and to the Marshal Streider Endowed Lecture Series."

Marshal flushed. He had been so overwhelmed by the Club that he had forgotten to thank Peter.

"Peter, the endowed lectureship—what an honor. I meant to thank you first thing, but I've been preoccupied with my last patient."

"Your last patient? That surprises me. Somehow I had the feeling that when patients exit, they never reenter the therapist's mind until they arrive for their next hour."

"It would be best that way. But—and this is a trade secret—even the most disciplined analysts carry patients around and have silent conversations with some between sessions."

"At no extra fee!"

"Ah, alas, no. Only lawyers charge for thinking time."

"Interesting, interesting! You may possibly be talking for all ther-apists, Marshal, but I have a hunch you're talking about yourself. I've often wondered why I've gotten so little from other therapists. Maybe it's because you're more dedicated—maybe your patients mean more to you."

The salmon en croute arrived, but Peter ignored it while he

proceeded to relate how Adriana, too, had been greatly dissatisfied with her previous therapists.

"In fact, Marshal," he continued, "that's one of the two things I wanted to discuss with you today. Adriana would like very much to work with you for a few sessions: she's got to iron out some things in her relationship with her father, especially now that he may not have long to live."

Marshal, a close observer of class differences, had long known that the upper class deliberately delayed taking the first mouthful of food; in fact, the older the wealth, the longer the delay before the first forkful. Marshal did his best to pause along with Peter. He, too, ignored the salmon, sipped his Calistoga, listened intently, nodded, and assured Peter that he would be glad to see Adriana in brief therapy.

Finally, Marshal could stand it no longer. He dug in. He was glad he had followed Peter's recommendation of the salmon. It *was* delicious. The delicate buttered crust crackled and melted in his mouth; the salmon needed no chewing—with the slightest pressure of tongue on palate, the rosemary-laced flakes separated and, on a bed of warm, creamy butter, glided gently down his throat. The hell with cholesterol, Marshal thought, feeling positively wicked.

Peter, for the first time, looked at his food, almost surprised to see it there. He took one hearty bite, then lay down his fork and resumed speaking.

"Good. Adriana needs you. I'm very relieved. She'll phone this afternoon. Here's her card. If the two of you can't make phone contact, she'd appreciate your phoning her to leave an appointment time for next week. Any time you have free: she'll work her schedule around you. Also, Marshal—and I've cleared this with Adriana—I'd like to pay for Adriana's hours. This will cover five sessions." He handed Marshal an envelope containing ten hundred-dollar bills. "I can't tell you how grateful I am that you'll see Adriana. And of course this adds impetus to my desire to repay my debt to you."

Marshal's interest was piqued. He had supposed that the endowed lecture series signaled that his window of opportunity had closed forever. Fate, it seemed, had decided to tempt him once again. But he knew his professionalism would prevail: "Earlier you spoke of two issues you wanted to discuss. One was my seeing Adriana in therapy. Is your continuing feeling of indebtedness the second issue?"

Peter nodded.

"Peter, you've got to let this go. Or else—and this is a major threat—I'm going to have to suggest you delay your trip for three or four years so we can resolve this in analysis. Let me repeat: *there is no outstanding debt.* You contracted for my services. I charged an appropriate fee. You paid that fee. You even paid more than my fee. Remember? And then you were gracious and generous enough to endow a lectureship in my name. There never *was* an outstanding debt. And, even if there were, your gift clearly settled it. More than settled it: *I* feel indebted to *you*!"

"Marshal, you taught me to be true to myself and to express my feelings openly. So I'm going to do just that. Humor me for a couple of minutes. Just hear me out. Five minutes. Okay?"

"Five minutes. And then we bury it forever. Agreed?"

Peter nodded. With a smile Marshal took off his watch and placed it between them.

Peter picked up Marshal's watch, studied it intently for a moment, returned it to the table, and began.

"First thing: let me clear the air about something. I'd feel like a fraud if I let you think that the university bequest was really a gift to you. The truth is, I make a moderately sized gift to the university almost every year. Four years ago I endowed the very chair in economics that my father holds. So I would have made the gift anyway. All I did differently was earmark it for your lecture series.

"Second thing: I understand entirely your feelings about gifts, and I respect them. However, I have a suggestion that you may find acceptable. How much time left?"

"Three minutes and counting." Marshal grinned.

"I haven't told you much about my business life, but what I do primarily is buy and sell companies. I'm an expert in pricing companies—I did it for Citicorp for several years before striking out on my own. I guess I've been involved in the purchase of over two hundred companies over the years.

"I've recently identified a Dutch company that is so amazingly underpriced and with such powerful profit potential that I've purchased it for myself—perhaps I'm being selfish, but my new partnership is not yet complete. We're raising two hundred fifty million. The opportunity to purchase this company is brief and, I'll be honest, it's too good to share."

Despite himself, Marshal was intrigued. "So?"

"Wait, let me finish. This company, Rucksen, is the world's second leading manufacturer of bicycle helmets, with fourteen percent of the market. Sales were good last year—twenty-three million—but I am certain I can quadruple that in two years. Here's why. The largest share of the market—twenty-six percent—is held by Solvag, a Finnish company, and it just so happens that my consortium owns controlling interest in Solvag! And I own controlling interest in the consortium. Now Solvag's main product is motorcycle helmets, and that division is far more profitable than the bicycle helmet division. My plans are to streamline Solvag by merging it with an Austrian motorcycle helmet company that I'm bidding on now. When that happens, I'll discontinue Solvag bicycle helmets and convert their plant into full motorcycle-helmet capacity. Meanwhile I'll have stepped up Rucksen production capacity and positioned it to move right into the gap left by Solvag. You see the beauty of this, Marshal?"

Marshal nodded. Indeed he did. Insider beauty. And he also saw the futility of his pathetic attempts to time the stock market or to buy a stock with the worthless crumbs of information that made their way down to outsiders.

"Here's what I propose." Peter glanced at the watch. "A couple more minutes. Hear me out." But Marshal had forgotten all about the five-minute limit.

"I leveraged the purchase of Rucksen and need put up only nine million cash. I expect to go public with Rucksen in approximately twenty-two months and have very good reasons to expect more than five hundred percent return. Solvag's departure from the field will leave them with no powerful competitors—which of course no one knows but me, so you must keep this confidential. Also I have information—I can't reveal the source, even to you—of legislation making bicycle helmets mandatory for minors that will be introduced imminently in three European countries.

"I propose you take a portion of the investment, say, one percent—no wait, Marshal, before you refuse: this is *not* a gift, and I am no longer a patient. This is a bona fide investment. You give me a check and you become part owner. With one proviso, however—and here's where I'm asking you to stretch yourself: I do *not* want to find myself in another Dr. Black scenario. You remember how much aggravation that caused me?

"So," Peter continued, sensing Marshal's growing interest and speaking more confidently now, "here's my solution. For the sake of *my* mental health, I want this to be risk-free for *you*. If at any time you feel unhappy about the investment, I will buy back your shares at your cost. I propose to give you my personal promissory note— fully secured and payable upon demand in an amount equal to one hundred percent of your investment plus ten percent interest annually. But you must give *me* your promise that you will exercise this note in the event of some unforeseen incident—who knows what? . . . presidential assassination, my accidental death, or anything else that you feel puts you at risk. In other words, you are obligated to exercise this note."

Peter sat back, lifted Marshal's watch, and handed it back to him. "Seven and a half minutes. Now I'm finished."

All of Marshal's gears were spinning at once. And now, finally, the gears did not grind. *Ninety thousand dollars,* he thought. *I make, say, seven hundred percent—that's over six hundred thousand dollars profit. In twenty-two months. How can I, how could anyone, turn that down? Invest that at twelve percent and that's seventy-two thousand dollars a year for the rest of my life. Peter's right. He's no longer a patient. This is no transference gift—I put up money; it's an investment. So what if it's risk-free! It's a private note. There's no professional misconduct here. This is clean. Squeaky-clean.*

Marshal stopped thinking. It was time to act. "Peter, I only saw part of you in my office. Now I know you better. Now I know why you've been so successful. You set a goal and you go after it—go after it with a tenaciousness and intelligence that I have rarely seen . . . and a graciousness, too." Marshal extended his hand. "I accept your offer. And with gratitude."

The rest of the transaction was completed quickly. Peter offered to take Marshal in as a partner for any amount up to one percent of the company. Marshal decided, now that he had come this far, to grab the brass ring and invest the maximum: ninety thousand. He would raise the money from selling his Wells Fargo and his Fidelity select electronic stock and wire the money to Peter's Zurich bank within five days. Peter was going to close the purchase of Rucksen in eight days and was required by Dutch law to have all parties listed. Meanwhile Peter would prepare a secured note and leave it off at Marshal's office before he left for Zurich.

Later that afternoon, after Marshal had seen his last patient of the day, there was a knock on his door. A pimpled adolescent bicycle messenger, in a denim jacket with magenta fluorescent armbands and the mandatory San Francisco Giants baseball hat worn backward, handed him a manila envelope containing a notarized letter specifying all the aspects of the transaction. A second note for Marshal's signature specified that he was obligated to request a full repayment of his investment should, for any reason, the value of Rucksen fall below its purchase price. A memo from Peter was also enclosed: "For your full peace of mind, a secured note from my attorney will reach you by Wednesday. Enjoy my celebratory token of our partnership signing."

Marshal reached into the envelope and extracted a Shreve's Jewelry Store box. He opened it, gasped, and gleefully put on his first jewel-spangled Rolex watch.

T E N

*J*ust before six o'clock on a Tuesday evening, Ernest received a phone call from the sister of Eva Galsworth, one of his patients.

"Eva told me to call you and just to say, 'It's time.'"

Ernest wrote a message of apology to his 6:10 patient, taped it to his office door, and rushed to the home of Eva, a fifty-one-year-old woman with advanced ovarian cancer. Eva was a creative writing teacher, a graceful woman of great dignity. Ernest often imagined, with pleasure, living his life side by side with Eva, had she been younger and had they met under different circumstances. He thought her beautiful, admired her deeply, and marveled at her commitment to life. For the past year and a half, he had unstintingly devoted himself to easing the pain of her dying.

With many of his patients, Ernest introduced the concept of regret into his therapy. He asked patients to examine regrets for their past conduct and urged them to avoid future regrets. "The goal," he'd say, "is to live so that five years from now you won't look back on these five years filled with regret."

Occasionally Ernest's "anticipatory regret" strategy fell flat. Generally it proved meaningful. But no patient ever took it more seriously than Eva, who dedicated herself to, as she put it, "sucking the marrow out of the bones of life." Eva packed a great deal into the two years following her diagnosis: she left a joyless marriage, had whirlwind affairs with two men she had long desired, took a wildlife safari in Kenya, finished two short stories, and traveled around the country visiting her three children and some of her favorite former students.

Throughout all these changes, Ernest and she had worked closely and well. Eva regarded Ernest's office as a safe haven, a place to bring all her fears about dying, all the macabre feelings she dared not express to friends. Ernest promised to face everything directly with her, to flinch from nothing, to treat her not as a patient but as a fellow traveler and sufferer.

And Ernest kept his word. He took to scheduling Eva for the last hour of the day because he often ended the hour flooded with anxiety about Eva's death, and his own as well. He reminded her over and over that she was not entirely alone in her dying, that he and she were both facing the terror of finitude, that he would go with her as far as he was humanly able. When Eva asked him to promise he would be with her when she died, Ernest gave his word. She had been too ill for the past two months to come to his office, but Ernest kept in touch by telephone and made occasional home visits, for which he chose not to bill.

Ernest was greeted by Eva's sister and ushered into her bedroom. Eva, heavily jaundiced because her tumor had invaded her liver, was gasping for breath and perspiring so heavily that her soaked hair was plastered to her head. She nodded and in a whisper between breaths told her sister to leave. "I want one more private session with my doctor."

Ernest sat down next to her. "Can you talk?"

"Too late. No more words. Just hold me."

Ernest took Eva's hand, but she shook her head. "No, please, just hold me," she whispered.

Ernest sat on the bed and leaned over to hold her but could find no workable position. There was nothing to do but to get on the bed, lie next to her, and put his arms around her. He kept his suit jacket and shoes on and nervously eyed the door, worried that some misunderstanding person would enter. He felt awkward at first and was grateful for the layers between them—sheet, comforter, coverlet, suit jacket. Eva pulled him to her. Gradually his tension dissipated. He loosened up, took off his jacket, pulled back the comforter, and clutched Eva closely. She clutched back. For an instant he felt an unwelcome warm purring inside, the foreshadowing of sexual arousal, but, furious at himself, managed to banish it and to devote himself to hugging Eva in a loving fashion. After a few minutes he asked: "Is this better, Eva?"

No answer. Eva's breathing had become labored.

Ernest jumped up from the bed, bent over her, and called out her name.

Still no answer. Eva's sister, hearing his call, rushed into the room. Ernest reached for Eva's wrist but could feel no pulse. He put his hand on her chest, gently pressing her heavy breast aside, and felt for an apical pulse. Discovering her heartbeat to be thready and wildly irregular, he pronounced: "Ventricular fibrillation. It's very bad."

The two of them sat vigil for a couple of hours, listening to Eva's heavy, erratic breathing. "Cheyne-Stokes" breathing, Ernest thought, surprised at how the term had floated up from the deep unconscious flotsam of third-year medical school. Eva's eyes trembled from time to time but never reopened. Dry spittle-foam formed continuously on her lips, and Ernest wiped it away with Kleenex every few minutes.

"That's a sign of pulmonary edema," Ernest pronounced. "Because her heart is failing, fluid is accumulating in her lungs."

Eva's sister nodded and looked relieved. Interesting, Ernest thought, how these scientific rituals—naming and explaining phenomena—ease terror. So I give a name to her breathing? So I explain how the weakening left ventricle causes fluid to back in the left auricle and then in the lungs, causing the foam? So what? I've offered nothing! All I've done is to name the beast. But I feel better, her sister feels better, and, if poor Eva were conscious, she'd probably feel better too.

Ernest held Eva's hand as her breathing grew more shallow and irregular and, after about an hour, stopped entirely. Ernest could feel no pulse. "She's gone."

He and Eva's sister sat silently for a few minutes and then began making plans. They generated a list of phone calls to be made—to children, friends, the newspaper, the funeral parlor. After a while Ernest stood to leave, as her sister prepared to wash Eva's body. They briefly discussed how to dress her. She would be cremated, her sister said, and she thought the funeral parlor would supply some type of shroud. Ernest agreed, though he knew nothing whatever about it.

He knew very little about any of this, Ernest thought, on the way home. Despite his lengthy medical experience and cadaver dissection in medical school, he, like many physicians, had never before been present at the actual moment of death. He remained calm and clinical; though he would miss Eva, her death had been mercifully easy. He knew he had done all he could, but he continued to feel the pressure of her body against his chest through a very troubled night.

He awoke just before five in the morning clutching at the remnants of a powerful dream. He did exactly what he always told his patients to do after a disturbing dream: he stayed in bed motionless and recollected the dream before even opening his eyes. Reaching for a pencil and notepad by his bed, Ernest wrote down the dream.

I was walking with my parents and my brother in a mall, and we decided to go upstairs. I found myself on an elevator alone. It was a long, long ride. When I got off, I was by the seashore. But I couldn't find my family. I looked and looked for them. Though it was a lovely setting . . . seashore is paradise . . . I began to feel pervasive dread. Then I started to put on a nightshirt that had a cute, smiling face of Smokey the Bear. That face became brighter, then brilliant . . . soon the face became the entire focus of the dream—as though all the energy of the dream was transferred onto that cute grinning little Smokey the Bear face.

The more Ernest thought about it, the more important this dream appeared. Unable to return to sleep, he dressed and went to his office at six A.M. to enter it into the computer. It was perfect for the chapter on dreams in the new book he was writing, *Death Anxiety and Psychotherapy*. Or perhaps *Psychotherapy, Death, and Anxiety*. Ernest couldn't decide on the title.

There was no mystery about the dream. The events of the previous night made the meaning crystal-clear. Eva's death had hurled him into a confrontation with his own death (represented in the dream by the pervasive dread, by his separation from his family, and by his long elevator ascent to a heavenly seashore). How annoying, Ernest thought, that his own dream-maker had bought into the fairy tale of an ascent to paradise! But what could he do? The dream-maker was its own master, formed in the dawn of consciousness, and obviously shaped more by popular culture than by volition.

The power of the dream resided in the nightshirt with the bright Smokey the Bear emblem. Ernest knew that symbol was prompted by the discussion of how to dress Eva in preparation for cremation— Smokey the Bear representing cremation! Eerie, but instructive.

The more Ernest thought about it, the more useful this dream might be in teaching psychotherapists. For one thing it illustrated a point of Freud's that a primary function of dreams was to preserve sleep. In this instance, a frightening thought—cremation—is transformed into something more benign and pleasing: the adorable, cunning figure of Smokey the Bear. But the dream was only partially successful: though it enabled him to continue sleeping, enough death anxiety seeped out to soak his entire dream in dread.

Ernest wrote for two hours, until Justin arrived for his appointment. He loved writing in the early morning hours, even though it meant he'd be exhausted by early evening.

"Sorry about Monday," said Justin, walking straight to his chair and avoiding eye contact with Ernest. "I can't believe I did that. About ten o'clock, I was on my way to the office, whistling, feeling in a pretty good mood, when suddenly it hit me like a ton of bricks: *I'd forgotten my hour with you.* What can I say? I have no excuses. None at all. Just flat-out forgot. It's never happened before. Do I get charged?"

"Well . . ." Ernest hesitated. He hated to charge a patient for a missed hour, even when, as in this case, it was obviously because of resistance. "Well, Justin, being that, in all our years together, this is the first time you've ever missed . . . uh, Justin, why don't we say that from today on, I'll charge you for missed sessions without twenty-four hours notice."

Ernest could hardly believe his own ears. Did he really say that? How could he *not* charge Justin? He dreaded his next supervision session. Marshal was going to climb all over him about this! Marshal accepted no excuse—auto accident, illness, hailstorm, flash flood, broken leg. He would charge patients if they missed to attend their mother's funeral.

He could hear Marshal now: "You in this to be a nice guy, Ernest? Is that the point? So your patients will one day say to someone, 'Ernest Lash is a nice guy'? Or are you still guilty because you were irritated at Justin for leaving his wife without telling you first? What kind of capricious, inconsistent frame are you providing for therapy?"

Well, there was nothing to be done about it now.

"Let's go into it further, Justin. There's more going on than just missing Monday's session. In our last session, you were a couple of minutes late, and also we've had some silences, long silences, in the last couple of sessions. What do you think is happening?"

"Well," said Justin with uncharacteristic forthrightness, "there'll be no silence today. There's something important I want to talk about: I've decided to raid my home."

Justin, Ernest noted, was speaking differently: he had more directness and less deference in his voice. However, he was still evading a discussion of their relationship. Ernest would come back to that later—for now he was awash in curiosity about Justin's words. "What do you mean, *raid*?"

"Well, Laura feels I should take what belongs to me—no more, no less. Right now I've only got the stuff I crammed into one suitcase the night I left. I've got a huge wardrobe. I've always indulged myself when it comes to clothes—God, the beautiful ties I've got at home; it breaks my heart. Laura thinks it's stupid to go out and buy all kinds of new stuff when I own so much—besides, we need the money for about twenty other things, starting with food and shelter. Laura thinks I should just march right into my own house and take what's mine."

"Big step. How do you feel about that?"

"Well, I think Laura's right. She's so young and unspoiled—and unanalyzed—she brushes aside a lot of crap and sees right into the center of issues."

"And Carol? Her reaction?"

"Well, I've called her twice—about seeing the kids and about getting some of my stuff. I've got some of next month's payroll stuff on my home computer—my dad'll kill me. I didn't tell her about the computer data—she'd trash it." Justin fell silent.

"And?" Ernest was getting in touch with some of the irritation he had felt toward Justin the previous week. After five years of treatment, he shouldn't have to work so goddamn hard tugging out every byte of information.

"Well, Carol was Carol. Before I could say anything, she asked when I was coming home. When I told her I wasn't coming back, she called me a fucking asshole and hung up."

"Carol was Carol, you say."

"You know, it's funny, she's helping me by being her usual bitchy self. After she screamed and hung up, I felt better. Each time I hear her shriek on the phone, I'm more sure I was right to walk out. More and more, I've been thinking what an idiot I was to have thrown away nine years of my life in that marriage."

"Yeah, Justin, I hear your regrets, but the important thing is not to look back, ten years from now, and be overcome with similar regrets. And look at the start you're making! How wonderful that you've left this woman. How wonderful that you've had the courage to take such a step."

"Yeah, Doc, you said it all along: 'avoid future regrets,' 'avoid future regrets.' I used to say it in my sleep. But I couldn't really hear it before."

"Well, Justin, just put it this way, you weren't ready to hear it. And now you're ready to hear it *and* act on it."

"How wonderful," Justin said, "that Laura came along when she did. I can't tell you what a difference it is to be with a woman who actually *likes* me, who even admires me, who's on my side."

Though Ernest was irritated that Justin continually invoked Laura, he had himself under good control—the supervisory session with Marshal had really helped. Ernest knew he had no other recourse than to ally himself with Laura. Still, he didn't want Justin to give away his power completely to her. After all, he had just taken his power back from Carol, and it would be a good thing for him to own it for a while.

"It *is* wonderful that Laura's entered your life, Justin, but I don't want you to downplay yourself in this—*you* made the move, it was *your* feet that walked out of Carol's life. But earlier you said something about a 'raid'?"

"Well, I took Laura's advice and drove over to the house yesterday to pick up my possessions."

Justin noted Ernest's surprise and added: "Don't worry—I haven't completely lost my mind. I phoned first to be sure Carol had left for work. Well, can you believe Carol locked me out of my own house? The witch changed the locks. All night Laura and I talked about what to do. She thinks I ought to pick up a crowbar from one of my dad's stores and go back, bust open the door, and just take what belongs to me. The more I think about it, the more I think she's right."

"Many locked-out husbands have done such things," Ernest said, astounded at Justin's newfound power. He imagined, for a moment, Justin in a black leather jacket and ski mask, crowbar in hand, tearing apart Carol's new house locks. Delicious! Ernest was beginning to like Laura more. Still, reason prevailed: he knew he'd better cover himself because later he'd have to describe this interview to Marshal. "What about the legal consequences, though? Have you considered seeing an attorney?"

"Laura's against any delay: looking for an attorney will just give Carol more time to pillage and destroy my things. Besides, her courtroom viciousness is well known—I'd have a hard time finding an attorney in this city who'd be willing to take her on. You know, this business of getting my things back is not optional: Laura and I are running out of money. I don't have money to pay for anything—and I'm afraid that includes your bill!"

"All the more reason to seek professional legal help. You've told me that Carol earned far more than you—in California that means you're entitled to spousal support."

"You're joking! Can you see Carol paying me spousal support?"

"She's like everyone else; she has to obey the laws of the land."

"Carol will never pay me alimony. She'd take it to the Supreme Court, she'd flush the money down the toilet, she'd go to jail, before paying me."

"Fine, she goes to jail, Justin, and you'd walk in, get your things, your kids, and your house back. Don't you see how unrealistically you view her? Listen to yourself! Listen to what you're saying: Carol's got supernatural powers! Carol inspires so much terror that no attorney in California would dare oppose her! Carol is beyond all law! Justin, we're talking about your wife, not God! Not Al Capone!"

"You don't know her as I do—even after all these years of therapy, you still don't really know her. And my folks aren't much better. If they were paying me a fair salary, I'd be okay. I know, I know, you've been pushing me for years to demand a realistic salary. I should have done it long ago. But now's not the time—they're really pissed at me for all this."

"Pissed? How come?" asked Ernest. "I thought you said they hated Carol."

"Nothing would please them more than never to lay eyes on her again. But she's got them hamstrung: she's holding the kids for ransom. Since I left, she hasn't allowed them to see their grandchildren—not even to talk to them on the phone. She's warned them that if they aid and abet me now, they can kiss their grandchildren good-bye forever. They're quaking in their boots—afraid to do anything to help me."

For the rest of the session, Justin and Ernest talked about the future of their therapy. Missing a session and coming late obviously reflected a diminishing commitment to treatment, Ernest commented. Justin agreed and made it clear that he could no longer afford therapy. Ernest counseled against stopping therapy in the midst of so much upheaval and offered to allow Justin to postpone payment until his finances had straightened out. But Justin, sporting his newly found assertiveness, disagreed because he couldn't foresee his finances straightening out for years—not until his parents died. And Laura felt (and he agreed) that it was not a good idea to begin their new life with a big debt.

But it was not only money. Justin told Ernest that he no longer needed therapy. Talking to Laura provided all the help he needed. Ernest didn't like that, but was assuaged by remembering Marshal's words that Justin's rebellion was a sign of real progress. He accepted Justin's decision to end therapy but gently argued against stopping so suddenly. Justin was obstinate but finally agreed to return for two more sessions.

✕

Most therapists take a ten-minute break between patients and schedule appointments on the hour. Not Ernest—he was far too undisciplined for that, and often started late or ran over the fifty minutes. Ever since he started practice, he had arranged a fifteen- or twenty-minute break between sessions and scheduled patients at odd times: 9:10, 11:20, 2:50. Naturally, Ernest kept this unorthodox practice secret from Marshal, who would have criticized his inability to maintain boundaries.

Generally Ernest used the break time to enter notes in the

patient's chart or to jot down ideas in a journal for his current book project. But he made no notes after Justin left. Ernest simply sat quietly, contemplating Justin's termination. It was an incomplete ending. Though Ernest knew he had helped Justin, he had not taken him far enough. And, of course, it was irritating that Justin attributed his entire improvement to Laura. But somehow that no longer mattered as much to Ernest. His supervision had helped attenuate those feelings. He must be sure to tell Marshal that. Individuals as supremely self-confident as Marshal usually get few strokes—most people don't think they need anything. But Ernest had a hunch he would appreciate some feedback.

Despite his wish that he might have taken Justin a bit further, Ernest was not displeased with the termination. Five years was enough. He was not made for holding chronic patients. He was an adventurer, and when patients lost the appetite to strike out for new, unexplored territory, Ernest lost interest in them. And Justin had never been the exploring kind. Yes, it was true that, finally, Justin had broken his chains and liberated himself from that abomination of a marriage. But Ernest gave Justin little credit for that move—that wasn't Justin but a new entity: Justin-Laura. When Laura vanished, as she was sure to, Ernest suspected Justin would be stuck with the same old Justin.

ELEVEN

*T*he following afternoon, Ernest hastily scribbled some clinical notes before Carolyn Leftman arrived for her second session. It had been a long day, but Ernest wasn't tired: he was always invigorated by doing good therapy and, so far, he was satisfied with his day.

At least satisfied with four of his five patient hours. The fifth patient, Brad, used the time, as he always did, to give a detailed, and boring, report of his week's activities. Many such patients seemed constitutionally unable to use therapy. After failing in every attempt to guide him to deeper levels, Ernest began to suggest that another approach to therapy, perhaps a behavioral one, might offer Brad more help for his chronic anxiety and crippling procrastination. However, each time he began to utter the words, Brad would gratuitously comment on how enormously helpful this therapy had been, how his panic attacks had subsided, and how much he treasured his work with Ernest.

Ernest was no longer satisfied with containing Brad's anxiety. He had grown as impatient with Brad as he had been with Justin. Ernest's criteria of good therapy work had changed: now he was satisfied only if his patients revealed themselves, took risks, broke new ground, and, more than anything else, were willing to focus on and explore the "in-betweenness"—the space between patient and therapist.

At their last supervisory session, Marshal had chided Ernest for his chutzpah in thinking that a focus on the in-betweenness was something original; for the last eight decades analysts had been focusing microscopically on the transference, on the patient's irrational feelings toward the therapist.

But Ernest would not be squelched and doggedly continued to take notes for a journal article on the therapeutic relationship entitled *In-betweenness—The Case for Authenticity in Therapy*. Despite Marshal, he was convinced he was bringing something new into therapy by focusing not on the transference—the unreal, distorted relationship—but on the *authentic, real* relationship between himself and the patient.

Ernest's evolving approach demanded that he reveal more of himself to patients, that he and the patient focus on their real relationship—the *we* in the therapy office. He had long thought that the work of therapy consists of understanding and removing all the obstacles that diminish that relationship. Ernest's radical self-disclosure experiment with Carolyn Leftman was simply the next logical step in the evolution of his new approach to therapy.

Not only was Ernest pleased with his day's work, but he had received a special bonus: patients had described to him two chilling dreams that, with their permission, he might use in his book on death anxiety. He still had five minutes before Carolyn was due to arrive, and he turned on his computer to enter the dreams.

The first was only a snippet:

I came to your office for an appointment. You weren't there. I looked around and saw your straw hat on the hat rack—it was all filled with cobwebs. An oppressive wave of great sadness came over me.

Madeline, the dreamer, had breast cancer and had just learned that it had spread to her spine. In Madeline's dream the target of death shifts: it is not *she* who is faced with death and decay but the therapist, who has disappeared and left behind only his cobweb-filled hat. Or, Ernest thought, the dream might reflect her sense of loss of world: if her consciousness is responsible for the form and shape and meaning of all "objective" reality—her entire, personally meaningful world—then the extinguishing of her consciousness would result in the disappearance of everything.

Ernest was accustomed to working with dying patients. But this particular image—his beloved Panama hat encased in cobwebs—sent a shiver down his spine.

Matt, a sixty-four-year-old physician, supplied the other dream:

I was hiking along a high cliff on the Big Sur coast and came upon a small river running into the Pacific. As I got closer I was amazed to see that the river was flowing away from the ocean, running backwards. Then I saw an old stooped man, who resembled my father, standing alone and broken in front of a river cave. I couldn't get closer to him since there was no trail down, so I continued following the river from on high. A short while later I came upon another man, even more stooped, perhaps my grandfather. I couldn't find a way to get to him, either, and woke up unsettled and frustrated.

Matt's greatest fear was not of death per se but of dying alone. His father, a chronic alcoholic, had died a few months previously and, though they had had a long, conflicted relationship, Matt could not forgive himself for allowing his father to die alone. He feared that his destiny, too, would be to die alone and homeless, as had all the men in his family. Often, when he was overcome with anxiety in the middle of the night, Matt soothed himself by sitting next to his eight-year-old son's bed and listening to him breathing. He was drawn to a fantasy of swimming in the ocean, far from shore, with his two children, who lovingly help him slip beneath the waves forever. But, since he had not helped his father or his grandfather die, he wondered if he deserved such children.

A river flowing backward! The river, carrying pinecones and brown brittle oak leaves, running *uphill*, away from the ocean. A river flowing backward to the golden age of childhood and the reunion of the primeval family. What an extraordinary visual image for time turned backward, for the yearning for an escape from the fate of aging and diminishment! Ernest was full of admiration for the latent artist in all his patients; often he wanted to doff his hat in homage to the unconscious dream-maker who, night after night, year after year, spun masterpieces of illusion.

In the waiting room on the other side of the wall, Carol wrote also: notes of her first therapy session with Ernest. She stopped and reread her words:

FIRST SESSION
Feb. 12, 1995

Dr. Lash—inappropriately informal. Intrusive. Insisted, over my protests, that I call him Ernest . . . touched me in the first thirty seconds—my elbow, as I entered the room . . . very gentle—touched me again, my hand, when he handed me a tissue . . . took history of my major problems and my family history . . . pressed hard for repressed sexual abuse memories in first session! Too much, too fast—I felt overwhelmed and confused! Revealed his personal feelings to me . . . tells me it's important that we get very close . . . invites me to ask him questions about himself . . . promises to reveal all about himself . . . expressed approval of my affair with Dr. Cooke . . . ran ten minutes over the hour . . . insisted on giving me a good-bye hug . . .

She felt satisfied. *These notes will come in very handy,* she thought. *Not sure how. But someday, someone—Justin, my mal-practice attorney, the state ethics board—will find them of great interest.* Carol closed her notebook. She needed to get focused for her session with Ernest. After the events of the last twenty-four hours, she wasn't thinking too well.

She had come home yesterday to find a note from Justin taped to the front door: "*I came back for my things.*" The back door had been pried open, and he had taken everything that she had not yet destroyed: his racquetball racquets, clothing, toiletries, shoes, books, as well as some jointly owned possessions—books, camera, binoculars, portable CD player, most of their CD collection, and several pots, pans, and glasses. He had even pried open her cedar chest and taken his computer.

In a frenzy Carol had called Justin's parents to tell them she intended to see Justin behind bars and that she would put them in the next cage if they, in any way, aided their felon son. Phone calls to Norma and Heather were of no help—made things worse, in fact. Norma was preoccupied with her own marital crisis, and Heather, in her annoying, gentle way, reminded her that Justin had the right to his own things. No breaking-and-entering charge could be filed— it was his own home and she had no legal right to change the locks or attempt to exclude him in any other fashion without a restraining order.

Carol knew Heather was right. She hadn't secured an order from the court restraining Justin from entering the premises because never—not in her wildest dreams—could she imagine him taking such action.

As if the missing objects were not bad enough, when she dressed that morning she found the crotch neatly cut out of all her underpants. And just so there could be no confusion about how it had happened, Justin had left, in each pair, a small section of one of the neckties she had sliced and thrown back into his closet.

Carol was stunned. This was not Justin. Not the Justin she knew. No, there was no way Justin could do that alone. He didn't have the guts. Or the imagination. Only one way it could have happened . . . only one person who could have orchestrated this: Ernest Lash! She looked up and there he was in the flesh—nodding his fat head to her and inviting her into his office! *Whatever it takes, you son of a bitch,* Carol resolved, *however long it takes, whatever I have to do, I am going to put you out of business.*

"So," Ernest said after he and Carol were seated, "what seems important today?"

"So many things. I need a moment to collect my thoughts. I'm not sure why I'm feeling so agitated."

"Yes, I see from your face there's a lot going on inside today."

Oh, brilliant, brilliant, you asshole, Carol thought.

"But I'm having a hard time reading you, Carolyn," Ernest continued. "Somewhat perturbed, perhaps. Somewhat sad."

"Ralph, my late therapist, used to say there were four basic feelings . . . "

"Yes," Ernest rushed in quickly, "bad, sad, mad, and glad. That's a good mnemonic."

Good mnemonic? This field is a real brain trust—a one-syllable profession, Carol thought. *You fuckers are all alike!* "I guess I've been feeling some of each, Ernest."

"How so, Carolyn?"

"Well, 'mad' at the bad breaks of my life—at some of the things we discussed last time: my brother, my father, especially. And 'bad'—anxious—when I think of the trap I'm in now, waiting for my husband to die. And 'sad' . . . I guess 'sad' when I think of the years I wasted on a bad marriage."

"And glad?"

"That's the easy one—'glad' when I think about you and about how lucky I was to find you. Thinking about you and about seeing you today was the main thing keeping me going this week."

"Can you say more about that?"

Carol took her purse out of her lap, placed it on the floor, and gracefully crossed her long legs. "I'm afraid you're going to make me blush." She paused, demurely, thinking: *Perfect! But slow, play it slow, Carol.* "The truth is, I've been having daydreams all week about you. Sexy daydreams. But you're probably used to your women patients finding you attractive."

Ernest was flustered at the thought of Carolyn having daydreams, probably masturbatory fantasies, about him. He considered how to respond—how to respond *honestly.*

"*Aren't* you used to it, Ernest? You said I should ask you questions."

"Carolyn, there's something about your question that makes me uncomfortable, and I'm trying to figure out why. I think it's because it assumes that what happens here between us is something standardized—something predictable."

"I'm not sure I understand."

"Well, I consider you unique. And your life situation unique. And this meeting between you and me unique. Therefore, a question about what *always* happens seems off somehow."

Carol screwed her eyes into a starry-eyed gaze.

Ernest savored his own words. *What a great answer! I must try to remember it—it'll fit right into my 'in-betweenness' article.* Ernest also realized, however, that he had steered the session into abstract, impersonal territory, and hastened to correct that: "But, Carolyn, I'm getting away from your real question . . . which is . . . ?"

"Which is how you feel about my finding you attractive," replied Carol. "I've been spending so much time thinking about you this past week . . . of what it might be like if we had, by chance—perhaps at

one of your readings—met as man and woman instead of as therapist and client. I know I should talk about it but it's hard . . . it's
embarrassing . . . maybe you'll find it—I mean *me*—repugnant. I *feel*
repugnant."

Very, very good, Carol thought. *Damn, I'm good at this!*

"Well, Carolyn, I promised honest answers. And the truth is, it's
very pleasant for me to hear that a woman—a very attractive
woman, I might add—finds me attractive. Like most people, I have
doubts about my physical attractiveness."

Ernest paused. *My heart is racing. I've never said anything so personal to a patient. I liked telling her she was attractive—gave me a
charge. Probably a mistake. Too seductive. Yet she regards herself as
repugnant. She doesn't know she is a good-looking woman. Why
not offer her some affirmation, some reality testing, about her
appearance?*

Carol, for her part, was elated—for the first time in weeks. *"A
very attractive woman." Bingo! I remember Ralph Cooke uttering
the same words. That was his first move. And it was the exact words
that disgusting Dr. Zweizung had used. Thank God I had enough
sense to call him a scumbag and walk out of that office. But both of
them are probably still at it with other victims. If only I had had the
sense to get evidence, to blow the whistle on those bastards. Now I
can make up for it. If only I had brought a tape recorder in my
purse. Next time! I just didn't believe he'd be so lascivious so soon.*

"But," Ernest continued, "to be fully honest with you, I don't
take your words too personally. There may be a little of me in your
words but, to a much greater extent, you're not responding to me;
you're responding to my role."

Carol was taken aback. "What do you mean?"

"Well, move back a few steps. Let's look dispassionately at recent
events. You've had some awful things happen to you; you've kept
everything inside, sharing little with anyone. You've had disastrous
relationships with the important men in your life, one after the
other—your father, your brother, your husband, and . . . Rusty,
wasn't it? Your high school boyfriend. And the one man you felt
good about, your former therapist, abandoned you by dying.

"And then you come to see me and, for the first time, take a risk
and share everything with me. Given all that, Carolyn, is it surprising that you develop some strong feelings toward me? I don't think
so. That's what I mean when I say it's the role, not me. And also

those powerful feelings toward Dr. Cooke? It's not surprising that I inherit some of those feelings—I mean, they get transferred to me."

"I agree with that last part, Ernest. I *am* starting to feel the same feelings toward you as I did toward Dr. Cooke."

A brief silence. Carol gazed at Ernest. Marshal would have waited it out. Not Ernest.

"We've discussed the 'glad,'" said Ernest, "and I appreciate your honesty there. Could we take a look at the other three feelings? Let's see, you said 'mad' at the circumstances of your past—especially the men in your life; 'bad' at the trap in which you find yourself with your husband; and 'sad,' because . . . because . . . remind me, Carolyn."

Carol flushed. She had forgotten her own story. "I've forgotten myself what I said—I'm too agitated to concentrate well." *This won't do,* she thought. *I have got to stay in my role. Only one way to avoid these slips—I've got to be honest about myself—except, of course, about Justin.*

"Oh, I remember," said Ernest: "'sad' because of the accumulated regrets in your life—'the years wasted,' I think you put it. You know, Carolyn, that mnemonic of 'mad, sad, glad, and bad' is pretty simplistic—you're obviously an intelligent woman and I fear insulting your intelligence: yet it *was* useful today. The issues associated with each of these four feelings are absolutely core—let's pursue them."

Carol nodded. She felt disappointed that they had moved so quickly away from his comments about her being attractive. *Patience,* she reminded herself. *Remember Ralph Cooke. This is their modus operandi. First they win your confidence; next they make you totally dependent and themselves absolutely indispensable. And only then do they make their move. There's no way to avoid this charade. Give him a couple of weeks. We have to go through it at his pace.*

"How shall we start?" asked Ernest.

"Sad," said Carolyn, "sad to think of all the years I've spent with a man I can't stand."

"Nine years," said Ernest. "A big chunk of your life."

"A very big chunk. I wish I had it back."

"Carolyn, let's try to find out why you gave away nine years."

"I've done a lot of rummaging around in the past with other therapists. Never helped. Won't looking at the past take us away from my present situation, my dilemma?"

"Good question, Carolyn. Trust me, I'm not a rummager. Nonetheless, the past is part of your present consciousness—it forms the spectacles through which you experience the present. If I'm to know you fully, I need to see what you see. I also want to find out how you've made decisions in the past, so we can help you make better decisions in the future."

Carol nodded. "I understand."

"So, tell me about your marriage. How did it come about that you decided to marry and stay married for nine years to a man you detested?"

Carol followed her plan of staying close to the truth, and gave Ernest an honest history of her marriage, changing only geography and any factual details that might alert Ernest's suspicion.

"I met Wayne before I graduated from law school. I was working as a clerk in an Evanston law firm and assigned to a case representing Wayne's father's business, a highly successful chain of shoe stores. I spent a lot of time with Wayne—he was good-looking, gentle, devoted, contemplative, and poised to take over his father's five-million-dollar business in a year or two. I had no money at all and had accumulated enormous student loans. I made a quick decision to marry. It was a very stupid decision."

"How so?"

"After a few months of marriage, I began to see Wayne's qualities in more realistic ways. 'Gentle' I soon learned was not kindness, but cowardice. 'Contemplative' became monstrous indecision. 'Devoted' turned into clinging dependency. And 'rich' turned to ashes when his father's shoe business went bankrupt three years later."

"And the good looks?"

"A good-looking, poor male dolt plus a dollar fifty buys you a cup of cappuccino. It was a bad decision in every way—a life-wrecking decision."

"What do you know about making that decision?"

"Well, I know what it followed. I told you that my high school sweetheart, Rusty, dumped me in my sophomore year of college with no explanation. Throughout law school I kept steady company with Michael. We were a dream team; Michael was second in the class . . . "

"How did that make you a dream team?" Ernest interrupted. "Were you a good student also?"

"Well, we had a bright future. He was second in the class and I was first. But Michael ended up dumping me to marry the airhead daughter of the senior partner of New York's largest corporate law firm. And then, during my summer internship at the district court, there was Ed, an influential assistant to a district court justice, who tutored me on his office couch in the nude almost every afternoon. But he wouldn't be seen in public with me and, after the summer was over, never responded to my letters or calls. I hadn't gotten close to a man for a year and a half when I met Wayne. I guess marrying him was a rebound decision."

"What I'm aware of is a long skein of men who have betrayed you or abandoned you: your father, Jed—"

"Jeb. It's a *b.*" *B, b, b, you jerk,* Carol thought. She forced a friendly smile. "Think of *b* for brother—a two-syllable mnemonic. Or for betrayer, or bullshitter, or butcher."

"Sorry, Carolyn. *Jeb,* Dr. Cooke, and Rusty, and then today we add Michael and Ed. That's quite a list! I guess when Wayne came along you must have been relieved to find someone who seemed safe and reliable."

"No danger of Wayne abandoning me—he was so clinging, he was scarcely willing to go to the bathroom without me."

"Maybe 'clinging' had an allure to it at the time. And this skein of male losers? Is it an unbroken skein? I haven't heard of any exceptions, any men who were good for you. And good to you."

"There was just Ralph Cooke." Carol hastened to move into the safety of deception. A few moments before, as he listed the men who had betrayed her, Ernest was beginning to stir up painful emotions just as he had last session. She realized she had to be on guard. She had never appreciated how seductive therapy was. And how treacherous.

"And he died on you," said Ernest.

"And now there's you. Are you going to be good to me?"

Before Ernest could answer, Carol smiled and posed another question: "And how's *your* health?"

Ernest smiled. "My health is excellent, Carolyn. I plan on being around a long time."

"And my other question?"

Ernest looked at Carol quizzically.

"Will you be good to me?"

Ernest hesitated, then chose his words carefully: "Yes, I will try to

be as helpful as I can. You can count on that. You know, I'm thinking of your comment that you were law school valedictorian. I had
to almost tug it out of you. First in the class at the University of
Chicago Law School—that's no mean achievement, Carolyn. You
take pride in that?"

Carol shrugged her shoulders.

"Carolyn, humor me. Please tell me again: How did you do
scholastically in the University of Chicago Law School?"

"Did pretty well."

"How well?"

Silence and then, in a small voice, Carol said, "I was first in my
class."

"Come again. How well?" Ernest cupped his ear with his hand to
indicate he could barely hear.

"First in my class," Carol said loudly. And added, "And editor of
the law review. And no one else, including Michael, was even close
to me." And then she burst out crying.

Ernest handed her a Kleenex, waited until the heaving of her
shoulders subsided, and then gently asked: "Can you put some of
those tears into words?"

"Do you know, do you have *any* idea, what vistas were open to
me then? I could have done anything—I had a dozen good offers—
I could have picked my firm. I could even have done international
law, since I had a good offer to work in the general counsel's office
of the U.S. Agency for International Development. I could be doing
something very influential in governmental policy. Or if I had gone
to a prestigious Wall Street firm, I'd be earning five hundred thousand dollars a year now. Instead, look at me: doing family law, wills,
two-bit tax work—and earning peanuts. I've squandered everything."

"For Wayne?"

"For Wayne and also for Mary, who was born ten months after
our wedding. I love her dearly, but she was part of the trap."

"Tell me more about the trap."

"What I really wanted to do was international law, but how can
you do international work when you have a young child and a husband who's too immature even to be a decent househusband—a husband who freaks out if he's left alone a single night, who can't decide
what to wear in the morning without a consultation with me first?
So I settled for less, turned down my opportunities, and took an

offer from a smaller firm to stay in Evanston so that Wayne would be near his father's headquarters."

"How long ago did you realize your mistake, did you know, really know, what you had gotten into?"

"Hard to say. I had my suspicions within the first couple of years, but there was an incident—the great camping debacle—that removed even the shadow of a doubt. That was about five years ago."

"Tell me about that."

"Well, Wayne decided the family should indulge in America's favorite pastime: a camping trip. I once almost died, in my teens, from a bee sting—anaphylactic shock—and I have malignant poison-oak reactions; so there was no way I could go camping. I suggested a dozen other trips: canoeing, snorkeling, inland waterway trip to Alaska, sailing in the San Juans, Caribbean, or Maine—I'm a good sailor. But Wayne decided his whole manhood was at stake and would have nothing else but a camping trip."

"But how could he expect you to go camping with a bee sting sensitivity? He expected you to put your life at risk?"

"He could only see that I was trying to control him. We fought pitched battles. I told him I would never go, and then he insisted on taking Mary without me. I had no problem with his going back-packing and urged him to go with some male friends—but he had no friends. I felt it was unsafe for him to take Mary—she was only four. He's so inept, so cowardly, that I feared for her safety. I believe he wanted Mary there for his protection rather than vice versa. But he wouldn't budge. Finally he wore me down and I agreed.

"And that's when things got bizarre," Carol continued. "First he decided he had to get in shape and lose ten pounds—thirty pounds would have been more to the point. Incidentally that's the answer to your question about good looks: he blimped up soon after our wedding. He started going to the gym daily to lift weights and lose weight, which he did, but then he threw out his back and gained the weight back. He'd get so anxious, he'd often hyperventilate. Once, at the dinner honoring me when I made full partner in our firm, I had to leave to take him to the emergency room. So much for the macho camping trip. That's when the horror of my mistake fully dawned on me."

"Whew, what a story, Carolyn." Ernest was struck by the similarities between this account and Justin's story about his backpacking fiasco with his wife and twins. Fascinating to hear two such similar stories—but from very different perspectives.

"But tell me, when you really realized your mistake—let's see, how long ago was that camping trip? You say your daughter was four?"

"About five years ago." Every few minutes Carol pulled herself up short; despite loathing Ernest, she found herself engaged in his inquiry. *Amazing,* she thought, *how bewitching the therapy process becomes. They can hook you in an hour or two, and once they have you they can do as they wish—get you coming every day, charge you what they wish, fuck you on their rug and even charge you for that. Maybe it's too dangerous to play myself honestly. But I have no other option—if I invented a persona, I'd be tripped up time and again by my own lies. This guy's a prick, but he's no dummy. No, I have to play myself. But careful. Careful.*

"So then, Carolyn, five years ago you realized your mistake—yet you stayed in the marriage nonetheless! Maybe there were more positive parts of the marriage you haven't discussed yet."

"No, it was a hideous marriage. I had no love for Wayne. Nor respect. Nor he for me. I got nothing from him." Carol dabbed at her eyes. "What kept me in the marriage? Christ, I don't know! Habit, fear, my daughter—though Wayne has never bonded to her—I'm not sure . . . the cancer and my promise to Wayne . . . nowhere else to go—I've had no other offers."

"Offers? From men, you mean?"

"Well, no offers from men, for sure, and, please, Ernest, let's talk about that today—I've got to do something about my sexual feelings—I'm starving, I'm desperate in that area. But that's not what I meant just then—I meant no interesting professional offers. Not like those golden offers I had when I was young."

"Yes, those golden offers. You know, I'm still thinking of your tears a few minutes ago when we talked about being first in your class and about the unlimited career vista ahead of you . . . "

Carol steeled herself. *He's trying to get back in,* she thought. *Once they find the vulnerable area, they keep drilling into it.*

"There's a lot of pain in there," Ernest continued, "about what your life could have been. I was thinking of that wonderful Whittier lyric: 'of all sad words of tongue or pen, / The saddest are these: "It might have been."'"

Oh, no, Carol thought. *Spare me. Now it's poetry. He's pulling out all the stops. Next, he'll tune up the old guitar.*

"And," Ernest continued, "you gave up all those possibilities for a life with Wayne. A bad bargain—no wonder you try not to think about it . . . you see the pain that comes up when we face it head-on? I think that's why you haven't left Wayne—it would have put the stamp of reality on it. There would have been no denying any longer that you gave up so much, your whole future, for so little."

Despite herself, Carol shivered. Ernest's interpretation rang true. *Goddamnit, get off my case, will you? Who asked you to pontificate on my life?* "Maybe you're right. But that's over; how can this help now? This is exactly what I meant by rummaging around in the past. What's past is past."

"Is it, Carolyn? I don't think so. I don't think it's just that you made a bad decision in the past: I think you're still making bad choices. Right now in your life today."

"What choice do I have? Abandon a dying husband?"

"It feels stark like that, I know. But that's the way bad choices are always set up—by convincing yourself that there's no other choice to be made. Maybe that might be one of our goals."

"What do you mean?"

"Helping you to understand that maybe there are more possible choices, a wider range of choices."

"No, Ernest, it still comes down to the same thing. There are only two choices: I either abandon Wayne or stay with him. Right?"

Carol regained her composure: this invented Wayne was far removed from Justin. Still, watching Ernest try to help her leave him revealed his methods of brainwashing Justin into leaving her.

"No, not at all. You're making a lot of assumptions that aren't necessarily true. For example, that you and Wayne will always have contempt for each other. You've omitted the possibility that people may change. The confrontation with death is a great catalyst for change—for him, possibly for you. Possibly marital couple therapy might help—you mentioned you haven't tried that. Maybe there's some buried love that you or he might rediscover. After all, you have lived together and raised a child for nine years. How would it be for you if you left him or if he died and you knew you might have tried harder to improve things in your marriage? I'm certain you'd be better off feeling that you've left no stone unturned.

"And another way to look at it," Ernest continued, "is to question your basic assumption that accompanying him to the very end of his life is a good thing. Is that necessarily true? I wonder."

"It's better than for him to die alone."

"Is it?" Ernest asked. "Is it a good thing for Wayne to die in the presence of one who holds him in contempt? And still another possibility is to keep in mind that divorce need not be synonymous with abandonment. Is it not possible to imagine a scenario in which you build a different life for yourself, even with another man, and still do not abandon Wayne? You might even be able to be more present with him if you didn't resent him so much for being part of the trap. You see, there are all sorts of possibilities."

Carol nodded, wishing he would stop. Ernest looked like he could go on forever. She looked at her watch.

"You look at your watch, Carolyn. Can you put that into words?" Ernest smiled slightly as he recalled the supervisory session in which Marshal confronted him with the identical words.

"Well, our time is almost up," said Carol, dabbing at her eyes, "and there are other things I wanted to talk about today."

Ernest was chagrined to think he had been so directive that his patient had not been able to address her own agenda. He moved quickly. "A few minutes ago, Carolyn, you mentioned the sexual pressure you were experiencing. Is that one of the things?"

"It's the main thing. I'm out of my mind with frustration—I'm sure it's the root of all this anxiety. Our sex life was not much before but, since Wayne had his prostate surgery, he's been impotent. I understand that's not uncommon after surgery." Carol had done her homework.

Ernest nodded. And waited.

"So, Ernest . . . you sure it's okay to call you Ernest?"

"If I call you Carolyn, you must call me Ernest."

"All right, *Ernest* it is. So, Ernest, what should I do? Lots of sexual energy and nowhere to direct it."

"Tell me about you and Wayne. Even though he's impotent, there are still ways for you and him to be together."

"If by 'being together' you're thinking of some way for him to get me off, forget it. There's no solution there. Our sex life was over long before the surgery. That was one of the reasons I wanted to leave him. Now I'm completely turned off by any kind of physical contact with him. And he couldn't be less interested himself. He's never found me attractive—said I'm too thin, too bony. Now he tells me to go out and get laid somewhere."

"And?" asked Ernest.

"Well, I don't know what to do and how to do it. Or where to go. I'm in a strange city. I know no one. I'm not about to go into a bar to get picked up. It's a jungle out there. Dangerous. I'm sure you'd agree that the last thing in the world I need is to be abused again by a man."

"That's for sure, Carolyn."

"Are you single, Ernest? Divorced? The jacket of your book mentions no wife."

Ernest drew a breath. He had never talked about his wife's death to a patient. Now his commitment to self-disclosure was going to be put to the test. "My wife was killed six years ago in an auto accident."

"Oh, I'm sorry. That must have been hard."

Ernest nodded. "Hard . . . yes."

Dishonest. Dishonest, he thought. *Though it's true that Ruth was killed six years ago, it's also true that my marriage would never have lasted anyway. But does she need to know that? Stay with what will help the patient.*

"So, you're also struggling in the singles world now?" Carol asked.

Ernest felt jammed. This woman was unpredictable. He had not anticipated such rough sailing for his maiden voyage of total disclosure, and was strongly tempted to head for the calm waters of analytic neutrality. He knew that course by rote: it would be simple enough to say, "I wonder why you're asking these questions," or "I wonder what your fantasies are about my being in the singles world." But such devious neutrality, such inauthenticity, was precisely what Ernest had vowed to avoid.

What to do? He wouldn't be surprised if next she inquired into his dating strategies. For a moment he imagined Carolyn, a few months or years hence, telling some other therapist about Dr. Ernest Lash's approach to therapy: "Oh, yes, Dr. Lash often discussed his personal problems and his techniques of meeting single women."

Yes, the more Ernest thought about it, the more he realized that herein lay a major problem of therapist self-disclosure. *The patient has confidentiality, but the therapist has none!* Nor can a therapist demand it: if patients enter therapy in the future with someone else, they absolutely must have the freedom to discuss everything, including the quirks of their former therapists. And though therapists can be trusted to protect the confidentiality of the patient, they often gossip among themselves about the foibles of colleagues.

Several weeks ago, for example, Ernest referred the wife of one of his patients to another therapist, a friend named Dave. Recently the same patient requested another referral for his wife; she had terminated therapy with Dave because of his habit of *smelling her* as a way of apprehending her mood! Ordinarily Ernest would have been horrified at this behavior and would never again have referred a patient to him. But Dave was such a good friend that Ernest asked him what had happened. Dave said that the patient had left therapy because of her anger at him for refusing to prescribe Valium, which she had secretly been abusing for years. "And what about smelling?" Dave was at first bewildered but, a few minutes later, remembered one occasion when, early in therapy, he made a casual compliment about a new, particularly heavy perfume she was wearing.

Ernest added another item to his rules of disclosure: *reveal yourself to the extent that it will be helpful to your patient; but if you want to stay in practice, have a care about how your self-disclosure will sound to other therapists.*

"So you too are struggling in the singles world," Carol repeated.

"I'm single but not struggling," Ernest responded. "Not at the moment, at least." Ernest strove for an engaging, yet nonchalant smile.

"I wish you would tell me more about how *you* deal with the singles life in San Francisco."

Ernest hesitated. There's a difference between spontaneity and impulsivity, he reminded himself. He must not, willy-nilly, respond to every question. "Carolyn, I'd like you to tell me more about why you're asking this question. I made you a couple of promises: to be as helpful as I possibly can—that's primary—and, in the service of that, to be as honest as possible. So now, from the standpoint of my primary objective—being helpful to you—let's try to understand your question: tell me, what is it that you're really asking me? And why?"

Not bad, Ernest thought, *not bad at all.* To be transparent does not mean to be a slave to all the patient's whims and flights of curiosity. Ernest jotted down his response to Carolyn; it was too good to lose—he could use it in his journal article.

Carol was prepared for his question and had silently rehearsed this sequence. "I would feel more completely understood by you if I knew that you were dealing with similar issues. And especially if you have passed through them successfully. I can experience you as more like me."

"That makes sense, Carolyn. But there must be more to your question, since I've already said that I'm dealing—and dealing satisfactorily—with being single."

"I was hoping you could give me direct guidance—point me in the right direction. I'm feeling really paralyzed—to be honest, I'm horny and terrified at the same time."

Ernest looked at his watch. "You know, Carolyn, we're out of time. Before our next session, let me suggest you work on developing a series of options to meet men and then we'll consider the pros and cons of each. I'm very uncomfortable giving you concrete suggestions or, as you put it, 'pointing you in the right direction.' Take my word for it—I've been through it countless times: that type of direct guidance rarely proves helpful to the patient. What's good for me or someone else may not be good for you."

Carol felt thwarted and angry. *You smug, self-righteous bastard,* she thought. *I'm not going to end this hour without some definite progress.* "Ernest, I'm going to have a hard time waiting for another whole week. Could we schedule something earlier; I need to see you more often. Remember, I'm a good cash customer." She opened up her purse and counted out a hundred and fifty dollars.

Ernest was disconcerted by Carol's comment about money. *Customer* seemed a particularly ugly word: he disliked facing any part of the commercial aspect of psychotherapy. "Oh . . . ah . . . Carolyn, that's not necessary . . . I know you paid cash at the first session, but from now on I'd prefer sending you a bill at the end of each month. And actually I'd prefer a check to cash—easier for my primitive bookkeeping methods. I know a check is less convenient because you don't want Wayne to know that you're seeing me, but perhaps a cashier's check?"

Ernest opened up his appointment book. The only time slot available was Justin's newly vacated eight A.M. hour which Ernest wanted to reserve for writing. "Let's play this by ear, Carolyn. I'm pressed for time at the moment. Wait a day or so and if you feel like you absolutely must see me before next week, give me a call and I'll make time. Here's my card; leave a message on my voice mail and I'll call back and leave an appointment time."

"It's awkward if you call. I'm still not working and my husband's always home . . . "

"Right. Here, I'll write my home number on the card. You can generally reach me there between nine and eleven in the evening." Unlike many of his colleagues, Ernest had no concerns about giving out his home number. He had learned long ago that, in general, the easier it was for anxious patients to reach him, the less likely they were to call.

As she was leaving the office, Carol played the last card in her hand. She turned to Ernest and gave him a hug, a little longer, a little tighter, than the last one. Sensing his body tensing up, she commented: "Thank you, Ernest. I needed that hug if I'm going to get through another whole week. I need to be touched so bad, I can hardly stand it."

As she descended the stairs Carol wondered, *Is it my imagination or is my pigeon taking the bait? He got into that hug just a bit?* She was halfway down when the ivory-sweatered jogger came flying up the stairs, almost knocking her over. He grasped her arm firmly to steady her, lifted his white yachting cap by the bill, and flashed a brilliant smile at Carol. "Hey, we meet again. Sorry for almost running you over. I'm Jess. We seem to share a shrink. Thanks for keeping him over the hour; otherwise he'd be interpreting my lateness half the session. He in good form today?"

Carol stared at his mouth. Never had she seen such perfect white teeth. "Good form? Yeah, he's in good form. You'll see. Oh, I'm Carol." She turned to watch Jess bound up the remaining stairs two at a time. *Great buns!*

TWELVE

On Thursday morning a few minutes before nine, Shelly closed his racing form and tapped his foot impatiently in Marshal Streider's waiting room. Once he was finished with Dr. Streider, he had a good day ahead of him. First, some tennis with Willy and his kids, who were home for Easter break. Willy's kids played so well now that it felt less like coaching and more like competitive doubles. Then lunch at Willy's club: some of those langoustines grilled with butter and anise or perhaps that soft shell crab sushi. And then to Bay Meadows with Willy for the sixth race. Ting-a-ling, Willy and Arnie's horse, was running in the Santa Clara stakes. (Ting-a-ling was the name of Shelly's favorite poker game: a high-low five-card stud game where a sixth card could be bought at the end for two hundred and fifty dollars.)

Shelly had little use for shrinks. But he felt well disposed to Streider. Though he had yet to meet him, Streider had already served him well. When Norma—who, despite everything, really loved him—

came home the night after receiving his faxes, she was so grateful not to have to end the marriage that she leaped into Shelly's arms and tugged him into the bedroom. They pledged vows again: Shelly to make good use of therapy for help with his gambling habit, and Norma to give Shelly an occasional day of rest from her voracious sexual demands.

Now, thought Shelly, *all I have to do is go through the motions with this Dr. Streider and I'm home free. But maybe there's an angle. There's got to be something. As long as I've got to put in the time, probably several hours, to humor Norma—and to humor the shrink, too—maybe there's some real use I can make of this guy.*

The door opened. Marshal introduced himself, shook hands, and invited him in. Shelly buried his racing form in his newspaper, entered the office, and began appraising its contents.

"Quite a collection of glass you got there, Doc!" Shelly gestured toward the Musler pieces. "I like that big orange guy. You mind if I touch it?"

Shelly had already risen and at Marshal's be-my-guest gesture stroked the Golden Rim of Time. "Cool. Very soothing. I bet you have patients who'd like to take that home. And that jagged rim— you know, it looks something like the Manhattan skyline! And those glasses? Old, eh?"

"Very old, Mr. Merriman. About two hundred and fifty years. You like them?"

"Well, I like old wine. I don't know about old glasses. Valuable, eh?"

"Hard to say. There's hardly a booming market in antique sherry glasses. Well, Mr. Merriman . . ." Marshal adopted his formal, session-opening voice, "please take a seat and let's begin."

Shelly caressed the orange globe one last time and took his chair.

"I know little about you except that you were once a patient of Dr. Pande's and that you told the institute's secretary that you had to be seen immediately."

"Well, it's not every day you read in the newspapers that your therapist is a fuck-up. What's the charge against him? What is it he did to me?"

Marshal took firmer control of the session: "Why don't we begin with your telling me a bit about yourself and why you began treatment with Dr. Pande."

"Whoa, Doc. I need more focusing. General Motors doesn't put a notice out saying there's something seriously wrong with your car and then let the owner guess what it is, do they? They say there's some something wrong with your ignition system or fuel pump or automatic transmission. Why don't we begin with your telling me about the defect in Dr. Pande's therapy?"

Startled for a moment, Marshal quickly regained his balance. This was no ordinary patient, he told himself: this was a test case—the first recall treatment case in psychiatric history. If flexibility were necessary, he could be flexible. Ever since his linebacker days he took pride in his ability to read the opposition. Respect Mr. Merriman's need to know, he decided. Give him that . . . and nothing more.

"Fair enough, Mr. Merriman. The Psychoanalytic Institute has determined that Dr. Pande often offered interpretations that were idiosyncratic and entirely unfounded."

"Come again?"

"Sorry, I mean that he gave patients wild and often troubling explanations for their behavior."

"I'm still not with you. What kind of behavior? Give me a for instance."

"Well, for example, that all men may crave some type of homosexual union with their father."

"*What?*"

"Well, they may want to enter their father's body and merge with him."

"Yeah? Their father's *body*? What else?"

"And that wish may interfere with their comfort and their friendships with other men. That ring any bells for you from your work with Dr. Pande?"

"Yeah. Yeah. The bells. It's beginning to come back to me. It was many years ago and I've forgotten stuff. But is it true that we never really forget stuff? Everything's upstairs in storage, everything that's ever happened to us?"

"Exactly," Marshal nodded. "We say it's in the *unconscious* mind. Now tell me what you recall about your therapy."

"Just that—that stuff about making it with my father."

"And your relationships with other men? Problems there?"

"Big problems." Shelly was still groping but slowly he was beginning to discern the contours of an angle. "Big, big problems! For example, I've been looking for a job ever since my company went belly-up some months ago, and every time I go in for an interview—almost always with men—I fuck up, one way or the other."

"What happens in the interviews?"

"I just blow it. I get upset. I think it must be that unconscious stuff with my father."

"How upset?"

"Real upset. Whaddaya call it? You know—panic. Breathing fast and all."

Shelly watched Marshal jot down some notes and figured he was hitting pay dirt. "Yeah, panic—that's the best term for it. Can't catch my breath. Sweating like hell. The interviewers look at me like I'm crazy and they gotta figure, 'How's this guy gonna sell our products?'"

Marshal jotted that down, too.

"Yeah, the interviewers show me the way out pretty fast. I'm so jumpy they get jumpy. So I been out of work a long time. And there's something else, Doc, I've got this game of poker—been playing with the same guys for fifteen years. Friendly game, but big enough stakes to drop a bundle . . . this is confidential, isn't it? I mean, even if at some point you meet with my wife, it stays confidential, doesn't it? You're sworn to secrecy?"

"Of course. Everything you say stays here in this room. These notes are for my use only."

"That's good. I wouldn't want my wife to know about my losses—my marriage is already rocky. I *have* dropped a bundle and, now that I think of it, I started losing about the time I saw Dr. Pande. Ever since my therapy with him I lost my ability—anxiety around guys, just like we were talking about before. You know, before therapy I used to be a good player, better than average—after therapy I started getting all knotted up—tense—gave away my hand . . . lost every game. You play poker, Doc?"

Marshal shook his head. "We have a lot to cover. Maybe we ought to talk a bit about why you first visited Dr. Pande."

"In a sec. Lemme finish first, Doc. What I was going to say was that poker isn't about luck: poker is about nerves. Seventy-five percent of playing poker is psychology—how you handle your emotions, how you bluff, how you respond to bluffs, the signals you flash—unintentionally—when you got good hands and bad hands."

"Yes, I see your point, Mr. Merriman. If you're uncomfortable with your fellow players, you're not going to be successful at the game."

"'Not successful' at the game means losing my ass. Big money."

"So, let's turn to the question of why you first saw Dr. Pande. Let's see . . . what year was that?"

"So, the way I figure it, between poker and being made unhirable, this Dr. Pande and his wrong interpretations has ended up costing me money—a great, great deal of money!"

"Yes, I understand. But tell me why you first consulted Dr. Pande."

Just as Marshal began growing alarmed at the direction the session was taking, Shelly suddenly relaxed his grip. He had learned what he needed. Not for nothing had he been married for nine years to a crack tort attorney. From this point on, he figured, there was everything to gain, nothing to lose, by being a cooperative patient. He sensed he would have a much stronger case in court if he demonstrated that he was entirely responsive to conventional psychotherapy techniques. He therefore proceeded to answer all of Marshal's questions with great honesty and thoroughness—except questions, of course, about his treatment with Dr. Pande, about which Shelly remembered absolutely nothing.

When Marshal asked about his parents, Shelly delved deeply into the past: into his mother's unwavering glorification of his talents and beauty, which stood in stark contrast to her persistent disappointment with his father's many schemes and many failures. His mother's devotion notwithstanding, Shelly was convinced that his father had been the major player in his life.

Yes, the more he thought about it, the more disturbed he was, he told Marshal, about Dr. Pande's interpretations about his father. Despite his father's irresponsibility, he felt a deep connection with him. When he was young he worshiped his dad. He loved to see him with his friends, playing poker, going to the races—to Monmouth in New Jersey, to Hialeah and Pimlico when they vacationed in Miami Beach. His dad bet on any sport—the greyhounds, jai alai, football pools, basketball—and played any game: poker, pinochle, hearts, backgammon. Some of Shelly's favorite childhood moments, he related, had been sitting on his dad's lap and picking up and arranging his dad's pinochle hands. His initiation into adulthood occurred when his father allowed him to join the game. Shelly winced when he recalled his smart-assed request, at age sixteen, for the pinochle stakes to be raised.

Yes, Shelly agreed with Marshal's comment that his identification with his father had been very deep, very extensive. He had his father's voice and often sang all the Johnnie Ray songs his father used to sing. He used the same shaving cream and aftershave lotion his father used. He brushed his teeth with baking powder, too, and never, ever failed to end his morning shower with a couple of seconds of cold spray. Liked his potatoes crispy and, just like his dad, in a restaurant would often ask the waiter to take the potatoes back and *burn* them!

When Marshal asked about his father's death, tears flooded Shelly's eyes as he described his father dying of a coronary at fifty-eight, surrounded by his cronies, while pulling in a fish on a deep-sea fishing cruise off Key West. Shelly even told Marshal about how ashamed he was at his father's funeral for being preoccupied with the last fish his father caught. Had he landed it? How big was it? The guys always had a giant betting pool for the largest catch, and maybe there was some cash coming to his dad—or to his heir. He might never see his father's fishing friends again and was sorely tempted to pose these questions at the funeral. Only shame had prevented him.

Since his father's death, Shelly, in one way or another, thought about him every day. When he dressed in the morning and looked at himself in the mirror, he noticed his bulging calf muscles, his shrinking buttocks. At thirty-nine, he was, more and more, beginning to resemble his father.

When the end of the hour came, Marshal and Shelly agreed that, since they were on a roll, they should meet again soon. Marshal had several open hours—he had not filled Peter Macondo's—and arranged to meet with Shelly three times the following week.

THIRTEEN

"*S*o, this analyst has two patients who happen to be close friends . . . you listening?" Paul asked Ernest, who was engrossed in deboning a braised sweet-and-sour rock cod with his chopsticks. Ernest had a book reading in Sacramento and Paul had driven down to meet him. They were sitting at a corner table in the China Bistro, a large restaurant with roasted caramelized ducks and chicken displayed on a central chrome and glass island. Ernest was dressed in his book-reading uniform: a double-breasted blue blazer worn over a white cashmere turtleneck.

"Of course I'm listening. You think I can't eat and listen at the same time? Two close friends are in analysis with the same analyst and . . . "

"And after tennis one day," Paul continued, "they compare notes about their analyst. Exasperated with his pose of serene omniscience, they cook up some entertainment: the two friends each agree to tell him the same dream. So the following day one tells the analyst the dream at eight A.M., and at eleven A.M. the other describes the identical dream. The analyst, unruffled as usual, exclaims, 'Isn't it remarkable? That's the *third* time I've heard that dream today!'"

"Good story," said Ernest, guffawing, nearly choking on his chow fun, "but apropos of what?"

"Well, for one thing, apropos of the fact that it's not only therapists who conceal themselves. Many patients have been caught lying on the couch. Did I tell you about the patient I've been seeing who, a couple of years ago, saw two therapists at the same time without telling either about the other?"

"His motive?"

"Oh, some kind of vindictive triumph. He'd compare their comments and silently ridicule both for proclaiming, with great certainty, completely opposite, equally preposterous interpretations."

"Some triumph!" said Ernest. "Remember what old Professor Whitehorn would have called that?"

"A Pyrrhic victory!"

"*Pyrrhic,*" said Ernest, "his favorite word. We heard it every time he talked about patients resisting psychotherapy!

"But you know," Ernest continued, "your patient who saw two therapists—remember when we were at Hopkins and we'd present the same patient to two different supervisors and joke about their lack of agreement on anything? Same thing. I'm intrigued by your story about the two therapists." Ernest laid down his chopsticks. "I wonder—could it happen to me? I don't think so. I'm pretty sure I know when a patient is leveling with me. Initially sometimes there's doubt, but there comes a moment when there can be no further doubt we're together in truth."

"*Together in truth*—sounds good, Ernest, but what does it mean? I can't tell you how often I've seen a patient for a year or two and then something happens or I learn something that causes me to reevaluate everything I know about the patient. Sometimes I see a patient in individual therapy for years and then put him in a therapy group and I'm astonished at what I see. Is this the same person? All those parts of himself he hadn't shown me!

"For three years," Paul continued, "I've been working with a patient, a very intelligent woman, about thirty, who started— through absolutely no urging from me—spontaneously recovering memories of incest with her father. Well, we worked on this for about a year and I was convinced that, to use your words, we were together in truth. I held her hand through months of terror as the memories reappeared, I supported her through some hairy scenes in the family after she tried to confront her father about this. Now—maybe in rhythm with the public media blitz—she's suddenly beginning to doubt all these early memories.

"I tell you, my head's spinning. I've no idea what's truth, what's fiction. Moreover, she's growing critical of me for being so gullible. Last week she dreamed she was in her parents' home and a Goodwill truck drives up and starts battering away at the foundations of her home. Why are you smiling?"

"Three guesses who's the Goodwill truck?"

"Right. No mystery about that. When I asked for her associations about the truck, she said jokingly that the name of the dream was: The Helping Hand Strikes Again. So the dream's message is that, under the guise, or belief, of helping, I am undermining the very foundations of her house and family."

"The ingrate."

"Right. And I was stupid enough to try and defend myself. When I pointed out that it was *her* memories I was analyzing, she called me simplistic for believing everything she said."

"And you know," Paul continued, "maybe she's right. Maybe we're too gullible. We're so used to patients paying us to listen to their truth that we're probably naive about the possibility of lying. I heard about some recent research that showed that psychiatrists, and FBI agents as well, were particularly inept at spotting liars. And the incest controversy gets even more bizarre . . . you listening, Ernest?"

"Go on. You were saying the incest controversy gets bizarre . . . "

"Right. It gets really bizarre when you get into the world of Satanic ritual abuse. I'm the attending doc this month on the county inpatient unit. Six of the twenty patients on the unit claim ritual abuse. You can't believe what goes on in the therapy groups: these six patients describe their Satanic ritual abuse—including human sacrifice and cannibalism—with so much vividness and persuasiveness that no one dares to voice any skepticism. And that includes the staff! If group therapists were to challenge these accounts, they'd be stoned by the groups—absolutely rendered ineffective. To tell you the truth, several of the staff actually believe these accounts. Talk about an insane asylum."

Ernest nodded as he deftly flipped his fish over and started on the other side.

"Same problem with multiple personality disorder," Paul continued. "I know therapists, really good ones, who have reported two hundred cases of it, and I know other good therapists who have been in practice for thirty years and still claim they have never encountered a single case."

"You know Hegel's comment," Ernest replied: "'The owl of Minerva flies only at dusk.' Maybe we're just not going to discover the truth about this epidemic until it passes and we can take a more objective look. I agree with what you've been saying about incest survivors and multiple personalities. But leave them aside for a moment and look at your everyday outpatient therapy case. I think that a good therapist recognizes the truth with patients."

"With sociopaths?"

"No, no, no, you know what I mean—your everyday therapy patient. When do you ever have a sociopath in therapy—one who pays for therapy and is not ordered there by the courts? You know that new patient I told you about, the subject of my great experiment with total disclosure? Well, in our second session last week I couldn't read her for a while . . . we were so far apart . . . like we weren't in the same room. And then she started talking about being first in her class at law school and then suddenly she burst into tears and moved into a state of exquisite honesty. She talked about big-time regrets . . . about blowing all her golden career chances and choosing instead a marriage that soon turned rotten for her. And, you know, exactly the same thing, the same kind of breakthrough into truth, happened the first session when she talked about her brother and some abuse—or possible abuse—when she was young.

"My heart went out to her each time . . . you know, we really touched. We touched in such a way that dishonesty is now impossible between us. In fact, right after that moment in the last session she moved incredibly deep into truth . . . started talking in a remarkably candid manner . . . about sexual frustration . . . about going nuts if she doesn't get laid."

"Well, I see you two have a lot in common."

"Yeah, yeah. I'm working on it. Paul, stop with the bean sprouts. You in serious training for the anorexic Olympics? Here, try some of these sizzling scallops—house specialty. Why is it always left to me to do the work of two at dinner? Look at this halibut—it's beautiful."

"No, thanks, I get my mercury from chewing on thermometers."

"Very funny. Christ, what a week! My patient Eva died a couple of days ago. You remember Eva—I told you about her—the wife, or the mother, I wish I had? Ovarian cancer? A writing teacher. A great lady."

"She the one who had that dream of her father saying, 'Don't stay home and eat chicken soup like me—go, go to Africa.'"

"Oh, yes. I'd forgotten that. Yeah, that was Eva, all right. I'm going to miss her. This death hurts."

"I don't know how you work with cancer patients like that. How do you bear it, Ernest? You go to her funeral?"

"No. That's where I draw the line. I've got to protect myself—have a buffer zone. And I keep limits on the number of dying patients I see. I'm treating a patient now who is a psychiatric social worker in the oncology clinic and sees *only* cancer patients—all day long—and let me tell you, this woman is hurting."

"It's a high-risk profession, Ernest. You see the suicide rates for oncologists? As high as for psychiatry! You've got to be masochistic to keep doing it."

"It doesn't have to be all dark," Ernest replied. "You can get something out of it, too. If you work with dying patients and you're in therapy yourself, you get in touch with different parts of yourself, reorder your priorities, trivialize the trivia—I know I usually come out of therapy hours feeling better about myself and my life. This social worker had had a successful five-year analysis, but after working with dying patients all kinds of new material emerged. Her dreams, for example, were filled with death anxiety.

"She had a lulu last week after one of her favorite patients died. She dreamed she was present at a committee meeting that I was conducting. She had to bring me some folders and had to pass by a large open window that reached all the way to the floor. She was angry at my indifference to the risk she had to take. Then a storm arose and I took charge of the group and led everyone up a staircase with metal stairs, like a fire escape. They all climbed up, but the stairs dead-ended at the ceiling—no place to go—and everyone had to come back down again."

"In other words," replied Paul, "you and no one else are going to be able to protect her or to lead her out of this sickness unto death."

"Exactly. But the point I wanted to make is that, in five years of analysis, the topic of her mortality never even surfaced."

"It almost never does with my therapy patients either."

"You have to go after it. It's always percolating under the surface."

"So, what about you, Ernest, with all this ontological confrontation? New material coming up—does that mean more therapy in store?"

"That's why I'm writing the book on death anxiety. Remember Hemingway used to say that his Corona was his therapist."

"Corona cigar?"

"Typewriter. Before your time. And, in addition to my writing, *you're* giving me good therapy."

"Right, and here's my bill for the night." Paul signaled for the check and gestured that it be given to Ernest. He looked at his watch. "You've got to be at the bookstore in twenty minutes. Brief me quickly about your self-disclosure experiment with that new patient. What's she like?"

"Strange lady. Highly intelligent, competent, yet strangely naive. Bad marriage—I'd like to get her to the point where she can find a way out of it. Wanted to divorce a couple of years ago, but her husband came down with prostatic cancer and now she feels bound to him for his remaining years. Her only successful previous therapy was with an East Coast psychiatrist. And—now catch this, Paul— she had a long sexual affair with this guy! He died a few years ago. Damnedest thing, she insists it was healing—she swears by this guy. That's a first for me. I've never known a patient who claimed sex with a therapist was helpful. Have you?"

"Helpful? Helped the therapist get his rocks off! But for the patient—always bad news for the patient!"

"How can you say 'always'? One minute ago I told you about a case where it was helpful. Let's not let the facts stand in the way of scientific truth!"

"Right, Ernest. I stand corrected. Let me try to be objective. Let's see, let me think. I remember that case you were involved with a few years ago as expert witness—Seymour Trotter, wasn't it? He claimed it helped his patient—that it was the only way he could treat her successfully. But that guy was so narcissistic—a menace—who can believe him? Years ago I once worked with a patient who had slept a couple of times with her aging therapist after his wife died. A 'mercy fuck,' she called it. Claims it neither particularly hurt nor helped—but, if anything, it was more positive than negative.

"Of course," Paul continued, "there have been many therapists who got involved with patients and then married them. Gotta count them, too. I've never seen any data on that. Who knows about the fate of those marriages—maybe they work out better than we'd predict! The truth is, we just don't have the data. We know about the casualties only. In other words we just know the numerator, but not the denominator."

"Strange," said Ernest, "that's exactly—word for word—the argument my patient presented."

"Well, it's obvious: We know the casualties but not the total pool from which they spring. Maybe there are patients out there who profited from such a relationship and we never hear about them! The reasons for their silence are not hard to imagine. First, it's not the kind of thing you talk publicly about. Second, maybe they were helped and we don't hear about them because they don't come for more therapy. Third, if it were a good experience, then they would try to protect their therapist-lover with silence.

"So, Ernest, there's the answer to your question about scientific truth. Now I've paid my homage to science. But, for me, the question of therapist-patient sex is a moral question; there's no way science is going to prove to me that immorality is moral. I believe sex with your patients is not therapy or love—it's exploitation, violation of a trust. Yet, I don't know what to do with your series of one patient who says otherwise—no reason why this patient should lie to you!"

Ernest paid the check. As they left the restaurant for the short walk to the bookstore, Paul asked, "So . . . tell me more about the experiment. How much are you revealing?"

"I'm breaking new ground with my own transparency, but it's not going the way I had hoped. Not what I had in mind."

"Why not?"

"Well, I had wanted a more human, more existential, kind of revelation—one that would result in a 'here we are together facing the exigencies of existence.' I thought I'd be talking about my here-and-now feelings about her, about our relationship, about my own anxieties, the fundamental concerns she and I share. But she doesn't ask about anything deep or meaningful; instead she's pressing me on trivial stuff: my marriage, my dating practices."

"How do you answer her?"

"I'm struggling to find my way. Trying to differentiate between responding authentically and satisfying prurient curiosity."

"What does she want from you?"

"Relief. She's caught up in a miserable life situation but generally fixates narrowly on her sexual frustration. She's got a real sexual itch. And she's taken to hugging me at the end of each session."

"Hugging? And you go along with that?"

"Why not? I'm experimenting with a complete relationship. In your hermitage you may be losing sight of the fact that in the real world people touch all the time. It is not a sexual hug. I know sexual."

"And I know you. Careful, Ernest."

"Paul, let me set your mind at ease. Do you remember the passage in *Memories, Dreams, Reflections* where Jung says that the therapist must invent a new therapy language for each patient? The more I think about his words, the more inspired they seem. I think it's the most interesting thing Jung ever said about psychotherapy, except that I don't think he took it far enough, didn't realize it wasn't the invention of a new language or, indeed, a new therapy for each patient but the *inventing* that was important! In other words, what's important is the process of the therapist and patient working, inventing together in honesty. That's something I learned from old Seymour Trotter."

"Great teacher," Paul replied. "Look where he ended up."

On a beautiful Caribbean beach, Ernest was tempted to say, but said instead: "Don't dismiss everything about him. He knew a thing or two. But with this patient—it'll be easier to talk about her if I give her a name; let's call her Mary—with Mary I'm taking all of this very seriously. I'm committed to being totally honest with her, and so far the result feels pretty authentic. And the hug is just one part of that—it's no big deal. This is a touch-deprived woman, and touch is just a symbol of caring. Trust me, the hug represents agape, not lust."

"But, Ernest, I believe you. I believe that's what the hug represents *for you*. But *to her*? What's it mean to her?"

"Let me answer by telling you about a talk I heard last week on the nature of the therapeutic bond. The speaker described a terrific dream of one of his patients toward the end of therapy. The patient dreamed that she and her therapist were attending a conference together at a hotel. At some point the therapist suggested she get a room adjoining his, so they could sleep together. She goes to the desk and arranges it. Then a little later the therapist changes his mind and says it's not a good idea. So she then goes back to the desk to cancel the transfer. But it's too late. All of her things had been moved to the new room. It turns out that the new room is a much nicer room—larger, higher, better view. And, numerologically, the room number, 929, is more propitious."

"Nice. Nice. I get the point," said Paul: "with the hope of sexual union the patient makes some important positive changes—the better room. By the time the hope of sex proves to be mere illusion, the changes are irreversible—she can't change back again, any more than she could get her old hotel room again."

"Exactly. So that's my answer to you. It's the key to my strategy with Mary."

They strolled in silence for a few minutes and then Paul said, "When I was a medical student at Harvard, I remember Elvin Semrad—a marvelous teacher—saying something very similar . . . about the advantages, even the necessity, of some patients to have some sexual tension in the relationship. Still, it's a risky strategy for you, Ernest. I hope you got a big enough margin of safety. She attractive?"

"Very! Not necessarily my style, but, no question, a neat-looking woman."

"Is it possible you're misreading her? Is it possible she's coming on to you? Wants a therapist to love her just like the last one?"

"She does want that. But I'm going to use that for leverage in therapy. Trust me. And, for me, the hug is nonsexual. Avuncular."

They stopped in front of Tower Bookstore. "Well, here we are," said Ernest.

"We're early. Ernest, let me ask you one more thing before you go in. Tell me the truth: You enjoy the avuncular hugs with Mary?"

Ernest hesitated.

"The truth, Ernest."

"Yes, I enjoy hugging her. I like this lady a lot. She wears this incredible perfume. If I didn't enjoy it, I wouldn't do it!"

"Oh? That's an interesting comment. I thought this avuncular hug was for the patient."

"It is. But if I didn't enjoy it, she'd sense it and the gesture would lose all authenticity."

"Talk about mumbo-jumbo!"

"Paul, we're talking about a quick friendly hug. I'm handling it."

"Well, keep zipped up. Otherwise your tenure on the State Medical Ethics Board will be embarrassingly short. When's that board meeting? Let's meet for dinner."

"Two weeks from tonight. I hear there's a new Cambodian restaurant."

"My turn to select. Trust me, I've got a treat in store for you—a big macrobiotic surprise!"

FOURTEEN

The following evening Carol called Ernest at home, saying she felt panicked and needed an emergency session. Ernest spoke to her at length, gave her an appointment for the next morning, and offered to phone in a prescription for an anxiety-relieving drug to an all-night pharmacy.

As she sat in the waiting room, Carol read through her notes of the previous session.

> *Called me an attractive, a very attractive, woman . . . gave me his home phone, asks me to call him there . . . probed deeply into my sex life . . . . reveals his personal life, his wife's death, dating, singles world . . . hugged me at end of session—longer than last time . . . says he enjoys me having sex fantasies about him, runs ten minutes over . . . strangely uncomfortable at accepting my money.*

Things were progressing well, Carol thought. Inserting a micro-cassette into her miniature recorder, she slipped it into a porous straw purse bought especially for the occasion. She entered Ernest's office excited by the knowledge that the trap was set, that every word, every irregularity, would be captured.

Seeing that the urgency of the previous evening had disappeared, Ernest turned his attention to understanding the panic attack. He and his patient, it quickly became apparent, held very different viewpoints. Ernest thought Carolyn's anxiety had been evoked by the previous session. She, on the other hand, claimed she was exploding with sexual tension and frustration, and continued her attempts to pry suggestions about possible sexual outlets from him.

When Ernest inquired more systematically into Carol's sexual life, he got more than he bargained for. She described, in graphic detail, many masturbatory fantasies in which he played a prominent role. Without a trace of self-consciousness, she related her arousal at unbuttoning his shirt, kneeling before his chair in the office, unzipping his pants, slipping him into her mouth. She enjoyed the thought of bringing him, again and again, just to the point of orgasm and then slowing and waiting till he softened and then beginning over again. That, she said, was usually sufficient to bring her to orgasm as she masturbated. If not, she continued the fantasy by dragging him to the floor and imagining him lifting her skirt and hurriedly sliding her underpants to the side and pounding into her. Ernest listened attentively and tried not to squirm.

"But masturbation," Carol continued, "has never really been satisfying to me. Partly, I believe, it's the shame attached to it. Except once or twice with Ralph, this is the first time I've talked about it with anyone—man or woman. The problem is that often it doesn't culminate in a full orgasm but, instead, I get a lot of minor sexual spasms that leave me still in a state of heightened arousal. I'm beginning to wonder if it might be my masturbation technique. Could you give me some instruction about that?"

Carol's question brought the blood to Ernest's face. He was getting used to her casualness about sex. In fact, he admired her ability to speak of her sexual practices—for example, the way she had, in the past, picked up men in bars whenever she traveled or was angry with her husband. It seemed all so easy, so natural for her. He thought of the hours of agony—and futility—he had endured in singles bars and at parties. He had spent a year in Chicago during his internship. *Why, oh why,* Ernest thought, *couldn't I have run into Carolyn when she was prowling Chicago bars?*

As for her question about masturbatory technique, what did he know about that? Virtually nothing, except for the obvious necessity of clitoral stimulation. People so often assumed psychiatrists knew more than they did.

"I'm no expert in that, Carolyn." Where, Ernest wondered, did she imagine he could have learned about female masturbation? Medical school? Perhaps his next book should be *Things They Didn't Teach You in Medical School*!

"The only thing that comes to mind now, Carolyn, is a lecture I heard by a sex therapist recently on the advisability of freeing the clitoris of all adhesions."

"Oh, is that something you can check in a physical examination, Dr. Lash? That's okay with me."

Ernest flushed again. "No, I hung up my stethoscope and did my last physical exam seven years ago. I'd suggest you bring this up with your gynecologist. Some women find it easier to speak of such things to a female gynecologist."

"Is it different for men, Dr. Lash, I mean do you . . . do men have a problem in masturbation with partial orgasm?"

"Again, I'm no expert but I believe men generally have an all-or-nothing experience. Have you discussed this with Wayne?"

"With Wayne? No, we don't talk about anything. That's why I ask you these questions. You're it. Right now you're the main man, the only man, in my life!"

Ernest felt lost. His resolution to be honest offered no direction. Carolyn's aggressiveness was confusing him; he was losing his bearings. He turned to his touchstone, his supervisor, and tried to imagine how Marshal might have responded to Carolyn's question.

The proper technique, Marshal would have said, was to obtain more data: to conduct a systematic, dispassionate sexual history, including the details of Carolyn's masturbation practice and accompanying fantasies—both current and past.

Yes, that was the right approach. But Ernest had a problem: Carolyn was beginning to arouse him. All his adult life Ernest had felt unattractive to women. All his life he believed he had to work hard, to use his intellect, sensitivity, and charm, to overcome his nerdy appearance. It felt wildly exciting to hear this lovely woman describe masturbating to the thought of undressing him and dragging him to the floor.

Ernest's arousal limited his freedom as a therapist. If he asked Carolyn for more intimate details of her sexual fantasies, he could not be clear of his motives. Would he be doing this for her benefit or for his own titillation? It would feel like voyeurism, like getting off on verbal sex. On the other hand, if he avoided her fantasies, would he be shortchanging his patient by not allowing her to talk about what was uppermost in her mind? And wouldn't avoidance be saying to her that her fantasies were too shameful to discuss?

And what about his self-disclosure contract? Should he not simply share with Carolyn exactly what he was thinking? But, no, he was certain that would be an error! Was there another principle of therapist transparency in there? Perhaps therapists should not share things about which they are heavily conflicted. Best that the therapist first work out those issues in personal therapy. Otherwise the patient gets saddled with the task of working on the therapist's problems. He jotted that principle down on his notepad—it was worth remembering.

Ernest grasped the first opportunity to shift the focus. He returned to Carolyn's anxiety attack the previous night and wondered whether she might also have been anxious because of some of the hard questions he had raised in the previous session. For example, why she had stayed so long in a bitter, loveless marriage? And why she had never tried to improve the marriage in couples therapy?

"It's hard to convey how utterly, utterly hopeless I feel about my marriage, or about marriage in general. There hasn't been a spark of happiness or respect in our marriage for years. And Wayne is as nihilistic as I am: he's had many, many expensive, fruitless years of therapy."

Ernest was not to be so easily thwarted.

"Carolyn, as I think about your despair about your marriage, I can't help wondering what role the failed marriage of your parents has played in your own. When I asked you last week about your parents, you said that you never heard your mother mention your father in any but a hateful and contemptuous manner. Maybe your mother did you no service by feeding you such a steady hateful diet. Maybe it wasn't in your best interests to have drilled into you day after day, year after year, that no man could be trusted to look after anything but his own self-interests?"

Carol wanted to get back to her sexual agenda but couldn't help rushing to her mother's defense: "No picnic for her, raising two children, all alone, no help from anyone."

"Why all alone, Carolyn? What about her own family?"

"What family? Mother was all alone. My mother's father took off, too, when she was young—one of the pioneer deadbeat dads. And she had little help from her mother—a bitter, paranoid woman. They hardly ever spoke."

"Your mother's social network? Friends?"

"Nobody!"

"Did your mother have a stepfather? Your grandmother remarry?"

"No—out of the question. You'd have to know Grandma. Wore black forever. Even black handkerchiefs. Never saw her smile."

"And your mother? Other men in her life?"

"Are you kidding? I never saw a man in our house. She hated men! But I've been over all this before in therapy. This is ancient history. Thought you said you weren't a rummager."

"Interesting," said Ernest, ignoring Carol's protests, "how closely your mother's life script followed *her* mother's. As though there's this legacy of pain in the family being passed down, like a hot potato, from one generation of women to the next."

Ernest caught Carol's impatient look at her watch. "I know we're out of time, but stay with me on this a minute longer, Carolyn. You know, this is really important. I'll tell you why . . . because it raises the urgent question of what you may be passing on to your daughter! You see, maybe the best thing we can do in your therapy is to help you break the cycle! I want to help you, Carolyn, and I'm committed to that. But perhaps the real, the major beneficiary, of our work together is going to be your daughter!"

Carol was absolutely unprepared for this comment and it stunned her. Despite herself, tears welled up and overflowed. Without another word, she rushed out of the office, still weeping, and thinking, *Goddamn him, he's done it again. Why am I letting the bastard get to me?*

Descending the stairs, Carol tried to sort out which of Ernest's comments applied to the fictional persona she had created and which truly applied to her. She was so shaken and so lost in thought that she almost stepped on Jess, who was sitting on the bottom step.

"Hello, Carol. Jess. Remember me?"

"Oh, hi, Jess. Didn't recognize you." She wiped away a tear. "Not used to seeing you sitting still."

"I love jogging, but I've been known to walk. The reason you always see me running here is because I'm chronically late—a tough problem to work on in therapy because I always get there too late to talk about it!"

"Not late today?"

"Well, I've changed my hour to eight A.M."

Justin's hour, Carol thought. "So you don't have an hour with Ernest now?"

"No. I stopped by to speak to you. Wonder if we could talk sometime—perhaps jog together. Or lunch? Or both?"

"I don't know about jogging. Never done it." Carol swiped at her tears.

"I'm a good teacher. Here's a handkerchief. I can see you've had one of those hours today. Ernest gets to me, too—uncanny how he knows where the pain is. Anything I can do? Take a walk?"

Carol started to return Jess's handkerchief but began sobbing again.

"No, keep the handkerchief. Look, I've had those kind of sessions, too, and I almost always want time by myself to digest things. So I'll take off. But might I call you? Here's my card."

"And here's mine." Carol fished a card out of her purse. "But I want my reservations about jogging to go on record."

Jess looked at the card. "Noted and entered, counselor." With that he tipped his yachting cap and took off jogging down Sacramento Street. Carol stared after him, at his long blond hair flowing in the wind and at the white sweater tied around his neck which rose and fell with the undulations of his powerful shoulders.

Upstairs Ernest entered his notes on Carolyn's chart:

Progressing well. Hard working hour. Heavy self-disclosure about sex and her masturbatory fantasies. Erotic transference increasing. Need to find a way to address that. Worked on relationship to mother, on family role modeling. Defensive about any perceived criticism of mother. I ended session with comment about the type of family model she will pass on to her daughter. Ran weeping out of office. Expect another emergency phone call? Error to end hour with such a powerful message?

Besides, Ernest thought, as he closed his folder, *I can't have her charging out of my office like that—I missed my hug!*

FIFTEEN

After Marshal's lunch with Peter Macondo the previous week, he immediately sold ninety thousand dollars' worth of stock with the intent of wiring the money to Peter as soon as it cleared. But his wife insisted that he discuss the investment with his cousin Melvin, a tax attorney for the Department of Justice.

Shirley generally played no part in the Streider family finances. As she had become involved in meditation and in ikebana, she had grown not only unconcerned about material goods but increasingly contemptuous of her husband's obsession with acquiring them. Whenever Marshal reveled in the beauty of a painting or glass sculpture and lamented the fifty-thousand-dollar price tag, she would respond simply by saying, "Beauty? Why don't you see it there?" And then point to one of her ikebana arrangements—a graceful minuet of a swirling oak branch and six Morning Dawn camellia blossoms—or to the elegant sloping lines of a gnarled and proud five-needle-pine bonsai.

Though indifferent to money, Shirley was fiercely interested in one thing money could provide: the finest education possible for her children. Marshal had been so expansive, so grandiose, in describing the future returns of his investment in Peter's bicycle helmet factory that she grew concerned and, before agreeing to the investment (all stocks were held jointly), she insisted that Marshal call Melvin.

For years, Marshal and Melvin had had an informal, mutually profitable barter arrangement: Marshal offered Melvin medical and psychological advice and Melvin reciprocated with investment and tax guidance. Marshal phoned his cousin about Peter Macondo's plan.

"I don't like the smell of it," Melvin said. "*Any* investment promising that rate of return is suspect. Five hundred, seven hundred percent return—come on, Marshal! Seven hundred percent! Get real. And the promissory note you faxed to me? You know what that's worth? Zilch, Marshal! Exactly zilch!"

"Why zilch, Melvin? A promissory note signed by a highly visible businessman? This guy's known everywhere."

"If he's such a great businessman," Melvin said in his rasping voice, "tell me, why does he give you an unsecured piece of paper—an empty promise? I don't see any collateral. Say he decides not to pay you? He can always create defenses to payment—excuses not to pay. You would have to sue him—that would cost thousands and thousands—and then you would only have another piece of paper, a judgment, and you would still have to find his assets to collect. That would cost you even more money. The note does *not* remove this risk, Marshal. I know what I'm talking about. I see this stuff all the time."

Marshal dismissed Melvin's comments out of hand. First, Melvin was paid to be suspicious. Second, Melvin had always thought small. He was just like his father, Uncle Max, who, alone of all the relatives who had come from Russia, had failed to prosper in the new country. His father had begged Max to go partners in a grocery store, but Max scoffed at the idea of getting up at four in the morning to go to the market, working sixteen hours, and ending the day by throwing out rotting, cockroach-brown apples and grapefruits with green ulcers. Max had thought small, had chosen the safety and security of a civil service job, and Melvin, his gawky, gorilla-eared schlemiel of a son with arms that practically reached the floor, had followed in his father's footsteps.

But Shirley, who had overheard their conversation, did not so easily dismiss Melvin's warnings. She grew alarmed. Ninety thousand dollars would pay for an entire college education. Marshal tried to conceal his annoyance at Shirley's interference. During their nineteen-year marriage, not once had she shown the slightest interest in any of his investments. And *now,* when he was poised to grab the economic opportunity of his life, now she chose to stick her uninformed nose in. But Marshal calmed himself—he understood that Shirley's alarm grew out of her ignorance of financial affairs. It would have been different had she met Peter. Her cooperation, however, was essential. To obtain it, he would have to placate Melvin.

"All right, Melvin, tell me what to do. I'll follow your recommendations."

"Very simple. What we want is a bank to guarantee the payment of the note—that is, an irrevocable and unconditional commitment by a prime bank to honor the note *whenever you demand your money.* If this man's holdings are as extensive as you describe, he should have no difficulty obtaining this. If you wish I'll personally draw up an iron-clad note from which Houdini couldn't escape."

"That's good, Melvin. Do that," said Shirley, who had joined the discussion on the extension phone.

"Whoa, wait a minute, Shirley." Marshal was now growing angry at these small-minded obstructions. "Peter promised me a secured note by Wednesday. Why don't we just wait and see what he sends? I'll fax it to you, Melvin."

"Okay. I'll be around all week. But don't send money till you hear from me. Oh, and one other thing: you say that Rolex came in a Shreve's Jewelry Store box? Shreve's is a reputable jeweler. Do me a favor, Marshal. Take twenty minutes, take the watch to Shreve's and let them verify it! Fake Rolexes are the rage—they sell them on every street corner in downtown Manhattan."

"He'll go, Melvin," said Shirley, "and I'll go with him."

The trip to Shreve's reassured Shirley. The watch was, indeed, a Rolex—a thirty-five-hundred-dollar Rolex! Not only had it been purchased there but the salesman remembered Peter well.

"Fine-looking gentleman. Most beautiful coat I've ever seen: double-breasted gray cashmere, reached almost to the floor. He was on the verge of buying a second, identical watch for his father but then thought better of it—said he was going to fly to Zurich that weekend and he'd buy a watch there."

Marshal was so pleased he offered to buy Shirley a gift. She chose an exquisite two-mouthed green ceramic vase for ikebana.

On Wednesday, as promised, Peter's note arrived and, to Marshal's great pleasure, it met Melvin's specifications precisely—a note guaranteed by Crédit Suisse for ninety thousand dollars plus interest at prime, payable upon demand at any of the hundreds of worldwide branches of Crédit Suisse. Even Melvin could find no fault with it and grudgingly admitted it did, indeed, appear to be iron-clad. Just the same, Melvin reiterated, he was uneasy with any investment that hinted at that rate of return.

"Does that mean," Marshal said, "you wouldn't want a part of this investment?"

"You offering a piece of it?" asked Melvin.

"Let me think about it! I'll get back to you." *Fat chance,* Marshal thought, as he hung up the phone. *Melvin'll have a long wait to get a piece of this.*

The following day the money from Marshal's stock sale entered his account, and he wired ninety thousand to Peter in Zurich. He played great basketball at noon and had a quick lunch with Vince, one of the players, a psychologist whose office adjoined his. Although Vince and he were confidants, Marshal did not speak about the investment with him. Or with anyone in his field. Only Melvin knew. And yet, Marshal reassured himself, this transaction was squeaky-clean. Peter was not a patient; he was an ex-patient, and an ex–brief therapy patient at that. Transference was not an issue. Even though he knew there was no professional conflict of interest, Marshal reminded himself to tell Melvin to keep this entirely confidential.

Later that afternoon, when he met with Adriana, Peter's fiancée, Marshal took care to maintain the boundaries of their professional relationship by avoiding any discussion of his investment with Peter. He graciously acknowledged her congratulations for his endowed lectureship, but when she informed him that she had learned yesterday from Peter that a bill requiring juvenile bicyclists to wear helmets had been placed before the legislature in both Sweden and Switzerland, he nodded only briefly and then immediately turned to her issues: an investigation of her relationship with her father, a basically benevolent man who, however, was so intimidating that no one dared confront him. Adriana's father had very positive feelings toward Peter—indeed, he was one of Peter's group of investors—but he nonetheless strongly opposed a marriage that would take not only his daughter but his future grandchildren and heirs out of the country.

Marshal's comments to Adriana about her relationship with her father—about how good parenting consists of preparing children to individuate, to become autonomous, to be able to leave their parents—proved useful. For the first time Adriana began to comprehend that she did not necessarily have to accept the guilt that her father laid upon her. It was not her fault that her mother had died. Not her fault that her father was growing old or that his life was so unpeopled. They ended the hour with Adriana raising the question of whether she might continue for longer than the five hours Peter had requested.

"Might it also be possible, Dr. Streider," Adriana asked as she rose to leave, "for you to meet jointly with me and my father?"

The patient had not yet been born who could force Marshal Streider to extend a session. Even by a minute or two. Marshal prided himself on that. But he couldn't resist a reference to Peter's gift and gestured toward his wrist, saying, "My new watch, accurate to a millisecond, says two-fifty precisely. Shall we begin our next session with your questions, Miss Roberts?"

SIXTEEN

*M*arshal was pumped up as he prepared to see Shelly. What a great day, he thought. It doesn't get much better than this: the money finally wired to Peter, a brilliant session with Adriana, and glorious basketball—that final driving lay-up, lane opening up like magic, no one daring to get in his way.

And he was looking forward to seeing Shelly. It was their fourth hour. Their two sessions earlier in the week had been extraordinary. Could any other therapist possibly have worked so brilliantly? He had begun a deft, efficient sector analysis on Shelly's relationship with his father, and with the precision of a surgeon had methodically replaced Seth Pande's corrupt interpretations with correct ones.

Shelly entered the office and, as always, stroked the orange bowl of the glass sculpture before taking his seat. Then, with no coaxing from Marshal, he immediately began.

"You remember Willy, my poker and tennis chum? I talked about him last week. He's the one who's worth about forty, fifty million. Well, he's invited me to La Costa for a week to be his partner in the annual Pancho Segura invitational doubles tournament. I thought I was okay with that, but . . . well, there's something about it that doesn't sit right. I'm not sure what."

"What are your ideas about it?"

"I like Willy. He's trying to be a good buddy. I know the couple thou he'll be laying out for me at La Costa is nothing for him. He's so loaded, there's no way he can even spend the interest on his money. Besides, it's not like he's not getting something back. He's set his sights on a national ranking at senior doubles and, let me tell you, he's not going to find a better partner than me. But I don't know. This still doesn't explain the way I feel."

"Try something, Mr. Merriman. I'd like you to do something different today. Focus on your bad feeling and focus, too, on Willy and just let your thoughts run free. Say anything that comes into your mind. Don't try to prejudge or select things that make sense. Don't try to make sense of anything. Just think out loud."

"*Gigolo*—that's the first word that comes—I'm a kept gigolo, a call boy for Willy's entertainment. Yet I like Willy—if he weren't so goddamned rich, we could be close friends . . . well, maybe not . . . I don't trust myself. Maybe if he weren't rich, I'd lose interest in him."

"Keep going, Mr. Merriman, you're doing fine. Don't select, don't censor. Whatever comes to mind, let it in and then talk about it. Whatever you think or whatever you see, describe it to me."

"Mountain of money . . . coins, bills . . . the money looms . . . whenever I'm with Willy I'm scheming . . . always scheming . . . how can I use him? Get something from him? You name it . . . I want something: money, favors, gourmet lunches, new tennis racquets, business tips. I'm impressed with him . . . his success . . . makes me bigger to be seen with him. Makes me smaller, too . . . I see me holding my father's big hand . . . "

"Stay with that image of you and your father. Focus on it. Let something happen."

"I see this scene, I must have been younger than ten because that's when we moved across town—Washington, D.C.—to live on top of my father's store. My father held my hand as he took me to Lincoln Park on Sunday. Dirty snow and slush on the streets. I can remember my dark gray corduroy pants rubbing when I walked and making that ratchety sound. I had a bag of peanuts, I think, and I was feeding the squirrels, throwing peanuts to them. One of them bit my finger. Bad bite."

"What happened then?"

"Hurt like hell. But can't remember anything else. Nothing."

"How did one bite you if you were throwing peanuts?"

"Right! Good question. It don't make sense. Maybe I held my hand down to the ground and they ate out of my hand, but I'm guessing—I don't remember it."

"You must have been scared."

"Probably. Don't remember."

"Or remember getting treated? Squirrel bites can be serious—rabies."

"That's right. Rabies in squirrels used to be a big deal on the East Coast. But nothing comes. Maybe I remember jerking my hand back in pain. But I'm pushing it."

"Just keep describing your stream of consciousness."

"Willy. How he makes me feel smaller. His success makes my own failures stand out more. And you know, the truth is that when I'm around him I don't just feel smaller, I *perform* smaller . . . he talks about his real estate condominium project and how sales are slow . . . I've got some good ideas about promotion, I'm great at that—but when I tell him about my ideas, my heart starts pumping and I forget half of 'em . . . even happens with tennis . . . when I play as his doubles partner . . . I play within his range . . . I could do better . . . I'm holding back, just pushing my second serve . . . when I play anyone else I rip that twist into the backhand corner—I can hit the chalk nine out of ten times . . . I don't know why . . . don't want to show him up . . . got to change that when we play in doubles tourney. It's funny, I want him to succeed . . . but I want him to fail . . . last week he told me about an arbitrage investment going sour and . . . shit, you know what I felt? Happy! Can you believe that? Happy. Feel like a piece of shit . . . some kind of friend I am . . . this guy has been nothing but good to me . . . "

Marshal listened to Shelly's associations for half the session before offering an interpretation.

"What strikes me, Mr. Merriman, is your deeply ambivalent feelings toward both Willy and your father. I believe that your relationship to your father is the template by which we can understand your relationship to Willy."

"*Template?*"

"I mean that your relationship to your father is the key, the foundation, to your relationships to other 'big' or successful men. Over the last two sessions you've told me a great deal about your father's neglect or disparagement of you. Today, for the first time, you give me a warm, positive memory of your father and, yet, look how the episode ends—with a terrible injury. And look at the nature of the injury—a bite on the finger!"

"I don't get your point."

"It seems unlikely that that is an actual memory! After all, as you yourself point out, how can a squirrel bite your finger as you are flinging peanuts? And would a father allow his son to feed a rabies-bearing rodent by hand? Unlikely! So maybe that particular injury—getting bitten on the finger—is a symbol for some other kind of feared injury."

"Come again. What are you getting at, Doc?"

"Remember that early memory you described last session? The first memory that you can recall in your entire life? You said that you were on your parents' bed and that you put your toy lead truck in the light socket on the nightstand and that you got a terrible shock and that half of your truck melted away."

"Yeah, that's what I remember. Clear as day."

"So let's juxtapose these memories—you put your truck into Mother's socket and you get burned. There's danger there. Danger in getting too close to your mother—that's Father's territory. So how do you cope with the danger coming from your father? Maybe you try to get close to him, but your finger gets badly injured. And isn't it evident that these injuries—to your little truck and to your finger—seem symbolic: What else could they represent but some injury to your penis?

"You've said that your mother doted on you," Marshal continued, noting that he had Shelly's full attention. "She lavished affection on you and at the same time denigrated your father. That sounds like a dangerous position for a young child—to be set up against his father. So what do you do? How do you cope? One way is to identify with your father. And so you have, in all the ways you've described: imitating his tastes in burnt potatoes, his gambling, his carelessness with money, the way you feel about your body resembling his. Another way is to compete with him. And so you did. Pinochle, boxing, tennis; in fact, it was easy to defeat him, to be better than him, because he was so unsuccessful. And yet you felt very uncomfortable surpassing him—as if there's some danger in that, some danger in succeeding."

"What's the danger exactly? I honestly think the old man wanted me to succeed."

"The danger is not in succeeding per se, but in succeeding *over* him, besting him, replacing him. Perhaps, in your young boy's mind, you wanted him gone—that's only natural—you wanted him to disappear so you might have sole possession of Mother. But 'disappearing,' to the child, is equivalent to death. *So you had death wishes for him.* And that's not an indictment of you—that's what happens in every family, that's simply the way we're built. The son resents the obstruction of the father. And the father resents the son for attempting to replace him—in the family, in life.

"Think about it—it's uncomfortable to have death wishes. It feels dangerous. What's the danger? Look at your truck! Look at your finger! *The danger lies in your father's retaliation.* Now these are old events, old feelings—they happened decades ago. And yet these feelings haven't dissolved. They are buried inside of you, they still feel fresh, they still influence the way you live. That child's sense of danger is still in you—you've long forgotten the reason, but look what you've told me today: *you act as if success were very dangerous.* Hence, you don't let yourself be successful, or resourceful, around Willy. Can't even allow yourself to play good tennis. So all your skills, your talents, stay locked up, unused, inside of you."

Shelly didn't respond. Not very much of this made sense to him. He closed his eyes and sifted through Marshal's words, searching frantically for some scrap that might be useful.

"Little louder," Marshal said, smiling. "Can't quite hear you."

"I don't know what to think. You've said so much. I guess I've been wondering why Dr. Pande didn't point all this out to me. Your explanations seem so right on—so much more on target than that homosexual garbage with my father. In four sessions you've done more than Dr. Pande did in forty."

Marshal was soaring. He felt like an interpretive stud. Once every year or two he entered a "zone" in basketball: the basket looked like a huge barrel up there—three-pointers, twisting lay-ups, jump shots with either hand. He just couldn't miss. Now he was in a zone in his office—with Peter, Adriana, Shelly. He just couldn't miss. Every interpretation went whizzing—zzzooommmm—straight to the heart.

God, he wished Ernest Lash could have seen and heard this session. He had had another run-in with Ernest during their supervision yesterday. They were coming more frequently now—almost every time. Christ, what he had to put up with. All these therapists like Ernest, these amateurs, just don't understand—just don't get it—don't get that the therapist's task is to interpret, only to interpret. Ernest can't comprehend that interpretation isn't one of many options, isn't just one thing the therapist can do—it's *all* the therapist should do. It's an insult to wisdom and the natural order that someone at his level of development should have to put up with Ernest's juvenile challenge to the effectiveness of interpretation, Ernest's blather about authenticity and openness, and all that transpersonal horseshit about soul meetings.

Suddenly the clouds parted and Marshal saw all and understood all. Ernest, and all the critics of analysis, were correct, all right, about the ineffectiveness of interpretations—*their interpretations*! Interpretation, in their hands, was ineffective because its content was wrong. And surely, Marshal thought, it wasn't just the content that made him excel, but his manner of delivery, his ability to frame the interpretation in precisely the right language and the perfect metaphor for each patient, and his genius in being able to reach every patient in any walk of life: the most sophisticated academic, the Nobel laureate in physics, down to the lower lifes—gamblers and tennis bums—to Mr. Merriman, who was eating out of his hand. More than ever before, he saw what a superbly honed instrument of interpretation he was.

Marshal thought about his fees. Surely it was unnatural for him to charge the same as other therapists when he was obviously top of the line. Really, Marshal thought, *who* was his equal? Surely, if this session were watched by some heavenly tribunal of analytic immortals—Freud, Ferenczi, Fenichel, Fairbairn, Sullivan, Winnicott—they would marvel: "Wunderbar, amazing, extraordinary. That kid Streider is something. Give him the ball and get out of his way. No question, he's the world's greatest living therapist!"

It had been a long time since he had felt this good—perhaps since his glory linebacker years in college. Maybe, Marshal thought, he had been subclinically depressed all these years. Perhaps Seth Pande hadn't really analyzed in depth his depression and the graying of his grandiose fantasies. God knows Seth had blind spots in regard to grandiosity. But now, today, Marshal understood more clearly than ever before that *grandiosity need not be abandoned,* that it's the ego's natural way of staving off the limitations, the dreariness and despair of everyday life. What's needed is to find a way to channel grandiosity into adaptive, fulfillable, adult form. Like cashing a bicycle helmet check for six hundred thousand dollars or being sworn in as president of the International Psychoanalytic Association. And all that was coming. Soon!

Unwelcome grating words yanked Marshal out of his reverie.

"You know, Doc," Shelly said, "the way you got right to the bottom of things, the way you helped me so quickly, makes me even more pissed at the way this Seth Pande prick ripped me off! Last night I was making an inventory, adding up how much his treatment—what did you call it . . . his 'errant methods'?—cost me. Now this is between you and me—I don't want this made public—but I figure forty-thousand-dollar losses at poker. I explained to you how my tension around men—tension Pande caused with his nutty explanations—has screwed up my poker. By the way, you don't have to take my word about the forty thousand—I can easily prove that amount, to any investigator, in any courtroom, with the bank records and canceled checks of my poker account. And then there's the job and my inability to interview well because of the effects of bad psychiatric treatment—that's at least six months without salary and benefits, another forty thousand. So what are we talking about? We're talking, ballpark, eighty thou."

"Yes, I can understand your feelings of bitterness toward Dr. Pande."

"Well, it goes beyond feelings, Doc. And it goes beyond bitterness. To put it in legal terms, it's more like demand for reparation. I think, and my wife and her attorney friends agree, that I got a good case for a lawsuit. I don't know who should be sued—Dr. Pande, of course, but in these days the attorneys go after the 'deep pockets.' That might be the Psychoanalytic Institute."

When he had the right hand, Shelly was a good bluffer. And he was holding pretty good cards.

The entire recall scheme was Marshal's baby. He had jumped on the idea and hoped to ride it straight into the institute presidency. And here, the very first recall therapy patient was threatening to sue the institute in what would undoubtedly be a highly visible and embarrassing trial. Marshal tried to keep his cool.

"Yes, Mr. Merriman, I understand your distress. But will a judge or a jury understand it?"

"It seems to me this is an open-and-shut case. It'll never come to trial. I'd be very willing to give consideration, serious consideration, to a settlement offer. Maybe Dr. Pande and the institute might split it."

"I can only function as your therapist and have no authority to speak for the institute or anyone else, but it seems to me it would *have* to come to trial. First, I know Dr. Pande—he's tough. And stubborn. A real fighter. Trust me, there is no way in the world he would ever admit malfeasance—he'd fight to the bitter end, he'd hire the nation's best defense lawyers, he'd spend every cent he has on the fight. And the institute, too. They'd fight. They would never voluntarily settle because it would open the path to endless lawsuits—it would be their death knell."

Shelly called Marshal's bet and cavalierly raised. "Trial's all right with me. Cheap, too. All in the family. My wife's an incredible trial litigator."

Marshal reraised without a blink. "I've been through trials involving therapy malpractice. Let me tell you, the patient pays a high price emotionally. All that personal exposure—not only you but others. Including your wife, who might not be able to be your attorney, since she'd have to testify about the degree of your emotional pain. And then, what about the amount of your gambling losses? If that were made public, it wouldn't be great public relations for her legal practice. And, of course, all your fellow poker players would be called to testify."

Shelly confidently shot back, "They're not only poker players but close friends. No one, not a single one, would refuse to testify."

"But would you, if they are friends, ask them to testify—to go public with information that they're involved in gambling of this magnitude? May not be good for their own personal or professional life. Besides, private gambling is illegal in California, isn't it? You'd be asking each one of them to put his head in the noose. Didn't you say some were attorneys?"

"Friends do things like that for one another."

"When they do, they don't stay friends."

Shelly took another look at Marshal. *This guy's built like a brick shithouse,* he thought, *not an ounce of flab—he could stop a tank.* He stopped to take another look at his cards. *Shit,* he thought, *this guy's a player. He's playing it like an aces-high full boat against my flush. Better save something for the next hand.* Shelly folded his cards. "Well, I'll think about it, Doc. Talk it over with my legal advisers."

Shelly lapsed into silence. Marshal, of course, waited him out.

"Doc, can I ask you something?"

"You can ask anything. No promises about answering."

"Go back five minutes . . . our talk about the lawsuit . . . you hung in there pretty tough. How come? What happened there?"

"Mr. Merriman, I believe it's more important to explore the motivation behind your question. What are you really asking? And in which ways might it articulate with my interpretation earlier about you and your father?"

"No, Doc, that's not where I'm coming from. We finished that. I got it. Honest. I feel all sorted out about my mother's socket and my father and competition and death wishes. What I want to talk about now is this hand we just played. Let's go back and play the cards open. That's the way you can really help."

"You haven't told me *why* yet."

"Okay. *Why* is easy. We been working on the cause of my actions—what did you call it? The *temple key*?"

"Template."

"Right. And it looks like we got that down pat. But I'm still left with damaged patterns, bad habits of showing my tension. I'm not here for just understanding; I need help changing my bad patterns. You know I been damaged—otherwise you wouldn't be sitting here giving me free hundred-and-seventy-five-dollar sessions. Right?"

"Okay, I'm beginning to get your drift. Now tell me again what you're asking me."

"Back then, five or ten minutes ago when we were talking about the trial and jury and poker losings. You could have folded your hand. But you coolly called my bet. I want to know how I gave my cards away!"

"I'm not sure. But I think it was your foot."

"My foot?"

"Yes, when you tried to be most forceful you flexed your foot a lot, Mr. Merriman. One of the surest signs of anxiety. Oh, and your voice—a trifle louder, a half-octave higher."

"No kidding! Hey, that's great. You know, that's helpful. *That's* what I *really* call help. I'm getting an idea—an inspiration about how you can really heal the damage."

"I'm afraid, Mr. Merriman, you have already seen what I can do. I've exhausted my store of observations. I'm convinced I can be most useful doing just what we've been doing these last four hours."

"Doc, you've helped me through all that childhood father stuff. I've got new insight. Good insight! But I'm impaired: I can't join my friends for a friendly game of poker. A real effective therapy should be able to fix that. Right? A good therapy should free me up enough so that I can choose how I spend my free time."

"I don't get it. I'm a therapist, I can't help you play poker."

"Doc, you know what a 'tell' is?"

"A tell?"

"Let me show you." Shelly took out his wallet and extracted a wad of bills. "I'm going to take this ten-dollar bill, wad it up, put my hands behind me, and put it into one of my hands." Shelly did as he described and then held out his hands, fists clenched in front of him. "Now your job is to guess which hand. Guess right, you keep the ten bucks; guess wrong, and you give me ten bucks. I'm going to repeat this six times."

"I'll go along with this, Mr. Merriman, but no gambling on it."

"No! Trust me, it won't work without risk. There's got to be something riding on it or it won't work. Do you want to help me or not?"

Marshal acquiesced. He was so grateful that Shelly appeared to have dropped the idea of a lawsuit that he would have agreed to playing jacks on the floor if that was what Shelly wanted.

Six times Shelly held his hands out, and six times Marshal guessed. Three times he guessed right and three times wrong.

"Okay, Doc, you won thirty bucks and you lost thirty. We're even. That's natural order. Way it should be. Here, *you* take the ten. Put it in your hand. Now it's *my* turn to guess."

Six times Marshal hid the ten in one hand or the other. Shelly missed the first one and then guessed the next five correctly.

"You win ten bucks, Doc, and I win fifty. You owe me forty. Do you need change?"

Marshal reached into his pocket, fetched out a roll of bills bound by a heavy silver money clip—his father's clip. Twenty years ago his father had succumbed to a massive stroke. While waiting for the rescue squad to respond to the 911 call, his mother had removed his father's money from his pocket, put the bills in her purse, and given the clip to her son. "Here, Marshal, this is for you," she had said. "You use it and think of your father when you do." Marshal took a deep silent breath, peeled off two twenties—the most he had ever lost on a bet in his life—and handed them to Shelly.

"How did you do that, Mr. Merriman?"

"Your knuckles were a little white on the empty hand—you squeezed too tight. And your nose turned, very, very, slightly, to the ten-buck hand. *That* is a tell, Doc. Want a rematch?"

"A good demonstration, Mr. Merriman. No rematch necessary: I get the point. I'm still not sure where this is leading; however, I'm afraid our time is just up. See you on Wednesday." Marshal rose.

"I've got an idea, a fantastic idea, about where it's leading. Want to hear it?"

"Indeed, I do, Mr. Merriman." Marshal checked his watch again and rose. "On Wednesday at four P.M. sharp."

SEVENTEEN

*T*en minutes before their session, Carol tried to prepare herself mentally. No tape recorder today. The recorder, hidden in her purse the last session, had picked up nothing intelligible. To get a decent recording, she realized, she would have to invest in a professional-grade listening device—perhaps something she could buy in the spy store that had recently opened near Union Square.

Not that there had been anything worth recording. Ernest was being more cagey than she had expected. And more cunning. And more patient. He was devoting a surprising amount of time to winning her confidence and making her dependent on him. He seemed in no rush—probably contentedly humping one of his other patients. She, too, had to be patient: sooner or later, she knew the real Ernest would emerge, the leering, lascivious, predatory Ernest she had seen at the bookstore.

Carol resolved to be stronger. She could not keep breaking down like she did last week when Ernest made the comment about passing on her mother's rage to her children. That observation had been ringing in her ears for the last several days and, in unexpected ways, had sharply affected her relationship with her children. Her son had even commented that he was happy that she wasn't going to be sad anymore, and her daughter had left a drawing of a big smiling face on her pillow.

And then last night, something extraordinary occurred. For the first time in weeks, Carol experienced a rush of well-being. It had happened while holding her children and reading their nightly installment of *The Wonderful Adventures of Nils*—the same dog-eared book from which, decades ago, her mother had read to her every night. Memories returned of her and Jeb clinging to her mother and crowding their little heads together to see the pictures. Strange that from time to time in the last week she had thought about the unforgiven, banished Jeb. Not wanting to see him, of course—she had meant what she said about a life sentence—but just wondering about him: where he was, what he was doing.

But then, Carol wondered, *is it really necessary to stonewall my feelings from Ernest? Maybe my tears aren't such a bad thing—they serve a purpose: they increase the semblance of genuineness here. Although that's hardly necessary—Ernest, poor sap, hasn't a clue. Yet, still, this is a risky game; why give him any influence over me? On the other hand, why shouldn't I take something positive from him? I'm paying enough. Even he has to say something useful, sometimes. Even a blind pig finds an acorn once in a while!*

Carol rubbed her legs. Even though Jess, true to his word, had been a patient and gentle jogging guide, her calves and thighs ached. Jess had phoned last night and they had met early in the morning in front of the De Young Museum to jog through the rising mist around the lake and riding fields of Golden Gate Park. She had followed his advice and moved no more quickly than a fast walk, sliding, shuffling, rather than running, barely lifting her shoes from the dewy grass. After fifteen minutes, she was out of breath and looked pleadingly at Jess, gliding gracefully at her side.

"Just a few minutes more," he promised. "Keep it to a fast walk; find the pace where you can breathe easily. We'll stop at the Japanese Tea House."

And then twenty minutes into the jog, something wonderful had happened. Her fatigue vanished and Carol was suffused with a feeling of limitless energy. She looked over to Jess, who nodded and smiled beatifically as though he had been awaiting her second-wind enlightenment. Carol glided faster. She flew, weightless, over the grass. She lifted her feet higher, then higher. She could have gone on forever. And then, when they slowed and stopped in front of the tea house, Carol crumbled in a heap and was grateful for the support of Jess's powerful arm.

Meanwhile, Ernest, on the other side of the wall, was entering into his computer an incident from a therapy group meeting he had just led—a valuable addition to his article on therapist-patient in-betweenness. One of his group members had brought in a compelling dream:

> *All of us group members were sitting around a long table with the therapist at one end holding a piece of paper. We were all stretching, craning our necks, leaning over, trying to see the note, but he kept it hidden. Somehow we all knew that, on the slip of paper, was written the answer to the question: Which of us do you love best?*

This question—Which of us do you love best?—Ernest wrote, is indeed the group therapist's nightmare. Every therapist fears that someday the group will demand to know which of its members he or she most cares for. And it is precisely for this reason that many group therapists (and individual therapists, too) are disinclined to express their feelings to patients.

What was special about this session was that Ernest had been true to his resolution to be transparent and, in so doing, felt he had handled the situation brilliantly. First he had steered the group into a productive discussion of each member's fantasy of who was the favorite child of the therapist. That, of course, was the conventional ploy—many therapists would do that. But then he did something few therapists would: he openly discussed his feelings toward each person in the group. Not whether he liked or loved each person, of course—such global responses were never useful—but which characteristics of each drew him closer and which pushed him away. And the tactic had succeeded wonderfully: each person in the group decided to do the same thing with the others, and everyone had received valuable feedback. What a pleasure, Ernest reflected, to lead his troops from the front rather than from the rear.

He turned off his computer and quickly leafed through his notes on Carolyn's previous session. Before rising to fetch her, he also reviewed the principles of therapist self-disclosure he had so far formulated.

1. Reveal yourself only to the extent that it will be helpful to the patient.
2. Reveal yourself judiciously. Remember you are revealing for the patient, not for yourself.
3. Have a care, if you want to stay in practice, about how your self-disclosure will sound to other therapists.
4. Therapist self-disclosure must be stage-sensitive. Consider timing: some revelations helpful late in therapy may, at an early stage, be counterproductive.
5. Therapists should not share things about which they are heavily conflicted; they should work them out in supervision or personal therapy first.

Carol entered Ernest's office determined to get results that day. She took a few steps past the doorway but did not take her seat. Instead she simply remained standing by her chair. Ernest began his descent into his chair, glanced at Carolyn looming over him, stopped in midair, rose again, and looked at her quizzically.

"Ernest, on Wednesday I rushed out of here so moved by what you said that I forgot something: my hug. And I can't tell you how much difference that made. How much I've missed it the last two days. It's like I'd lost you, like you no longer existed. I thought of phoning you, but your disembodied voice doesn't do it for me. I need the physical contact. Can you humor me on this one?"

Ernest, not wanting to show his pleasure at receiving a make-up hug, hesitated for a moment and said, "As long as we have an agreement to talk about it," and gave her a brief, upper-body hug.

Ernest sat down, his pulse throbbing. He liked Carolyn and loved her touch: the fleecy feel of her cashmere sweater, her warm shoulder, the thin, demure strap of her brassiere across her back, the feel of her firm breasts against his chest. Clean though the hug was, Ernest returned to his chair feeling soiled.

"Did you notice that I left without a hug?" Carol asked.

"Yes, I noticed it."

"Did you miss it?"

"Well, I was aware that my comment to you about your daughter struck some deep chords in you. Unsettling chords."

"You promised you'd be straight with me, Ernest. Please, no evasive shrink tactics. Won't you tell me, did you miss the hug? Is a hug from me unpleasant for you? Or pleasant?"

Ernest was aware of the urgency in Carolyn's voice. Obviously the hug had tremendous meaning to her—as an affirmation both of her attractiveness and of his commitment to be close to her. He felt cornered, searched for the right response, and then, attempting a charming smile, replied: "When the day comes that I find a hug from an attractive woman like you—attractive in every sense of the word—to be unpleasant, then that's the day to call the mortician."

Carol was extremely encouraged. *"A very attractive woman— attractive in every sense of the word!" Shades of Dr. Cooke and Dr. Zweizung. Now the hunter is starting to make his move. Time for the prey to bait the trap.*

Ernest continued: "Tell me more about touching and its importance to you."

"Not sure how much more I can add," she said. "I know that I think about touching you for hours on end. Sometimes it is very sexual— sometimes I am dying to have you inside me, explode like a geyser, and fill me up with your heat and your wetness. And there are other times when it's not sexual, just warm, loving, holding. Most nights this week I've gone to bed early just to imagine being with you."

No, that's not good enough, Carol thought. I've got to be explicit, got to heat this up. But it's hard to really imagine being sexual with this creep. Fat and oily—that same stained tie day after day, those scuffed Rockport imitation dress shoes.

She continued: "My favorite scene is to imagine the two of us in these chairs and then I move over to you and sit on the floor next to you and you start to stroke my hair and then slip down to join me and stroke me all over."

Ernest had encountered other patients with an erotic transference, but none who expressed it so explicitly and none who stirred him so much. He sat silently, perspiring, weighing his options, and mightily focusing his will on not getting an erection.

"You asked me to speak honestly," Carol continued, "to say what I was thinking."

"And so I did, Carolyn. And you're doing exactly what you should be doing. Honesty is the chief virtue in the realm of therapy. We can, we must, speak about, express, *everything* . . . as long as we each stay in our own physical space."

"Ernest, that doesn't work for me. Speaking and words aren't enough. You know my history with men. The distrust runs so deep. I cannot trust words. Before I saw Ralph I saw a number of therapists, each for one or two sessions. They followed procedure, followed the formula to the letter, adhered to their professional code, remained correctly remote. And every one of them failed me. Until Ralph. Until I met a real therapist—someone willing to be flexible, to work with where I was, what I needed. He saved my life."

"Aside from Ralph, none offered you anything useful?"

"Just words. When I walked out of their office, I took nothing with me. It's the same now. When I leave you without touching you, the words just disappear, you disappear, unless I have some imprint of you on my skin."

I've got to make something happen today, Carol thought. *Got to get this show on the road. And over with.*

"In fact, Ernest," she continued, "what I really wish today is not to talk but to sit next to you on the couch and just feel your presence next to me."

"I wouldn't feel comfortable doing that—that's not the way I can best help you. We've got too much work to do, too many things to talk about."

Ernest was growing more impressed with the depth and power of Carolyn's need for physical contact. It was not, he told himself, a need from which he had to retreat in terror. It was a part of the patient that had to be taken seriously; it was a need that had to be understood and treated like any other need.

During the previous week Ernest had spent time in the library reviewing the literature on eroticized transference. He had been struck by some of Freud's cautionary words regarding the treatment of "women of an elemental passionateness." Freud referred to these patients as "children of nature" who refused to accept the spiritual instead of the physical and were amenable only to the "logic of gruel and the argument of dumplings."

Pessimistic about treating such patients, Freud claimed that the therapist had only two, unacceptable choices: returning the patient's love or being the target of the mortified woman's fury. In either case,

Freud said, one must acknowledge failure and withdraw from the case.

Carol was one of these "children of nature," all right. No doubt about that. But was Freud right? Were there only two possible, equally unacceptable, choices for the therapist? Freud reached those conclusions almost a hundred years ago while immersed in the zeitgeist of Viennese authoritarianism. Perhaps things might be different now. Freud might not have been able to imagine the late twentieth century—times of greater therapist transparency, times when patient and therapist could be *in truth* with each other.

Carol's next words pulled Ernest out of his reverie. "Could we just move to the couch and talk there? It's too cold, too oppressive, talking to you from this distance. Try it for a few minutes. Just sit next to me. I promise not to ask more of you. And I guarantee that it will help me talk and get in touch with deeper currents. Oh, don't shake your head; I know all about the APA codes of behavior, and standardized tactics and conduct. But, Ernest, isn't there a place for creativity? Doesn't the true therapist find a way to help every patient?"

Carol played Ernest like a violin: she chose all the perfect words: "American Psychiatric Association," "standardized," "treatment manuals," "codes of professional conduct," "rules," "creativity," "flexibility." Like waving red words before an iconoclastic bull.

As Ernest listened, some of Seymour Trotter's words came to his mind: *Formal approved technique? Abandon all technique. When you grow up as a therapist, you will be willing to take the leap of authenticity and make the patient's needs—not the APA professional standards—your therapy guide.* Strange how much he had been thinking lately of Seymour. Perhaps it was simply comforting to know a therapist who had once trod this same path. For the moment, Ernest had forgotten, however, that Seymour never found his way back.

Was Carolyn's transference getting out of hand? Seymour had said that it cannot be too powerful. *The stronger the transference,* he had said, *the more effective a weapon to combat the patient's self-destructiveness.* And God knows that Carolyn was self-destructive! Why else would she stay in a marriage like that?

"Ernest," Carol repeated, "please sit next to me on the couch. I need it."

Ernest thought of Jung's advice to treat each patient as individually as possible, to *create a new language of therapy for every patient.* He thought of how Seymour had taken that even further and claimed that the therapist must invent a new therapy for each patient. These words gave him strength. And resolve. He stood, walked over to the couch, eased himself into the corner, and said, "Let's try it."

Carol rose and sat next to him, as close as possible without touching him, and immediately began: "Today is my birthday. Thirty-six. And did I tell you that I have the same birthday as my mother?"

"Happy birthday, Carolyn. I hope the next thirty-six birthdays are going to get better and better for you."

"Thank you, Ernest. You are really sweet." And with that she leaned over and gave Ernest a peck on the cheek. *Yuck,* she thought, *lime soda pop aftershave. Disgusting.*

The need to be physically close, the sitting on the sofa, and now the kiss on the cheek—all eerily reminded Ernest of Seymour Trotter's patient. But, of course, Carolyn was much better put together than the impulse-driven Belle. Ernest was aware of a warm tingle inside. He simply let it be, enjoyed it for a minute, and then herded his growing arousal into a far corner of his mind, got back to work, and assumed his professional voice: "Tell me your mother's dates again, Carolyn."

"She was born in 1937 and died ten years ago at the age of forty-eight. I've been thinking this week that I'm three-quarters her age when she died."

"What feelings does that bring up?"

"Sadness for her. What an unfulfilled life she had. Abandoned by a husband at age thirty. Her whole life spent in bringing up her two children. She had nothing—so little pleasure. I am so glad she lived till I graduated from law school. And glad, too, that she died before Jeb's conviction and jailing. And before my life fell apart."

"This is where we left off last session, Carolyn. I'm struck, again, by your conviction that your mother was doomed at thirty, that she had no other choice but to be unhappy and to die laden with regrets. As though all women who lose their husbands are destined to the same fate. Is that true? Was there no other path possible for her? A more life-affirming path?"

Typical male shit, Carol thought. *I'd like to see him make a self-affirming life while stuck with two kids, with no education because he put his spouse through school, and then get no help from the deadbeat spouse, and Do Not Enter signs blocking every decent job in the country.*

"I don't know, Ernest. Maybe you're right. These are new thoughts for me." But then she couldn't help adding, "I worry, though, about men trivializing the trap most women are in."

"You mean *this* man? Here? Now?"

"No, I didn't mean that—reflex feminism. I know you're on my side, Ernest."

"I've got my blind spots, Carolyn, and I'm open to your pointing them out—more than that, I'm *desirous* of it. But I don't believe this is one of them. It seems to me you're not considering any of your mother's responsibility for her own life design."

Carol bit her tongue and said nothing.

"But let's talk more about your birthday, Carolyn. You know we usually celebrate birthdays as though they are occasions for joy, but I've always believed that the opposite is true—that birthdays are sad markers of our lives passing by and that the birthday celebration is an attempt to deny the sadness. Is any of that true for you? Can you talk about thoughts of being thirty-six? You say you're three-quarters your mother's age when she died. Are you, like her, trapped absolutely in the life you live now? Are you really sentenced forever to living in a joyless marriage?"

"I *am* trapped, Ernest. What do you think I should do?"

Ernest, in order to face Carolyn more easily, had rested his arm along the back of the sofa. Carolyn had surreptitiously undone the second button on her blouse, and now sidled up closer and leaned her head against his arm and shoulder. For a moment, just for a moment, Ernest allowed his hand to rest on her head and caress her hair.

Ah, the creep begins to creep, Carol thought. *Let's see how far he'll creep today. I hope I've got the stomach for this.* She pressed her head closer. Ernest felt the weight of her head on his shoulder. He inhaled her clean citrus scent. He stared down at her cleavage. And then, suddenly, he stood up.

"Carolyn, you know, I think it's better if we go back to our old seating arrangement." Ernest moved back to his chair.

Carol remained where she was. She seemed on the verge of tears as she asked, "Why won't you stay on the couch? Because I just put my head on your shoulder?"

"It's not the way I feel I can best be useful to you. I think I need to keep some space and distance to be able to work with you."

Carol reluctantly moved back to her chair, took off her shoes and folded her legs beneath her. "Perhaps I shouldn't say this—maybe it's unfair to you—but I wonder if you would feel differently if I were a really attractive woman."

"That's absolutely not the issue." Ernest tried to compose himself. "In fact, it's the other way around; the very reason I *cannot* stay in close physical contact with you is that I *do* find you attractive and arousing. And I can't be erotically attracted to you and be your therapist at the same time."

"You know, Ernest, I've been thinking. I told you, didn't I, that I went to one of your readings at Printer's Inc. bookstore about a month ago?"

"Yes, you said that was when you made the decision to come see me."

"Well, I was watching you there before the reading, and I couldn't help noticing that you were coming on to that attractive woman sitting next to you."

Ernest shuddered. *Shit! She saw me with Nan Carlin. This is a goddamn quagmire. What have I gotten myself into?*

Never again would Ernest take therapist transparency so lightly. There was no longer any point in his trying to think of how Marshal, or other mentors, might respond to Carolyn's statement. He was so far out on a limb, so far beyond what traditional technique decreed, so far beyond acceptable clinical practice, that he knew he was entirely on his own—lost in the wilderness of wildcat therapy. His only choice was to continue being honest and to follow his instincts.

"And . . . your feelings about that, Carolyn?"

"How about *your* feelings, Ernest?"

"Embarrassment. To be honest with you, Carolyn, this is a therapist's worst nightmare. It's extremely uncomfortable to be talking to you, or any patient, about my personal life with women—but I'm committed to working *in truth* with you, and I'll try to stay with you on this, Carolyn. Now *your* feelings?"

"Oh, all kinds of feelings. Envy. Anger. Unfairness. Unlucky."

"Can you go into these? For example, anger or unfairness."

"It's just all so arbitrary. If only I had done what she did—moved and sat next to you. If only I had had the nerve, the courage, to speak to you."

"And . . . then?"

"Then everything might have been different. Tell me the truth, Ernest, what would have happened if I had approached you, if I had tried to pick you up? Would you have been interested in me?"

"All these conditional questions—these 'ifs' and 'would haves'— what are you really asking, Carolyn? I've mentioned more than once I consider you an attractive woman. I can't help wondering—are you wanting to hear me say that again?"

"And I'm wondering if you're avoiding my question with your question, Ernest."

"Whether I might have responded to your advances? The answer is, it's very possible I might have. I mean, yes. I probably would have."

Silence. Ernest felt naked. This was such a wildly different type of discourse than he had ever had with a patient that he was seriously considering whether he could continue treating Carolyn. Certainly not only Freud, but the consensus of the psychoanalytic theorists he had been reading during the week, would have decreed that a patient with an eroticized transference like Carolyn was untreatable—certainly by him.

"So, what do you feel now?" he asked.

"Well, this is exactly what I mean by arbitrary, Ernest. A slightly different toss of the dice and you and I might be lovers now, rather than therapist and patient. And I honestly believe you could do more for me as a lover now than as a therapist. I wouldn't ask much of you, Ernest, just meet once or twice a week—to hold me and get rid of this sexual frustration that's killing me."

"I hear you, Carolyn, but I am your therapist and *not* your lover."

"But that is purely arbitrary. Nothing is necessary. Everything could be otherwise. Ernest, let's roll back the clock—go back to the bookstore and toss the dice again. Become my lover; I am dying with frustration."

As she spoke, Carol slipped off her chair, glided over to Ernest, sat on the floor next to his chair, and rested her hand on his knee.

Ernest once again placed his hand on Carolyn's head. *God, I like to touch this woman. And her burning desire to make love to me— Christ knows I can empathize. How many times have I been overcome by lust? I feel sorry for her. And I understood what she means about the arbitrariness of our meeting. It's too bad for me, too. I'd rather be her lover than her therapist. I'd love to crawl off this chair and take off her clothes. I'd love to caress her body. And who knows? Suppose I had met her in the bookstore? Suppose we had become lovers? Maybe she's right—maybe I would have offered her more that way than as a therapist! But we'll never know—that's an experiment that can't be run.*

"Carolyn, what you're asking—roll back the clock, become your lover . . . I'll be honest with you . . . you're not the only one who is tempted—that sounds wonderful to me, too. I think we could enjoy each other very much. But I'm afraid *this* clock," Ernest said, pointing to the unobtrusive clock in his bookcase, "can't be turned backward."

As Ernest spoke he began to stroke Carolyn's hair again. She leaned more heavily against his leg. Suddenly he withdrew his hand and said: "Please, Carolyn, go back to your chair again, and let me say something important to you."

He waited while Carol planted a quick kiss on his knee and took her seat. *Let him make his little speech of protest, go through with his game. He's got to pretend to himself that he's resisting.*

"Let's take a few steps back," Ernest said, "and examine what's happening here. Let me review things as I see them. You were in distress. You sought out my assistance as a mental health professional. We met and I entered into a covenant with you—a covenant in which I committed myself to help you in your struggles. As a result of the intimate nature of our meetings, you've developed loving feelings toward me. And I fear that I'm not wholly innocent here: I believe my behavior—hugging you, touching your hair—is fanning the flames. And I'm worried about that. At any rate, I cannot now suddenly change my mind, take advantage of those loving feelings of yours, and decide to pursue my own pleasure with you."

"But, Ernest, you're missing the point. What I'm saying is that being my lover is to be the best possible therapist for me. For five years Ralph and I—"

"Ralph is Ralph and I am me. Carolyn, we're out of time and we'll have to continue this discussion next session." Ernest rose to signify the end of the hour. "But allow me one last observation. I hope that in our next session you will begin to explore more ways of taking what I *do* have to offer rather than continue to knock up against my limits."

As Carol was getting her good-bye hug from Ernest, she said: "And a last comment from me, Ernest. You have argued—eloquently—that I not go the route of my mother, that I not abdicate responsibility for the course of my life. And here, today, I am enacting your counsel—I am trying to make things better for myself. I see what—and who—I need in my life and I am trying to seize the day. You told me to live in such a way as to eliminate future regrets—and that is just what I am trying to do."

Ernest could find no suitable reply.

EIGHTEEN

*M*arshal sat on his deck during a free hour and enjoyed his maple grove bonsai: nine tiny beautiful maples, their scarlet leaves beginning to burst their bud jackets. Last weekend he had repotted them. With the gentle prods of a chopstick, he had cleaned the soil from the roots of each tree and then positioned them in the large blue ceramic basin in traditional fashion: two unequal clusters, of six and three trees, separated by a tiny gray-pink boulder, imported from Japan. Marshal noticed that one of the trees in the larger cluster was beginning to deviate, and in a few months would cross the plane of its neighbor. He cut off a six-inch piece of copper wire, carefully wrapped it around the trunk of the wayward maple, and gently bent it back into a more vertical position. Every few days he would bend the wire a little more and then, five or six months hence, remove the wire before it scarred the trunk of the impressionable maple. Ah, he thought, if only psychotherapy were so straightforward.

Ordinarily he would have called upon his wife's green thumb to adjust the course of the errant maple, but he and Shirley had had a blow-up over the weekend and had not spoken for three days. This latest episode was only symptomatic of an estrangement that had been growing for years.

It had all started, Marshal believed, several years ago when Shirley had enrolled in her first ikebana course. She developed a passion for the art and displayed unusual skill. Not that Marshal could judge her ability himself—he knew nothing about ikebana and made it a point to continue knowing nothing—but there was no denying the roomful of prizes and ribbons that she had won in competitions.

Shirley soon centered her entire life around ikebana. Her circle of friends consisted exclusively of fellow ikebana devotees, while she and Marshal shared less and less. To make matters worse, her eighty-year-old ikebana master, to whom she was slavishly devoted, encouraged her to begin the practice of Buddhist Vipassnia meditation, which soon placed even more demands on her time.

Three years ago Marshal had grown so concerned about the impact of ikebana and Vipassnia (about which Marshal also chose to remain uninformed) on their marriage that he pleaded with Shirley to enter graduate school in clinical psychology. He hoped that sharing the same field would bring them closer together. He hoped also that, once Shirley entered his field, she would be able to appreciate his professional artistry. Then, too, it would not be long before he could refer patients to her, and the idea of a second income was sweet.

But things had not gone as he had wished. Shirley did enter graduate school, but she didn't give up her other interests. Now her graduate studies plus the time spent in the collection and preparation of flowers or in meditation at the Zen Center left virtually no time for Marshal. And then, three days ago, she had devastated him by informing him that her doctoral dissertation, in its final stages of preparation, was a study of the effectiveness of ikebana practice in the management of panic disorder.

"Perfect," he had told her. "The perfect spousal support for my candidacy for presidency of the Psychoanalytic Institute—a flake wife doing flake flower-arranging therapy!"

They spoke little. Shirley returned home only to sleep—and they slept in different rooms. Their sex life had been nonexistent for months. And now Shirley had gone on strike in the kitchen; each night all that greeted Marshal on the kitchen table was a new flower arrangement.

Tending to his small maple grove provided Marshal some sorely needed tranquillity. There was something deeply serene about the act of wrapping the maple with copper. Pleasant . . . yes, the bonsai were a pleasant diversion.

But not a way of life. Shirley had to magnify everything, to make flowers her raison d'être. No sense of proportion. She had even proposed that he introduce bonsai care into his long-term therapy practice. Idiotic! Marshal clipped some new downward-heading slips of the juniper and watered all the trees. It was not a good time for him. Not only was he aggravated with Shirley; he was also disappointed with Ernest, who had precipitately terminated supervision. And then there were other inconveniences.

First, Adriana had not shown for her appointment. Nor phoned. Very strange. Very unlike her. Marshal had waited a couple of days, then phoned her, left her an appointment time on her voice mail for the same hour the following week, and requested that she notify him if the time was not convenient.

And the fee for Adriana's missed hour? Ordinarily Marshal would, without a second thought, charge her for the missed hour. But these were not ordinary circumstances, and Marshal ruminated about the fee for days. Peter had given him one thousand dollars—the fee for five sessions with Adriana. Why not simply deduct two hundred for the missed session? Would Peter even know about it? If he did, would he be affronted? Would he feel that Marshal was being disloyal or petty? Or ungrateful for Peter's largess—the bicycle helmet company investment, the endowed lecture series, the Rolex?

On the other hand, it might be better to handle the fee just as he would with any other patient. Peter would respect his professional consistency and adherence to his own standards. In fact, had not Peter chided him more than once for not placing a proper value on his services?

In the end Marshal decided to bill Adriana for the missed session. It was the right thing to do—he was certain of it. But, then, why was he so fretful? Why could he not shake the dark, lingering feeling that he would live to regret this decision?

This annoying attack of ruminitis was a minor dusky cloud compared to the storm that was breaking around Marshal's role in the institute's expulsion of Seth Pande. Art Bookert, an eminent humor columnist, had picked up the recall story in the *San Francisco Chronicle* (MOVE OVER, FORD, TOYOTA, CHEVROLET; NOW PSYCHIATRISTS RECALL PRODUCT) and had written a satirical piece predicting that therapists would soon be opening offices in auto repair shops where, in marathon sessions, they would treat clients waiting for automobile service. In their new partnership, the column said, therapists and auto repair shop operators would offer a joint, five-year warranty guaranteeing brakes and impulse control, ignition systems and assertiveness, automatic lubrication and self-soothing mechanisms, steering and mood control, muffler/exhaust systems and gastrointestinal tranquillity, and main shaft integrity and priapic potency.

Bookert's column (HENRY FORD AND SIGMUND FREUD AGREE ON MERGER) appeared prominently in both *The New York Times* and *The International Herald Tribune*. The besieged institute president, John Weldon, immediately washed his hands of the business by referring all inquiries to Marshal, the executor of the recall plan. Psychoanalyst colleagues throughout the country, who were not amused, phoned Marshal all week. In a single day the presidents of four psychoanalytic institutes—New York, Chicago, Philadelphia, and Boston—had phoned to express their alarm.

Marshal had done his best to soothe them with the news that only one patient had responded, that he, himself, was treating this patient in a highly effective course of brief therapy, and that the recall notice would not be reprinted.

But no such soothing was possible when a highly irritated Dr. Sunderland, the president of the International Psychoanalytic Association, called with the disturbing news that Shelly Merriman had repeatedly, and aggressively, faxed and phoned his office claiming that he had been damaged by Dr. Pande's errant methods and would soon institute legal action if his demands for financial settlement were not met immediately.

"What the hell's going on out there?" Dr. Sunderland had asked. "The entire country is laughing at us. Again! Patients are bringing in copies of *Listening to Prozac* to their analytic hours; drug companies, neurochemists, behaviorists, and critics like Jeffrey Masson are pickaxing our foundations; recovered-memory suits and implanted-memory countersuits are nipping at our heels. Goddamnit, this is not—NOT, I repeat—what the analytic enterprise needs! By whose authority did you place that recall notice?"

Marshal calmly explained the nature of the emergency facing the institute and the necessity for the recall action.

"I'm chagrined that you haven't been informed of these events, Dr. Sunderland," Marshal added. "Once you are fully appraised of everything, I am certain you'll appreciate the logic behind our actions. Furthermore, we followed proper protocol. The day following our institute vote, I checked this all out with Ray Wellington, the secretary of the International."

"Wellington? I've just learned that he's moving his office and his entire clinic to California! Now I'm beginning to understand the logic. Southern California sprouts-and-spinach logic. This whole catastrophe has been scripted in Hollywood."

"San Francisco, Dr. Sunderland, is in Northern California, four hundred miles due north of Hollywood—about the same distance as between Boston and Washington. We are not in Southern California. Trust me when I say there is northern logic behind our actions."

"Northern logic? Shit! Why didn't your northern logic inform you that Dr. Pande is seventy-four years old and dying of lung cancer? I know he's a pain in the ass, but how much longer can he last? One year? Two years? You are the conservator of the psychoanalytic seedbed: a little more patience, a little more continence, and nature would have weeded your garden.

"All right, enough of this!" Dr. Sunderland continued. "What's done is done. The future is pressing in on me: I have an immediate decision to make and I want your input. This Shelly Merriman is threatening suit. He's willing to back off for a seventy-thousand settlement. Our attorneys believe he'd settle for half of that. We fear precedent setting, of course. What's your reading on this? How serious is the threat? Will seventy or even thirty-five thousand dollars make Mr. Merriman go away? And stay away? Will that money buy silence? How discreet is your Mr. Merriman?"

Marshal responded quickly, in his most self-assured voice: "My advice is to do nothing, Dr. Sunderland. Leave this to me. You may count on me to handle the matter effectively and efficiently. The threat is empty, I assure you. The man is bluffing. And as for money buying his silence and discretion? No chance of that. Forget it—there is significant sociopathy. We must take a firm stance."

It was only later that afternoon as he escorted Shelly into his office that Marshal realized he had made an egregious error: for the first time in his professional career, he had violated patient-therapist confidentiality. He had panicked while on the phone with Sunderland. How could he have made that comment about sociopathy? He should have told Sunderland nothing about Mr. Merriman.

He was beside himself. If Mr. Merriman found out, he would either sue him for malpractice or, being told of the International's uncertainty, escalate his demands for financial settlement. The situation was spiraling into full catastrophe.

There was only one sensible course, Marshal decided: get on the phone to Dr. Sunderland as soon as possible and acknowledge his indiscretion—a momentary, understandable lapse emanating from a conflict of loyalty: wishing to serve both the International and his patient. Surely Dr. Sunderland would understand and would be honor-bound to repeat his remarks about his patient to no one. Of course, none of this was going to repair his reputation in national or international psychoanalytic circles, but Marshal could no longer concern himself with his image or his political future: his goal now was damage control.

Shelly entered the office and lingered at the Musler sculpture longer than usual.

"Love that orange globe, Doc. You ever want to sell it, let me know. I'd feel it up, get cool and soothed before every big game." Shelly plopped into his seat. "Well, Doc, I'm doing a little better. Your interpretations have helped. Better tennis for sure; I've cut loose like crazy on my second serve. Willy and I have been practicing three, four hours a day, and I think we've got a good shot at winning the La Costa tourney next week. So that part's good. But still got a ways to go on the other stuff. That's what I want to work on."

"Other stuff?" asked Marshal, though he knew full well what other stuff.

"You know. The stuff we were working on last time. The tells. Want to try all that again? Refresh your memory? Ten-dollar bill . . . you guess five times, I'll guess five times."

"No. No. Won't be necessary. I've gotten the concept . . . you made your point effectively. But you said at the end of the last session you had some ideas about how to continue the work."

"Very definitely. Here's my plan. Just like you had some tells last time and it cost you forty bucks in our little game, well, I am certain I am flashing tells all the time in my game, poker. And what's the reason I'm flashing tells? Because of stress, because of all Dr. Pande's 'errant therapy'—wasn't that the way you put it?"

"Something like that."

"I think those were your words."

"Errant methods, I believe I said."

"Okay, 'errant methods.' Same difference. Because of Pande's errant methods I've developed bad nervous habits in poker. Just like you had your tells last week, I've got a ton of bad tells in poker. I'm sure of it—that's absolutely got to be why I lost that forty thousand dollars in my friendly social game."

"Yeah, go on," said Marshal, growing wary. Though absolutely committed to placating his patient in every possible manner and to bring therapy to an immediate and satisfying conclusion, he was beginning to smell real danger.

"How does therapy fit in with this?" he asked Shelly. "I trust you're not expecting me to play poker with you. I'm not a gambler, certainly not a poker player. How could you possibly learn anything from playing poker with me?"

"Hold on, Doc. Whoever said anything about playing poker with you? Though I won't deny it passed through my mind. No, what's needed is the real situation—to have you observe me play in a real game, with the high stakes and the tension that goes along with it—and use your observation skills to point out to me what I'm doing to give away my hands—and my money."

"You want me to go to your poker game and watch you play?" Marshal felt relieved. As bizarre as this request was, it was not as bad as what he had feared a few minutes ago. Right now he'd accede to any request that would get Dr. Sunderland off his back, and get Shelly out of his office forever.

"Are you kidding? You come to the game with the guys? Man, that would be a scene—coming to the game with my own private shrink!" Shelly slapped his knees as he guffawed. "Oh, man . . . great . . . Doc, that would make us legends, you and me—me bringing my shrink and his couch to the game . . . the guys would be talking about that into the next millennium."

"Glad you find this so amusing, Mr. Merriman. I'm not sure I get it. Maybe you ought to tell me: what's your plan?"

"There's only one way. You have to come with me to a professional gambling casino and observe me play. No one would know us. We'd go incognito."

"You want me to go to Las Vegas with you? Cancel my other patients?"

"Whoa, Doc. There you go again. You *are* jumpy today. First time I've seen you like this. Who said anything about Las Vegas or canceling anything or anybody? This is simple-like. Twenty minutes south from here, just off the highway to the airport, there's a first-class game room called Avocado Joe's.

"What I'm asking from you—and this is my last request of you—is one evening of your time. Two or three hours. You watch everything I do at the poker game. At the end of each hand I'll flash you my down cards so you will know exactly what I was playing. You watch me: how I act when I've got a good hand, when I'm bluffing, when I'm pulling for a card trying to make a boat or a flush, when I'm set and don't care what cards get turned. You watch everything: my hands, gestures, facial expressions, my eyes, how I play with my chips, when I pull my ear, scratch my balls, pick my nose, cough, swallow—everything I do."

"And you said 'last request'?" Marshal asked.

"That's it! Your job will be over. The rest is up to me—to take in what you give me, to study it, and then use it in the future. You're off duty after Avocado Joe's; you'll have done all that a shrink can possibly do."

"And . . . uh . . . we could formalize that somehow?" Marshal's wheels were turning. A formal letter of satisfaction from Shelly might be his salvation: he'd fax it immediately to Sunderland.

"You mean some kind of signed letter saying it's been a successful course of treatment?"

"Something like that, something very informal, just between you and me, something saying that I've treated you successfully, that there are no remaining symptoms," said Marshal.

Shelly hesitated while his wheels turned, too. "I could agree to that, Doc . . . in exchange for a letter from you expressing your satisfaction with my progress. Might prove useful in patching up some marital wounds."

"Okay, let me go over it again," said Marshal. "I go to Avocado Joe's, spend two hours there observing you play. Then we exchange letters and our business together is at an end. Agreed? Shake hands on this?" Marshal extended his hand.

"Probably closer to two and a half hours—I need time to prepare you before the game, and we need some time after the game for you to debrief me."

"Okay. Two and a half hours, then."

The two men shook hands.

"Now," asked Marshal, "the timing of our rendezvous at Avocado Joe's?"

"Tonight? Eight o'clock? Tomorrow I leave for the week at La Costa with Willy."

"Can't tonight. I have a teaching commitment."

"Too bad, I'm really primed to get started. Can't finesse the teaching?"

"Out of the question. I've made a commitment."

"Okay. Let's see, I'm back in a week; how about a week from Friday—eight o'clock at Avocado Joe's? Meet you at the restaurant there?"

Marshal nodded. After Shelly left he collapsed in his chair and felt a wave of relief sweep over him. Amazing! How had this happened? he wondered. That he, one of the world's premier analysts, should feel relieved, should look forward with gratitude to a rendezvous with a patient at Avocado Joe's?

A knock on the door and Shelly entered and sat down again. "Forgot to tell you something, Doc. It's against the rules to stand around and watch poker at Avocado Joe's. You will have to play in the game with me. Here, I brought you a book."

Shelly handed Marshal a copy of *Texas Hold 'Em—the Texas Way.*

"No sweat, Doc," said Shelly in response to the look of horror on Marshal's face. "Simple game. Two down and then five open common cards. The book will explain all. I'll tell you what you need to know next week, before we play. You drop out of every hand—you just lose the ante. Won't amount to much."

"Are you serious? I have to play?"

"Tell you what, Doc—I'll share your losses. And if you have a ballbreaker hand, stay in and bet and you can keep the winnings. Read the book first and I'll explain more to you when we meet. It's a good deal for you."

Marshal watched Shelly rise and saunter out of his office, caressing the orange globe as he passed it.

A good deal, he calls it. *Mr. Merriman, what I call a good deal is when I will have seen the last of you and your good deals.*

NINETEEN

*F*or weeks Ernest sweated through hour after hour with Carol. Their sessions crackled with erotic tension and, though Ernest strove mightily to defend his boundaries, Carol began to breach them. They met twice weekly but, unbeknownst to Carol, she occupied far more than her allocated fifty minutes. On the days of their appointment Ernest awoke in the morning with a keen sense of anticipation. He imagined Carolyn's face in his mirror observing him as he scrubbed his cheeks with extra vigor, shaved more closely, and splashed on the Royall Lyme aftershave.

"Carolyn days" were dress-up days. Ernest saved his best pressed pants for Carolyn, his crispest, most colorful shirts, and his most stylish ties. A couple of weeks ago Carolyn had attempted to give him one of Wayne's neckties—her husband was now too ill to go out, she explained, and since their San Francisco apartment contained little storage space, she was discarding much of his formal wardrobe. Ernest, to Carolyn's great irritation, had, of course, declined the gift, even though Carolyn had spent the entire hour trying to persuade him to change his mind. But the next morning, while dressing, Ernest had the strongest craving for that necktie. It was exquisite: a Japanese motif of small dark glowing flowers layered around a bold central forest-green iridescent blossom. Ernest had gone out shopping for one like it, but in vain—it was clearly one of a kind. At times he puzzled about how he might learn where she had gotten it. Perhaps, if she were to offer it again, he might say that a necktie at the end of therapy, a couple of years down the road, might not be entirely inappropriate.

Carolyn days were new clothes days as well. Today it was a new vest and pair of trousers he had purchased at the Wilkes Bashford annual sale. The beige-heather hopsack vest was superb over his pink button-down shirt and brown herringbone trousers. Perhaps, he thought, the vest might be better displayed without a jacket. He would leave the jacket draped over a chair and wear just a shirt, tie, and vest. Ernest inspected himself in the mirror. Yes, that worked—a bit daring, but he could carry it off.

Ernest loved to observe Carolyn: that graceful walk as she entered his office, the way she moved her chair closer to him before she sat, that sexy swishing sound of her stockings as she crossed her legs. He loved that first moment when they looked into each other's eyes before starting the hour's work. And, most of all, he loved the way she adored him, the way she described her masturbatory fantasies about him—fantasies that grew ever more graphic, ever more evocative, ever more thrilling. An hour never felt long enough, and when the session was over Ernest, more than once, hurried to his window to snatch one last look at Carolyn as she descended his front steps. One surprising thing he noticed after the last two sessions was that she must have changed into sneakers in his waiting room because he saw her jog down his front stairs and up Sacramento Street!

What a woman! God, what bad luck that they *hadn't* met socially at that bookstore instead of becoming therapist and patient! Ernest liked everything about Carolyn: her quick intelligence and intensity, the fire in her eyes, her bouncy walk and limber body, her sleek, patterned stockings, her absolute ease and candor in discussing sex—her longings, her masturbation, her one-night stands.

And he liked her vulnerability. Although she had a tough and quick external persona (probably necessitated and reinforced by her courtroom work), she was also willing, with a tactful invitation, to enter the areas of her pain. For example, her fears of passing on her bitterness toward men to her daughter, her early abandonment by her father, her grief for her mother, her desperation about being trapped in a marriage to a man she detested.

Despite his sexual attraction to Carolyn, Ernest clung resolutely to his therapeutic perspective and kept himself under continuous personal surveillance. As far as he could tell, he was still doing excellent therapy. He was highly motivated to help her, had stayed focused, and, time and again, had brought her to important insights. Lately he had confronted her with all the implications of her lifelong bitterness and resentment—and her lack of awareness that others experienced life differently.

Whenever Carolyn introduced distractions to the therapy work— and it happened every hour, with extraneous inquiries into his personal life or pleading for more physical contact—Ernest had skillfully and vigorously resisted. Perhaps too vigorously in the last session, when he had responded to Carolyn's request for a few minutes of "couch time" with a dose of existential shock therapy. He had drawn a line on a sheet of paper, denoted one end of the line as her birthday and the other end as her death day. He handed her the paper and asked her to put an X on the line to indicate where in her life span she was at this moment. Then he asked her to meditate a few moments on her response.

Ernest had used this device with other patients, but had never encountered such a powerful response. Carolyn placed a cross on the line three-quarters of the way to the end, stared at it silently for two or three minutes, then said, "Such a small life," and burst into tears. Ernest asked her to say more, but all she could do was shake her head and say, "I don't know. I don't know why I'm crying so hard."

"I think I know, Carolyn. I think you're crying for all the unlived life inside of you. I hope, as a result of our work, we'll help unshackle some of that life."

That had made her sob even harder, and once again she left the office in a hurry. And without a hug.

Ernest always enjoyed the good-bye hug that had become a standard part of their hour, but he had staunchly refused all of Carolyn's other demands for touch, aside from her occasional request to sit next to him for a brief period on the couch. Ernest invariably ended these sitting interludes after a few minutes, or earlier if Carolyn edged too close or he got too aroused.

But Ernest was not blind to disturbing warning signals from within. He realized that his excitement about the Carolyn days was portentous. And so was Carolyn's insidious incursion into his fantasy life and particularly into his masturbatory fantasies. And the self-observing part of Ernest found it even more ominous that the setting of his fantasies was invariably his office. It was irresistibly exciting to imagine Carolyn sitting across from him in his office discussing her problems and then for him to beckon her closer with a mere hook of his finger, instruct her to sit in his lap and continue talking as he slowly unbuttoned her blouse, uncoupled her brassiere, caressed and kissed her breasts, gently removed her panty hose, and slowly slid to the floor with her, deliciously entering her while she continued to speak to him as a patient, and then taking long slow strokes toward muffled orgasm.

His fantasies both aroused and disgusted him—they offended the very foundation of the life of service to which he had dedicated himself. He understood perfectly that the sexual excitement in his fantasy was heightened by the sense of absolute power he wielded over Carolyn, by the forbiddenness of the clinical situation. Breaking sexual taboos was always exciting: Hadn't Freud pointed out, a century ago, that there would be no need of taboos if forbidden behavior were not so enticing? But such lucid understanding of the source of the excitement in his fantasies did little to diminish their power or allure.

Ernest knew he needed help. First, he turned again to the professional literature on erotic transference and found more there than he expected. For one thing, he was comforted by the knowledge that, for generations, other therapists had struggled with his dilemma. Many had pointed out, as Ernest had concluded on his own, that the therapist must not avoid the erotic material in therapy or respond in a disapproving or condemning fashion lest the material be driven underground and the patient feel that her wishes are dangerous and damaging. Freud had insisted that there was much to be learned from the patient's erotic transference. In one of his exquisite metaphors, he said that to fail to explore erotic transference would be analogous to summoning a spirit from the spirit world and then sending it away without asking it a single question.

It was sobering for Ernest to read that the great majority of therapists who had become sexually involved with patients claimed they were offering love. "But don't mistake this for love," many therapists had written. "This is not love—it is but another form of sexual abuse." It was also sobering to read that many offending therapists had felt, as he had, that it would be cruel to withhold sexual love from a patient who craved and needed it so much!

Others suggested that no intense erotic transference could persist for long if the therapist did not unconsciously collude. A well-known analyst suggested that the therapist attend to his own love life and ensure that his "libidinal and narcissistic budget be sufficiently positive." That rang true for Ernest and he set about balancing his libidinal budget by resuming a relationship with Marsha, an old friend with whom he had had a nonpassionate but sexually satisfying arrangement.

The idea of unconscious collusion troubled Ernest. It was not unlikely that he was, in some covert fashion, conveying his lustful feelings to Carolyn—confusing her by giving her one message verbally and an opposing message nonverbally.

Another psychiatrist, whom Ernest particularly respected, wrote that some grandiose therapists sometimes resort to sexual relationships when they are in despair about their inability to cure the patient, when their belief in themselves as an omnipotent healer is frustrated. That didn't fit him, Ernest thought—but he knew someone it did fit: Seymour Trotter! The more he thought about Seymour—his hubris, his pride in being thought of as "the therapist of last resort," his belief that, if he set himself the task, he could cure every patient—the more it clarified what had happened between Seymour and Belle.

Ernest turned for help to his friends, especially to Paul. Speaking to Marshal was out of the question. Marshal's reaction would have been entirely predictable: first censure, then outrage at Ernest's departure from traditional technique, and finally absolute insistence that he terminate therapy with the patient and reenter personal analysis.

Besides, Marshal was no longer in the picture. Last week Ernest had to terminate his supervision because of a curious set of events. Six months before, Ernest had accepted a new patient, Jess, who had abruptly terminated treatment with a San Francisco analyst whom he had been seeing for two years. When Ernest inquired about the circumstances of his termination, Jess described a peculiar incident.

Jess, an indefatigable runner, had one day, while jogging through Golden Gate Park, seen a strange disturbance deep in the branches of a scarlet weeping Japanese maple. When he approached, he saw it was his analyst's wife locked in a passionate embrace with a saffron-robed Buddhist monk.

What a dilemma. There was no doubt it was his analyst's wife: Jess had been taking training in ikebana, and she was a well-known master in the Sogetsu school, the most innovative of ikebana traditions. He had met her twice before at flower-arranging competitions.

What should Jess do? Though his analyst was a formal, distant man for whom Jess felt no great affection, still he was competent, decent, and had been so helpful that Jess was reluctant to hurt him by telling him the painful truth about his wife. Yet, on the other hand, how could he possibly continue his analysis while bearing such an enormous secret? Jess saw only one course of action: to terminate analysis under the pretext of some unavoidable scheduling conflict.

Jess knew he still needed therapy and at the recommendation of his sister, a clinical psychologist, began work with Ernest. Jess was the scion of a wealthy old San Francisco family. Exposed to the driving ambition of his father and the expectation that he would eventually enter the family banking business, Jess had rebelled on every front: flunking out of college, surfing for two years, abusing alcohol and cocaine. After the painful dissolution of a five-year marriage, he had slowly begun to put his life back together. First, a prolonged hospitalization and outpatient recovery program for substance abuse, then training in landscape architecture, a profession of his own choice, then two years of analysis with Marshal, and a rigorous physical conditioning and running regimen.

In his first six months of therapy with Ernest, Jess described why he had stopped therapy but refused to name his previous therapist. Jess's sister had told too many stories about how therapists love to gossip about one another. But, as the weeks went by, Jess grew to trust Ernest and, one day, suddenly divulged the name of his previous therapist: Marshal Streider.

Ernest was stunned. Not Marshal Streider! Not his impregnable, Rock of Gibraltar supervisor! Ernest was plunged into the same dilemma Jess had faced. He could neither tell Marshal the truth—he was bound by professional confidentiality—nor continue supervision with Marshal while possessing this burning secret. The incident was not entirely inconvenient, however, since Ernest had been building the resolve to terminate supervision and Jess's revelation provided the necessary impetus.

And so, with much trepidation, Ernest told Marshal of his decision. "Marshal, for some time now I've been feeling it's time to cut the cord. You've brought me a long way and now, finally, at age thirty-eight, I've decided to leave home and be on my own."

Ernest braced himself for a vigorous challenge from Marshal. He knew precisely what Marshal would say: Surely he would insist on analyzing his motives for such a precipitate termination. Without doubt, he would inquire about the timing of Ernest's decision. As for Ernest's pathetic desire to be on his own, Marshal would cut the ground out from under that in an instant. He would suggest it was more evidence of Ernest's juvenile iconoclasm; he might even intimate that this impetuousness suggested that Ernest lacked the maturity and the drive for self-knowledge so necessary for candidacy in the psychoanalytic institute.

Curiously, Marshal did none of these things. Appearing weary and distracted, he responded in a perfunctory fashion: "Yes, perhaps it's time. We can always pick up again in the future. Good luck to you, Ernest! My very best."

But it was not with relief that Ernest heard these words and ended his supervision with Marshal. Instead, puzzlement. And, yes, disappointment. Disapprobation would have been far preferable to such indifference.

After spending a half-hour reading a long article on therapist-patient sexual behavior faxed to him by Paul, Ernest picked up the phone.

"Thanks for 'Office Romeos and Lovesick Doctors'! Good God, Paul!"

"Ah, I see you got my fax."

"Unfortunately, yes."

"Why 'unfortunately,' Ernest? Wait a minute, let me switch to the cordless phone and into my comfortable chair. I've got a feeling this is going to be a histrionic conversation. . . . Okay . . . now again, why 'unfortunately'?"

"Because 'Office Romeo' is not what's happening. That article demeans something very precious, something of which it has no comprehension. Trivializing language can be used to vulgarize any finer sentiment."

"That's the way it seems to you because you're too close to see what's happening. But it's important for you to see what it looks like from the outside. Ernest, since our last talk I've worried about you. Listen to all the things you're saying: 'being in deep truth, loving your patient, her being touch-deprived, you being flexible enough to give her the physical closeness she needs to work in therapy.' I think you're going off your fucking rocker! I think you're heading for serious trouble. Look, you know me—I've been ridiculing orthodox Freudians ever since we entered this field, right?"

Ernest grunted assent.

"But when the doyen said 'finding a love object is always *refinding* one,' he was onto something. That patient is stirring up something in you that comes from elsewhere—far away and long ago."

No response from Ernest.

"Okay, Ernest, here's a riddle for you: What woman do you know who unconditionally loved every little molecule of your body? Three guesses!"

"Oh, no, Paul. You're not getting on the mother shtick again? I never denied I had a good nursing mother. She gave me a good start the first couple of years; I developed lots of good basic trust—that's probably where my promiscuous self-revealing comes from. But she wasn't a good mother when I started off on my own; never, till the day she died, could she forgive me for leaving her. So what's your point? That in the dawn of life I was imprinted like a young duckling and have been searching for my mother-duck look-alike ever since?

"And even so," Ernest continued—he knew his lines well; Paul and he had had similar conversations in the past—"I'll give you that. Part of it! But you're being so reductionistic—that I'm *nothing but* a grown-up still searching for the all-accepting mother. That is bullshit! I am, all of us are, so much more than that. Your mistake, and the mistake, too, of the entire analytic enterprise, is to forget that there's a real relationship in the present that's not determined by the past, that exists in the moment, two souls touching, influenced more by the future than by the early past—by the not-yet, by the destiny that awaits us. By our camaraderie, by our huddling together to face and endure the hard existential facts of life. And that this form of relationship—pure, accepting, mutual, equal—is redemptive and the most potent force we have for healing."

"Pure? Pure?" Paul knew Ernest too well to be intimidated or swayed by his oratorical flights. "*A pure relationship?* If it were pure, I wouldn't be ragging on you. You're getting off on this woman, Ernest. For chrissakes, admit it!"

"An asexual hug at the end of the session—that's it. And I've got this under control. Yes, I've got fantasies. I've admitted that. But I keep them in fantasyland."

"Well, I bet your fantasies and her fantasies are doing a moist minuet in fantasyland. But the truth, Ernest, reassure me. No other touching? The time sitting next to her on the couch? A harmless kiss?"

The thought of caressing Carolyn's fine hair as she leaned against him wafted through Ernest's mind. But he knew that wouldn't be understood, that Paul would vulgarize that as well. "No, that's it. No other contact. Paul, believe me, I'm doing good therapy with this woman. I'm handling this."

"If I thought so, I wouldn't be nagging you about it. There's something about this woman that I can't understand. To keep on coming after you like that hour after hour. Even after you are clear and firm about boundaries. Or you think you are. Now I'm not questioning that you're gorgeous—who could resist that cute little ass of yours? But something else is going on: I'm convinced you are unconsciously encouraging her . . . you want my advice, Ernest? My advice is to bail out. Now! To transfer her to a female therapist. And to abandon your self-disclosure experiment as well! Or confine it to male patients—at least for now!"

After he hung up, Ernest paced around his office. He always told Paul the truth, and this rare lapse left him feeling alone. To distract himself he turned to his correspondence. To renew his malpractice insurance, he had to fill out a questionnaire teeming with queries about his relationship with patients. It posed explicit questions. Did he ever touch patients? If so, in which way? Both sexes? For how long? Which part of the patient's body did he touch? Had he ever touched a patient's breast, buttocks, or other sexual body parts? Ernest had an impulse to rip the form to shreds. But he did not dare. No one dared, in these litigious days, to conduct therapy without malpractice insurance. He picked up the form again and checked "yes" to the question, "Do you touch patients?" To the question, "In which way?" he answered, "To shake hands only." For all other questions he checked no.

Ernest then opened Carolyn's folder to prepare for his upcoming hour. His thoughts wandered briefly back to his conversation with Paul. *Transfer Carolyn to a female therapist? She wouldn't go. Give up the experiment? Why? It's proceeding; it's in process. Give up being honest with patients? Never! The truth got me into this and the truth will get me out!*

TWENTY

*O*n Friday afternoon, before locking his office, Marshal surveyed the things he loved. Everything was in its place: the gleaming rosewood cabinet that contained the twisted-stem sherry glasses, the glass sculptures, the Golden Rim of Time. Yet nothing lightened his dark mood or eased the tightness in his throat.

As he closed the door, he paused and tried to analyze his disquiet. It did not emanate solely from his anticipated rendezvous with Shelly at Avocado Joe's in three hours—though, God knows, that was worrisome enough. No, it was about another matter entirely: Adriana. At the beginning of the week she had, once again, not shown for her appointment and not phoned to cancel. Marshal was baffled. It simply didn't compute: a woman of such excellent breeding and social presence simply does not behave in this fashion. Marshal paid himself another two hundred dollars out of the cash Peter had given him, this time without much deliberation. He had phoned

Adriana immediately and left a message asking her to contact him as soon as possible.

Perhaps he had made a tactical mistake in agreeing to treat her, even for brief therapy. She may have harbored more reservations about marriage than she had acknowledged to Peter, and perhaps felt awkward discussing them. After all, he was Peter's ex-therapist, he had been paid by Peter, and he was now an investor with Peter. Yes, the more Marshal thought about it, the more he suspected that he had made an error in judgment. That, he reminded himself, is precisely the problem with boundary violations—the slippery slope: one slip begets another.

Three days had passed since his call to Adriana, and still no response. It was not his style to phone a patient more than once, but Marshal unlocked the door, went back into the office, and dialed her number again. This time he was told that the line had been disconnected! The phone company could give him no other information.

As Marshal drove home he considered two diametrically opposed explanations. Either Adriana and Peter, possibly with the provocation of her father, had had a severe falling-out and she wished nothing to do with a therapist connected with Peter. Or Adriana had gotten fed up with her father and impulsively jumped on a plane to join Peter in Zurich—she had hinted during her last session that it was going to be difficult to remain apart from Peter.

But neither of these hypotheses accounted for Adriana's failure to phone him. No, the more Marshal thought about it, the more certain he became of something deeply portentous. Illness? Death? Suicide? His next step was obvious: he had to phone Peter in Zurich! Marshal glanced at his Rolex, accurate to the millisecond. Six P.M. That meant three A.M. in Zurich. He would have to wait until after his rendezvous with Shelly and call Peter at midnight—nine A.M. Swiss time.

As Marshal opened his garage door to park, he noted that Shirley's car was gone. Out for the evening. As usual. It happened so often now that Marshal had lost track of her schedule: whether she was working late at her clinical internship, taking one of her few remaining clinical psychology classes, teaching ikebana, participating in some ikebana exhibition, or sitting for meditation at the Zen Center.

Marshal opened the refrigerator door. Nothing there. Shirley was still not cooking. As usual she had left a new flower arrangement on the kitchen table for him. Under the bowl was a note stating she'd be back before ten. Marshal glanced quickly at the arrangement: a simple motif containing three calla lilies, two white, one saffron. The long graceful stalks of a white and a saffron calla lily were entwined and separated by a dense growth of crimson nambia berries from the third lily, which swooped away as far as possible from the other lilies and leaned dangerously far over the edge of the crackled lavender ceramic basin.

Why did she leave him these flower arrangements? For a moment, just for a moment, the thought occurred to Marshal that Shirley had been using saffron and white calla lilies a great deal lately. Almost as though she were sending him a message. But he dismissed the thought quickly. The time spent on such evanescent nonsense galled him. So many better ways to use one's time. Like cooking dinner. Like sewing some buttons on his shirts. Like finishing her dissertation, which, flaky as it was, had to be completed before she could start billing patients. Shirley was very good at demanding equal rights, Marshal thought, but was good also at giving her time away and, as long as her husband was around to pay the bills, was content to postpone indefinitely the moment of entry into the adult, billable world.

Well, *he* knew how to use time. Pushing the flower arrangement out of the way, he unfolded the afternoon *Examiner* and calculated his daily stock profits. Then, still tense and jittery, he decided on a Nautilus workout, grabbed his gym bag, and headed off to the YMCA. Later, at the restaurant at Avocado Joe's, he'd grab a bite.

⌇

Shelly whistled "Zip-a-dee-doo-dah, zip-a-dee-ay" all the way to Avocado Joe's. He had had a dynamite week. Playing the tennis of his life, he had carried Willy to the California senior doubles championship and a shot at the national championship. But there was more, much more.

Willy, riding a crest of euphoria, had made Shelly an offer that, with one quick stroke, solved all Shelly's problems. Willy and Shelly had decided to stay in Southern California an extra day to catch the races at Hollywood Park—Willy had a two-year-old named Omaha running in the feature race, the Hollywood Juvenile Derby. Willy was hot on Omaha, as well as the jockey riding him; he'd already bet a bundle and urged Shelly to do the same. Willy bet first, while

Shelly lingered behind in the clubhouse, doping out a show horse for a second bet on the race. When Willy returned, Shelly left to place his bets. However, Willy, after viewing the horses in the saddling paddock and admiring the sleek black muscular haunches of Omaha and noting, too, that the race favorite was sweating heavily— "washing out"—suddenly rushed back to the betting window. He had just put down another five thousand when he saw Shelly placing his bets at the twenty-dollar window.

"What gives, Shelly? We've been going to the races for ten years and I've never seen you hit anything but the hundred-dollar window. Here I am, swearing by my mother, my daughter, my whore, on this horse and you're at the twenty-dollar window?"

"Well . . ." Shelly blushed. "Cutting down . . . you know . . . for marital harmony . . . little belt tightening . . . job market bad . . . of course, lots of offers, but waiting for the right thing . . . you know, money only small part of it—got to feel I'm using myself in the right way. Tell you the truth, Willy, it's Norma . . . uptight, *very uptight* about my gambling action when she's the family honcho earner. We had a big blowup last week. You know, my income was always the family income . . . her big salary she always considers *her* money. You know how the broads bitch and moan about not getting opportunities, but as soon as they get them they ain't so crazy about the burden."

Willy slapped himself on the head. "*That's* why you weren't at the last two games! Shit, Shelly, I must be fucking blind not to have figured—whoa, wait, wait, they're off! Watch Omaha! Watch that fucking horse fly! Number five, McCarron's wearing the yellow jacket, yellow hat; he's gonna stay with the pack on the outside till the three-quarter pole and then shift that horse into another gear! Now, here, they're coming up to it now—Omaha's making his move—taking off. Look at those strides—he's barely touching the ground! Have you *ever* seen a horse move like that? The place horse looks like it's running backwards. He's pumped up—I tell you, Shelly, he could do a second mile."

After the race—Omaha paid eight eighty—when Willy returned from the festivities at the winner's circle, he and Shelly went to the clubhouse bar and ordered Tsingtaos.

"Shelly, how long you been out of work now?"

"Six months."

"Six months! Christ, that's awful. Look, I was going to sit down and have a long talk with you soon, and it might as well be now. You know this big project I own in Walnut Creek? Well, we been going through the city council for about two years trying to get the go-ahead to condominiumize all four hundred units, and we're just about there. All my inside sources—and I'm telling you, I'm spreading a lot of money around—say we're a month away from approval. Our next step is to get the go-ahead from the residents—of course we've got to offer them first rights at deep discount prices—and then we start conversion construction."

"Yeah, so?"

"So . . . the bottom line is: I need a sales manager. I know you haven't done real estate, but I also know you're a fabulous salesman. A few years ago when you sold me a million-dollar yacht, you did it so smoothly I left the salesroom actually feeling you had done me a favor. You're a fast learn and you've got something going for you that no one else can duplicate: trust. Total trust. I trust you one thousand percent. I've played poker with you for fifteen years—and you know that bullshit we throw around that if the roads are ever closed by an earthquake we could still play poker on the phone?"

Shelly nodded.

"Well, you know what? That's not bullshit! I believe it—we may be the only poker group in the world who could do that. I trust you and all the guys—eyes closed. So, go to work for me, Shelly. Shit, I'm going to have you on the tennis courts for so many hours training for the nationals, you'd get fired from any other job."

Shelly agreed to go to work for Willy. At the same sixty-thousand-dollar salary he had in the last job. Plus commissions. But that wasn't all. Willy wanted to protect the game, wanted to insure that Shelly could continue to play.

"You know that million-dollar yacht? I've had some good times on it, but not million-dollar good times, not like the good times I've had in the game. It doesn't compare. If I had to give one up—the yacht or the game—the boat would be history in a flash. I want the game to go on and on and on, just like it's always been. And I'll tell you the truth, I didn't enjoy the last two games as much without you. Dillon took your place—he's tight, squeezing his cards so hard, the queens were crying. Ninety percent of the hands he drops without even staying for the flop. Dull evening. Some of the life was gone from the game. Lose one key guy like you and the whole thing collapses. So tell me, Shelly—and I swear to God, this is between you and me. What do you need to play?"

Shelly explained that a forty-thousand stake had carried him for fifteen years—and would be carrying him still if not for that card streak from hell. Willy readily offered to bankroll the forty thousand—a ten-year, renewable, interest-free loan to which Norma would not be privy.

Shelly hesitated.

"Let's call it," Willy said, "a signing bonus."

"Well . . ." Shelly waffled.

Willy understood and instantly sought a better way to offer the money without compromising their relationship.

"Wait, a better suggestion, Shelly. Let's cut ten thou off your official salary, the salary Norma would know about, and I'll give you a forty-thousand advance—hidden in a Bahamas offshore account—and we'll be square in four years. Commissions are gonna outweigh your salary anyway."

And that was how Shelly got his stake. And a job. And a ticket to the game forever and ever. And now even Norma could not deny the business advantages of his little social poker game. What a day, Shelly thought after their talk, as he stood in a long line to collect on his twenty-dollar win ticket. A near perfect day. Only one blemish: if only, if only, this conversation had happened last week! Or yesterday. Or even this morning! *I'd be standing in the hundred-dollar line with a fistful of tickets. Eight-eighty! Goddamn, what a horse!*

⟞

Marshal arrived early at Avocado Joe's, a large neon-gaudy casino with a flaming red Mazda Miata convertible on display just inside the front entrance—a promotional prize to be given away next month, the doorman explained. After plunging ten or fifteen steps deeper into the dense cloud of cigarette smoke, Marshal quickly looked around, then backed out immediately and returned to his car. He was seriously overdressed, and the last thing he wanted to do was to call attention to himself. The best-dressed players at Avocado Joe's were wearing San Francisco Forty-niner warm-up jackets.

Marshal cleared his lungs with a few deep breaths and then moved his car into a darker corner of the well-lit parking lot. After making sure there were no observers, he climbed into the backseat, pulled off his necktie and white shirt, opened his gym bag, and slipped on the top of his warm-up suit. Still not right, with polished black shoes and navy slacks: he would call less attention to himself if he went the whole way. So he put on his basketball sneakers and squiggled into his warm-up pants, hiding his face from two women who had pulled into an adjacent spot and whistled as they peered into his car.

Marshal waited till they had gone, took one last breath of clean air, and plunged back into Avocado Joe's. The enormous main gallery was divided into two gaming rooms, one for western poker, the other for Asian gambling. The western room contained fifteen green-felted horseshoe-shaped tables, each illuminated by a hanging imitation Tiffany light, and each ringed by ten seats for players and a central dealer's seat. Coca-Cola dispensers filled three corners of the room, and the fourth contained a large vending machine full of cheap dolls and stuffed animals. For four quarters you could purchase the privilege of maneuvering a large set of pincers in an attempt to clasp one of the prizes. Not since he was a kid walking the boardwalk of Atlantic City had Marshal seen one of those.

All fifteen tables played the same game: Texas Hold 'Em. They differed only in the size of the bet permitted. Marshal strolled up to a five- and ten-dollar table and, standing behind one of the players, watched a hand. He had read enough of the booklet Shelly left him to understand the rudiments of the game. Each player got two down cards. Then five communal cards were dealt faceup, the first three all at once ("the flop"), the next two singly ("fourth street" and "fifth street").

A lot of money was being bet on the hand. Marshal started to edge closer to the table for a better look when Dusty, the pit boss, a sandy-haired, cigarillo-smoking, Alan Ladd look-alike who needed no assertiveness training whatsoever, strode briskly over and looked Marshal up and down, focusing especially on his air-inflatable basketball sneakers.

"Hey, buddy boy," he said to Marshal, "what are you doing here? Halftime?"

"Watching," Marshal replied, "until my friend gets here and then we plan to play."

"Watching? You gotta be kidding! You think you can just stand here and watch? Ever think about how the players might feel about it? See, we worry about feelings here! What's your name?"

"Marshal."

"Okay, Marshal, when you're ready to play, come to me and I'll put your name on the waiting list. All the tables are full now."

Dusty started to walk away, but then turned back and smiled: "Hey, glad to have you here, Sheriff. No kidding. Welcome to Avocado Joe's. But, meanwhile, until you play, you want to do something, anything . . . *don't* do it. Come to me first. If you want to watch, go back there," he instructed, gesturing toward the distant gallery behind a glass partition, "or the Asian room—go there; plenty of action and it's hip to watch."

As he walked away, Marshal heard Dusty say to one of the dealers leaving a table for a break: "He wants to watch! Can you believe it? Surprised he didn't bring his camera!"

Feeling sheepish, Marshal stepped back unobtrusively into the gallery and surveyed the scene. At the center of each ten-player table sat the dealer, dressed in the house uniform of dark trousers and bright floral vest. Every few minutes Marshal saw the winner of each hand toss the dealer a chip, which the dealer clicked crisply on the table before dropping it into his inner vest pocket. A custom, Marshal figured out, meant to signal to the floor manager that the dealer was putting his personal tip money, rather than house money, into his pocket. It was an archaic custom, of course, since the action at each table was being fully televised for later scrutiny if any irregularities arose. Ordinarily not a sentimental man, Marshal welcomed this one tiny obeisance to ritual in Avocado Joe's fast-paced click-clacking temple of materialistic expediency.

At the onset of each hand of Texas Hold 'Em, three of the ten players, in rotation, were forced to ante. The dealer divided the ante into three parts: one part stayed in the hand, one part was deposited into the house slot—that was the house rental fee for the game—and the third went into the jackpot slot, which, according to a wall poster, was paid when someone had a hand that could beat a full boat of aces over tens. The jackpot was in the neighborhood of ten thousand dollars, most of which went to the winner and the second-best hand, but some of which was shared by the other players at the table. Every twenty minutes or so the dealer took a break and a replacement took over. Marshal saw players who had done well during a dealer's shift slip him a few extra chips as he was going on his break.

Marshal coughed and tried to fan some of the cigarette smoke away from his nostrils. Wearing a gym suit to Avocado Joe's was ironic, since the casino was a shrine to bad health. Everyone looked unhealthy. All around him were sallow, shadowy faces. Many of the players had been at it ten or fifteen consecutive hours. Everyone was smoking. The flesh of several obese individuals poured through the slats in their chairs. Two anorexic waitresses flitted by, each fanning herself with an empty tray; several players had miniature electric fans set before them to blow away the smoke; a number of players wolfed down food as they played—shrimp with jellied lobster sauce was the dinner special. Dress code was casual-bizarre: one man with a scraggly white beard wore Turkish slippers with curled, pointed toes and a red fez; there were others with hefty cowboy boots and monstrous Stetsons; someone was in a Japanese sailor suit, circa 1940; many were in blue-collar work clothes; and several elderly women wore tidy, floral, 1950s-style dresses, buttoned up to the chin.

Everywhere, gambling talk. Couldn't get away from it. Some talked about the California state lotto; Marshal heard someone entertaining a small group by describing how the El Camino stakes had been won that afternoon by a ninety-to-one long shot who finished the race on three legs. Nearby, Marshal saw a man give a roll of bills to his girlfriend and say, "Remember, no matter what I do, no matter what—if I beg, threaten, curse, cry, whatever—tell me to fuck off, knee me in the balls, use your karate if you have to. *But don't give this roll back to me!* This is our Caribbean holiday. Run outta here and take a taxi home first." Another yelled to the floor manager to put the Sharks' hockey game on. There were a dozen TV sets, each showing a different basketball game, each surrounded by clients who had action on that game. Everyone was betting on something.

Marshal's Rolex showed five minutes before eight. Mr. Merriman was due to arrive momentarily and Marshal decided to wait for him in the restaurant, a small, smoky room dominated by a large oak bar. Imitation Tiffany glass everywhere: lamps, ashtrays, glass cabinets, panels. One corner of the room housed a pool table around which a large crowd of betting spectators watched an intense game of eight ball.

The food was as unhealthy as the air. No salads on the menu; Marshal studied the offerings again and again, searching for the least toxic dish. The anorexic waitress responded only "Huh?" when Marshal inquired about the possibility of steamed veggies. And "Huh" again when he asked about the type of oil used in the shrimp and lobster sauce. Finally he ordered roast beef without gravy and sliced tomatoes and lettuce—the first beef he had had in years, but at least he would know what he was eating.

"Hey, Doc, how ya doin'? Hey, Sheila," Shelly said as he bounced in, blowing a kiss to the waitress, "bring me whatever the Doc's eating. He knows what's good. But don't forget the gravy." He leaned over to the next table and shook hands with a diner reading the racing form. "Jason, do I have a horse for you! Del Mar derby in two weeks. Save up. I'm gonna make you rich—and all your descendants, too. Catch you later; got some business with my pal here."

This was definitely his element, Marshal thought. "You look buoyant tonight, Mr. Merriman. Good tennis tournament?"

"The best. You're breakin' bread with half the California doubles championship team! But, yeah, I'm feeling good, Doc, thanks to tennis, thanks to my friends, and thanks to you."

"So, Mr. Merriman . . . "

"Shh, Doc. None of this 'Mr. Merriman.' Gotta blend in. Gotta pass. 'Shelly' here. 'Shelly' and 'Marshal'—okay?"

"Okay, Shelly. Shall we proceed with our agenda tonight? You were going to brief me about my duties. I need to tell you that I have patients starting early tomorrow morning, so I can't stay till all hours. Remember: two-and-a-half-hour limit, a hundred and fifty minutes, and I'm off."

"Got ya. Let's get to work."

Marshal nodded as he cut away every nodule of fat from the roast beef, made a sandwich, covered it with sliced tomato and wilted lettuce, poured on ketchup, and munched while Shelly outlined the evening's activities.

"You read the booklet I gave you on Texas Hold 'Em?

Marshal nodded again.

"Good. Then you understand enough to get by on. Mainly all I want is for you to know enough not to call attention to yourself. I don't want you to focus on your own cards, and I don't want you to play: I want you to watch me. Now there's a twenty-forty-dollar table coming open soon. Here's how it works: the ante rotates—three guys have to put up money each hand. One guy puts up five dollars—that's called the 'butt' and that's the house cut: the rental on the table and the dealer. Another guy, the 'blind,' puts up twenty dollars. The guy next to him, the 'double blind,' puts up ten bucks. *Capisce* so far?"

"Does that mean," Marshal asked, "the twenty-dollar guy then gets to see the flop without putting more money?"

"Right. Unless there's a raise. That means you've paid for the flop and should get to see it once a round. There'll probably be nine players—so once every nine hands. The other eight you fold—*do not call the first bet*. I repeat, Doc, *do not*. This means that on every round you'll have to ante up three times for a total of thirty-five bucks. The entire round of nine hands should take about twenty-five minutes. So you should lose seventy bucks an hour, max. Unless you do something stupid and try to play a hand."

"You want out in two hours?" Shelly continued, as the waitress brought his roast beef floating in rich gravy. "Tell you what. Let's play for an hour and thirty or forty minutes and then talk for a half-hour after. I've decided to cover all your losses—I'm feeling generous today—so here's a hundred bucks." He fished a hundred-dollar bill out of his wallet.

Marshal took the bill. "Let's see . . . one hundred . . . does that compute?" He took out a pen and scribbled on the napkin. "Thirty-five dollars every twenty-five minutes, and you want to play for an hour and forty minutes—a hundred minutes. That comes out to one hundred forty dollars. Right?"

"Okay, okay. Here's another forty. And, here, here's a couple hundred more—a loan, only, for the evening. Best to buy three hundred worth of chips to start with—it looks better, won't call attention to yourself as a local yokel. You'll cash 'em in when we leave."

Shelly continued, wolfing down his roast beef and gravy-soaked bread. "Now listen carefully, Doc: if you lose more than one hundred forty, you're on your own. 'Cause the *only* way that can happen is to play your cards. And I wouldn't advise that—these guys are good. Most of 'em play three, four times a week—many of them make their living doing this. *Plus,* if you play your cards, you can't watch what I'm doing. And that's the point of this caper. Right?"

"Your book," said Marshal, "says there are certain treasure hands that should see the flop every time: high pairs, ace-king same suit."

"Shit, no. Not on my time. After I leave, Doc, you have a ball. Play all you want."

"Why *your* time?" Marshal asked.

"Because I'm paying all your antes to see all those cards. And besides this is still my official therapy time—even though it's the last session."

Marshal nodded. "Well, I guess so."

"No, no, wait, Doc. I see where you're coming from. Who under-stands better than me how hard it is to fold a good hand? That would be cruel and unusual punishment. Let's compromise. Any time your first two cards are a pair of aces, kings, or queens, you call the bet to see the flop. If the flop doesn't improve your hand—that is, if you don't hit three of a kind or two pair on the flop—*then* you fold: you do not see another bet. And then, of course, we go fifty-fifty on any winnings."

"Fifty-fifty?" asked Marshal. "Is it legal for players at the same table to split winnings? And are we fifty-fifty on any losses I incur?"

"Okay. Right. I'm feeling generous—you keep any winnings but you must agree to play only pairs of aces, queens, or kings. Fold every other hand. Even ace-king same suit! Do it any other way and the losings are all yours. We okay now?"

"Okay."

"Now let's talk about the main thing—the reason you're here. I want you to watch me when I bet. I'm going to bluff a lot tonight, so watch to see if I give it away with some kind of 'tell'—you know, the kind of stuff you picked up in your office: foot moving, stuff like that."

A few minutes later Marshal and Shelly heard their names called on the loudspeaker to join the twenty-forty game. Everyone wel-comed them courteously. Shelly greeted the dealer, "How ya doin', Al? Here, give me five hundred bucks of those round ones and take good care of my friend here—a beginner—I'm trying to corrupt him, and I need your help."

Marshal bought three hundred dollars' worth of chips—a stack of red five-dollar chips and a stack of blue-and-white-striped twenty-dollar chips. On the second hand Marshal was the "blind"—he had to bet twenty dollars on the two down cards and got to see the flop: three small spades. Marshal held two spades—a two and a seven—and thus had a flush on five cards. And the next up card, fourth street, was also a low spade. Marshal, dazzled by his flush, defied Shelly's instructions and stayed in for the rest of the hand, twice call-ing forty-dollar bets. At the end of the hand all the players turned their cards over. Marshal displayed his two and seven of spades and proudly said, "Flush." But three other players had higher flushes.

Shelly leaned over and said, as gently as possible, "Marshal, four spades in the flop—that means *everyone* holding even one spade has a flush. Your six spades are no better than anyone else's five spades, and your seven of spades is bound to get beaten by some higher spade. Why did you think the other players stayed in the betting? Always ask yourself that. They've *got* to have flushes! At this rate, my friend, I calculate you will lose approximately nine hundred dollars an hour of *your*"—Shelly emphasized "your"—"hard-earned money."

Overhearing these comments, one of the players who had been counting his chips—a tall black man wearing a gray Borsalino and a Rolex on his wrist—said, "Man, ah was about to cash in and check out . . . get some sleep . . . but . . . hmm, dude's playing seven-high flush . . . ah just might stick around some longer."

Marshal reddened at the attention, and the dealer said in a soothing manner, "Don't let 'em get to you, Marshal. I got a feeling you'll get on to it reeaalll soon—and when you do, you're going to kick some ass." As Marshal was to learn, a good dealer was a group therapist manqué and could always be counted on to soothe feelings and offer support: table tranquillity always meant greater tips.

After that Marshal played conservatively and folded every hand. A few good-natured jibes came his way for playing so tight, but Shelly and the dealer defended him and urged patience until he got the hang of it. Then, a half hour later, he held a pair of aces and the flop was an ace and pair of deuces, giving him an aces full boat. Not many players called him on his hand, but still Marshal collected a two-hundred-fifty-dollar pot. The rest of the time Marshal watched Shelly like a hawk, occasionally jotting discreetly in a small notepad. No one seemed to mind his taking notes except a small Asian woman, almost completely hidden by towering stacks of winning chips, who stretched up, leaned over her pile of black-and-white twenty-dollar chips, and said to Marshal, gesturing toward his notepad, "And don't forget, a big straight beats a little teeny full boat! Hee-hee-hee."

Shelly was by far the most active bettor at the table and seemed to know what he was doing. Yet when he had a winning hand, few players stayed in on his bets. And when he bluffed, even with the best possible table position, one or two players with marginal hands always called and beat him. When someone else bet a lock hand, Shelly foolishly stayed in. Though Shelly had above-average cards, his stack of chips steadily declined and, at the end of ninety minutes, he had gone through his five hundred dollars. It didn't take Marshal long to find out why.

Shelly stood up, threw the dealer his few remaining chips as a tip, and headed for the restaurant. Marshal cashed in his chips, left no tip, and followed Shelly.

"Pick up anything, Doc? Any tells?"

"Well, Shelly, you know I'm an amateur, but it seems to me that the only way you could have told them more about your hands is semaphorically."

"Huh? Come again."

"You know, that flag system ships use to signal other ships."

"Oh, yeah. That bad, eh?"

Marshal nodded.

"How about examples? Give me specifics."

"Well, to start, you remember the very big hands you had—I counted six: four full houses, a high straight, and a high flush?"

Shelly smiled wistfully, as if recalling old loves. "Yeah, I remember every one. Weren't they gorgeous?"

"Well," Marshal continued, "I noticed that anyone else at the table who had big hands always won more money than you did with comparable hands—a lot more money: at least twice or three times as much. In fact, I shouldn't even call your hands 'big hands,' maybe just high hands, because you never won a big pot with any of them."

"Meaning?"

"Meaning when you had a high hand the news spread like wildfire around the table."

"How'd I flag it?"

"Well, let me go over my observations. It seems to me that when you have great cards you squeeze them."

"Squeeze 'em?"

"Yeah, guard them as though you've got Fort Knox in your hand. Squeeze so hard, you bend the bicycle wheels. And another thing, when you've got a boat you keep looking at your chips before you bet. Let's see, there was something else . . ." Marshal studied his notes. "Yeah, here it is. Every time you've got a great hand, you look away from the table, off into the distance, as if you're trying to watch one of the TV basketball games—trying, I guess, to make the other players think you aren't too interested in the hand. But if you're bluffing, you're right in everyone's face, as though you're trying to stare them down, intimidate them, dissuade them from betting."

"You're kidding, Doc? I do this? I can't believe it. I know all this stuff—it's all in *Mike Caro's Book of Tells*. But I didn't know I did it." Shelly stood up and gave Marshal a bear hug. "Doc, this is what I call therapy! Big-time therapy! I can't wait to get back to that game—I'm going to reverse all my tells. I'll put such a spin on it, those jokers won't know what hit them."

"Wait! There's more. You want to hear it?"

"Of course. But let's move quick. I want to make sure I get that spot back at the table. On second thought, let me reserve it." Shelly trotted up to Dusty, the pit boss, slapped him on the shoulder, whispered something to him, and slipped him a ten. Quickly back to Marshal, Shelly was all ears.

"Keep going—you're on a roll."

"Two things. If you look at your chips, maybe do a quick count, then no question—you got a great hand. I guess I already said that. But I didn't say this: when you bluff you never look at your chips. And then something more subtle—low level of confidence in this one . . . "

"Run it by me. Anything you have to say, Doc, I want to hear! Let me tell you, you're spitting gold!"

"Well, it seems to me that when you've got a good hand, you put your bet on the table very gently. And very close to you—you don't extend your arm very far. And when you bluff, you do the opposite—more aggressive and you plunk the chips exactly in the center of the table. Also when you bluff, often—but not every time—you seem to look at your hole cards again and again, as though you're hoping they've changed. One last thing: you hang in there to the end when everyone else at the table seems to know the guy's got a lock hand—so I guess you're playing your cards too much and not playing the other guy. Well, that's it." Marshal started to tear up his page of notes.

"No, no, Doc. Don't tear that. Let me have it. I'm going to frame it. No, no, I'll seal it in plastic and carry it with me—good luck charm, the touchstone of the Merriman fortune. Listen, I've got to go—that unique opportunity . . ." Shelly beckoned toward the poker table they had just left. "That unique gathering of pigeons may never come again. Oh, yeah, I almost forgot. Here's the letter I promised you."

He handed over a letter, and Marshal scanned it:

To Whom It May Concern:
   This is to testify that I have received excellent treatment
from Dr. Marshal Streider. I consider myself completely
recovered from all ill effects I suffered from my treatment with
Dr. Pande.

                                        Shelly Merriman

"How's that?" asked Shelly.
"Perfect," said Marshal. "Now, if you would just date it."
Shelly dated the note and then, expansively, added a line:

   I herewith drop any legal claims against the Golden Gate
   Psychoanalytic Institute.

"How's that?"
"Even better. Thank you, Mr. Merriman. Tomorrow I'll mail you
the letter I promised."
"That will make us square. One hand washes the other. You
know, Doc, I've just been thinking—early stages, not planned
through yet—but you might have another whole career in poker
counseling. You're fantastic at it. Or I think you are—let me see
what happens when I get back to the table. But let's do lunch sometime. I could be persuaded to act as your agent. Just look around
this place—hundreds of losers with their little pipe dreams, dying to
improve. And other casinos are much larger . . . Garden City, Club
101 . . . they'd pay anything. I could fill your practice in an instant—
or could fill an auditorium for a workshop—couple hundred players, hundred bucks a head, twenty thou a day—I'd get regular
agent's fees, of course. Think about it. I gotta go. I'll call ya. Opportunity beckons."
And with that Shelly sauntered back to the hold 'em table,
singing, "Zip-a-dee-doo-dah, zip-a-dee-ay."
Marshal walked out of Avocado Joe's and into the parking lot.
The time was eleven-thirty. In a half hour he would call Peter.

TWENTY-ONE

*T*he night before his next session with Carolyn, Ernest had a vivid dream. He sat up in bed and jotted it down: *I am rushing through an airport. I spot Carolyn in a throng of passengers. I am glad to see her and I run up to her and try to give her a big hug but she keeps her purse in the way, making it a bulky and unsatisfactory hug.*

As he thought about his dream in the morning, he remembered his resolution after the conversation with Paul: "The truth got me into this and the truth will get me out." Ernest decided to do something he had never before done. He would share his dream with his patient.

In their next session, Carol was intrigued by Ernest's relating his dream about hugging her. After the last session she had begun to wonder whether she may have misjudged Ernest; she was losing hope that she could ever entice him into compromising himself. And here, today, he tells her he dreamed about her. Perhaps this might lead somewhere interesting, Carol thought. But without conviction: she no longer felt she had any control in the situation. For a shrink, Ernest was entirely unpredictable, she thought; almost every session he did or said something that surprised her. And almost every session he showed her something about herself she hadn't known.

"Well, Ernest, this is very strange because I had a dream about you last night. Isn't that what Jung called 'synchronicity'?"

"Not exactly. By 'synchronicity' I think Jung referred to a concordance of two related phenomena, one occurring in the subjective world, the other in the physical, objective world. I recall he described somewhere working with a patient's dream involving an ancient Egyptian scarab and then noting that a live beetle was flying against the windowpane as though it were trying to get into the room.

"I've never understood the significance of that concept," Ernest continued. "I think that many people are so uncomfortable at the sheer contingency of life that they find comfort by believing in some form of cosmic interconnectedness. I've never been drawn in by this. Somehow the idea of randomness or nature's indifference has never unsettled me. Why is simple 'coincidence' such a horror? Why must it be viewed as something other than coincidence?

"As for our dreaming of each other, is that worthy of wonder? It seems to me that, given the amount of contact we have and the intimacy of our connection, it would be surprising if we *didn't* enter into each other's dreams. Sorry to go on like this, Carolyn, I must sound like I'm lecturing. But ideas like 'synchronicity' stir up a lot of feeling for me: I often feel lonely trudging in the no-man's-land between Freudian dogmatism and Jungian mysticism."

"No, I don't mind when you talk about these things, Ernest. In fact, I like it when you share your thoughts like that. But you have one habit that does make things seem like a lecture: you keep using my name every other minute."

"I was absolutely unaware of it."

"You mind my saying that to you?"

"Mind? I'm delighted. Makes me feel you're starting to take me seriously."

Carol leaned over and gave Ernest's hand a squeeze.

He squeezed back for a second and said, "But we've got work to do. Let's go back to the dream. Can you tell me your thoughts about it?"

"Oh, no! It's *your* dream, Ernest. What do *you* think?"

"Fair enough. Well, often psychotherapy is symbolized in dreams as some form of a journey. So I think the airport represents our therapy. I try to be close to you, to hug you. But you put something in the way: your purse."

"And so, Ernest, what do you make of the purse? I feel a little weird—it's like we're switching roles."

"Not at all, Carolyn, I encourage it; nothing is more important than our being honest with each other. So let's stay with it. Well, what comes to mind is that Freud points out repeatedly that a 'purse' is a common symbol for female genitals. As I've mentioned, I don't ascribe to Freudian dogma—but still I try not to pour out the baby with the bathwater. Freud had so many correct insights that it would be foolish to ignore them. And once, years ago, I participated in an experiment where women were asked, under hypnosis, to dream that a man they desire comes to their bed. But they're instructed to disguise the explicit sexual act in the dream. A surprising number of women used a purse symbol—that is, a man coming to them and inserting something into their purse."

"So then, Ernest, the dream means . . . ?"

"I think that the dream is saying that you and I are embarking on therapy, but that you may be inserting sexuality between us in a fashion that prevents us from truly being intimate."

Carol fell silent for a few moments, then commented: "There's another possibility. A simpler, straightforward interpretation—that, deep inside, you want me physically, that the hug is a sexual equivalent. After all, wasn't it you who initiated the hug in the dream?"

"And," Ernest asked, "what about the purse as an obstacle?"

"If, as Freud said, a cigar can sometimes be a cigar, what about the feminine equivalent—that a purse can sometimes just be a purse . . . a purse containing money?"

"Yes, I see what you mean . . . you're saying that I desire you as a man desires a woman, and that money—in other words, our professional contract—gets in the way. And that I feel frustrated with that."

Carol nodded. "Yes, how about *that* interpretation?"

"It's certainly more parsimonious, and I have no doubt there is truth in it—that if we hadn't met as therapist and patient, I would have enjoyed knowing you in a personal, nonprofessional way—we talked about that at our last session. I've made no secret that I think you're a handsome, engaging woman with a wonderfully lively, penetrating mind."

Carol beamed. "I'm beginning to like this dream more and more."

"Yet," Ernest continued, "dreams are generally overdetermined—there's no reason to think my dream isn't depicting both wishes: my desire to work with you as a therapist without the intrusion and disruption of sexual desire *and* the desire to know you as a woman without the intrusion of our professional contract. That's the dilemma I have to work with."

Ernest marveled at how far he had come in his truth telling. Here he was—matter-of-factly, unself-consciously—saying things to a patient that he would, a few weeks ago, never have imagined saying. And, as far as he could tell, he had himself under control. He no longer felt he was being seductive to Carolyn. He was being open, but at the same time responsible and therapeutically helpful.

"What about the money, Ernest? Sometimes I see you glance at the clock and I think I just represent a paycheck to you, and that each tick of the clock is just another dollar."

"Money is not an important matter to me, Carolyn. I make more than I can spend, and I rarely ever think about money. But I have to keep track of the time, Carolyn. Just like you do when you see a client and must keep to a schedule. Yet I have never wanted our time to pass quickly. Not once. I look forward to seeing you, I value our time together, and more often than not, I am sorry when our time has run out."

Carol fell silent again. How annoying it was that she felt flattered by Ernest's words. How annoying that he appeared to be speaking the truth. How annoying that at times he no longer appeared repulsive.

"Another thought I had, Carolyn, was about the contents of the purse. Of course, as you suggest, money immediately comes to mind. But what else could be stuffed in there that gets in the way of our intimacy?"

"I'm not sure what you mean, Ernest."

"I mean that perhaps you may not be seeing me as I really am because of some preconceived ideas or biases getting in the way. Maybe you're toting some old baggage that's blocking our relationship—wounds from your past relationships with other men, your father, your brother, your husband. Or perhaps expectations from another era: think of Ralph Cooke and of how often you've said to me: 'Be like Ralph Cooke . . . be my lover-therapist.' In a sense, Carolyn, you're saying to me: Don't be *you*, Ernest, be something else, be someone else."

Carol couldn't help thinking how on target Ernest was—but not exactly for the reasons he thought. Strange how much more intelligent he had gotten recently.

"And your dream, Carolyn? I don't think I can do more with mine right now."

"Well, I dreamed that we were in bed together fully dressed and I think that we were . . . "

"Carolyn, would you start again and try to describe your dream in the present tense—just as though it's happening right now? Often that revivifies the emotion of the dream."

"Okay, here's what I remember. You and I were sitting—"

"You and I *are* sitting—stay in present tense," Ernest interjected.

"Okay, you and I are sitting or lying in bed fully clothed, and we are having a session. I want you to be more loving, but you stay uptight and keep your distance. Then another man comes into the room—a grotesque, ugly, squat, coal-black man—and I immediately decide to try to seduce him. I do that very easily, and we have sex right in front of you in the same bed. All the while I am thinking that if you see how good I am sexually with him, you'll get more interested in me and come around yourself and have sex with me, too."

"The feelings in the dream?"

"Frustration with you. Revulsion at the sight of this man—he was disgusting, he emanated evil. I didn't know who he was—and yet I did know. It was Duvalier."

"Who?"

"Duvalier. You know, the Haitian dictator."

"What's your connection with Duvalier? Mean anything to you?"

"That's the curious thing. Absolutely nothing. I haven't thought of his name in years. I'm astounded he comes to mind."

"Free-associate to Duvalier for a while, Carolyn. See what comes up."

"Nothing. Not sure I ever saw a picture of the man. Tyrant. Brutal. Dark. Bestial. Oh, yes, I think I read an article recently about him living in poverty in France somewhere."

"But the old man's long dead."

"No, no, it's not the old man. It's the younger Duvalier. The one they called 'Baby Doc.' I'm sure it was Baby Doc. I don't know how I knew it, but I knew it was him. That name came to my mind as soon as he entered. I thought I just told you that."

"No, you didn't, Carolyn, but I think it's the key to the dream."

"How?"

"Well, first, you ruminate about the dream. It's better to get your associations—just as we did in my dream."

"Let's see. I know I was feeling frustrated. You and I were in bed, but I wasn't getting anywhere with you. Then this base man comes along and I had sex with him—ugh; strange I would do that—and the weird logic in the dream was that you'd see my performance and somehow be won over. That doesn't make sense."

"Say more, Carolyn."

"Well, it doesn't. I mean, if I have sex with some grotesque man in front of you—let's face it, I'm not going to win your heart. Far more likely you'd be repelled, not attracted, by that."

"That's what logic would tell you, if we took the dream at face value. But I know a way the dream *would* make sense. Let's suppose that Duvalier is not Duvalier but instead represents someone or something else."

"Like?"

"Think of his name: 'Baby Doc'! Imagine that this man stands for some part of me: the baby, the more primitive or base part of me. In the dream, then, you hope to consort with this part of me in the hope that the rest of me, the more mature part of me, would be captivated, too.

"You see, Carolyn, in that way the dream would make sense—if you could seduce some part, some alter ego, of me, then the rest of me might easily follow suit!"

Silence from Carol.

"What do you think, Carolyn?"

"Clever, Ernest, a very clever interpretation." And to herself Carol said: *More clever than you know!*

"So, Carolyn, let me summarize: my readings of both dreams—yours and mine—point to a similar conclusion: that, though you come to see me and you profess strong feelings toward me, and want to touch and hug me, still you do not really want to be close to me.

"And, you know, those dream messages are similar to my overall feelings about our relationship. Several weeks ago I made it clear that I would be entirely open to you and would honestly address all of your questions to me. Yet you have never really pursued this opportunity. You say you want me to be your lover, yet, aside from questions about my life in the singles world, you have made no attempt to know who I am. I'm going to keep nagging you on this point, Carolyn, because it's so central, so close to the core. I'm going to keep urging you to relate honestly with me—and to do that, you will have to know me and to trust me enough to let yourself unfold fully in my presence. And that experience will be prelude to your becoming yourself, in its deepest meaning, with another man whom you have yet to meet."

Carol remained silent and looked at her watch.

"I know our time is up, Carolyn, but take another minute or two. Can you go any further with this?"

"Not today, Ernest," she said, then rose and quickly left the office.

TWENTY-TWO

*M*arshal's midnight call to Peter Macondo provided little comfort—he merely reached a recording, in three
languages, stating that the Macondo Financial
Group was closed for the weekend and would reopen Monday
morning. Nor did the Zurich information operator have a home
phone for Peter. That, of course, was no surprise: Peter had often
spoken of the Mafia and the necessity for the ultra-wealthy to guard
their privacy. It was going to be a long weekend. Marshal would
have to wait it out and call again at midnight on Sunday.

At two A.M., unable to sleep, Marshal began rummaging through
some pharmaceutical samples in his medicine cabinet looking for a
sedative. This was highly uncharacteristic—he often inveighed
against pill popping and insisted that the properly analyzed individual should deal with psychological discomfort only through intro-
spection and self-analysis. But, on this night, no self-analysis was
possible: his tension was sky-high and he needed something to calm

himself. Finally, he found some Chlor-Trimeton, a sedating antihistamine, gulped two tablets, and slept for a few uneasy hours.

As the weekend wore on, Marshal's restlessness grew. Where was Adriana? Where was Peter? Concentration was impossible. He flung the latest issue of *The American Journal of Psychoanalysis* across the room, couldn't generate interest in his bonsai trimming, even failed to compute his weekly stock profits. He put in a strenuous hour at the gym with free weights, played in a pickup basketball game at the Y, jogged over the Golden Gate. But nothing loosened the grip of the apprehension enveloping him.

He pretended he was his own patient. *Calm down! Why such uproar? Let's sit down and appraise what has really happened. Only one thing: Adriana failed to keep her appointments. So? The investment is safe. In a couple of days . . . let's see . . . in thirty-three hours . . . you will be talking to Peter on the phone. You have a note from the Crédit Suisse guaranteeing the loan. Wells Fargo stock has dropped almost two percent since you sold it: the worst that could happen is you call in the bank's note and repurchase your stock at a lower price. Yes, there may have been something going on with Adriana that you didn't pick up. But you're not a seer; you can miss something, sometimes.*

Solid therapeutic interventions, Marshal thought. But ineffective coming from himself to himself. There are limits to self-analysis; how did Freud do it all those years? Marshal knew he needed to share his concerns with someone. But who? Not Shirley: they spoke little enough these days about anything, and the topic of his investment with Peter was incendiary. She had opposed it from the beginning. When Marshal had mused aloud on how they would spend seven hundred thousand dollars' profit, she would respond with an impatient, "We live in two separate worlds." The word *greed* fell from Shirley's lips more and more now. Two weeks ago she had even suggested that Marshal seek guidance from her Buddhist adviser to address the greed that was inundating him.

Besides, Shirley had plans to hike up Mount Tamalpais on Saturday to search for ikebana material. That afternoon, as she was leaving, she said she might spend the night away: she needed some personal time, a mini ikebana/meditation retreat. Alarmed at the idea of spending the rest of the weekend alone, Marshal considered telling Shirley he needed her and asking her not to go. But Marshal Streider didn't beg; that was not his style. Besides, his tension was so palpable and contagious that, undoubtedly, Shirley needed to escape.

Marshal glanced impatiently at an arrangement Shirley had left behind: a forked lichen-covered apricot branch, one arm stretching far out parallel to the table, the other arm reaching up vertically. At the end of the horizontal branch rested a single white apricot blossom. The upward stretching arm was collared by swirls of lavender and sweet pea, which tenderly embraced two calla lilies, one white and the other saffron. *Damnit,* thought Marshal, *for this she has time!* Why does she do this? Three flowers . . . a saffron and white calla lily again . . . he studied the arrangement for a full minute, shook his head, and then shoved it under the table out of sight.

Who else can I speak to? My cousin Melvin? No way! Melvin can offer good advice sometimes, but would be useless now. I couldn't bear the sneer in his voice. A colleague? Impossible! I have violated no professional boundaries, but I'm not certain I can trust others—especially others who envy me—to reach the same conclusion. One word of this leaking out and I can kiss the presidency of the institute good-bye forever.

I need someone—a confidant. If only Seth Pande were still available! But I've kissed off that relationship. Maybe I shouldn't have been so hard on Seth. . . . No, no, no, Seth deserved it; it was the right thing to do. He got exactly what was coming to him.

One of Marshal's patients, a clinical psychologist, often spoke about his support group of ten male therapists, who met for two hours every other week. Not only were the meetings always useful, his patient claimed, but the other members often called one another in times of need. Of course, Marshal disapproved of his patient attending a group. In more conservative times he would have forbidden it. Support, affirmation, consolation—all these pathetic crutches merely reinforce pathology and slow down the work of real analysis. Nonetheless, now, at this moment, Marshal hungered for such a network. He thought of Seth Pande's words at the institute meeting about the lack of male friendships in contemporary society. Yes, that was what he needed—a friend.

At Sunday midnight—nine A.M. Monday, Zurich time—he phoned Peter only to hear a disturbing taped message: "You have reached the Macondo Financial Group. Mr. Macondo is on a cruise for nine days. The office will be closed during that time, but, if the matter is urgent, please leave a message. Messages will be checked and every effort will be made to reach Mr. Macondo."

A cruise? An office of that magnitude closing for nine days? Marshal left a message asking Mr. Macondo to call him on a truly urgent matter. Later, as he lay awake, the idea of a cruise made more sense. *Obviously some falling-out has occurred,* he thought, *either between Peter and Adriana or between Adriana and her father and, in a reparative effort, Peter made an impetuous decision to get away—to take off with or without Adriana on a Mediterranean cruise. It's nothing more than that.*

But, as the days went by with no word from Peter, Marshal grew more apprehensive about his investment. There was always the option of redeeming the banknote, but that meant the end of any possibility of profiting from Peter's largess: it would be foolish to panic and to sacrifice this unique opportunity. And for what? Because Adriana fails to show for an appointment? Stupid!

On Wednesday at eleven, Marshal had a free hour. Ernest's supervisory hour had still not been filled. He took a walk on California Street, passed the Pacific Union Club where he had lunched with Peter and then, a block later, suddenly turned back and climbed the stairs, passed through the marble doorway, past the rows of burnished brass mailboxes, into the diaphanous light of the soaring, glass-domed rotunda. There, surrounded on three sides by mahogany leather sofas, stood Emil, the gleaming, tuxedoed majordomo.

Thoughts of Avocado Joe's drifted into Marshal's mind: the Forty-niner jackets, the dense cigarette smoke, the black, bejeweled dude with the gray Borsalino, and Dusty, the pit boss, admonishing him about watching because "we worry about feelings here." And the sounds: the hum of action at Avocado Joe's, the chips clicking, pool balls clacking, the joshing, the gambling talk. The Pacific Union Club sounds were more subdued. The silverware and crystal lightly tinkled as waiters set the luncheon tables; the members genteelly whispered about stock market purchases, Italian leather shoes tapped smartly on polished oak floors.

Which of these was home? Or did he have a home? Marshal wondered, as he had so many times before. Where did he belong—Avocado Joe's or the Pacific Union Club? Would he drift forever, unanchored, in between, spending his life trying to leave the one, trying to reach the other? And if some imp or genie commanded him, *It's your time now to decide; choose one or the other—your home for all eternity*, what would he do? Thoughts of his analysis with Seth Pande came to mind. We never worked on this, Marshal thought. Not on "home," nor on friendship, and, according to Shirley, not on money or greed, either. What the hell *did* we work on for nine hundred hours?

For now Marshal feigned being at home in the Club and walked smartly up to the majordomo.

"Emil, how are you? Dr. Streider. My lunch companion, Mr. Macondo, a few weeks ago told me of your prodigious memory, but even you may not remember a guest after only a single meeting."

"Oh, yes, Doctor, I remember you very well. And Mr. Maconta . . . "

"Macondo."

"Yes, sorry, *Macondo*. There, so much for my prodigious memory. But, actually, I *do* remember your friend very well. Though we met only once, he left an indelible impression. A fine and very generous gentleman!"

"You mean, you met only once *in San Francisco*. He told me about meeting you when you were the majordomo at his club in Paris."

"No, sir, you must be mistaken. It is true I worked at the Cercle Union Interalliée in Paris, but I never met Mr. Macondo there."

"Then, Zurich?"

"No, nowhere. I am quite certain I have never met the gentleman before. The day the two of you lunched here was the first time I ever saw him."

"Then, well . . . what do you mean? . . . I mean how did he know you so well . . . I mean . . . how did he even know you worked at the club in Paris? How did he qualify for lunch here? No, I mean, does he even have an account here? How does he pay?"

"Is there some problem, sir?"

"Yes, and it is related to your pretending to know him so well, pretending to be such old friends."

Emil looked troubled. He glanced at his watch, then looked about him. The rotunda was empty, the club quiet. "Dr. Streider, I have a few free moments before luncheon. Please, let us sit and talk for a few moments." Emil gestured to a closet-sized room just off the dining room. Inside, Emil invited Marshal to sit down and asked permission to light a cigarette. After exhaling deeply he said, "May I speak, frankly, sir? And off the record, so to speak?"

Marshal nodded. "Of course."

"For thirty years I've worked at exclusive clubs. Majordomo for the past fifteen. I am witness to everything. Nothing escapes me. I can see, Dr. Streider, that you are unfamiliar with such clubs. Forgive me if I presume too much."

"No, not at all," Marshal said.

"One thing you should know is that, in private clubs, one person is always trying to get something—some favor, an invitation, an introduction, an investment, something—from another person. And to . . . let us say . . . to lubricate that process, one person has to make a certain impression upon the other. I, like every majordomo, must play my role in that process; I have an obligation to be certain that everything runs harmoniously. Thus, when Mr. Macondo chatted with me earlier that morning and asked whether I had worked at any other European club, naturally I responded cordially and told him I had worked in Paris for ten years. And when he seemed extremely friendly in greeting me in your presence, what was I expected to do? Turn to you, his guest, and say, 'I never saw this man before'?"

"Of course not, Emil. I see your point exactly. No criticism meant. It was only that I was astonished at your not knowing him."

"But, Dr. Streider, you mention a problem. Not a serious one, I hope. I should like to know if it is. The club should like to know."

"No, no. A minor matter. Only that I have misplaced his address and wish to contact him."

Emil hesitated. Obviously he did not believe it was a minor matter but when Marshal volunteered no further information, he rose. "Please, wait for me in the rotunda. I shall do what I can to get some information for you."

Marshal sat down, chagrined at his own awkwardness. It was a long shot, but perhaps Emil could help.

The majordomo returned in a few moments and handed Marshal a slip of paper on which was written the same address and phone in Zurich that Marshal already had. "According to the desk, Mr. Macondo was given a courtesy membership here, since he was a member of the Baur au Lac Club in Zurich. If you wish, we can fax them and request more current information."

"Please. And, if you will, please fax the reply to me. Here is my card."

Marshal turned to leave but Emil stopped him and added, in a whisper: "You asked about payment. I tell you this, also in confidence, Doctor. Mr. Macondo paid by cash, and generously. He gave me two hundred-dollar bills, instructed me to pay for lunch, leave the waiter a generous tip, and keep the rest for myself. On such matters as these my prodigious memory is entirely dependable."

"Thank you, Emil, you've been most helpful." Marshal reluctantly tugged a twenty from his money clip and pressed it into Emil's talcumed hand. He turned to leave and then suddenly remembered something else.

"Emil, may I ask one final favor of you? Last time I met a friend of Mr. Macondo, a tall gentleman dressed somewhat flamboyantly—orange shirt, red-checked jacket, I believe. I have forgotten his name, but his father was once mayor of San Francisco."

"That could only be Mr. Roscoe Richardson. I saw him earlier today. He's either in the library or the game room. A suggestion, Doctor: do not speak to him if he's at backgammon. That will make him cross. He's rather intense about his gaming. Good luck, and I will personally see to your fax. You may count on me." Emil bowed his head and waited.

"Again, thank you, Emil." And, again, Marshal had no choice but to peel off another twenty.

As Marshal entered the oak-paneled game room, Roscoe Richardson was just leaving the backgammon table and heading toward the library for his preluncheon newspaper.

"Ah, Mr. Richardson, perhaps you may remember me: Dr. Streider. I met you a few weeks ago when I lunched here with an acquaintance of yours, Peter Macondo."

"Ah, yes, Dr. Streider. I remember. The endowed lecture series. My congratulations. Wonderful honor. Wonderful. Join me for lunch today?"

"Alas, no. I have a full schedule of patients this afternoon. But a favor, please. I'm trying to reach Mr. Macondo and wonder if you know of his whereabouts."

"Heavens, no. I never saw him before that day. Delightful chap, yet, odd thing, I sent him material about my new start-up but FedEx returned it as undeliverable. Did he say he knew me?"

"I thought so, but now I'm not sure. I do remember his saying that your father and his, a professor of economics, played golf together."

"Well, who knows? That's very possible. My father played with every well-known man in the Western world. And . . . "—here he scrunched his heavily jowled face and produced a large wink—"and with quite a few women, too. Well, eleven-thirty. *Financial Times* should be arriving. There's always a mad rush for it, so I'll be on my way to the library. Good luck to you, Doctor."

Though the conversation with Roscoe Richardson provided no comfort, it did provide some ideas for action. As soon as he arrived at his office, Marshal opened his Macondo folder and extracted the fax announcing the Marshal Streider Endowed Lecture Series. What was the name of that provost at the University of Mexico? Here— Raoul Gomez. Within moments he had Mr. Gomez on the phone— the first thing to go well in days. Though Marshal's Spanish was limited, it was sufficient to understand Mr. Gomez's denial that he had ever even heard of a Peter Macondo, let alone received a large grant from him for a Streider lecture series. Furthermore, as for Peter Macondo's father, there was no Macondo on the faculty of the Department of Economics, nor, for that matter, in any department of the university.

Marshal collapsed into his chair. He had absorbed too many blows and now leaned back, trying to clear his head. After only a few moments his efficient temperament took over: he reached for pen and paper and made a "to do" list. The first item was to cancel his afternoon patients. Marshal placed calls and left messages for four patients canceling their hours. He did not, of course, cite a reason. The proper technique, Marshal was certain, was to remain silent and to explore the patients' fantasies of why he had canceled. And the money! Four hours at one hundred seventy-five dollars. Seven hundred dollars in fees lost—money that could never be made up.

Marshal wondered whether canceling his afternoon schedule represented some turning point in his life. The thought entered his mind that this was a watershed decision. Never before in his career had he canceled a clinical hour. In fact, he had never missed anything—a football practice, a day of school. His scrapbook was full of attendance awards going back to grammar school. It was not that he was never injured or sick. He got sick just like the next man. But he was tough enough to gut it out. But one cannot gut out an analytic hour in a state of panic.

Next item: call Melvin. Marshal knew what Melvin would say, and Melvin didn't miss a beat: "It's bank time—take that note immediately to the Crédit Suisse. Ask them to make a ninety-thousand-dollar direct deposit into your bank account. And be grateful,

Marshal, kiss my boots, that I insisted upon this note. You owe me. And remember—Christ, I shouldn't have to tell you this, Marshal—you're treating meshuganahs: Don't invest with them!"

An hour later Marshal, bank guarantee in hand, was walking down Sutter Street on his way to the Crédit Suisse. En route he grieved lost dreams: wealth, additions to his art collection, the leisure to give written expression to his fertile mind, but most of all he grieved the key to the insider world, the world of private clubs, brass mailboxes, and insider bonhomie.

And Peter? Was he of that world? He would not profit financially, of course—or, if he did, that was between him and the bank. But, Marshal thought, *if Peter had no financial motive, what were his motives? To ridicule psychoanalysis? Could there be a tie-in with Seth Pande? Or Shelly Merriman? Or even the whole breakaway faction of the Psychoanalytic Institute? Could this possibly be a prank? Sheer sociopathic maliciousness? But, whatever the game, whatever the motive, why hadn't I spotted it earlier? I've been a fucking fool. A fucking, greedy fool!*

The Crédit Suisse was a bank office, not a commercial working bank, on the fifth floor of an office building on Sutter Street. The bank officer who greeted Marshal inspected the note and assured him that they were fully authorized to deal with it. He excused himself, saying that the branch manager, who was tied up with another client, would attend to him personally. Besides, there would be a slight delay while they faxed the note to Zurich.

Ten minutes later, the manager, a slim, solemn man with a long face and a David Niven mustache, invited Marshal into his office. After inspecting Marshal's identification and copying numbers from his driver's license and banking cards, he examined the bank guarantee note and then rose to make a photocopy. When he returned, Marshal asked, "How will I receive payment? My attorney has informed me—"

"Excuse me, Dr. Streider, may I have your attorney's name and address?"

Marshal gave him the relevant information about his cousin Melvin and continued, "My attorney advised me to request a direct deposit into my Wells Fargo account."

The manager sat silently for several moments, inspecting the note.

"Is there some problem?" Marshal asked. "Doesn't that guarantee payment upon demand?"

"This is indeed a note from the Crédit Suisse guaranteeing payment upon demand. Here, as you see"—and here he pointed to the signature line—"it is issued from our Zurich office and signed by Winfred Forster, a senior vice president. Now I know Winfred Forster quite well—very well, indeed: the two of us spent three years together at our Toronto branch—and, yes, Dr. Streider, there is a problem: this is not Winfred Forster's signature! Moreover, Zurich has confirmed this by fax: there is hardly any resemblance. I'm afraid it is my unpleasant duty to inform you that this note is a forgery!"

TWENTY-THREE

*A*fter leaving Ernest's office, Carol changed into jogging clothes and shoes in the restroom on the first floor and drove to the marina. She parked near Green's, a trendy vegetarian restaurant efficiently run by the San Francisco Zen Center. There was a path by the yacht harbor that followed the bay for two miles and ended at Fort Point under the Golden Gate. It was Jess's favorite run and had become hers as well.

The run started at the old Fort Mason buildings which house small galleries, a library-overflow bookstore, an art museum, a theater, and a drama workshop. It continued past the boat slips and along the bay where brazen gulls dared runners to trample them. It passed the grassy field where kite fliers launched kites, not the simple triangular or box kites she and her brother, Jeb, had flown, but avant-garde models shaped like Superman or a pair of women's legs, or sleek, high-tech metallic triangles that hummed as they sharply veered, changed directions, or plunged straight down, braking instantly to pirouette delicately on their tails. After that, a tiny beach containing a few sunbathers surrounding a surreal sand sculpture of a mermaid, then a long stretch by the water where wet-suited wind-surfers prepared their pleasure crafts; then a rocky shore with dozens of stone sculptures—mounds of stones exquisitely chosen and precariously balanced by some unknown artist to resemble fantastical Burmese pagodas; next a long pier teeming with diligent, somber Asian fishermen, not one of whom, as far as Carol could tell, ever caught anything. Then the final stretch to the underbelly of the Golden Gate where one can watch the long-haired, sexy surfers bobbing in the cold water waiting to mount tall dark waves.·

Almost every day now, she and Jess ran, sometimes along trails in Golden Gate Park or along the beach south of Cliff House, but the marina trail was their regular route. She often saw Jess several evenings as well. Generally when she returned home after work, he was there preparing dinner and chattering with the twins, who were growing very fond of him. Despite her pleasure in Jess, Carol worried. Jess seemed too good to be true. And what would happen when he got closer yet, close enough to see what she was really like? Her insides, her inner thoughts were not pretty. Would he back off? She distrusted the easy way he had insinuated himself so deeply into her home—and the way he made himself so important to the children. Would she have a free choice if she decided Jess was not the man for her? Or would she be trapped by what was best for the children?

On the rare occasion when Jess's work precluded his running dates with her, Carol took the hour-long run on her own. She was astonished how much she had come to love jogging: perhaps it was the buoyant feel it gave to her body for the rest of the day, or that exquisite exhilaration that swept through her when her second wind appeared. Or perhaps it was simply that she had come to care so much for Jess that she liked the activities he liked.

Jogging alone was not as magical as jogging with Jess, but it provided something else: time for self-reflection. At first when she jogged alone she had listened to a Walkman—country music, Vivaldi, Japanese flute music, the Beatles—but lately she had been leaving the Walkman in the car in favor of a jogging meditation.

The idea of devoting time to think about her life was revolutionary for Carol. For most of her life she had done the opposite, filling every patch of free time with distractions. What was the difference now? she wondered, as she glided along the path, scattering gulls with every step. One difference was the new breadth of her emotional life. In the past, her inner landscape had been monotonous and bleak, consisting of a narrow, negative range of emotions: anger, resentment, regret. Most of it had been directed toward Justin, the rest toward most other people who crossed her daily path. Aside from her children, she almost never had a good thought about anyone. In that, she followed the family tradition: she was her mother's daughter and her grandmother's granddaughter! Ernest had made her aware of that.

And if she hated Justin so much, why *had* she, in God's name, imprisoned herself in that marriage and thrown away the key? She might as well have tossed it into the rolling swells of the Pacific, now just a few feet away as she approached the fishing pier.

She knew she had made a hideous mistake, and she had known it soon after she married. As Ernest—damn him!—had forced her to acknowledge, she had choices just like anyone else: she could have left the marriage, or she could have tried to change it. She had chosen, deliberately chosen—so it seemed now—to do neither. Instead she wallowed in a miserable mistake.

She remembered how Norma and Heather had insisted, on that evening after Justin had slithered out of her life, that he had done her a favor. They were right. And her rage that he, not she, had taken the initiative? Stupid! In the long skein of things—Ernest's pretentious phrase—what difference did it make who left whom? They were both better off out of that marriage. She felt better than she had in a decade. And Justin looked better—doing his feeble, pathetic best to be a decent father. The week before he had even agreed, with no questions asked, to baby-sit the twins when she and Jess went to Mendocino for the weekend.

How ironic, she thought, that the unsuspecting Ernest was working so hard with her now to do something about her fictitious marriage with Wayne—how indefatigable he was in his insistence that she confront her life situation and do something about it—either to change the marriage or to end it. What a joke; if only he knew that he was doing exactly the same thing with her that he did with Justin, only siding with *her* now, planning strategy with *her* in the war room, giving *her* the same advice he must have given Justin!

Carol was breathing hard when she arrived at the Golden Gate. She jogged up to the end of the trail, touched the furthermost wire barrier under the bridge, and, without stopping, turned back toward

Fort Mason. The wind, as usual, was sweeping in from the Pacific and now, with the wind at her back, she flew effortlessly back past the surfers, the fishermen, the Burmese pagodas, the Superman kite, and the brazen gulls.

After lunching on a crisp Red Delicious apple in her car, Carol drove back to the law offices of Jarndyce, Kaplan, and Tuttle, where she showered, and prepared to see her new client, referred to her by Julius Jarndyce, the senior partner. Mr. Jarndyce, busy lobbying in Washington, had asked her to take particularly good care of this client, an old friend, Dr. Marshal Streider.

Carol saw her client, pacing, obviously highly agitated, in the waiting room. When she invited him into her office, Marshal entered quickly, perched on the edge of a chair, and began: "Thank you for seeing me today, Mrs. Astrid. Mr. Jarndyce, whom I've known for many years, offered me an appointment next week, but this is too urgent a matter to delay. To go right to the bottom line: yesterday I learned I've been swindled out of ninety thousand dollars. Can you help me? What recourse is open to me?"

"Being swindled is an awful feeling and I completely understand your sense of urgency, Dr. Streider. Let's start from the beginning. First, tell me what you think I need to know about you and then let's review, in meticulous detail, exactly what's happened."

"Gladly, but first may I get clear about the frame of our contract?"

"The frame, Dr. Streider?"

"Sorry—an analytic term—I mean I'd like to be clear, before we start, about several things. Your availability? Fees? And confidentiality. Confidentiality is extremely important to me."

Yesterday, as soon as he had learned of the forgery, Marshal had panicked and dialed Melvin's number. As he listened to the phone ring, he made a sudden decision that he didn't want Melvin; he wanted a more sympathetic and high-powered attorney. He hung up the phone and immediately dialed Mr. Jarndyce, a former patient, one of San Francisco's most eminent attorneys.

Later, about three A.M. that night, Marshal realized that it was imperative to keep this whole incident as quiet as possible. He invested with an ex-patient—many would be critical of him. That, itself, was bad enough, but he felt like an idiot to have been hood-winked in this fashion. All in all, the fewer people who knew of this the better. In fact, he should never have called Jarndyce—that, too, was an error in judgment, even though therapy with him had ended many years ago. His disappointment, therefore, that Mr. Jarndyce was unavailable had now changed to relief.

"I'm available for this matter for as long as you need me, Dr. Streider. I have no travel plans, if that's what you mean. My fees are two hundred fifty an hour, and confidentiality is total, the same as in your profession—if anything, even tighter."

"I'd like that to include Mr. Jarndyce. I want everything to remain strictly between the two of us."

"Agreed. You can count on that, Dr. Streider. Now let's begin."

Marshal, still leaning forward on the edge of his chair, proceeded to tell Carol the entire story. He spared not a single detail, save his concern about professional ethics. After thirty minutes he finished and sank back in his chair, exhausted and relieved. He did not fail to note how consoling it was to share everything with Carol and how attached to her he already felt.

"Dr. Streider, I appreciate your honesty. I know it wasn't easy to relive all these painful details. Before we proceed, let me ask you something: I noticed the forcefulness with which you said, more than once, that this was an investment and *not* a gift and that Mr. Macondo was an *ex-patient*. Is there some question in your mind about your behavior—I mean, about professional ethics?"

"Not in *my* mind. My actions are beyond reproach. But you're right to call attention to that. It may be an issue to others. I have been highly vocal in my field about upholding professional standards of ethical behavior—been on the state medical ethics board, and head of the psychoanalytic task force on professional ethics— and therefore my position in these matters is a delicate one; my behavior must not only *be* above reproach, but *appear* above reproach."

Marshal was perspiring heavily and took out a handkerchief to wipe his brow. "Please understand . . . and this is reality, not paranoia . . . I have rivals and enemies, individuals who would be only too eager to misinterpret some piece of my behavior, who would be delighted to see me fall."

"So," Carol said, lifting her eyes from her notes, "let me ask again, is it true that you have absolutely no personal doubts about violation of therapist-patient financial boundaries?"

Marshal stopped wiping his forehead and looked, with surprise, at his attorney. Obviously, she was well informed about such matters.

"Well, it goes without saying, in retrospect, I wish I had behaved differently. I wish I had been a stickler, like I usually am, for such matters. I wish I had said to him that I *never* invest personally with patients *or* ex-patients. Now, for the first time, it dawns on me that such rules are protective not only of the patient but of the therapist as well."

"These rivals or enemies, do they represent . . . I mean, are they an important consideration?"

"I'm not sure what you mean . . . well, yes . . . I have real rivals. And, as I have implied, I am most anxious . . . no, let me change that . . . I'm *desperate* . . . for privacy in this matter . . . for my practice, for my professional associations. So, the answer is yes; I want this whole nasty business kept quiet. But why do you persevere on this particular aspect?"

"Because," Carol responded, "your need for secrecy bears directly upon the recourses available to us—the greater your wish for secrecy, the less aggressive we can be. I'll explain that more in a minute. But there's another reason I ask about secrecy—it's academic, since it's after the fact, but it may be of interest to you. I don't want to be presumptuous, Dr. Streider, in telling *you* about psychological matters, but let me point out something about the way the professional con man always works. He makes a point of getting his victim involved in a scheme in which the victim feels that he, *also,* is engaged in something marginally dishonest. In that fashion the victim becomes—what shall we say?—almost a co-conspirator and enters a different state of mind, a state in which he abandons his ordinary caution and discrimination. Furthermore, since the victim feels even slightly conspiratorial, he is disinclined to seek input from the reliable financial advisers he might ordinarily employ. And, for the same reason, after the swindle, the victim is disinclined to prosecute vigorously."

"This victim has no problems in that sphere," said Marshal. "I am going to get that bastard and nail him to the wall. No matter what it takes."

"Not according to what you've just told me, Dr. Streider. You've said that privacy is a priority. Ask yourself this question, for example: Would you be willing to be involved in a public trial?"

Marshal sat silently, head bowed.

"Sorry, Dr. Streider, I've got to point this out to you. I don't mean to discourage you in any way. I know that's not what you need now. But let's go on. We've got to look closely at every detail. It seems to me from everything you've said that Peter Macondo is a pro—he's done this before, and it's highly unlikely that he's left us a good trail. First, tell me what investigations you, yourself, have made. Can you list the people he's talked about?"

Marshal recounted his conversations with Emil, Roscoe Richardson, and the University of Mexico provost. And his inability to contact Adriana and Peter. He showed her the fax he had received that morning from the Pacific Union Club—a copy of a fax from the Baur au Lac Club in Zurich stating that they had no knowledge of a Peter Macondo. They verified that the fax had been sent on their stationery and from the fax machine in their library, but they stressed that any member, any guest, or even former guest, or even a guest at the hotel that adjoins the club, could easily have walked in, borrowed their stationery, and used that fax machine.

"Is it possible," Marshal asked as Carol read, "that incriminating evidence may be found on that fax, or on the fax from the University of Mexico?"

"Or, that *alleged* fax from the University of Mexico!" Carol replied. "He probably sent that to himself."

"Then maybe we can find the location of the machine it came from. Or fingerprints? Or interview the jewelry store salesman again—the one who sold him my Rolex? Or the airline records to Europe? Or passport control?"

"If, indeed, he went to Europe at all. You only know what he told you, Dr. Streider—what he wanted you to know. Think about it: *there is not a single independent source of information.* And he paid cash for everything. No, there's no question—your man is a real professional. Naturally we must inform the FBI—undoubtedly the bank has already done so: they are required to report international fraud. Here is the number to call; simply ask for the on-duty agent. I could assist you with this, but it would only run up your legal expenses.

"Most of the questions you're asking," Carol continued, "are investigative, not legal, and best answered by a private detective. I can give you a referral to a good one, if you wish, but my advice is, be careful; don't plunge too much more of your money and energy in what will probably be an empty chase. I've seen too many of these cases. This kind of criminal rarely gets caught. And if they do, they rarely have any money left."

"What happens to them ultimately?"

"They're basically self-destructive. Sooner or later your Mr.

Macondo will do himself in—take too great a risk, perhaps try to swindle the wrong person and find himself dead in the trunk of a car."

"Maybe he's already starting to do himself in. Look at the risk he took here, look at his target—a psychoanalyst. I admit it worked on me, but still he's picking a highly trained observer of human behavior—one very likely to spot deception."

"No, Dr. Streider, I disagree. I've had a great deal of experience which suggests exactly the opposite. I'm not at liberty to discuss my sources, but I have evidence that psychiatrists may be among the most gullible of people. I mean, after all, they are accustomed to people telling them the truth—people *paying* them to listen to their true stories. I think psychiatrists are easy to swindle—you may not be his first victim. Who knows? Swindling therapists might even be his modus operandi."

"That suggests he's trappable. Yes, Mrs. Astrid, I *do* want the name of your detective. I was an all-American linebacker; I know how to pursue and I know how to tackle. I'm so caught up, so tense—it's up to my eyeballs now—I can't let it go. I can't think of anything else, I can't see patients, I can't sleep. I have only two thoughts in my mind now: first, ripping him apart and, second, getting my ninety thousand dollars back. I am devastated by the loss of that money."

"All right, let's turn to that. Dr. Streider, give me a picture, if you will, of your financial situation: income, debts, investments, savings—everything."

Marshal spelled out his entire financial situation while Carol rapidly took notes on sheet after sheet of lined yellow paper.

When he had finished, Marshal pointed toward Carol's notes and said, "So, you can see, Mrs. Astrid, I'm not a wealthy man. And you can see what it means to me to lose ninety thousand dollars. This is devastating—the worst thing that's ever happened to me. When I think of the months and months I worked for this, waking up at six to squeeze an extra patient in, following and trading my stocks, daily phone calls with my broker and financial adviser, and . . . and . . . I mean . . . I don't know how I can recover from this. This is going to scar me and my family permanently."

Carol studied her notes, put them down, and in a soothing voice said: "Let me try to put this into perspective for you. First, try to understand that this is *not* a ninety-thousand-dollar loss. With the record of a forged bank-guaranteed note, your accountant will treat this as a capital loss and offset the substantial capital gains you've had in the past year and are likely to have in the future. What's more, three thousand a year may be used to offset *regular* income for the next ten years. So, in one stroke, we've just cut your loss substantially—down to less than fifty thousand.

"The second, and the last point I'm going to have time to make today—I've another client waiting—is that, as I look over your financial situation from the information you've supplied me, I see no devastation. You've been a good provider—an excellent provider—for your family, and you've been a successful investor. The truth is, this loss will not materially change your life in any fashion!"

"You don't understand—my son's education, my art—"

"Next time, Dr. Streider. I must stop now."

"When is the next time? Do you have any time tomorrow? I don't know how I'm going to get through the next few days."

"Yes, three o'clock tomorrow? Is that okay?"

"I'll make it okay. I'll cancel whatever I have. If you knew me better, Dr. Astrid—"

"*Mrs.* Astrid, but thanks for the promotion."

"Mrs. Astrid . . . but I was going to say that if you knew me, you'd appreciate that the situation must be grave indeed for me to cancel patients. Yesterday was the first time I've done that in twenty years."

"I'll make myself available to you as much as possible. However, we also want to keep costs down. I feel awkward saying this to a psychiatrist, but the best thing for you now is to speak intimately to a confidant—a friend, a therapist. You are stuck in a perspective that is increasing your panic, and you need other points of view. What about your wife?"

"My wife lives in another world—an ikebana world."

"Where? Ike . . . what? Sorry—I don't understand."

"Ikebana—you know, Japanese flower arrangement—she's addicted to it and to her Buddhist meditating cronies. I hardly ever see her."

"Oh, oh . . . I see . . . what? Oh, yes, ikebana . . . yes, I've heard of that . . . Japanese flower arrangement. I understand. And she's away—you say lost in that world? Not home much? . . . Why, that must be awful for you. Dreadful. And you're alone . . . and you need her now. Dreadful."

Marshal was surprised, but touched, by Carol's nonlawyerly response. He and Carol sat silently for a few moments until it was Marshal who had to say, "And you say you have another client now?"

Silence.

"Mrs. Astrid, you say—"

"Sorry, Dr. Streider," Carol said as she rose, "my mind wandered for a minute. But we meet tomorrow. Hang in there. I'm on your side."

TWENTY-FOUR

After Marshal's departure, Carol sat stunned for several minutes. Ikebana! Japanese flower arrangement! There could be no doubt about it—her client, Dr. Streider, was Jess's ex-therapist. Jess had, from time to time, talked about his previous therapist—always in highly positive terms, always emphasizing his decency, dedication, helpfulness. At first, Jess had evaded Carol's questions about starting therapy with Ernest, but as their relationship deepened, he told her of that April day when, deep in the boughs of the weeping scarlet maple, he came upon the shocking sight of his therapist's wife locked in deep embrace with a saffron-robed Buddhist monk.

But Jess had made a point of honoring his former therapist's privacy, and hadn't revealed his name. But there could be no mistake about it, Carol thought: it *had* to be Marshal Streider. How many therapists have a wife who is an ikebana expert and a Buddhist?

Carol could hardly wait to see Jess at dinner; she could not remember the last time she had been so eager to share some news with a friend. She imagined Jess's expression of incredulity, his soft, round mouth saying, "No! I can't believe it! How awful—ninety thousand dollars! And, believe me, this man works hard for his money. And of all the people in the world, he came to you!" She imagined him listening to every word. She would stretch the details out to extend the juicy story as long as possible.

But then she abruptly cut herself short when she realized she couldn't tell Jess this. *I can't tell him anything about Marshal Streider,* she thought. *I can't even reveal that I've seen him. I'm explicitly sworn to professional secrecy.*

Yet she ached to tell him. Maybe, someday, there would be a way. But for now she had to be content with whatever meager nourishment she could extract from the thin gruel of honoring her professional code of behavior. And to be content, also, with behaving as Jess would have wanted her to behave—to offer all possible aid to his former therapist. This would not be easy. Carol had never met a shrink she liked. And she liked this particular shrink, Dr. Streider, less than most: he whined too much, took himself too seriously, and resorted to puerile macho football images. And, even though he was momentarily humbled by this swindle, she could sense his underlying arrogance. Not hard to understand why he had enemies.

Yet Jess had received much from Dr. Streider, and so Carol, as a gift to Jess, made a commitment to extend herself to help this client in every way possible. She liked giving Jess gifts, but a secret gift—to be a covert good Samaritan, for Jess not even to know of her good deeds—that was going to be difficult.

Secrets had always been her strong suit. Carol was a master of manipulation and intrigue in her litigation work. No litigator liked to oppose her in the courtroom; she had accrued a reputation for being ingeniously and dangerously devious. Deception had always come easy to her and she made few distinctions between her professional and personal behavior. But in the last few weeks she had grown weary of deviousness. There was something deliciously refreshing in being honest with Jess. Every time she saw him, she tried to take some new risk. After only a few weeks, she had revealed more to Jess than she had ever shared with any other man. Save for one topic, of course: Ernest!

Neither talked much about Ernest. Carol had suggested that life would be less complicated if they did not speak of their therapy to each other and not speak of each other to Ernest. At first she would have liked to turn Jess against Ernest, but she dropped that plan quickly—there was no mistaking that Jess was benefiting greatly from therapy and liked Ernest enormously. Carol, of course, revealed none of her devious behavior or her feelings about Ernest.

"Ernest is an extraordinary therapist," Jess exclaimed one day after a particularly good session. "He is so honest and human." Jess went on to describe their session that day. "Ernest really homed in on something important today. He told me that whenever he and I got closer, whenever we moved into greater intimacy, then I invariably pulled away, either by making some homophobic joke or by launching into an intellectual diversion.

"And he's right, Carol, I do that all the time with men, especially my father. But I'll tell you what was amazing about him—he went on to acknowledge that *he, too,* found intense male intimacy uncomfortable, that he had colluded with me by being distracted by my jokes or by joining me in some intellectualized discussion.

"Now isn't that an uncommon kind of honesty from a therapist," Jess said, "especially after so many years with distant, uptight shrinks? What is even more amazing is how he can maintain this level of intensity, hour after hour."

Carol was startled to hear how self-revealing Ernest was with Jess and, in a strange way, almost disappointed to learn that it was not just with her that he was. In some odd way she felt tricked. Yet Ernest had never implied that he treated her any differently than his other patients. The thought grew stronger that she might have been mistaken about him, that his intensity was not, after all, a prelude to seduction.

In fact, her whole Byzantine project with Ernest was turning into a quagmire. Sooner or later, Jess would *have* to bring her up in his therapy, and then Ernest would learn the truth. And her goal of discrediting Ernest, of putting him out of business, and rupturing his relationship to Justin no longer made much sense. Justin had faded into irrelevance, and Ralph Cooke and Zweizung had receded again into the past. Any injury to Ernest would result in nothing but pain for Jess and, ultimately, for her. Rage and revenge had driven Carol for so long that now, without them, she felt lost. Whenever she contemplated her motives—and she did so more and more—she felt confused about what she was doing and why she was doing it.

Nonetheless, she continued, as though on automatic pilot, to be sexually seductive with Ernest. A couple of sessions ago, during their parting hug, she pulled him tightly against her. He immediately froze up and said sharply, "Carolyn, it's clear you still want me to be your lover, just the way that Ralph was. But it's time now for you to drop it. Hell will freeze over before I get involved sexually with you. Or with any of my patients!"

Ernest had immediately regretted his testy response and, the following session, returned to it.

"I'm sorry about my sharpness last session, Carolyn. I don't often lose it like that, but there's something so strange, so driven, about your persistence. And so self-destructive, it seems to me. I think we can do good work together, I'm sure I have much to offer you—but what I don't get is why you continue to try to sabotage our work."

Carol's response, her entreaties about needing more of him, her references to Ralph Cooke, sounded hollow even to her, and Ernest responded hastily: "I know this must feel repetitious but, as long as you keep pushing against my boundaries, we've got to keep going over it, time and time again. First, I'm convinced that becoming your lover will ultimately be harmful to you—I know you believe otherwise and I've tried every way I know to persuade you. You cannot believe that I might have genuine concern for you. So today I'm going to try something else. I'm going to talk about our relationship from my own selfish point of view, from the perspective of what's good for me.

"The bottom line is that I'm going to avoid acting in a way that will cause me pain later on. I *know* what the ultimate result of any sexual involvement will be for me: I will feel bad about myself for years to come, probably forever. And I'm not going to treat myself in that manner. And this doesn't even touch upon the legal risks. I could lose my license. I've worked too hard to get where I am, I love what I'm doing, and I'm not willing to jeopardize my entire career. And it's time for you to start to examine why you're asking this of me."

"You're mistaken. There is no legal risk," Carol countered, "because no legal action can exist without a claim being filed, and I will never, never do that. I want you to be my lover. I could never harm you."

"I know you feel that way. *Now*. But there are hundreds of claims filed every year and in every case—without exception—the patient once felt exactly as you do at this moment. So let me put it very frankly and very selfishly: I am behaving in my own self-interest!"

No response from Carol.

"Well, that's about it, Carolyn, I've laid it on the line. I can't be clearer. You have a decision ahead of you. Go home. Think deeply about what I've said. Believe me when I tell you I will never be physically intimate with you—I am dead serious about it—and then decide whether you still want to continue to see me."

They parted on a somber note. No hug. And this time, no regrets on Ernest's part.

Carol sat down in Ernest's waiting room to change into her running shoes. She opened her purse and read over some of her session notes:

> *Urges me to call him "Ernest," to phone him at home, says that I am attractive in every way, sits next to me on sofa, invites me to question him about his personal life, caresses my hair, says that if we met elsewhere he'd want to be my lover . . .*

She thought about Jess, who would be waiting for her in front of Green's Restaurant. *Goddamnit.* She tore up the notes and took off running.

TWENTY-FIVE

*M*arshal's visit to Bat Thomas, the private investigator Carol recommended, started off promisingly. He looked the part: craggy-faced, wrinkled clothes, crooked teeth, sneakers, slightly overweight and out of shape—probably the result of too much alcohol and too many sedentary stakeouts. His manner was brusque and tough, his mind powerful and disciplined. In his office, a rugged fourth-floor walkup off Fillmore, sandwiched between a produce market and a bakery, the necessary accoutrements were all in place: a sagging, battered green leather couch, bare wood floors, and a scratched-up wooden desk with a book of matches wadded under one leg to prevent tottering.

Marshal enjoyed running up the stairs—he had been too agitated to play basketball or to jog the past few days and missed his exercise. And, at first, he liked talking to the straight-shooting investigator.

Bat Thomas was entirely in agreement with Carol. After hearing

Marshal describe the entire incident—including his anguish about his stupidity, the magnitude of the loss, and his terror about public exposure—he commented, "Your attorney's right—she rarely misses and I've worked with her for years. The guy's a pro. I'll tell you what part I like: that bit about the Boston surgeon and asking you to help him work on his guilt . . . hey, hey, dynamite technique! Also buying your silence with that thirty-five-hundred-dollar Rolex—cute stuff, very cute! An amateur would have given you a fake watch. And taking you to the Pacific Union Club—great! He got an angle on you. Quick. You gave something away. Sharp guy. You're lucky he didn't take more. But let's see what we can get on him. You got any other names he's mentioned? How'd he get to you in the first place?"

"Said that a friend of Adriana's had recommended me," Marshal replied. "No names given."

"You've got phone numbers for him and his fiancée? I'll start with those. And his phone number in Zurich, too. He had to provide some identification to have gotten the phone service, so let me track that down today. But don't get your hopes up—probably bogus. How'd he travel? You see a car?"

"Don't know how he arrived at my office. Rented car? Taxi? When we left the P.U. Club he walked to his hotel—just a couple of blocks. How about tracking the University of Mexico fax?"

"Faxes lead nowhere, but give it to me and I'll take a look— undoubtedly he made up a logo on his computer and faxed it to himself or had his girlfriend fax it. I'll track down their names and see if they light up anything in the NCIC computer—that's the National Crime Information Center. I got someone who, for a small payoff, can get into the computer to look him up. Worth a try, but don't get your hopes up—your man's using an alias. He probably does this three or four times a year—maybe only with shrinks. I've never heard of that M.O. before but I'll check around. Or he might go after bigger money—surgeons, maybe—but even with small fry like you, he nets four or five hundred K a year. Not bad when you consider it's tax-free! This guy's good; he'll go far! I'll need a retainer of five hundred just to start."

Marshal wrote out a check and asked for a receipt.

"Okay, Doc, we're in business. I'm gonna get right to it. Come back this afternoon around five or six and we'll see what we have."

That afternoon Marshal returned only to learn that nothing had panned out. Adriana had obtained a phone service by using a stolen Arkansas driver's license and credit card. Peter had paid cash for everything at the Fairmont Hotel and used a phony American Express card as collateral. The faxes all originated locally. The Zurich phone was set up with the same AMEX card.

"No leads," said Bat. "Zip! The guy's smooth, very smooth—you gotta respect him."

"I get the picture. You like this guy's work. I'm glad the two of you are getting along so well," said Marshal. "But remember *I'm* your client, and I want to nail him."

"You want him? There's only one thing to do—I've got friends in the fraud squad. Let me go to them, have lunch with my friend Lou Lombardi—he owes me. We can check out similar cons, other shrinks or docs who have been done to the same way—the wealthy, grateful, cured client, the insistence on rewarding the miracle-working surgeon, the Rolex, the endowed lectureship, the overseas investment, and the guilt about past unsuccessful tips to docs. That line is too good not to have been used before."

"Go after the bastard any way you can."

"There's a hitch: you got to go with me to file a complaint—it's the San Francisco fraud squad territory; you made the transaction in this city. But you've got to use your name, and there's no way it can be kept from the press—can't be done—you gotta be prepared—you know that newspaper shit—some newspaper heading like PSYCHIATRIST'S WALLET SHRUNK BY EX-PATIENT!"

Marshal, holding his head in his hands, groaned. "That's worse than the swindle—it'd ruin me! Newspaper accounts of my accepting a Rolex from a patient? How could I be so stupid? How could I?"

"It's your money and your call. But I can't help you if you tie my hands."

"That fucking Rolex cost me ninety thousand dollars! Stupid, stupid, stupid!"

"Let up on yourself, Doc. No assurance the fraud squad could track him . . . chances are, he's out of the country. Here, sit back, let me tell you a story." Bat lit up a cigarette, tossing the match on the floor.

"Couple of years ago I fly into New York on business and to see my daughter, who just gave birth to my first grandchild. Nice fall day, crisp weather, I'm walking down Broadway around Thirty-ninth or Fortieth thinking maybe I should've brought a gift—kids always thought I was stingy. Then I see myself in a TV monitor on the street—some lowlife hawking a brand-new mini Sony camcorder for a hundred and fifty bucks. I use these all the time in my work—they run around six hundred. I knock him down to seventy-five, he sends a little kid running off, and five minutes later an old Buick drives up to the curb with about a dozen camcorders in original Sony packing boxes on the backseat. They're looking furtively around all the time, telling me that typical shit about them falling out of a truck. Stolen, obviously. But greedy asshole that I am, I buy it anyway. I give 'em the seventy-five bucks, they take off, and I take the box back to the hotel. Then I begin to get paranoid. I was a key investigator in a megabucks bank fraud case and had to stay clean. Felt I was being tailed. Once back in the hotel I get even more convinced I'm being set up. I'm afraid to leave the stolen camcorder in my room. I lock it in a suitcase and check it downstairs in the hotel. Next day I pick up the suitcase, take it to my daughter's home, cut open the brand-new Sony camcorder box, and there it is: a big brick!

"So, Doc, lighten up on yourself. It happens to pros—to the best of us. You can't live a life always looking over your shoulder, always thinking your friends are going to screw you. Sometimes you're just going to be unlucky enough to be in the way of a drunk driver. Sorry, Doc. But seven o'clock—I got a job tonight. Send you a bill later, but your five hundred will just about cover it."

Marshal looked up. For the first time he truly understood that he had been robbed of ninety thousand dollars. "So? That's it? That's what I get for my five hundred bucks? Your quaint little tale about the brick and the camcorder?"

"Look, you been picked cleaner than a rat's ass, you come in here without a clue, without a lead, with nothing . . . you ask my help—I give you five hundred bucks of my time and my staff's time. It's not like I didn't warn you. But you can't tie my hands—not let me do my job—and then bitch you're not getting your money's worth. I know you're pissed. Who wouldn't be? But let me go after him with everything I got or you gotta drop it."

Marshal remained silent.

"You want my advice? The meter's turned off—no further charge for this: *kiss that money off*. Consider it one of life's hard lessons."

"Well, Bat," Marshal said over his shoulder as he walked out of the office. "I don't give up that easy. That fucker's picked the wrong guy."

"Doc," Bat called down the stairs as Marshal descended, "if you're thinking of playing Lone Ranger—don't! That's guy's smarter than you are! A whole lot smarter!"

"Fuck you," Marshal muttered as he walked out of the doorway onto Fillmore.

⌁

Marshal took a long walk home, carefully considering his options. Later that evening he acted decisively. First he called Pac Bell and arranged for the installation of another home phone line with an unlisted number and voice mail. Next he faxed an ad to be placed in the next issue of the American Psychiatric Association's *Psychiatric News,* sent weekly to every psychiatrist in the country:

> WARNING: Are you treating a brief therapy patient (WM, wealthy, attractive, forty, slender) for problems with children and fiancée, involving estate dispersal and prenuptial arrangement, who offers great investment opportunity, gifts, endowed lectureship? You may be in great danger. Call 415-555-1751. Absolutely confidential.

TWENTY-SIX

*N*ights were especially hard for Marshal. He could sleep
now only with the help of heavy sedatives. During the
day nothing could halt the continual reliving of every
minute he had spent with Peter Macondo. Sometimes he sifted
through the debris of his memory for new clues, sometimes he
played out revenge fantasies in which he ambushed Peter in the
woods and beat him senseless, sometimes he just lay awake excori-
ating himself for his stupidity and imagining Peter and Adriana gaily
waving as they whizzed by in a new ninety-thousand-dollar Porsche.

Nor were the days easy. The sedative hangover, despite double
espressos, lasted till noon, and it was only with the greatest effort
that Marshal could get through his hours with patients. Again and
again he imagined breaking his role and intruding into the analytic
hour. "Stop whining," he wanted to say. Or, "You couldn't get to
sleep for an hour—you call *that* insomnia? I was awake half the
fucking night!" Or, "So, after ten years, you saw Mildred in the

grocery store and once again you had that magical feeling, that little pang of desire, that little flash of fear! Big deal! Let me tell you what pain is."

Nonetheless, Marshal carried on, drawing what pride he could from the knowledge that most therapists suffering his level of distress would have long since thrown in the towel and called in sick. When the going gets tough, he reminded himself, the tough get going. And so, hour after hour, day after day, he sucked in the pain and gutted it out.

Only two things kept Marshal going. First, the lust for revenge; he checked his voice mail several times a day hoping for a response to his ad in the *Psychiatric News,* hoping for some trail that would lead him to Peter. Second, his soothing visits with his attorney. An hour or two before each appointment with Carol, Marshal could think of little else; he rehearsed what he would say, he imagined their conversations. Sometimes, when he thought of Carol, his eyes filled with tears of gratitude. Each time he left her office, his burden seemed lighter. He didn't analyze the meaning of his deep feelings for her—he didn't much care. Soon, weekly meetings were not enough, he wanted to meet two, three times a week, even daily.

Marshal's demands taxed Carol. She soon exhausted all she had to offer as an attorney and was at a loss as to how to deal with Marshal's distress. Finally she decided that she could best fulfill her Good Samaritan vow by urging him to see a therapist. But Marshal would have none of it.

"I can't see a therapist for the same reasons that I can't have any publicity about this whole business. I've got too many enemies."

"You think a therapist couldn't maintain confidentiality?"

"No, it's not so much a question of confidentiality—more a question of visibility," Marshal replied. "You have to consider that anyone who's going to be of use to me will have to be analytically trained."

"You mean," Carol interrupted, "no other type of therapist but an analyst could help you?"

"Mrs. . . . . I wonder if you mind if we go on a first-name basis? Mrs. Astrid and Dr. Streider sounds so stiff and formal, considering the intimate nature of our discussion."

Carol nodded her approval, not failing to remember Jess's comment that the only thing he disliked about his therapist was his formality: he had snorted at Jess's suggestion of using first names and insisted on being addressed as Doctor. . . .

"Carol . . . yes, that's better . . . tell me the truth—can you see me consulting some flake therapist? Some past-lives specialist, or someone who's drawing diagrams of parent, child, and adult on a portable blackboard, or some young cognitive therapy jerk trying to correct my faulty thinking habits?"

"Okay, for the moment assume it is true that only an analyst could help. Now continue your argument: Why does that present such a problem to you?"

"Well, I know every analyst in the community, and I don't think there's one who could assume the necessary neutral attitude toward me. I'm too successful, too ambitious. Everyone knows I'm on course to become president of the Golden Gate Psychoanalytic Institute and that I've got my sights on national leadership."

"So, then, it's a question of envy and competition?"

"Of course. How could any analyst maintain therapeutic neutrality toward me? Any analyst I saw would secretly gloat about my misfortune. I probably would if I were in their place. Everyone likes to see the collapse of the mighty. And word would get around I was in therapy—in a month everyone in town would know about it."

"How?"

"No way to conceal it. Analytic offices are clustered together. Someone would spot me in the waiting room."

"So? Is it a disgrace to be in therapy? I've heard of people speak with admiration of therapists still willing to work on themselves."

"Among my colleagues, and at my age and level, it would be perceived as a sign of weakness—it would cripple me politically. And keep in mind that I've been highly critical of therapist misconduct: I've even engineered the disciplining and expulsion—a well-deserved expulsion, I might add—of my own analyst from the institute. You read about the Seth Pande catastrophe in the papers?"

"The psychiatric recall? Yes, of course!" Carol said. "Who could miss that flap? That was you?"

"I was a major player in it. Maybe *the* major player. And, between you and me, I saved the institute's ass—a long and confidential story, I can't go into it—but the point is this: How could I ever again speak up about therapist misconduct when there might be someone in the audience who knows that I accepted a Rolex from a patient? I'd be forced into silence—and political ineffectiveness—forever."

Carol knew there was something seriously wrong with Marshal's argument, but she couldn't find a way to challenge it. Perhaps his distrust of therapists was too close to her own. She tried another tack.

"Marshal, go back to your statement that *only* an analytically trained therapist could help you. Where does that leave you and me? Look at me—a totally untrained person! How is it that you consider me helpful?"

"I don't know *how*—I only know you *are*. And right now I don't have the energy to figure out why. Maybe all you have to do is just be there in the room with me—that's all. Just let me do the work."

"Still," said Carol, shaking her head, "I'm uncomfortable with our arrangement. It's unprofessional; it may even be unethical. You're spending money to see someone who has no special expertise in the area you need. And it's a good bit of money—after all, I charge more than a psychotherapist."

"No, I've thought all that through. How can it be unethical? Your client is requesting it because he finds it helpful. I'll sign an affidavit to that effect. And it's not expensive if you take into consideration the tax consequences. Moderate medical expenses at my level of income are not deductible, but legal expenses are. Carol, you are one hundred percent deductible. You're actually cheaper than a therapist—but that's not the reason for seeing you! The real reason is that you're the one person who can help me."

And so Carol was persuaded to continue her meetings with Marshal. She had no difficulty spotting Marshal's problems—one by one he spelled them out for her. Like so many excellent attorneys Carol took pride in her beautiful penmanship, and her meticulous notes on legal-sized paper soon contained a cogent list of issues. Why was it so impossible for Marshal to turn to anyone else for help? Why so many enemies? And why so arrogant, so judgmental, about other therapists and other therapies? He was omnivorously judgmental; he spared no one, not his wife, not Bat Thomas, not Emil, not Seth Pande, not his colleagues, not his students.

Carol couldn't help insinuating a question about Ernest Lash. Under the pretext that one of her friends was considering entering therapy with him, she asked for his recommendation.

"Well—and, remember, this is confidential, Carol—he's not the first person I would recommend to you. Ernest's a bright, thoughtful young man who has an excellent background in drug research.

In that area he's top-notch. No question. But as a therapist . . . well . . . let's just say he's still developing, still undifferentiated. The main problem is, he's had no real analytic training aside from limited supervision with me. Nor, I think, is he sufficiently mature yet to undertake proper analytic training: too undisciplined, too irreverent and iconoclastic. And even worse, he flaunts his unruliness, attempts to dignify it under the name of 'innovation' or 'experimentation.'"

Unruly! Irreverent! Iconoclastic! As a result of these accusations, Ernest's stock rose several points in her estimation.

Next on Carol's list, after distrust and arrogance, came Marshal's shame. Deep shame. Maybe arrogance and shame went together, Carol thought. Maybe, if Marshal weren't so judgmental of others, he wouldn't be so hard on himself. Or did it work the other way? If he weren't so hard on himself, might he be more forgiving of others? Funny, now that she thought of it, that was exactly the way Ernest had put it to her.

Actually, in many ways she recognized herself in Marshal. For example, his rage—its white heat, its tenacity, his obsession with revenge—reminded her of the meeting she had had with Heather and Norma that awful night after Justin left. Had she really entertained the idea of a hit man, a tire-iron beating? Had she really destroyed Justin's computer files, his clothing, his souvenirs from his youth? None of it seemed real now. It happened a thousand years ago. Justin's face was fading from memory.

How had she changed so much? she wondered. The chance meeting with Jess, probably. Or maybe just getting away from the strangulation of the marriage? And then Ernest crossed her mind . . . could it have been that, despite everything, he had managed to bootleg some therapy into their sessions?

She tried to reason with Marshal about the uselessness of his rage, and pointed out its self-defeating character. But to no avail. Sometimes she wished she could transfuse some of her newly developed temperateness into him. Other times she lost patience and wanted to shake some sense into him. "Let it go!" she wanted to yell. "Don't you see what your idiotic rage and pride are costing you? Everything! Your peace of mind, your sleep, your work, your marriage, your friendships! Just let it go." But none of these approaches would help. She remembered only too vividly the tenacity of her own vengefulness just a few weeks ago, and so could easily empathize with Marshal's anger. But she didn't know how to help him let it go.

Some of the other items on her list—for example, Marshal's pre-occupation with money and status—were alien to her. She had no personal concourse with them. Nonetheless she appreciated their centrality to Marshal: after all, it was his greed and ambition that had gotten him into this mess.

And his wife? Carol waited patiently hour after hour for Marshal to speak of her. But scarcely a word, other than to say that Shirley was away on a three-week Vipassnia retreat at Tassajara. Nor did Marshal respond to Carol's questions about their marriage other than to say that their interests had diverged and that they had been going their separate ways.

Often while jogging, while researching other clients' cases, while lying in bed, Carol thought about Marshal. So many questions. So few answers. Marshal sensed her disquiet and reassured her that merely helping him to formulate and discuss his basic problems was sufficient to ease some of his pain. But Carol knew it wasn't enough. She needed help; she needed a consultant. But who? And then one day it occurred to her: she knew exactly where to turn.

TWENTY-SEVEN

*I*n Ernest's waiting room, Carol decided she would devote her entire therapy hour to getting advice about how to help Marshal. She made a checklist of the areas in which she needed help with her client and planned how best to present them to Ernest. She knew she had to be careful: Marshal's remarks made it clear that he and Ernest knew each other and she would have to bury Marshal's identity very deeply. That didn't daunt Carol; *au contraire,* she moved easily and cheerfully in the halls of intrigue.

But Ernest had quite a different agenda. As soon as she entered the office, *he* opened the hour.

"You know, Carolyn, I feel that the last session was unfinished. We ended in the middle of something important."

"What do you mean?"

"It seemed to me that we were in the midst of a more searching look at our relationship and you began to get agitated. You practically bolted out of here at the end of the hour. Can you talk about the feelings you experienced on your way home from our session?"

Ernest, like most therapists, almost always waited for the patient to begin the hour. If he ever broke that rule and introduced the first topic, it was invariably for the purpose of exploring some issue left hanging from the last session. He had learned from Marshal long before that the more therapy sessions flow from one to the other, the more powerful did therapy become.

"Agitated? No." Carol shook her head. "I don't think so. I don't remember much about the last session. Besides, Ernest, today is today and I want to talk to you about something else. I need some advice about a client I'm seeing."

"In a minute, Carolyn, first let me follow through with this for a few minutes. There are some things that feel important to me that I want to say."

Whose therapy is this, anyway? Carol mumbled to herself. But she nodded amiably and waited for Ernest to continue.

"You remember, Carolyn, that in our first session, I told you that nothing was more important in therapy than for us to have an honest relationship? For my part, I gave you my word that I would be honest with you. Yet the truth is that I haven't lived up to that. It's time to clear the air, and I'll start with my feelings about the erotic . . . there's been a lot of that in our relationship and that's been disturbing to me."

"What do you mean?" Carol felt concerned; Ernest's tone made it clear this was not going to be an ordinary hour.

"Well, look at what's happened. From the first session forward, a great deal of our time has been devoted to your talking about your sexual attraction to me. I've become the center of your sexual fantasies. Again and again, you've asked me to take Ralph's place as your lover-therapist. And then there are the hugs at the end of the hour, the attempts to kiss me, the 'couch time' where you want to sit close to me."

"Yes, yes, I know all that. But you used the word *disturbing*."

"Yes, definitely disturbing—and in more ways than one. First, because it was sexually arousing."

"You're disturbed because I was aroused?"

"No, that *I* was. You've been very provocative, Carolyn, and since the name of the game here, and especially today, is honesty, I'll tell you honestly that it's been disturbingly arousing to me. I've told you before that I consider you a very attractive woman; it's very difficult for me, as a man, not to be affected by your seductiveness. You've entered into *my* fantasies, as well. I think about seeing you hours before you come in, I even think about what to wear on the days I see you. I've got to own up to this.

"Now, obviously, therapy can't go on like this. You see, rather than help you resolve these . . . these—what shall I say?— powerful but unrealistic feelings toward me, I believe I've colluded in them, I've encouraged them. I've enjoyed hugging you, touching your hair, having you sit next to me on the sofa. And I believe you know I've enjoyed it. You shake your head 'No,' Carolyn, but I believe I've fanned the flames of your feelings to me. I've been saying 'No, no, no,' all along but, in a softer but audible voice, I've also been saying, 'Yes, yes, yes.' And that has not been therapeutic for you."

"I haven't heard the 'Yes, yes, yes,' Ernest."

"Maybe not consciously. But if I feel these feelings, I'm certain you've sensed them at some level and been encouraged by them. Two people locked together in an intimate relationship—or a relationship that is *trying* to be intimate—always communicate everything to each other, if not explicitly, then on a nonverbal or unconscious level."

"I'm not sure I buy into that, Ernest."

"I'm sure I'm right on this. We'll come back to it again. But I want you to hear the gist of what I've said: your erotic feelings toward me are not good for therapy, and I, with my own vanity and my own sexual attraction to you, must take the responsibility for encouraging those feelings. I have not been a good therapist for you."

"No, no," Carol said, shaking her head vigorously. "None of this is your fault—"

"No, Carolyn, let me finish. . . . There's something more I want to say to you. . . . Before I even met you I had made a conscious decision that I was going to be totally self-revealing with my next new patient. I felt, and still feel, that the basic flaw in most traditional therapy is that the relationship between patient and therapist is not genuine. My feelings about this are so strong that I had to break with an analytic supervisor I greatly admired. It's for this very reason that I've recently made a decision not to pursue formal psychoanalytic training."

"I'm not sure what the implications of this are for our therapy."

"Well, it means my treatment of you has been experimental.

Maybe, in my own defense, I should say that that's too strong a term since, over the past few years, I have tried to be less formal and more human with all my patients. But with you there's a bizarre paradox: I committed myself to an experiment of total honesty and yet never told you about that experiment. And now, as I take stock of where we are, I don't believe this approach has been helpful. I've failed to create the type of honest, authentic relationship that I know is necessary if you're going to grow in therapy."

"I don't believe that any of this is your fault—or the fault of your approach."

"I'm not sure *what* went wrong. But *something* has. I feel an enormous gulf between us. I feel great suspicion and distrust coming from you, which alternates suddenly with some expression of great affection and love. And I always feel baffled because most of the time I don't sense you feel warm or even positive to me. Surely, I'm not telling you something you don't know."

Carol, head bowed, stayed silent.

"So, my concern is growing: I have not done the right thing by you. In this case honesty may *not* have been the best policy. It would have been better if you had seen a more traditional therapist, someone who would foster a more formal therapist-patient relationship, someone who would keep clearer boundaries between a therapeutic and a personal relationship. Sooo, Carolyn, I guess that's what I wanted to say to you. Any response?"

Carol started to speak twice but fumbled for words. Finally she said, "I'm confused. I can't speak—don't know what to say."

"Well, I can guess what you're thinking. In the light of all I've said, I'd expect that you'd be thinking you'd be better off with another therapist—that it's time to bring this experiment to an end. And I think you may well be right. I'll support you in this, and I'll be glad to make suggestions for another therapist. You might even be thinking that I've improperly charged you for an experimental procedure. If so, let's talk about that; maybe returning your fees is the proper thing to do."

The end of the experiment—a certain lilt to that, Carol thought. *And the perfect way out of this whole sticky farce. Yes, it's time to go, time to stop the lie. Leave Ernest to Jess and Justin. Perhaps you're right, Ernest. Perhaps it is time for us to stop therapy.*

That's what she should have said; instead, she found herself saying something quite different.

"No. Wrong on all counts. No, Ernest, it is not your therapy approach that's at fault. I don't like the idea of your changing it because of me . . . that troubles me . . . it troubles me a great deal. Surely one patient is not enough for you to reach such a conclusion. Who knows? Maybe it's too early to tell. Maybe it's the perfect approach for me. Give me time. I like your honesty. Your honesty has done me no harm. Maybe a lot of good. As for returning your fees, that's out of the question—and, incidentally, as an attorney, I want to advise you against such statements in the future. Leaves you vulnerable to litigation.

"The truth?" Carol continued. "You want the truth? The truth is, you've helped. More than you know. And, no, the more I think about it, I don't want to stop seeing you. And I won't see anyone else. Maybe we're over the tough period. Maybe, unconsciously, I was testing you. I think I was. And testing you severely."

"How did I do on the test?"

"I think you passed. No, better than that . . . top of your class."

"What was the test all about?"

"Well . . . I'm not sure I know . . . let me think about it. Well, I know a few things about it, but could we save that for another time, Ernest? There's something I *must* talk to you about today."

"Okay, but are we clean—you and I?"

"Getting cleaner."

"Let's go on with your agenda. You said it involved a client."

Carol described her situation with Marshal, revealing he was a therapist but, in all other ways, carefully disguising his identity and reminding Ernest of her professional commitment to confidentiality so that he wouldn't ask leading questions.

Ernest was not cooperative. He didn't like turning Carolyn's therapy hour into a consultation and posed a string of objections. She was resisting her own work; she was not making good use of her time or her money; and her client should be seeing a therapist, not an attorney.

Carol countered each of these deftly. Money was no issue—she was not wasting her money. She charged the client more than Ernest charged her. As for her client seeing a therapist—well, *he just wouldn't* and she couldn't explain further because of confidentiality. And she wasn't avoiding her own problems—she'd be willing to see Ernest more frequently to make up the hour. And since the client's problems mirrored her own, she was working indirectly on her issues by working on his. Her most powerful point was that by acting in a purely altruistic manner for her client, she was enacting Ernest's exhortation to break the cycle of selfishness and paranoia passed on to her by her mother and grandmother.

"You've persuaded me, Carolyn. You're a formidable woman. If ever I have to have a case argued, I want you as my counsel. Tell me about you and your client."

Ernest was an experienced consultant and listened carefully as Carol described what she was confronting in Marshal: rage, arrogance, loneliness, preoccupation with money and status, and withdrawal of interest in anything else in his life, including his marriage.

"What strikes me," Ernest said, "is that he's lost all perspective. He's so caught up by these events and these feelings that he's become identified with them. We need to find a way to help him take a few steps back from himself. We need to help him see himself from a more distant perch, even from a cosmic perspective. That's exactly what I was trying to do with you, Carolyn, whenever I asked you to consider something from the long skein of your life events. Your client's *become* these things—he has lost the sense of a persisting self who is experiencing these events for some small fraction of his existence. And what makes things worse is that your client is assuming that his present misery is going to be his permanent state—fixed for all time. Of course, that's the hallmark of depression—a combination of sadness plus pessimism."

"How do we break that up?"

"Well, there are many possibilities. For example, from what you've said, it's clear that accomplishment and effectiveness are central to his identity. He must feel absolutely helpless now, and terrified of that helplessness. What's happened is that he may have lost sight of the fact that he has choices and that these choices give him the power to change. He has to be helped to understand that his predicament is not the result of a predetermined destiny, but the result of his own choices—for example, his choice to revere money. Once he accepts that he is the creator of his situation, he can also be brought to the understanding that he has the power to extricate himself: his choices got him into this; his choices can get him out.

"Or," Ernest continued, "he probably has lost sight of the natural evolution of his present distress—that it exists now, that it had a beginning and will have an end. You might even review times in the past when he's felt this much rage and distress and help him remember how that pain has faded away—just as his current pain will, at some point, become a bleached memory."

"Good, good, Ernest. Terrific." Carol hastily scribbled notes. "What else?"

"Well, you say he's a therapist. There's some additional leverage there. When I treat therapists, I often find that I can use their own professional skills to good advantage. It's a good way to move them back from themselves, to look at themselves from a more distant perspective."

"How do you do that?"

"One simple way might be to ask him to imagine a patient with the same concerns as his walking into his office. How might he approach that patient? Ask him, 'What would you feel about this patient? How might you help him?'"

Ernest waited as Carol turned a page and continued her note taking.

"Be prepared for him to be annoyed at this; usually when therapists are in deep pain, they're like anyone else: they want to be taken care of, not to have to be their own therapist. But be persistent . . . it's an effective approach, it's good technique. In the business, it's what you call 'hard love.'

"Hard love is not my strong suit," Ernest continued. "My former supervisor used to tell me that I generally opted for the immediate gratification of my patients loving me, rather than the more important gratification of watching them get better. I think—no, I *know*— he was right. I owe him a lot for that."

"And arrogance?" asked Carol, looking up from her notes. "My client is so arrogant and grandiose and competitive that he has no friends at all."

"Usually 'upside down' is the best approach: his grandiosity is probably covering a self-image that is full of doubt and shame and self-derogation. Arrogant, hard-driving people usually feel they have to overachieve just to stay even. So I wouldn't think of exploring his grandiosity or self-love. Focus instead on his self-contempt—"

"Shh." Carol held up her hand to slow him down while she wrote. When she stopped he asked, "What else?"

"His preoccupation with money," Carol said, "and with insider status. And his isolation and narrowness. It's as though his wife and family play no role in his life."

"Well, you know, no one enjoys being swindled, but I'm struck by your client's catastrophic reaction: such panic, such terror . . . it's as though his very life is at stake, as though, without money, he would become nothing. I'd be inclined to wonder about the origins of that personal myth—and, incidentally, I'd deliberately and repeatedly refer to it as a 'myth.' When did he create this myth? Whose voice guided him? I'd like to know more about his parents' attitudes toward money. It's important because, from what you tell me, his reverence for status is what did him in—sounds like a clever con man who must have picked up on this and used it to entrap him.

"It's a paradox," Ernest continued. "Your client—I almost said *patient*—considers his loss as his ruination, yet, if you can guide him properly, the swindle may be his salvation. It may be the best thing that ever happened to him!"

"How do I make that happen?"

"I'd ask him to look very deep within himself and examine whether his essence, his very center, believes that the purpose of his existence is to compile money. Sometimes I've asked such patients to project themselves into the future—to the point of their death, to their funeral—even to imagine their grave and to compose an epitaph. How might he feel, your client, to have an account of his preoccupation with money chiseled on his gravestone? Is that the way he'd like his life summed up?"

"Scary exercise," said Carol. "Reminds me of that lifeline exercise you once asked me to do. Maybe I should tackle this one, too . . . not today, though . . . I'm not finished with questions about my client. Tell me, Ernest, what do you make of his indifference toward his wife? I've heard by sheer chance she may be having an affair."

"Same strategy. I'd ask what *he* would say to a patient who is this indifferent to the person closest to him in all the world. Ask him to imagine life without her. And what's happened to his sexual self? Where has that gone? When did it vanish? And isn't it strange how he seems far more willing to understand his patients than his wife? You say that she's also a therapist but that he ridicules her training and her approach? Well, I'd confront that head-on, as hard as I could. What's the basis of his ridicule? I'm sure it's not based on hard evidence.

"Let's see, what else? As for his incapacitation—if that continues, then maybe a sabbatical of a month or two from practice would be good for him, both for his sake and for his patients'. Maybe the best way to spend it would be a retreat with his wife. Perhaps they could see a couples counselor and attempt some listening exercises. I think one of the best things that could happen would be if he permitted her, even with her despised methods, to help him."

"One last question—"

"Not today, Carolyn, we're running out of time . . . and I'm running out of ideas. But let's spend just one minute looking at our session today. Tell me, underneath the words we've been exchanging today, what have you been feeling? About our relationship? And today I want to hear the full truth. I've leveled with you. Level with me."

"I know you have. And I'd like to level . . . but I don't know how to say it . . . I feel sobered, or humbled . . . or maybe 'privileged' is the right term. And cared for. And trusted. And your honesty makes it hard for me to conceal."

"Conceal what?"

"Look at the clock. We're running over. Next time!" Carol rose to leave.

There was an awkward moment at the door. They had to invent a new mode of leave-taking.

"See you Thursday," said Ernest as he held out his hand for a formal handshake.

"I'm not ready for a handshake," said Carol. "Bad habits are hard to break. Especially cold turkey. Let's cut down slowly. How about a paternal hug?"

"Settle for 'avuncular'?"

"What's 'avuncular'?"

TWENTY-EIGHT

*I*t had been a long day in the office. Marshal trudged home, lost in reverie. Nine patients seen that day. Nine times one hundred seventy-five dollars. Fifteen hundred and seventy-five. How long to earn back the ninety thousand dollars? Five hundred patient hours. Sixty full days at the office. Over twelve workweeks. Twelve weeks yoked to the plow, working for that fucking Peter Macondo! Not to mention the overhead during this time: the office rental, professional dues, malpractice insurance, medical license. Not to mention the fees lost when he canceled patients during the first couple of weeks after the swindle. Nor the five hundred the detective ripped off. Not to mention that Wells Fargo rallied last week and is four percent higher than when he sold it! And the attorney's fees! *Carol's worth it,* Marshal thought, *even though she doesn't understand that a man can't just drop this. I am going to string up that bastard if it takes the rest of my life!*

Marshal stomped into the house and, as always, dropped his briefcase in the doorway and rushed to his new phone line to check messages. Voilà! Sow and ye shall reap! There was a voice mail message.

"Hello, I saw your ad in the APA monitor—well, not your ad, your warning. I'm a psychiatrist in New York City and I'd like more information about the patient you describe. Sounds like someone I'm treating. Please call me at home at 212-555-7082 this evening. Very late is okay."

Marshal dialed the number and heard a "Hello" on the phone, a "Hello" that, God willing, would lead him directly to Peter. "Yes," Marshal replied, "I got your message. You say you're treating someone like the person I describe in the ad. Can you describe him to me?"

"Just a minute, please," said the caller. "Let's back up. Who are you? Before I tell you anything, I need to know who you are."

"I'm a psychiatrist and an analyst in San Francisco. And you?"

"A psychiatrist in practice in Manhattan. I need more information about your ad. You use the term *danger*."

"And I *mean* danger. This man is a swindler, and if you're treating him, you're in danger. Does he sound like your patient?"

"I'm not at liberty—professional rules of confidentiality—simply to talk to a stranger about my patient."

"Trust me, forget the rules—this is an emergency," said Marshal.

"I'd prefer that first you tell me what you can about this patient."

"No problem with that," said Marshal. "About forty, good-looking, mustache, went by the name of Peter Macondo—"

"Peter Macondo!" the voice on the phone interrupted. "That's *my* patient's name!"

"That's incredible!" Marshal fell into a chair, astounded. "Using the same name! *That* I never expected. The same name? Well, I saw this guy, Macondo, in brief individual therapy for eight hours. Typical problems of the mega-wealthy: estate issues with his two children and ex-wife, everyone wanted a piece of him, generous to a fault, wife alcoholic. You got the same script?" said Marshal.

"Yep, he told me he sent her to the Betty Ford Center too," Marshal replied. "And then I saw him and his fiancée together . . . That's right, tall, elegant woman. Name Adriana . . . She used the same name, too? . . . Yeah, that's right, to work on a prenuptial agreement . . . sounds like a carbon copy. You know the rest . . . successful therapy, wanted to reward me, complained about my low fee, endowed lectureship at University of Mexico—

"Oh, Buenos Aires? Well, nice to hear he is still improvising. He's brought up his new investment? Bicycle helmet factory?

"That's right—the chance of a lifetime—you're absolutely guaranteed against loss. No doubt you got the great moral dilemma? How he gave a bad financial tip to the surgeon who saved his father's life? How he flagellated himself for that? Couldn't deal with the guilt of injuring a benefactor. How he would never again allow that to happen?

"That's right . . . a heart surgeon . . . he spent a whole hour with me, too, working that through. A detective I saw . . . a pain in the ass . . . really got off on that part—called it an inspired ploy.

"So, how far along are you? Given him a check for the investment yet?

"Lunch next week at the Jockey Club—just before he leaves for Zurich? Sounds familiar. Well, you saw my ad just in time. The rest of the story will be short and bitter. He sent me a Rolex watch, which of course I refused to accept, and I suspect he'll do the same with you. Then he'll ask you to treat Adriana and pay you generously in advance for her therapy. You may see her a time or two. And then—poof—gone. Both will vanish from the face of the globe.

"Ninety thousand. And believe me I can't afford it. How about you? How much were you planning to invest?

"Yeah, only forty thousand? I know what you mean about your wife—I had the same problem with mine. Wants to bury gold coins under the mattress. In this case she was right—first time. But I'm surprised he didn't push for more.

"Oh, he offered to lend you another forty, interest-free, while you freed up more money over the next few weeks? Cute twist."

"I can't thank you enough for your warning," replied the caller. "In the nick of time. I'm in your debt."

"Yes—in the nick of time, all right. You're very welcome. Glad to be of help to a fellow professional. How I wish someone had done that for me.

"Whoa, whoa, wait, don't hang up. I can't tell you how glad I am to have saved you from a swindle. But that's not why . . . or only why . . . I placed the notice. This bastard's a menace. He's got to be stopped. He'll just go on to another psychiatrist. We've got to get this guy put away.

"APA? Well, I agree: getting the APA lawyers involved would be one way to go. But we don't have the time. This guy only surfaces briefly and then vanishes. I've had a private investigator working on it and, let me tell you, when Peter Macondo disappears, he disappears. Untraceable. You have any information, any clues, that might lead to his real identity? A permanent address? Ever seen a passport? Credit cards? Checking account?

"Yeah, cash for everything? Did that with me too. How about car license plates?

"Great—if you can get the car plates—great. So, that's how you met him? He rented the house down the street from your summer house on Long Island and gave you a ride in his new Jaguar? I know who paid for that Jag. But yes, yes, get that license number, any way you can. Or the dealer's name if it's still on the car. No reason at all we shouldn't be able to trap him.

"I agree completely. You *should* see a private investigator—or maybe a criminal attorney. Everyone I've consulted has gone out of their way to let me know what a pro this guy is. We need professional help. . . .

"Yes, much better to let the detective gather the information, not you. If Macondo sees you snooping around his house or car, he's off.

"Fees? My detective charged five hundred a day—the attorney two hundred-fifty an hour. In New York they'll rip you off for more.

"I don't follow you," said Marshal. "Why should *I* pay the fees?

"Neither do I have anything to gain. We're in the same boat—everyone has guaranteed me that I will never get a penny of my money back—that when Macondo's caught he'll have no assets and a mile-long string of claims against him. Believe me—my motives here are the same as yours: justice and the protection of others in our field. . . . Revenge? Well, yes, there's some of that—I'll own up to it. Okay, well, how about this? Let's go fifty-fifty with any expenses you run up. Remember, it's tax-deductible."

After a bit of a haggle, Marshal said, "Sixty-forty? I can live with it. So we're agreed? Next step is to see a detective. Ask your attorney for a recommendation. Then let the detective help us develop a plan to trap him. One suggestion, though: Macondo will offer to give you a secured note of your choice—ask him for a bank-guaranteed note; he'll produce one with a forged signature. And then we can nail him for bank fraud—a more serious offense. That can get the FBI involved. . . . No, I didn't. Not with the FBI. Not with the police. I'll square with you; I was too scared of bad publicity, of censure for boundary violations—for investing with a patient, or an ex-patient. A mistake—I should have gone after him with everything I had. But, see, you're not in that quandary. You have not yet invested, and when you do it will be only in order to trap Macondo."

"Not sure you want to get involved?" Marshal began pacing as he talked. He realized he could easily lose this precious opportunity and chose his words carefully.

"What do you mean? You *are* involved! What are you going to feel when you hear about other psychiatrists, maybe buddies of yours, getting stung and you know you could have stopped it? And how will *they* feel when they learn you were a victim and remained silent? Don't we tell our patients that? About consequences for actions—or inactions?

"What do you mean—'you're going to think about it'? We've no time. Please, Doctor . . . you know, I don't know your name.

"That's true, you don't know mine. We're in the same predicament—we're both afraid of exposure. We need to confide in one another. My name is Marshal Streider—I'm a training analyst in practice in San Francisco—psychiatric training at Rochester, Golden Gate Psychoanalytic Institute. That's right—when John Romano was chairman at Rochester. You?

"Arthur Randal—sounds familiar—St. Elizabeth's in Washington? No, don't know anyone there. So you've got mainly a psychopharm practice?

"Well, I'm starting to do more brief therapy, too, and a little couples work. . . . But please, Dr. Randal, back to what we were saying—there's no time for you to think about it—are you willing to participate?

"Are you kidding? Of course, I'll fly to New York. I wouldn't miss it. I can't come for the whole week—I've got a full schedule. But when the crunch time comes, I'll be there. Call me after you've seen the detective—I want to be involved with every part of this. You calling from home? What's the best number to reach you at?"

Marshal wrote down several numbers—home, office, and weekend number on Long Island. "Yeah, I'll call about this time at home. It's pretty impossible to reach me at my office, too. You break on the half hour? I usually break ten till the hour—we'll never connect during the day."

He hung up the phone feeling a mixture of relief, exhilaration, and triumph. Peter behind bars. Peter's drooped head. Adriana, downcast, in prison grays. The new Jag, good resale value, parked in his garage. Vindication at last! No one fucks over Marshal Streider.

Then he reached for the APA directory and turned to the picture of Arthur Randal—good features, blond hair combed straight back, no part, age forty-two, trained at Rutgers and St. Elizabeth's, research on lithium levels and bipolar illness, two kids. The office number checked. Thank God for Dr. Randal.

Cheap bastard, though, Marshal thought. *Someone saves me forty thousand, I wouldn't nickel-and-dime him about the detective's fees. Still, from his point of view, why should he lay out money? He's not been hurt. Peter's paid his fees. Why should he invest money to trap someone who has done him no wrong?*

Marshal's thoughts turned to Peter. Why would he use the same name in another scam? Maybe Macondo's starting to self-destruct. Everyone knows that sooner or later sociopaths do themselves in. Or did he just think that this clod Streider was so stupid that it wasn't worth the trouble of adopting an alias? Well, we will see!

Once set into motion by Marshal, Arthur moved quickly. By the next evening he had already consulted a detective who, unlike Bat Thomas, made himself useful. He recommended putting Macondo under surveillance for twenty-four hours (at seventy-five dollars an hour). He'd get the license plates and run a check on them. If circumstances permitted, he might enter Macondo's car in search of fingerprints and other identifying material.

There was no way, the detective had told Arthur Randal, to apprehend Macondo until he committed a crime in New York. Therefore he advised that they proceed with an entrapment plan, keeping careful records of every conversation, and contacting the New York Police Department Fraud Squad immediately.

The following night Marshal learned of more progress. Arthur had contacted the Midtown Manhattan Fraud Squad and was turned over to a Detective Darnel Collins who, having investigated a case with a similar M.O. six months before, expressed interest in Peter Macondo. He asked Arthur to wear a wire and to meet Peter, as planned, for lunch at the Jockey Club, hand the cashier's check over to him, and receive in return the forged bank guarantee. The fraud squad, having witnessed and televised the transaction, would move in for the arrest on the spot.

But the NYPD required good cause for such an extensive operation.

Marshal would have to cooperate. He would have to fly to New York, file an official complaint about Peter with the fraud squad, and personally identify him. Marshal shuddered at the thought of the publicity but, with his prey so close at hand, reconsidered his position. True, his name might make some of the New York smaller tabloids, but how likely was it that word would get back to San Francisco?

The Rolex watch? What Rolex? Marshal said aloud, as if in rehearsal. *Oh, the watch Macondo sent at the end of therapy? The watch I refused to accept and returned to Adriana?* As he spoke, Marshal slipped the watch off his wrist and buried it in his dresser drawer. Who would challenge him? Anyone going to believe Macondo? Only his wife and Melvin knew about the Rolex. Shirley's silence was secure. And Marshal was the guardian of so many of Melvin's bizarre hypochondriacal secrets that he had no concerns there.

Marshal and Arthur spoke for twenty minutes each night. What a relief for Marshal to have, finally, a real confidant and collaborator, perhaps eventually a friend. Arthur even referred one of his patients to Marshal, an IBM software engineer who was going to be transferred to the San Francisco Bay Area.

Their one disagreement concerned the money to be given Peter for the investment. Arthur and Peter had arranged to meet for lunch in four days. Peter had agreed to draw up a bank-guaranteed note, and Arthur would have a forty-thousand-dollar cashier's check. But Arthur wanted Marshal to put up the entire forty thousand dollars. Having just bought a summer home, Arthur had no available cash. His only recourse was money in his wife's estate left her by her mother who had died the previous winter. But his wife, a member of a family prominent in New York society for over two hundred years, was exquisitely sensitive to social appearance and placed extreme pressure on Arthur to have nothing whatsoever to do with this entire sordid mess.

Marshal, offended by the unfairness of the situation, had a long negotiation session with Arthur, during the course of which he lost all respect for his pusillanimous colleague. Ultimately Marshal, rather than risk Arthur's capitulation to his wife and total withdrawal, agreed again to a sixty-forty split. Arthur needed to present a single cashier's check, drawn on a New York bank. Marshal agreed to have twenty-four thousand dollars in Arthur's account the day preceding the luncheon—either he would bring it to New York or he would wire it. Arthur, reluctantly, agreed to put up the other sixteen thousand.

The following evening Marshal returned home to find a voice mail message from Detective Darnel Collins, New York City Midtown Manhattan Fraud Squad. Marshal got short shrift when he returned the call. The harried police operator told him to call back in the morning: Officer Collins was off duty, and Marshal's call seemed no emergency.

Marshal's first patient the next morning would be at seven A.M. He set the alarm for five and called New York again upon arising. The police operator said, "I'll page him. Have a good day," and slammed the phone down. Ten minutes later the phone rang.

"Mister Marshal Streider?"

"*Doctor* Streider."

"Well, 'scuse me. DOCTOR Streider. Detective Collins, New York fraud squad. Got *another* doctor here—Dr. Arthur Randal—says you had a little nasty run-in with someone we're interested in—goes sometimes by the name of Peter Macondo."

"Very nasty run-in. Robbed me of ninety thousand dollars."

"You got company on that. Other folks, too, annoyed with our friend Macondo. Give me details. Everything. I'm taping this—okay?"

Marshal took fifteen minutes to describe all that had happened with Peter Macondo.

"Man oh man, you mean to say, just like that, you handed him ninety thousand dollars?"

"You can't fully appreciate it if you don't understand the nature, the intricacies, of the psychotherapy situation."

"Yeah? Well, we know I'm no doctor. But tell you this: *I* never handed over money like that. Ninety thousand's a lot of money."

"I told you, I had a secured note. Ran it by my lawyer. That's the way all business is done. The banknote commits the bank to pay the note upon demand."

"A note which you got around to checking out two weeks after he was gone."

"Look, Detective, what is this? Am I on trial? You think I'm happy about this?"

"Okay, my friend, stay calm, and we'll all do okay. Here's what we do to make you well. We're gonna arrest this guy eating lunch—

chomping on his radicchio—next Wednesday, maybe twelve-thirty, one o'clock. But to make this stick we need you in New York to make an ID within twelve hours after the arrest—in other words, before Wednesday midnight. We got a tight agreement?"

"I wouldn't miss it."

"Okay, man, lot of people counting on you. Another thing—you still got the forged note and the receipt for the cashier's check?"

"Yes. You want me to bring those?"

"Yeah, bring the originals when you come, but I want to see copies of them right away. Can you fax them to me today? Two-one-two-five-five-five-three-four-eight-nine—put my name, Detective Darnel Collins, on them. One other thing. I'm sure I don't need to tell you—but *don't, don't, don't* show your face at the restaurant. You do and our bird flies, and everybody's very unhappy. Wait for me at the Fifty-fourth Street station—it's between Eighth and Ninth, or arrange with your buddy to meet him after the snatch and come down with him. Let me know which. Any other questions?"

"One other. Is this safe? That's a real check with mostly my money that Dr. Randal's giving him."

"*Your* money? I thought it was *his* money."

"We split it sixty-forty. I'm putting up twenty-four thousand."

"Safe? We got two men eating lunch at the next table and three others watching and televising every move. Safe enough. But *I* wouldn't do it."

"Why?"

"Always can be something—earthquake, fire, all three officers keel over together with heart attacks—I dunno, shit happens. Safe? Yeah, plenty safe. Still, I wouldn't do it. But I ain't a doctor."

⌐

Life became interesting again for Marshal. Back to jogging. Back to basketball. He canceled his hours with Carol because he felt sheepish about admitting that he had been stalking Peter. She had fully committed herself to the opposite strategy: pressing him to accept his loss and let go of his anger. It was a good object lesson, Marshal thought, on the perils of giving advice in therapy: if patients don't follow the advice, they won't come back.

Every night he spoke to Arthur Randal. As the meeting with Peter neared, Arthur got edgier and edgier.

"Marshal, my wife is convinced I'm going to tar myself in this whole affair. This will hit the papers. My patients will read it. Consider my reputation. I'll either be ridiculed or accused of investing with a patient."

"But that's the point: you're *not* investing with the patient. You're acting in consort with the police to trap a criminal. This will *enhance* your reputation."

"That's not what the press will say. Think about it. You know how they scratch for scandal—especially with psychiatrists. I'm feeling more and more I don't need this in my life. I've got a good practice, everything I've ever wanted."

"If you hadn't read my notice, Arthur, you'd be out forty thousand to this thug. And if we don't stop him he'll keep on going—victim after victim."

"You don't need me—*you* nail him, I'll identify him. I'm applying for a clinical faculty position at Columbia . . . even the hint of scandal—"

"Look, Arthur, here's an idea: cover yourself—write a detailed letter about the situation and your plans to the New York Psychiatric Society—do it *now,* before Macondo is arrested. If necessary you can provide a copy of that letter to your department at Columbia and to the press. That will provide you absolute insurance."

"No way I can write that letter, Marshal, without mentioning you—your ad, your involvement with Macondo. How's that stand with you? You were reluctant to have your name made public, too."

Marshal blanched at the idea of any further exposure but knew he had no choice. Anyway, it made little difference—his taped session with Detective Collins made his involvement with Peter a matter of public record anyway.

"If you got to do that, Arthur, do it. I have nothing to hide. The whole profession will feel nothing but gratitude to us."

Then there was the matter of wearing a wire so that the police could tape the closing of the deal with Macondo. With each passing day, Arthur grew more queasy.

"Marshal, there's got to be some other way to do this. This is not to be taken lightly—I'm placing myself in great jeopardy. Macondo is too smart and experienced for us to put this over on him. You talked to Detective Collins? Be honest—you think he's an intellectual match for Macondo? Suppose Macondo discovers the wire while we're talking?"

"How?"

"He'll pick it up, somehow. You know him—he's always ten steps ahead."

"Not this time. You got police at the next table, Arthur. And don't forget the sociopath's grandiosity, his sense of invulnerability."

"Sociopaths are also unpredictable. Can you say that Peter might not lose it and go for a gun?"

"Arthur, that's not his M.O. . . . it's inconsistent with everything we know about him. You are safe. Remember, you're in a fashionable restaurant surrounded by alert police. You can do this. It's got to be done."

Marshal had an awful premonition of Arthur backing out at the last moment, and in every evening's conversation he drew upon all his rhetorical powers to bolster his timid accomplice's courage. He relayed his concerns to Detective Collins, who joined with him in calming Arthur.

But, to his credit, Arthur conquered his qualms and anticipated his meeting with Macondo with resolve, even equanimity. Marshal wired the money from his bank on Tuesday morning, spoke to Arthur that evening to confirm its arrival, and caught the red-eye to New York.

The plane was delayed two hours, and it was three in the afternoon when he arrived at the Fifty-fourth Street police station for his meeting with Arthur and Detective Collins. The clerk informed him that Detective Collins was interviewing and directed him to a ratty leather chair in the hallway. Marshal had never before been in a police station and watched with great interest the steady stream of sallow-faced suspects led up and down the stairs by harried officers. But he was groggy—he had been so keyed up that he had not been able to sleep on the plane—and soon dozed off.

About thirty minutes later the clerk awakened him with a gentle shake on the shoulder and directed him to a room on the second floor where Detective Collins, a powerfully built black man, was writing at his desk. *Big man,* Marshal thought, *pro-linebacker size. Exactly as I imagined him.*

But nothing else was as he had imagined. When Marshal introduced himself he was struck by the detective's strange formality. In one horrific moment it became apparent the detective had no idea who Marshal was. Yes, he was Detective Darnel Collins. No, he had not spoken to Marshal on the phone. No, he had never heard of a Dr. Arthur Randal or a Peter Macondo. Nor had he heard anything about any arrest at the Jockey Club. He had never even heard of the

Jockey Club. Yes, *of course* he was absolutely certain he had not arrested Peter Macondo while he was chomping on radicchio. Radicchio? What's that?

The explosion in Marshal's mind was deafening, even louder than the explosion detonated by the discovery, weeks ago, that the bank guarantee had been forged. He grew light-headed and folded into the chair the detective offered.

"Easy, man. Easy. Put your head down. It might help." Detective Collins rose and returned with a glass of water. "Tell me what's happened. But I have a hunch I know."

Marshal dazedly told his whole story. Peter, hundred-dollar bills, Adriana, P.U. Club, bicycle helmets, the psychiatric newspaper ad, Arthur Randal's call, sixty-forty split, private eye, Jaguar, the twenty-four-thousand-dollar wire trap, the fraud squad—everything—the whole catastrophe.

Detective Collins shook his head as Marshal talked. "Man, that smarts, I know. Hey, you don't look good. You need to lie down?"

Marshal shook his head, and cradled it with his hands as Detective Collins spoke. "You okay to talk?"

"Men's room, quick."

Detective Collins led him to the men's room and waited in his office while Marshal vomited into the toilet, rinsed his mouth, washed his face, and combed his hair. Slowly he walked back to Detective Collins's office.

"Better?"

Marshal nodded. "I can talk now."

"Just listen for a minute. Let me explain what's happened to you," said Detective Collins. "This is the twice-bit gig. It's famous. I've heard about it lots, but I never, ever seen it. I learned about it in fraud school. Takes real skill to pull it off. Operator got to find a special victim: smart, prideful . . . and then, what he does is, *bites them twice* . . . first time hooks 'em by greed . . . second time hooks 'em by revenge. Real skill. Man, never seen it before. Takes cool nerve because anything can go wrong. Take one for instance—if you get only a little suspicious and check with Manhattan telephone information to get the real police station phone number, it's all over. Man—nerve. Major-league stuff."

"No hope, eh?" Marshal whispered.

"Give me those phone numbers, I'll run a check on 'em. I'll try everything I can. But the truth? You want the truth? . . . No hope."

"What about the real Dr. Randal?"

"Probably on vacation out of the country. Macondo got into his voice mail. Not hard to do."

"How about tracking the others involved?" Marshal asked.

"What others? Ain't no others. His girlfriend probably the police operator. He must have been the others himself. These guys are actors. The good ones do all the voices themselves. And this guy's good. And long gone by now. For sure."

Marshal stumbled downstairs, leaning on Detective Collins's arm, refused a ride to the airport in a police car, caught a cab on Eighth Avenue, went to the airport, caught the next plane to San Francisco, drove home in a daze, canceled his patients for the next week, and climbed into bed.

TWENTY-NINE

"Money, money, money. Can't we talk about anything else, Carol? Let me tell you a story about my father that will answer, once and forever, all your questions about me and money. Happened when I was a baby, but I've heard about it all my life—part of the family folklore." Marshal slowly unzipped his sweatsuit jacket, slipped it off, refused Carol's outstretched hand offering to hang it up, and dropped it in a heap on the floor next to his seat.

"He had a tiny, six-by-six, grocery store on Fifth and R streets in Washington. We lived over the store. One day a customer came in and asked for a pair of work gloves. My father pointed to the back door, saying he had to get them out of the back room and that it would take him a couple of minutes. Well, there was no back room. The back door opened onto an alley. My father galloped down the alley to the open market two blocks down, bought a pair of gloves for twelve cents, rushed back, and sold them to the customer for fifteen cents."

Marshal pulled a handkerchief out, blew his nose hard, and unabashedly wiped the tears from his cheeks. Since his return from New York, he had abandoned all attempts to conceal his vulnerability and wept almost every session. Carol sat in silence, respecting Marshal's tears and trying to recall when she had last seen a man cry. Jeb, her brother, refused to cry, though he had been abused routinely by everyone: father, mother, school bullies—sometimes for the specific purpose of making him cry.

Marshal buried his face in his handkerchief. Carol reached over and squeezed his hand. "The tears are for your father? He still alive?"

"No, he died young, encoffined forever by that grocery store. Too much running. Too many three-cent deals. Whenever I think about making money, or losing money, or squandering money, I have a vision of my dear father dressed in his white apron blotched with chicken blood, flying down that grubby alley, wind in his face, black hair flowing, gasping for breath, triumphantly holding aloft, like some Olympic baton, a pair of twelve-cent work gloves."

"And you, Marshal, your place in that vision?"

"That vision is the cradle of my passions. Perhaps the critical defining incident of my life."

"It shaped the future course of your attitudes to money?" Carol asked. "In other words, make enough money and the bones of your father will stop clattering up and down the alleyway."

Marshal was startled. He looked up at his attorney with new respect. Her tailored mauve dress offsetting her gleaming complexion made him a little self-conscious about his unshaven face and grubby jogging suit. "That comment . . . takes my breath away. Need to think about clattering bones."

Then a long silence. Carol prodded, "Where do your thoughts go now?"

"To that back door. The glove story is not only about money; it's also about back doors."

"The back door to your father's store?"

"Yeah. And the pretense that the door opened onto another large storeroom rather than onto the alley—that's a metaphor for my whole life. I pretend that I contain other rooms; yet, deep in my heart, I know I have no storeroom, no hidden wares. I enter and exit through alleys and back doors."

"Ah, the Pacific Union Club," said Carol.

"Exactly. You can imagine what it meant, finally, finally, to enter through the front door. Macondo used the irresistible lure: the insider lure. All day long I treat wealthy patients. We're close, we share intimate moments, I am indispensable to them. Yet I know my place. I know if it weren't for my profession, if I had met them in any other context, they wouldn't give me the time of day. I'm like the parish priest from the poor family who ends up taking confession from the upper class. But the P.U. Club—*that* was the symbol of arrival. Out of the Fifth and R grocery store, up the marble stairs, banging the big brass knocker, marching through open doors into the inner, red-velvet chambers. I had aimed toward that goal all my life."

"And inside waited Macondo—a man more corrupt than any who entered your father's store."

Marshal nodded. "Truth is, I remember my father's customers with great fondness. You remember I told you about that patient who maneuvered me a few weeks ago into going to Avocado Joe's? I've never been in a place quite that . . . that low. Yet, you want to know the truth? I liked it there. No pretense—I felt at home, more comfortable than at the P.U. Club. I belonged there. It was like being with my father's customers in the Fifth and R store. But I hate liking it; I don't like sinking to that level—there's something alarming in being so thoroughly programmed by early life events. I'm capable of better things. All my life I've said to myself: 'I'm kicking the grocery store sawdust from my feet; I'm rising above all this.'"

"My grandfather was born in Naples," said Carol. "I don't remember much about him except that he taught me to play chess, and every time we finished and we were putting away the pieces he would say the same thing—I can hear his gentle voice now: 'You see, Carol, chess is like life: when the game is over, all the pieces—the pawns and the kings and the queens—all go back into the same box.'

"It's a good lesson for you, too, to meditate upon, Marshal: *pawns and kings and queens all go back into the same box at the end of the game.* See you tomorrow. Same time."

Every day since his return from New York, Marshal had met with Carol. For the first two meetings she had visited him at home, then he began dragging himself to her office and now, a week later, he had begun to emerge from his depressive stupor and was making an effort to understand his role in what had happened to him. Her associates noted the daily regularity of her meeting with Marshal and, more than once, inquired about the case. But Carol always responded, "Complex case. Can't say more—delicate issues of confidentiality."

All the while Carol continued to obtain consultation from Ernest. She used his observations and advice with good effect: almost every suggestion worked like a charm.

One day when Marshal seemed stuck, she decided to try Ernest's tombstone exercise.

"Marshal, so much of your life has been centered on material success, on making money and the objects money procures—your status, your art collections—that money seems to define who you are and what your whole life has meant. Will you want that to be your final insignia, the final summing up of your life? Tell me, have you ever thought what you would like to have inscribed on your tombstone? Would it be these attributes—the climbing, the accumulating, the money?"

Marshal blinked as a drop of sweat rolled into one of his eyes. "That's a tough question, Carol."

"Aren't I supposed to ask tough questions? Humor me—spend a couple of minutes on it. Say anything that comes into your mind."

"The first thing that comes to mind is what that New York detective said about me—that I was prideful, blinded by greed and blinded by revenge."

"*That's* what you want on your tombstone?"

"That's what I *don't* want on my tombstone. My worst horror. But maybe I deserve those words—maybe my whole life's been rolling toward that epitaph."

"You don't want that tombstone? Then," Carol said, checking her watch, "your future course is clear: you've got to change the way you're living. Our time's up for today, Marshal."

Marshal nodded as he picked up his jacket from the floor, slowly put it on, and prepared to leave. "Suddenly cold . . . I'm shivering . . . that tombstone question. That's a shocking question—devastating. Gotta be careful with heavy artillery like that, Carol. You know who I'm reminded of? Remember that therapist you asked me about once for your friend? Ernest Lash—my ex-supervisee. That's the kind of thing he would be likely to ask. I'd always be reining him in from those questions. He referred to them as existential shock therapy."

Carol had already half risen, but her curiosity got the best of her.

"Then you think it's bad therapy? You were pretty critical about Lash."

"No, I didn't say that it was bad therapy for me. On the contrary, it's excellent therapy. A good wake-up call. And as for Ernest Lash—I shouldn't have been so hard on him. I want to take back some of the things I said."

"How come you were so hard?"

"My arrogance. It's just what we were discussing all last week. I was intolerant of him: I was so convinced that my way was the only way. I wasn't a good supervisor. And I didn't learn from him. I don't learn from anyone."

"So, the truth about Ernest Lash?" Carol asked.

"Ernest's all right. No, better than all right. Truth is—he's a *good* therapist. I used to kid him that he needed to eat so much because he gave too much to patients—gets overinvolved, lets himself be sucked dry. But if I had to see a therapist, I'd choose one now who erred on the side of giving too much of himself. If I don't climb out of this pit soon and have to refer out some of my patients, I'd consider sending some of them to Ernest."

Marshal rose to leave. "Past time. Thanks for running over for me today, Carol."

⤖

Session after session passed without Carol's bringing up the topic of Marshal's marriage. Perhaps she hesitated because of her own marital wasteland. Finally, one day, in response to one of Marshal's repeated statements that Carol was the only person in the world with whom he could speak honestly, she took the plunge and asked why he could not talk to his wife. Marshal's responses made it clear that he had not told Shirley about the New York swindle. Nor about the extent of his distress. Nor that he needed help.

The reason he hadn't spoken to Shirley, Marshal said, was that he didn't want to interrupt her month-long meditation retreat at Tassajara. Carol knew that was a rationalization: Marshal's actions were motivated less by consideration than by indifference and shame. Marshal acknowledged that he hardly ever thought about Shirley, that he was too preoccupied with his internal state, that he and Shirley now lived in different worlds. Emboldened by Ernest's advice, Carol persisted.

"Marshal, tell me, what happens if one of *your* patients repeatedly dismisses his relationship with his wife of twenty-four years so casually? How do *you* respond?"

As Ernest had predicted, Marshal bridled at that question.

"Your office is the one place where I don't *have* to be the therapist. Be consistent. The other day you confront me with how I don't let myself be cared for, and now you're trying to make me be the therapist *even here*."

"But, Marshal, wouldn't it be foolish of us not to take advantage of all the resources at our disposal, including your own extensive therapeutic knowledge and skill?"

"I'm paying you for your expert help. I'm not interested in self-analysis."

"You call me an expert and yet you reject my expert advice to use your own expertise."

"Sophistry."

Once again Carol applied Ernest's words.

"Isn't it true that you're not interested simply in getting nurtured? Isn't your *real* goal autonomy? Learning to nurture yourself? Becoming your own mother and father?"

Marshal shook his head in wonder at Carol's power. He had no choice but to feed himself the questions vital to his own recovery.

"All right. All right. The main question is what has happened to my love for Shirley? After all, we'd been wonderful friends and lovers since the tenth grade. So when and how did things deteriorate?"

Marshal tried to answer his own questions. "Things began to go sour a few years ago. About the time our children entered adolescence, Shirley grew restless. Common phenomenon. Over and over she talked about feeling unfulfilled, about my being so absorbed with my work. I thought the ideal solution would be for her to become a therapist and go into practice with me. But my plan backfired. In graduate school she grew critical of psychoanalysis. She chose to get involved with the very approaches I felt most critical of: the flaky alternative, spiritually oriented approaches, especially those based on Eastern meditative approaches. I'm sure she did this deliberately."

"Keep going," Carol urged. "Identify other important questions I should pose to you."

Marshal grudgingly spit out several: "Why does Shirley make such little effort to learn about psychoanalytic treatment from me? Why does she so deliberately defy me? Tassajara is only three hours away—I guess I could drive up there, tell her how I feel, and ask her to talk about her choice of therapy schools."

"Even so, that's not what I'm getting at. Those are questions of *her*," Carol said. "How about questions of yourself?"

Marshal nodded, as though to indicate to Carol that her approach was sound.

"Why have I talked so little to her about her interests? Why have I made such little effort—no effort at all—to understand her?"

"In other words," Carol asked, "why are you so much more willing to understand your patients than your wife?"

Marshal nodded again. "You might put it that way."

"Might?" Carol asked.

"You definitely could put it that way," Marshal acquiesced.

"Other questions you might ask a patient in your situation?"

"I'd ask my patient some sexual questions. I'd ask about what has happened to his sexual self. And to his wife's. I'd ask whether he wants this unsatisfying situation to endure permanently. If not, why hasn't he pursued marital therapy? Does he want to divorce? Or is it just pride and arrogance—just waiting for his wife to come groveling?"

"Good work, Marshal. Shall we dig into some answers?"

Answers came tumbling out. Marshal's feelings toward Shirley were not unlike those he had toward Ernest, he said. Both had wounded him by rejecting his professional ideology. Yes, there was no doubt that he felt injured and unloved. And there was no doubt also that he was waiting to be soothed, waiting for some form of massive apology and reparation.

No sooner had he said these words than Marshal shook his head and added, "That's what my heart and my wounded vanity say. My intellect says something different."

"Says what?"

"Says that I shouldn't consider a student's proclivity for independent thought as a personal attack. Shirley must be free to develop her own interests. Ernest, too."

"And must be free from your control?" Carol asked.

"That, too. I remember my analyst telling me that I play life like I played football. Relentless pushing, blocking, moving forward, imposing my will on my opponent. That's how Shirley must have felt about me. Yet it wasn't just that she rejected psychoanalysis. That would have been bad enough, but I could have lived with it.

What I couldn't live with was her choosing the flakiest possible wing of the field, the most harebrained Marin County idiotic approach to therapy. Obviously she was deliberately and publicly mocking me."

"So, because she chooses a different approach, you assume she mocks you. And, consequently, you mock her in return."

"My mocking is not retaliatory; it's substantive. Can you imagine treating patients through flower arranging? It's hard to exaggerate the ridiculousness of this idea. Be honest with me, Carol—is this or is this not ridiculous?"

"I don't think I can give you what you want, Marshal. I don't know much about it, but my boyfriend is an ikebana aficionado. He's been studying ikebana for years and tells me he has profited in many ways from the practice."

"What do you mean, *profited*?"

"He's had a lot of therapy over the years, including analysis, which he says has helped him, but he says that he has gained as much from ikebana."

"You're still not saying *how* it helps."

"What he's told me is that ikebana offers an escape from anxiety—a refuge of tranquillity. The discipline helps him feel centered, offers a sense of harmony and balance. Let me remember . . . what else did he say? Oh, yes—that ikebana inspires him to express his creativity and his aesthetic sensibility. You're so quickly dismissive of it, Marshal. Remember, ikebana is a venerable practice, going back several centuries, practiced by tens of thousands. You know much about it?"

"But ikebana therapy? Good God!"

"I've heard of poetry therapy, music therapy, dance therapy, art therapy, meditation therapy, massage therapy. You said yourself that working with your bonsai these last weeks has saved your sanity. Isn't it possible that ikebana therapy might be effective for certain patients?" asked Carol.

"I think that's what Shirley's trying to determine in her dissertation."

"What are her results?"

Marshal shook his head and said nothing.

"I assume that means you've never inquired?" asked Carol.

Marshal nodded almost imperceptibly. He took off his glasses and looked away, as he always did when he felt ashamed.

"So you feel mocked by Shirley and she feels . . . ?" Carol gestured for Marshal to speak.

Silence.

"She feels . . . ?" Carol asked again, her hand cupping her ear.

"Devalued. Invalidated," Marshal answered *sotto voce*.

A long silence. Finally, Marshal said: "Okay, Carol, I acknowledge it. You've made your point. I've got things to say to her. So where do I go from here?"

"I have a feeling you know the answer to that question. A question ain't a question if you know the answer. Seems to me like your course is clear."

"Clear? Clear? To you, maybe. What do you mean? Tell me. I need your help."

Carol remained silent.

"Tell me what to do," Marshal repeated.

"What would *you* say to a patient who pretends not to know what to do?"

"Dammit, Carol, stop acting like an analyst and tell me what to do."

"How would you respond to *that* kind of statement?"

"Goddamnit," said Marshal, holding his head between his hands and rocking back and forth. "I've created a goddamned monster. Pity. Pity. Carol, ever heard of pity?"

Carol hung tough, just as Ernest had advised. "You're resisting again. This is valuable time. Go ahead, Marshal, what would you say to that patient?"

"I'd do what I always do: I'd interpret his behavior. I'd tell him that he has such a craving for submission, such a lust for authority, that he refuses to heed his own wisdom."

"So you *do* know what to do?"

Marshal nodded resignedly.

"And when to do it?"

Another nod.

Carol looked at her watch and rose. "It's two-fifty sharp, Marshal. Our time is up. Good work today. Call me when you return from Tassajara."

~

At two in the morning at Len's house in Tiburon, Shelly hummed "Zip-a-dee-doo-dah, zip-a-dee-ay" as he raked in another pot. Not only had the cards turned—flushes, full houses, and perfect lows had been dealt to him all evening—but by cannily reversing every one of the tells that Marshal had identified, Shelly had confused the other players and built enormous pots.

"No way I could have figured Shelly for a full house," mumbled Willy. "I would have bet a thousand dollars against it."

"You *did* bet a thousand against it," Len reminded him. "Look at that mountain of chips—it's going to totter the table. Hey, Shelly, where are you? You still there? I can barely see you behind those stacks."

As Willy reached into his pocket for his wallet, he said, "Last two hands you bluff me out, this hand you suck me in; what the hell is going on, Shelly? You taking lessons or something?"

Shelly embraced his mountain of chips, pulled them closer, looked up, and grinned, "Yeah, yeah, lessons—you got it. It's like this: my shrink, a bona fide psychoanalyst, is giving me a few pointers. He totes his couch down every week to Avocado Joe's."

⌐

"So," Carol said, "last night in this dream you and I were sitting on the edge of a bed and then we took off our dirty socks and shoes and sat facing each other touching our feet together."

"Feeling tone of the dream?" Ernest asked.

"Positive. Exhilarating. But a little scary."

"You and I sit touching our bare feet together. What's that dream saying? Let your mind drift. Think about you and me sitting together. Think about therapy."

"When I think about therapy, I think about my client. He's left town."

"And . . . " prompted Ernest.

"Well, I've been hiding behind my client. Now it's time for me to come out, to get started on myself."

"And . . . just let your thoughts run free, Carolyn."

"It's like I'm just beginning . . . good advice . . . you know, you gave me good advice for my client . . . damned good . . . and watching how much he was getting made me envious . . . made me long for something good for myself . . . I need it. . . . I need to start talking to you about Jess, whom I've been seeing a lot of lately—problems coming up as I get closer to him . . . hard time trusting that something good can happen to me . . . starting to trust you . . . passed every test . . . but it's scary too—don't quite know why . . . yes, I do . . . can't quite say why. Yet."

"Perhaps the dream says it for you, Carolyn. Look at what you and I are doing in the dream."

"I don't get it—touching the soles of our bare feet. So?"

"Look at how we're sitting—sole to sole. I think the dream is expressing a wish to sit soul to soul—spelled *s-o-u-l*. Not sole touching but *soul* touching."

"Oh, cute. *Soul,* not sole. Ernest, you can be very clever if I give you half a chance. Soul touching—yes, that feels right. Yes, that's what the dream is saying. It *is* time to begin. A new beginning. The cardinal rule here is honesty, right?"

Ernest nodded. "Nothing more important than our being honest with each other."

"And anything I say here is acceptable, right? *Anything* is acceptable as long as it's honest."

"Of course."

"Then I have a confession to make," said Carol.

Ernest nodded, reassuringly.

"You ready, Ernest?"

Ernest nodded again.

"You sure, Ernest?"

Ernest smiled knowingly. And a little smugly—he had always suspected that Carolyn had kept some parts of herself concealed. He picked up his notepad, snuggled back cozily into his chair, and said, "Always ready for the truth."